SECOND CHANCES

B.D. STOREY

COPYRIGHT

FOREWARD

If someone had told me that I was going to write and publish a 100,000+ word love story, I'd have laughed in their faces.

Yet here we are!

I hope you enjoyed Josie and Jacobs' story. This book is a result of a challenge I set myself in July of 2020. I've always been a puttering kind of writer. Small stories here and there, usually a result of some game I was playing or some small moment that caught my eye or popped into my head.

One evening in July, my lovely wife and I were watching a Hallmark movie. We enjoyed watching them as they always make you feel good and we had our favorite sets of actors/actresses.

For some reason, that one night, I turned to my wife and said "You know, I think I could write one of these stories. I'd make it a bit more edgy, but I could do this. Guy, gal, plot, love story, conflict, happy ever after. I could do that."

She looked at me with that quirky smile of hers and said "You probably could." Then she went back to her reading.

For the next couple of days I let my mind wander over story ideas. This story was not the original idea. Josie and Jacob were always the characters, and always in Northeast Washington. It was the original plot that morphed from logging and land owning to what I published.

I do have plans to visit these guys and gals again. I am fleshing out Jacob/Kara and Josie/Gregs backstories that got them up to this telling. No timeline on that project.

If you enjoyed the book, please leave a review at your favorite ebook purchasing site and tell all your friends and Facebook followers. Follow me on Facebook or Instagram for further updates. I still work a day job, so please don't be upset if it takes me time to respond to your emails or messages.

Bob

Website:
   https://BDStorey.com
   Facebook:
   https://www.facebook.com/BDStoreyAuthor/
   Instagram:
   https://instagram.com/bdstoreyauthor/

WARNING

This book contains discussion and references to rape, sexual assault, and violence. The author does not condone the actions depicted as part of this story.

PROLOGUE

Jacob

M ist from the early morning rain clung to the trees and mixed with the light breeze to cool the sweat on my face as I walked up the small trail.

Just past the halfway point to the glade, I stepped over the roots of old Splitjaw. At some point in its past, the aged fir tree had been bent over and broken, creating a neck-like structure where the shattered ends split open, making the trunk look like the opened jaws of an alligator. Kara, my fiancé, named it Splitjaw during our first hike in this area.

I smiled, thinking back to that day and her silliness. She'd insisted that Splitjaw needed to be fed. She had dug through her backpack and pulled out some beef jerky, which she opened and stuck in its jagged "mouth." Pleased with herself, she'd shouldered her pack and continued with our trek.

Digging into one of the cargo pouches on my pants, I pulled out the strips of beef jerky I brought with me for this very moment. I unwrapped them and placed them into Splitjaw's mouth. Pocketing the wrapper, I patted the tree and proceeded on my way. Tradition satisfied.

It was close to noon when I stepped out of the trees and into the clearing. Sunlight bathed the meadow. The tall, waving grasses forming a sea of green, almost like a calm lake. The lone Oregon white oak dominated the center of the clearing, a soldier standing guard over the meadow and its denizens. I had no idea how that acorn made it to this area, but I was happy that it had found a home here.

Its branches spread outward to provide shelter and shade to all those who gathered below them, perfect for the task I had given it.

I drew in a cleansing breath, shaking myself from my reverie, and continued walking until I stood under the oak's branches. I unshouldered my backpack and set it down against the tree before letting one hand rest gently on its trunk.

"Sorry I'm late. I was finishing up some drywall in one of the upstairs bedrooms and lost track of time."

I bent down, opened up the pack, and pulled out a collapsible rake. Unfolding it as I stood, I began clearing the detritus of small limbs and leaves from around the area.

"It took longer than I planned, but I got the flooring finished in the kitchen. I know we talked about that white checkered slate tile, but it was out of stock and the backorder was going to take too long. So, I ended up doing a grey, sixteen-inch tile that has four small black diamonds in the center. I think it looks fantastic against the backsplash."

I continued my rundown of my construction highlights as I kept raking.

Satisfied that no limbs or leaves remained, I collapsed the rake, stowed it back in the pack, and pulled out a small set of shears. I squatted down on one knee and began trimming the grass around the two small bronze markers. I worked in thoughtful silence, letting the metallic *snip-snip* of the trimmers soothe my mind and heart as I cleared back the grass and weeds that had grown since my last visit.

Once everything was pruned to my liking, I stowed the shears and retrieved a small rag and bottle of brass cleaner. Pouring a small bit of the solution onto my cloth, I began scrubbing the bird droppings off the markers.

With the bronze gleaming again, I stowed all of my tools and supplies and gazed down at the markers, telling myself I wouldn't cry even as the first tear worked its way down my cheek. Every time I thought I had cried myself out, I found that with these two, I never would.

Kara Berman
  Loving Wife

Karen Berman
  Beloved Daughter

"I love you both," I whispered, letting my fingers lightly brush the metal.

I stood up, grabbing my backpack and swinging it up and onto my back. I shrugged my shoulders a couple of times to seat the straps comfortably, then fastened the belly band, tugging on it to make sure it was tight.

With a final, pained glance at the markers, I turned and headed east, passing quickly out of the meadow and into the trees beyond.

ONE

Josie

I shook the small handheld GPS unit in an attempt to make it work.
"You've got to be freaking kidding me! I will smash you into a million pieces, you worthless hunk of plastic!"

The small, yellow electronic devil was obviously unimpressed with my threat and mocked me with its refusal to comment. Looking up at the sky, I almost asked the heavens, '*What next?*' But I didn't want to tempt fate. Little did I realize at the time that the heavens could read minds, and fate could be a real bitch.

Sighing like a teenager being asked to do the dishes, I shoved the worthless plastic demon into my backpack and pulled out my trusty old compass. Flipping open the lid, I began turning in a small circle, talking to myself while the needle danced inside its glass case.

"Okay, let's see," I muttered to myself. "If that's north, then that way is west and towards the lake. If I can make it to the lake, I should be able to get to the marina and use their phone."

I nodded to myself, taking a deep, calming breath. This was good. Everything was going to be okay.

"I'm going to call Brianna Cranston and give her a piece of my mind. Wait, no. First, I'm going to get her to come pick me up and take me to my car, and while she's driving me to it, then I'm going to give her a piece of my mind. She'll be trapped then and can't escape my wrath. Nice plan, Josie. Less walking, more righteous satisfaction."

Brianna had been the one to talk me into this jaunt when I *should* have been helping Mom with the store. I knew that somewhere in those spreadsheets and invoices was the answer to our financial situation, something that would pull us up out of the hole we were spiraling into.

Apparently, I had been getting a tad bitchy with folks lately. Brianna cornered me in my small office Wednesday. Mom apparently let her slip back to harass me.

"Girl, you need to get away from the sheets of numbers and clear your head before you bite one of your worker's—or worse, Kaylin's head off," she told me, crossing her arms and skewering me with an icy glare.

I scrubbed my tired eyes, glancing up at her. "I don't have the time. We're losing money every day and if I don't figure out how to stop it, Mom and I are toast."

Brianna began lecturing me, using her finger like a conductor's baton. "Get your lazy butt out in the woods. You and your dad loved the woods and trails around here. Hell, you were a tomboy for most of your time here. Get out there, walk among the trees, and clear your mind. Maybe an acorn will fall on that head of yours and give you the idea you need!"

I had reluctantly agreed, more to get her to leave and to stop her nagging. And I had to admit … she had a point. I needed a break.

Putting my compass in the pocket of my shorts, I began walking in the right direction, only slightly limping, thanks to the blister on my heel. Normally, I'd have fixed it with some moleskin, but since I was in such a hurry to leave this morning, I neglected to pack my first aid kit.

My pack contained everything else I might need. Bear whistle, snacks, water, and dry socks. I even had a copy of *Cosmo* that I had filched from the beauty shop. Figured it could double as emergency toilet supplies should the need arise.

No GPS, no moleskin, a squishy blister on my heel, and still a long way from my car. The day was just a winner all the way around.

"Just you wait, Brianna, I've got two sweaty socks with your name written all over them!"

I chuckled evilly at the thought of taking off my boots in her car and launching an odoriferous attack. If I were lucky, she'd puke. Hey, if you can't make your best friend puke, why are they your bestie?

While I might have thought Brianna gagging on sweaty socks would be funny, what galled me the most was that she was right.

About an hour into the hike this morning, I realized I actually felt better. The rich smell of the trees and the sounds of nature slowly eroded my stress level, lowering it to what most folks considered normal. I was bordering on darn near relaxed. Even with the blister and the evil GPS unit, I was feeling better than I had in several weeks.

"Okay, Brianna, maybe no socks this time." Nodding to myself, I continued on down the trail.

After another thirty or so minutes of walking, I came to a ridgeline. Taking a moment, I glanced down into what appeared to be about a fifty-foot drop-off. It wasn't a straight drop, more of a steep downhill, something you might ski on if there were snow, and if you didn't mind rocks and trees at the end of your run. Unhooking my water bottle, I took a small sip as I drank in the panoramic view. I could just see the lake on the horizon. Clipping the water bottle back to my pack, I took a deep, refreshing breath.

"Finally, something is going my way."

I began walking along the edge, hoping to find a way down that looked less like a blue diamond run and more like a bunny slope. I enjoyed skiing, but the lack of skis and snow put a damper on shooshing down the ledge. With my luck today, I'd fall and break an ankle.

At that exact moment, the heavens showed me that they had been paying attention to my thoughts. Just as I walked near a patch of scrub brush, a small rabbit burst out of it right at my feet, moving as if it was late for something.

Like any red-blooded girl seeing something that looks like a mouse on steroids flying at her, I screamed and high-stepped away from the impending rodent mauling that I just knew was coming my way.

Unfortunately, in my adrenaline-fueled rush to escape, I forgot about the ridgeline I had been admiring. I screamed again as I toppled over the edge. I smashed flat on my side and began tumbling end over end as the loose rocks and dirt gave way. I saw ground, sky, ground and then felt a sharp burst of pain in my leg and a punch to my stomach.

I barely had time to think, "Ow ... *shit,*" before blackness took me.

TWO

Jacob

As I emerged from the tree line about 500 feet from a small ridge, a shrill scream pierced the air. Someone, and I guessed a woman by the pitch of the scream, had a healthy set of lungs. I rushed over to an old tree stump, hopping up on it to get a better view just as a second terrified scream shredded the quiet.

Scanning the area, I saw a dust cloud billowing up from the lower face of the ridge. Hopping down from the trunk, I was already moving before the echoes of the second scream faded away. Adrenaline kicked in as instinct took over.

My eyes darted left and right through the scrub, looking for potential trip points even as my mind was processing likely injuries and the treatment each would need. Unlike my time in Afghanistan, there was little possibility of bullet or shrapnel wounds.

My head was on a swivel, my attention divided between the tricky terrain and the fading dust cloud still hanging in the air. Several times, larger tree trunks or rock piles that I couldn't climb, forced me to find alternate paths, including going backwards a few times.

Glancing at the ridge, I figured that most of this debris must have been part of the hillside before storms and winds caused it to slide downward. Regardless of how the ridge got here, moving around on it would be treacherous and would land me in awful shape if I wasn't careful.

I lucked out as I got to the bottom of the ridge. The force of all those trees and rocks falling down over the years had created a roughly fifteen-foot-wide strip of land that was basically a road. A quick glance showed it to be cleared all the way along the base of the ridge.

Reaching the area where I had seen the cloud, I turned back towards the scattered trunks and rocks and started looking in earnest. I hadn't taken more than ten steps when I spotted the body wedged up against some rocks.

Dropping to my knees, I unsnapped my backpack and let it slide to the ground beside me.

A young woman lay on her back, her side up against the rocks. Her right arm was flung back, as if she was asleep and had thrown it there to be out of the way. She was dressed in fairly standard hiking clothes: a light blue windbreaker, the kind designed to wick away moisture yet keep you dry in the event of a light rain, khaki shorts, and hiking boots.

I brushed her hair from her face, laying two fingers against her neck and carotid artery. Her pulse was strong, if a bit fast. Studying her face more closely, I knew that I had seen her around town but had never met her. A quick once-over of her limp form didn't find any bones sticking out of places that they shouldn't, nor any blood imitating a fountain. I looked down at her, sighing.

"Sorry, Miss. You're not able to give me permission, but I need to touch you to see where you're hurt. I can't move you till I know that much." I took her silence to mean she didn't have any reasonable objection to the idea.

Starting with her head, I began gently searching her for injuries. As I did, I noticed that even covered in dirt and with pieces of twigs and leaves stuck in her auburn hair, she was very attractive.

I paused as my fingers brushed across a small bump behind her right ear, but there was no blood flowing from it. I continued down her right arm and then crossed over to her left. Still no bones sticking out.

So far so good. I moved down to check out her legs and still didn't see anything at first glance except for some possible swelling on her lower right leg. I brought both hands up to her stomach and didn't feel any hardening or other indicators of internal bleeding. I started gently touching her lower ribs. Her breathing hadn't been labored or frothy, so I was reasonably comfortable that nothing in her ribcage was broken, but it never hurt to check and make sure.

Just as I had my hands right below her breasts, her chest rose quickly with a rush of air as she inhaled. I sighed in relief. If she was regaining consciousness, then this would go quicker, and I could get an accurate picture of her injuries.

"Be careful, Miss. Don't—"

My warning was interrupted by the right cross I never saw nor expected connecting with my jaw and snapping my head to the side.

THREE

-

Josie

I opened my eyes, blinking rapidly from the bright sunlight. My vision was blurry but clear enough that I could make out some strange man leaning over me. Not only leaning over me but had his hands damn near on my boobs.

Instinct kicked in as I screamed and threw a punch at his head. I had a moment's satisfaction at seeing the punch connect and his head snap to the side before my hand exploded in agony.

"Shit! Who … what …?"

I tried to scramble back away from him, but a crushing wave of pain gripped me, causing my teeth to clench and my eyes to tear up. My right leg let me know that it had a say in things when it came to moving and that it didn't want to move right now.

"Miss, please don't move," the man said. His hand was clutching his jaw as he worked it, testing its function. I could just make out the red imprints on his skin where my punch landed. "I didn't mean to startle you."

"Startle me? Get the fuck away from me!"

Once again, I tried to scramble away from this stranger and again the pain from my leg ripped through me.

"*Shit …*"

The guy put his hands up.

I could see the red mark on his jaw more clearly now. Good. I hoped it hurt.

"Please stop before you hurt yourself even more. You have to calm down or you're going to hyper-ventilate. Relax. Miss, I'm *not* going to hurt you."

"RELAX? What the fuck do you mean *relax*? You don't have some strange asshole groping you in the middle of … wait … where the *hell* am I?"

My lungs were heaving as I tried to get a breath, causing yet more pain from my chest. Glancing left and right, I tried to figure out where I was and how to get away from this stranger.

I caught sight of the ridge, and the memory rushed back in. Crap. That damn rabbit. My hand throbbed, my leg hurt, my chest was on fire, and I was pretty sure the burning feeling on my ass was a magnificent strawberry in the making. All because of that stupid bundle of demonic brown fur.

I tried to get up, but the guy shot forward, putting his hands against my shoulders, stopping me.

"Get your fucking hands off me!" I would have kicked him in the balls, but he was too far away from my knee for it to connect.

"WOULD YOU STOP!" he yelled in a voice loud enough that I'm sure they heard him at the marina. I froze, suddenly scared at the tone and force of that voice. His face immediately softened, and he smiled lightly. For the first time, I really looked at him, and my heart froze.

Cornflower blue eyes. Not just any blue but cornflower blue. The same color as Greg, my dead husband. Worse or amazing, not sure which. He also had the same sandy blond hair as Greg. The memories come surging up unbidden, the pain almost overpowering my senses. I closed my eyes, battering those agonizing feelings back into the prison that normally held them.

His voice brought me back from that painful recall. "Miss, please don't try to get up," he said in a more quiet and calm tone. "I'm not going to hurt you, but you really need to keep still so I can figure out how badly you're hurt."

I felt my lips curl up as I squinted at him, panting from my labors.

"And I suppose you're a doctor?"

If my disdain bothered him, he didn't show it. "Well," he chuckled and waved one hand around at our location. "Given our circumstances, I do think your choices in medical care are a bit limited. If it makes you feel better, I work part-time as a nurse down at the hospital."

Sure, like I was supposed to fall for that line.

"So, you know Maggie, the head nurse?"

He laughed again, shaking his head. "You mean Janey, the head nurse, who is engaged to Ken, the deputy sheriff. Maggie is the front desk receptionist. Do I pass the test?"

Grumpily, I had to admit he seemed to check out.

"For now."

I tried to sit up again, but pushing up against his hands was like pushing up against a brick wall. On top of everything else, this guy was strong. Unfortunately, I tried to use my right hand to add leverage to my push.

"*Shit!*" I gasped as fiery pain shot up my arm. His expression changed instantly. A look of intense concern swept across his face. As if someone had turned up a dimmer switch, those achingly familiar-colored eyes dialed up their intensity and bore straight into mine.

"Please?" he asked quietly.

I read somewhere that some of our most intense and long-lasting memories were tied to our senses. Smelling a fresh-baked apple pie that was cooling on a windowsill would transport you back to your grandmother's kitchen where you had baked pies as a girl.

For me, it was his eyes and that intense look. I'd be ninety and complaining about misplacing my teeth and I would still be able to recall that expression because it was tied to some of the happiest times in my life, moments with Greg. When he had looked at me with that same intense stare, I could deny him virtually nothing.

Staring back at the eyes now watching me that reminded me so much of my dead husband, I nodded my head and relaxed back to the ground.

"Now, let's figure out the damage." He zipped open his backpack and started pulling out various items. "I'm going to take the fact that you were able to land a decent right cross on my jaw as a sign that you've got movement in your limbs and no apparent damage to your neck or spinal cord," he said, bundling up a coat and beginning to wrap a t-shirt around it.

I winced slightly, more from embarrassment than pain. "Sorry about that punch." I was not sorry.

He grinned as he rubbed his jaw. "Oh, don't be," he replied. "Coming to, groggy, barely able to focus, and the first thing you see is some strange man bending over you with his hands on your chest as if to … Well, it's all good. In fact, I learned a very valuable lesson out of it."

"Oh yeah?" I watched as one corner of his mouth quirked up.

"Never, ever, piss you off," he said, waggling his eyebrows at me as he smiled.

For the first time, I really looked at this guy. Okay, for a potential forest molester, he didn't seem too bad. I was still trying to ignore the eyes.

"Damn straight," I remarked.

I tried glaring at him but found I couldn't pull it off. His smile was working on me. My shoulders relaxed as the tension slowly drained away.

"First things first, as your current medical provider, perhaps I should introduce myself. I'm Jacob. And you are?"

"Josie."

"Name remembrance. Excellent. Can you tell me what day it is?"

"Saturday."

"Awesome. Let's get you a bit comfier," he said.

He gently lifted my head just far enough off the ground that he could slide his t-shirt bundle under it. Once he had it positioned where he wanted, he let my head back down, pulling some twigs from my hair and flicking them to the side.

"So, where does it hurt?" Jacob asked.

"You mean other than my right hand feeling like I punched a wall?"

"Yeah, let's take that as a given." He flashed that infectious grin again.

"Right leg, right hand, and my head. Don't suppose you have an aspirin or twelve in that bag of yours?"

"Give me a sec and let me check out those areas you mentioned. I'd already checked your head before your spirited revival, so I'll give everything else a once over." He leaned towards me and brought his hands up, pausing with them still a few inches away. "I'm just going to touch you, Josie. Please don't hit me again. You're running out of working hands." He captured my gaze with his, his lips twitching upward slightly.

The female patients at the hospital must love this guy's bedside manner.

"I've never hit my medical provider before." I gave him a slight smile of my own. He laughed quietly, shaking his head. His face really lit up when he laughed. Maybe he wasn't such a bad guy after all. Time would tell.

For the next few minutes, he gently examined me, telling me each time he was going to move and where he was going to touch. I guess I didn't blame him. He was probably scared I'd knee him in the groin or something worse next, which was still not beyond the realm of possibility.

"Right. So, what do you want first? The good news or the bad news?" he asked.

"Wait, what about the aspirin?"

Jacob shook his head. "Sorry, without knowing if you have any internal bleeding going on, I can't risk it. I don't think you do, but I can't take the chance.

"In that case, let's have the good news first." Hopefully, it would help my head feel better.

"So then. Along with the right hand, you have a small bump behind your right ear. I don't see any blown pupils, so I think that bump is the only real head issue. Pretty sure you have at least two damaged ribs. You're not blowing bloody bubbles at me or gasping as you breathe, so I'm going to go with bruised versus broken. Last but most certainly not least, I think the fibula in your right leg has a deep bruise or is broken between your knee and ankle," Jacob explained, ticking off each item.

My mouth dropped open. That was what he thought to be *good news*? I must have looked like one of those clowns at the fair, the ones where you shoot water into their open mouth to inflate a balloon and win a cheap prize. What did he consider bad? Decapitation?

"What the fuck?" I barked at him. "We're stuck out here, miles from anything, I have a busted leg and ribs, and you think *that* is the good news? What the *hell* do you consider bad news?"

Okay, maybe it was a small temper tantrum, but with the attempted rabbit mauling and the 'agony of defeat' tumble down the ridge, I figured I was damn well due.

Jacob leaned over so he could look directly into my eyes, and his face took on a deeply serious look.

"I'll have to check to be sure, but I don't think I take your insurance."

FOUR

Jacob

I grinned as her mouth fell open and her eyebrows arched upwards to an impressive height. I watched as shock, disbelief, and even something I thought might be anger flew across her face. For the first time, I allowed myself to linger on her eyes.

Her emerald-green eyes. Another face with emerald-green eyes leapt to mind, one that I knew intimately. I buried that thought quickly before it could gain a hold on me.

Her jaw snapped shut, and her eyes turned into little green laser beams that I could swear were boring right into me.

"I'm lying here with a busted leg, a stick jamming me in my ass, and I'm pretty sure I have a boulder in my bra, and you're making *jokes?*" she demanded through gritted teeth. I'd never seen steam come out of anyone's ears, but I was pretty sure I was about to witness it for the first time.

I laughed even though I could tell she was pissed. Her face had a slight flush, and I could see a small, throbbing vein in her neck. Note to self: Don't *ever* be the target of this woman's anger. But some masochistic blip in my makeup couldn't help but poke the bear a bit more. Kinda the 'in for a penny, in for a pound' thing.

"Absolutely. It's all part of my bedside manner. No extra charge!"

The fire in her eyes slowly faded, and a glint of humor peeked through. She raised her left hand, beckoning me to come closer. Like a stupid man, I did.

"Jacob," she said softly. I couldn't help the small shit-eating grin I was currently sporting as I answered her just as softly.

"Yes?"

"One day, not today, but someday soon, I'm going to make you pay for that. It won't be pretty, and you won't like it. But you *will* pay." She smiled at me like a cat grinning at a mouse.

I slapped my thighs as I rocked back and straightened up. "Well then, guess we better get you out of here so you can plot my evil demise."

Delving back into my pack, I pulled out a small, collapsed buck-saw. Scrambling to my feet, I started picking my way over the boulders to a couple of young fir trees. Unfolding the saw, I locked the blade into place with a small click and began checking branches. It only took a moment to find one that would work for me, and the sharp saw made short work of removing it from the tree. I began trimming off the excess branches. Once done, I laid the limb across a small bolder and cut the long branch into several smaller sections. I flexed each piece, testing the strength before picking two that would work.

I carried my haul back to Josie and dropped the saw near my pack. Pulling my knife from its belt sheath, I trimmed off the branch stubs and other small bumps on the two sticks until they were as smooth as I could make them. Wiping the blade on my shorts to remove the sap, I slipped it back into its sheath, securing the snaps.

Kneeling down, I rummaged in my pack again, pulling out a bundle of parachute cord. Any good soldier would tell you that there is almost nothing that parachute cord can't fix. Rednecks might have their duct tape, but give me a few hundred feet of paracord and I could build a house.

I cut several lengths of cord and laid them next to my splint pieces before turning my attention back to her. I knew she wasn't going to like what I had to do next, but it was necessary. I had to get her out of here.

"Josie, there really is no good way to do this. I have to splint that leg, and it's going to hurt."

She nodded and gritted her teeth in anticipation.

I worked as quickly as I could. She hissed and blew her breath out each time I tied a cord in place. I sat back, surveying my work. It would hold until I could get her to the hospital. Unfortunately, my options for doing that were limited.

I held the water bottle out to her, and she took a few ragged gulps before handing it back.

"Damn … that … hurt," she managed to stutter out.

"Sorry." I didn't want to hurt her, but there was nothing to help that right now. "Hand next."

When I pulled out the paracord, I also pulled out an elastic bandage. I always kept one in my pack when hiking. You never knew when you might roll or twist an ankle while out enjoying nature.

I held my left hand out to her, palm up, and wiggled my fingers. She gingerly brought her injured right hand up to me. She winced and huffed a few times as I wrapped from wrist up to her first knuckles. Not too tightly, just enough to contain the swelling.

"Well, that's the best I can do with what I have in my pack. Now, let's get you to the hospital."

She gave me that 'you've lost your mind' look again. "I know I bumped my head when I did my tumbleweed impression," she said, "but unless you have a horse or a four-wheeler in that backpack, I'm not seeing how we're getting there."

"Oh, yee of little faith."

I rounded up all my supplies and shoved them back into my pack. Once done, I glanced around for her pack, spying it at the base of the cleared area. Scrambling up the slippery, shifting rocks, I retrieved it, reworking the straps so that I could fasten it to the back of mine. I slid back down the ridge face and moved back to her, kneeling down on her left side.

"Okay lazybones, let's go."

"Look," she replied with a sigh. "We've had this discussion—"

I cut her off, "I'm going to carry you."

She burst out laughing. I didn't know it was possible to have a belly laugh while laying down, but she proved me wrong. She was laughing so hard she began to snort and wheeze simultaneously. The only thing she hadn't done yet was piss her pants. I silently prayed she had good bladder control.

I sat there, waiting for the laughing fit to pass. I decided I liked her laugh. Her face flushed, and her emerald eyes sparkled again. I had done a good job so far of not noticing the color of her eyes and hair, and how they pulled at the pain I kept locked away, but I was losing the fight. The laugh was making it almost unbearable. I shoved those feelings back down into the basement of my mind, sealing them away with the pain they brought.

"Ow ... that hurts," she said with a wheeze, trying to speak and laugh at the same time. "Let me ... heehee ... ow ... ow ... see if I have this right. God that hurts ... I may have ... hehehe. You're going to pick me up and *carry* me out of here?"

"Yes." I kept my face serious with no hint of humor. She needed to understand that I wasn't kidding.

"To where?" asked the new queen of mirth.

"Well, my trailer and truck are about a mile or so that way, so we—"

"A MILE!" she exclaimed. "You're going to pick me up and carry me a *mile?*"

I nodded again. "That's the plan."

She snorted again. "Well, far be it from me to point out the flaws in your plan."

"Far be it. Now, to avoid any confusion and further injury to my face, I'm going to be picking you up. Okay?"

She nodded but kept laughing.

"As with the splinting, this might hurt a bit." I dreaded causing her anymore pain.

Working carefully, I raised her up to a sitting position. I knew it hurt because she began to pant slightly. I gave her a few moments to catch her breath, then slid my arms around her and lifted her up so that she sat on my knee.

She grunted once when her right leg shifted, but other than that was quiet. I was a bit impressed. I knew it had to hurt, but she gritted her teeth and bore it. Once she was on my knee, I repositioned my grip to grasp under her knees and around her back before standing up. I had her on her left side so she could rest her right hand on her belly.

She settled against me, and I felt those demons pounding at the walls I had wrapped around them. This was going to be the longest mile I had ever traveled.

FIVE

Josie

Holy shit! He wasn't joking. Lying there in the dirt and grass and listening to him casually mention picking me up and toting me a mile had me laughing so hard I almost peed my pants. God, did it make my ribs hurt.

I wasn't laughing now.

"You're going to hurt your back and drop me, you doofus!"

"Doofus," he said with a chortle. "I think the last time I heard that was in junior high."

"It's an oldie, but a goodie. Now put me down and let's come up with a different plan."

"Sorry, can't do that," he replied. "Now, without being too forward, can you help me out and put your left hand around my back and grasp my backpack to help hold on?"

I looked at him like he had grown another head. "You want me to snuggle up to you while you walk?" I almost laughed again as a blush started from his neck and worked its way up his face. This was like shooting fish in a barrel.

"It will help me and make it easier on you. Your call," he said, face still flaming. I slipped my arm around him and tried not to blush myself as I snuggled up to him. This would be a lot easier if he didn't feel so damn good when I laid my head against his shoulder. Hell, he even smelled good; a woodsy smell with a hint of manly sweat. I breathed him in quietly.

Jacob stepped off and started us down a small trail. I let him go another few steps before I changed my mind. I couldn't let him do this.

"Jacob, stop."

He stopped and turned his gaze on me. Damn it! Time to go on the offensive. Don't look at the eyes, girl.

"Look, it's cool what you're doing but you're gonna hurt yourself carrying me and then we will both be stuck out here. Just put me down near one of the trees and go get help. I'll be fine."

"Seriously?" he asked. "One, you want me to leave an injured woman parked under a tree in the middle of the woods. Two, hike the mile or so to my truck, drive the fifteen miles into town, get help, drive the fifteen miles back. Three, force an EMT team to hike all the way back here with a stretcher and all their gear. Four, hope that you are still safe and sound when I get back. Is that really what you're asking? Maybe that bump on your head was a bit harder than I thought."

I rolled my eyes and grumped a bit. "Yeah, but I promise I'll be—"

He interrupted me again, "Josie, let me ask you a personal question. Do you weigh more than 150 pounds?" I really didn't like to be interrupted, and I was really starting to get a bit pissed.

I glared at him, both for cutting in again and for his question. "Hasn't anyone ever told you that it's rude to ask a woman that question?"

"Yes, I'm taking my life into my hands, but I promise that I can easily carry you. Trust me?"

Those words caused me to snap my focus back to him. It was damn near an automatic response since it had been Greg's favorite way to ask me to do something he knew I wouldn't like. I smiled weakly at him and nodded my head.

"Good," he said before starting off again. He was using small animal paths and working around trees, so the path was not always straight.

As he walked, I gave him small glances. I already knew his chest felt good, but along with those eyes, he had everything else that could make you feel wonderful. Small dimples when he smiled, strong chin. Okay, so I may have snuggled into that amazing chest a bit more, but he said it was helping him, right?

Every fifteen minutes, Jacob would stop and go down on one knee, letting me sit on the other raised knee. During this small break he would roll his shoulders and shake out his arms, one at a time so as not to dislodge me. At the end of the break, he would stand and head off again.

His breathing only deepened, never quickened. I got the distinct impression that he could have carried me for hours. I suspected he was stopping so often more for me rather than him actually needing a break.

Shortly after the third break, the trail emptied out into a clearing. On the far side was what appeared to be a camping trailer and a truck. The right side of the clearing had several sheds and piles of wood, bricks, and cement blocks. It seemed we had finally made it to our destination.

Jacob carried me over to the trailer. One of those roll-out awnings was attached to the trailer and was hanging out over an old, faded picnic table. He carefully lowered me down to the tabletop, squirming around until he had me settled so that my legs hung over the end. Our packs hit the ground a second later.

"Stay," he ordered, pointing a finger at me and grinning.

"You're *soooo* funny."

He walked to the driver's side of the pickup truck and hopped up into the cab. The engine fired up with a roar before settling into a deep-throated rumble. He maneuvered the truck until the passenger side was as close to the table as the awning would allow.

Leaving the truck idling, he jumped out and came back to me. Unfortunately, to get me into the truck he would need to pick me up on the right side. I was already gritting my teeth in anticipation.

"Sorry," he whispered softly before picking me up. I could tell he was being as gentle as possible, but it still hurt.

"Fuckity … fu … fuuddgee …" I grunted out between clenched teeth. He maneuvered me into the passenger seat, causing yet another round of agony to shoot up from my leg, which of course meant I tensed up my ribcage, allowing the ribs to put in their two cents. I think they pooled their money and came up with more than two cents. I began huffing and heeing like I had during the Lamaze classes I had taken for the birth of my daughter, Kaylin.

Once I was safely in the seat, he tossed our backpacks in at my feet, fumbling around in his until he pulled out a cell phone. He reached behind my right shoulder and grabbed the seat belt end, pulling it over me and fastening it in place. After slamming my door shut, he ran back around the truck and climbed up in the driver's seat.

The drive to the paved road was slow, bumpy, and painful. He tried to avoid as many of the ruts and bumps as he could, but it still hurt like hell. Once we hit the smoother blacktop, the ride got a lot better, and the pain from my ribs and leg dulled. Without taking his eyes from the road, he hit a speed dial on his phone.

"Janey, good, you're on today. Listen, I'm on my way in with a patient. Josie … hang on a sec," he said, briefly turning to face me before shifting his gaze back to the road. "Sorry, I never asked your last name."

"Callison."

He nodded and started speaking to his phone again. "Janey, I'm on my way in with Josie Callison. Yes … Yes, I wouldn't know, Janey. Look, chat later."

I listened as he outlined my injuries and all the particulars from his examination of me.

"We're about twelve miles out, just passing the old Pierson logging road. Call Ken and let him know I'll be flying by him in about ten minutes." Janey must have started talking because he paused a few seconds before continuing. "Come on, Janey. It's Saturday. You know right where he's sitting. Tell him to be watching for me. See you soon," he told her, clicking off the call. With the call finished, he dropped the phone next to him on the seat and hit the gas, pushing me backwards from the sudden acceleration.

"Killing me on the way to the hospital defeats the purpose of bringing me, Mr. Speed Demon. And just where is Ken, and how do you know where he is?"

Jacob looked at me funny and nodded, even as he slowed the trucks speed down below ninety.

"He's in his patrol car near the old firebreak. He always parks there on Saturdays after lunch so he can watch for speeders. Least, that's what he tells folks. Everyone knows he's just taking a nap after eating Brianna's meatloaf special at the diner, which she only serves on Saturdays," he replied. "But I'm guessing you didn't know that?"

"I did know about the meatloaf, didn't know about Ken's nap spot. I don't normally get up this way very often."

"Huh," he said. There was a lot of innuendo in that little statement and if I wasn't hurting so bad, I would be addressing it. I made a mental note to kill him after I got even for that insurance gag.

My ribs were starting to really hurt, and a steady, painful throb had begun in my hand as we flew down the road. It seemed like hours, but it was really just a few minutes before flashing lights erupted ahead of us on the road. Ken must have seen us because the cruiser accelerated like a scalded cat. We quickly gained on the patrol car, forcing Jacob to slow down and let Ken lead the way with lights and sirens.

As we hit the outer edge of the town, the sheriff's cruiser pulled further ahead to make sure all the intersections were clear. When we turned off the main road to the hospital's ER entrance, Ken swung his cruiser away from the doors, allowing us to pull up under the overhang where a crew was waiting.

We had barely stopped before Jacob was out and at my side of the truck. He threw open the door. Apologizing again, he gently lifted me out of the truck. My leg bumped the edge of the door causing me to cry out from the pain.

Janey and another nurse moved up close to him with a gurney and watched as Jacob placed me gently on it. Once situated, they pushed me through the emergency room doors and straight into an exam room where two other nurses joined us.

With a precision that showed years of practice, they moved me from the gurney to the exam table and began doing all the usual ER things. Orders were snapped out. Ringers, IV, X-ray, STAT. I heard all the usual buzz words inherent in the medical field. My stick brace was cut off and tossed to the floor.

As they began fussing over me, Jacob and Ken slipped into the room. Jacob leaned against the wall, arms crossed, silently taking in the activity. Ken tucked his thumbs into his belt and became a statue.

Dr. Harper came in about that time, and Janey outlined my list of injuries along with the results of their prodding and poking. The doctor nodded as he pulled a small flashlight out of his coat pocket. He moved up beside my head and gave me a smile as he clicked on his small light.

"Well, Josie, not that I don't enjoy seeing you, but what happened to cause you to grace us with your presence today?" he asked, flicking the flashlight into and out of my left eye before moving to my right.

"Have you ever watched those old sports shows on TV where they talk about the agony of defeat and show a skier going ass over toes down a hill?" I asked him. He nodded, put away his flashlight and gently pressed my rib cage. I hissed at the pressure and the beeping on one of the monitors sped up a bit.

"I did my best impression of that today, managing to bang myself up and knock myself out. I woke up to Jacob there preparing to molest me." I had started to laugh at my joke but it died in my throat.

I've watched a ton of movies and TV shows in my time. I've seen countless scenes where a character says something so outlandish or shocking that a whole roomful of people just stop what they are doing or saying and stare at the speaker. The proverbial pin drop situation. I had seen it, but never been part of one.

Until now.

The exam room became deathly quiet. The only sound being the beeping of the monitor beside me. The nurses just stared at me. Dr. Harper froze in place. I glanced at Ken and cringed. He had fire in his eyes and looked like he was starting a slow boil. It was the complete opposite of Jacob.

His eyes looked … sad. That was the only word that came to mind. Intense sadness.

Ken started to say something, but Jacob laid a hand on his arm, shook his head, turned and left the room. Ken fixed me with a stare.

"Josie, you've been back, what, about a month or so?" he asked quietly. I nodded. "You ever met or talked to anyone about Jacob? Know anything about him?"

"No."

I didn't know what was going on, but something told me to keep my mouth shut until I got more information.

"Ah," he said. "That explains that."

With that simple statement, the movie of life started back up from pause, and sounds and actions resumed. Dr. Parker began giving directions to the nurses who started manipulating my table so they could get me to X-ray.

Ken stepped aside so they could wheel me through the door but held up a hand to stop them.

"I'll wait for them to finish and take you home," he said. I shook my head.

"I'll call Mom once I get out of here. She can come get me. No need to disrupt your meatloaf digestion any further."

He shot me a withering glance. Score one for me today. He stepped back out of the way so I could be wheeled out of the room.

SIX

Josie

Two hours later, I was out of the ER with my ribs wrapped up, my hand in an elastic wrap, and my foot in a walking boot, which was much more preferable than a cast. Fortunately, my leg hadn't been broken, just deeply bruised. The downside was that I needed to wear the boot for four weeks.

Ken had stayed for me anyway, and we now huddled into his patrol car. He backed us out of the hospital and headed back to the main road. I managed to fish my cell phone out of my backpack without dumping the contents all over the floorboard. I called Mom to give her a brief update, then I assured her I was fine and that Ken was bringing me home. As I was putting the phone away, I glanced out the windows at the buildings going by and realized we were not heading toward my house.

"Um, where are we going?"

"Just a quiet place for a quick chat. Shouldn't take more than a few minutes," he said, his attention on the road.

"Ken, it's been a really crappy day. I just want to go home, get clean, and lay down. You know Mom is going to have kittens if I'm not there soon. Not to mention what Janey will do to me if she finds me parking somewhere with you."

He just chuckled. "Leave your mom and Janey to me. If it gets too rough, I can put you in protective custody if you're scared," he stated with a slight glance my way. He couldn't quite hide his grin.

"Yeah, like that would stop either of them. Fine, be secretive."

We wound our way through town until we started going through familiar surroundings. My suspicions were confirmed when he pulled into the high school parking lot. He swung the big cruiser around and pointed us back towards the street before parking. He left the engine running, undid his seatbelt, and wiggled around until he was a bit more comfortable.

"You know much about Jacob?" he asked as he scanned the street in front of him.

"No, not really. I've had my head buried in the store and helping Mom since I got back. Haven't had time to get to know much of anyone I didn't already know. Today was the first day I've ever spoken to him."

Ken nodded as he pulled out a piece of peppermint candy from a pocket. He offered me a piece, but I wasn't in a candy mood. He unwrapped and popped the small disc in his mouth and sucked on it for a few moments.

"Jacob got here about, oh, three years before you. Nice guy. Kept to himself for the most part. He and the sheriff hit it off right from the start. Both are former military and have similar backgrounds.

"First time I had a beer with them, they were having the most confusing conversation I'd ever heard. They started talking about some really hairy shit. Firefights, ambushes, best way to set up booby traps. Scared the living piss out of me to hear them talk about this stuff so calmly." He started chuckling again. "Then they got to arguing and it was all 'Jarhead or Marine' from Jacob and 'Grunt this' or 'Grunt that' from the sheriff."

"Grunt?" Now I was confused.

"Yeah, seems 'Grunt' is what Army soldiers are sometimes called. Same with 'Jarhead' or 'Marine' for the Marines. They used some other names, but I'm not sure I want to say those in mixed company.

"Anyway, ask Jacob if you want any details about his military life. As you may now know, one of his skills is first aid. The military, among other things, trained him to be a combat medic." He stared at me, grinning. "You lucked out, girl. The absolute best person to find you after your fall found you. He keeps his skills and certifications up by helping at the hospital. Think he works one or two shifts every couple of weeks, fills in when he's needed."

Ken looked back out into the night, his candy clinking against his teeth. I don't know what he was thinking about, but I could feel the mood change in the car and a chill go up my arms.

"About eighteen months or so after he got here, we had a motor-cycle gang take up residence at that old campsite out on Pierson Road. Pretty much kept to themselves, came into town for beer and such. Didn't really bother folks. We got a few complaints but nothing major. They spent money in the town and folks just let them be."

He cleared his throat and twitched in his seat. Whatever this was, he was agitated thinking about it.

"One night, Jacob finished up a shift at the hospital and was heading home when he stopped at Johnson's Market. Before he could get in the store, he heard someone cry out. He walked around the side of the building and saw a foot sticking out from behind a dumpster. Rushing over he found nineteen-year-old Alice Branson, badly beaten. He ran back into the store, yelled at them to call 911, then ran back out to Alice. Best we can figure she was still conscious enough to talk to him before we got there.

"I pulled up just after the ambulance, about five minutes after I got the call from dispatch. I no sooner got out of the car when Jacob passed me at a dead run heading for his truck. I caught a glimpse of his face but even that sent a chill through me. I tried calling out to him, but he jumped in his truck and peeled out."

I watched as Ken paused, rubbing his hands up and down his pants leg. His jaw muscles were clenching and unclenching. He worked his jaw a few times before taking a deep breath and blowing it out noisily.

He continued, "Took us about twenty minutes to get Alice stable enough to get her on the gurney and another three minutes to the hospital. I'd radioed the sheriff, and he was waiting for us when we rolled up to the emergency room. He'd already sent a patrol car to get Alice's parents. They got there about fifteen minutes after us.

"We'd been waiting about an hour when the doctor came out. Given the circumstances, he briefed us all on Alice. She had been beaten badly and was in a coma. Mrs. Branson started wailing and wanted to be let in to see her daughter.

"It was Mr. Branson who finally asked about seventeen-year-old Jenny, his other daughter. It seems she and Alice had gone out together that night to meet up with friends."

Ken paused again. He was gripping the steering wheel so tight his knuckles were white. I placed my hand on his arm and gave it a light squeeze. He took a moment to get himself under control before continuing.

"The sheriff got up and was heading towards the door when he stopped and cursed. Before the rest of us could move, the doctor was yelling out orders. I turned, to see what the problem was, and I felt the bile rise up my throat.

"Jacob stood in the door with a blanket-wrapped figure in his hands. He was bleeding down one side of his head, a cut above one eye that was also bruising up to be a nice shiner, not to mention blood on his pants and shoes. An arm hung out of that blanket and what appeared to be long, blond, bloody hair.

"He moved right by the doctor and went straight into the back area of the ER, limping as he did, leaving red-tinged footprints in his path. The doc was trailing him, still calling out orders, but he was pale as a ghost. A couple of nurses met them at the doors with another gurney as the doctor began opening the blanket. Before the doors closed, we heard someone puke. A god damn nurse puked. What kind of shit do you have to see as a nurse to make you puke?

"Must have been about forty-five minutes later that Jacob came back out. He had been cleaned up and was sporting some new stitches. The sheriff got up close with him and began talking, low enough that I couldn't hear. I watched the sheriff's head snap back and his face go rigid in shock, then turned to stone. He looked at me and motioned me to follow as he turned and headed out the door. Jacob was already kneeling with the Bransons. The last sound I heard as the doors closed was Mrs. Branson crying out for her baby.

"I followed the sheriff up to the bikers' camp where we met two other cars he'd radioed for. Sheriff got out of his car, pulling his shotgun with him. He jacked a round home and motioned us to follow as we all drew weapons.

"We hadn't gone fifteen feet before we found the first body. Sheriff had us go back to the cars to get restraint ties. We made sure the first guy found was breathing, zipped up his hands and feet and made our way up to the small cabin. The next body, also still alive, was draped over the porch rails. He got the same treatment. The sheriff walked up to the front door, which was hanging on one hinge. He used his shotgun to push the door open. It fell off the frame, landing on the floor."

He paused, staring back out into the night.

"Josie, the sheriff always hinted at what Jacob was capable of, but holy hell. The inside of that cabin looked like the aftermath of the worst bar fight you have ever seen. Busted up furniture littered the floor, along with bodies. We found six bikers in the cabin, all alive but not moving. One guy was hanging halfway out of a side window. One was smashed into the fireplace, face buried in the ash. The others were just lumps on the floor. One large, ugly guy had two broken arms, a smashed face, and various other injuries. We found out later that he was Mad Dog, the leader of the gang.

"We had to wait eight weeks for those assholes to heal up enough to stand trial. Tried them all at one time and it took almost two months. They were all charged with possession of cocaine, heroin, aggravated assault, kidnapping, and aggravated rape. That was just for Jenny. A whole separate set of charges were for Alice.

"DNA evidence tagged everyone in that cabin to Jenny. Judge gave them all twenty years. The DA wanted thirty, but I think he had to settle to protect Jacob. I don't know what they worked out, but Jacob walked away scot-free. In the process, he became a town hero.

"As they were hauling the leader out of the room, he was screaming at Jacob. Said he was going to kill him when he got out, that this wasn't over. That he was going to kill his entire family. Jacob didn't blink. He looked that trash in the eye until they got him out of the courtroom. He turned and walked back and kneeled next to the Bransons, and they talked quietly for a few moments before both parents seemed to gasp and began shaking their heads. He handed them a small business card that they first refused but then took after he talked to them a bit more. Mrs. Branson hugged Jacob hard. Her and her husband left with Jacob following them.

"The Bransons were gone the next day. An unmarked truck and crew came a few days later and packed up their house. It went on the market immediately afterwards. Not even sure where they ended up, but I hope those two girls recovered."

Ken stopped speaking and turned to me. I stared back, the tears silently rolling down my cheeks.

"It's his story to tell why, but know this: Jacob *hates* rapists. In his mind, the only good rapist is a dead rapist. He could have killed those men easily, and honest to God I don't know why he didn't, but he could have killed every damn one of them and *never* lost a wink of sleep.

"I'm telling you this, Josie, so you know why everyone reacted that way back at the hospital. I got mad, but then I realized you just didn't know what had happened. But the hospital staff love him and they, as well as many in this town, are protective of him, so they didn't take the joke the right way, as you saw."

I sat there, stunned. I could hear the creak of Ken's leather belt as he fidgeted on the seat. Several cars motored by on the street in front of us.

I'd never felt this low or embarrassed before. Along with thanking him for helping me in the woods, I needed to beg his forgiveness for my crass remark. I couldn't wait until this crap day was over.

"Well, best get you to your mom's before she calls the sheriff on me."

He fired up the car and took me home. Mom and Kaylin swarmed me as soon as I got out of the car. Mom still managed to give Ken the stink eye, and he ducked his head and left quietly. Kaylin never left my side and waited on me hand and foot while I recapped the day, had dinner, and worked out with Mom on getting my car back from where I'd parked it.

That night in bed, I lay awake mulling through what Ken had told me about Jacob. Seems I had some apologizing to do and soon.

SEVEN

Josie

M om insisted I stay off my feet for at least a week. We
compromised, and I stayed home from work until
Wednesday.

When Greg had died, I stayed in North Carolina. I had friends and
a good job working for a finance company that allowed me to provide
a decent life for Kaylin and I. Greg's life insurance, both our personal
policy as well as through his work, gave me enough cushion to give me
time to think.

Then just over a year after Greg died, Dad passed quietly in his
sleep. The doctors suspected a stroke. Several months later, Mom
started making noises about the store being in trouble and asked if I
could help. I took a quick trip home to scope out the situation. Three
months after that trip, I moved back to Azton.

The store was in serious trouble, and I was wracking my brain
trying to come up with a plan to help resolve all the issues. The stress
of dealing with that was what forced Brianna to make her suggestion
about the hike.

Mom and Dad owned Martinson's Emporium, a business that had been in our family for over seventy-five years. The store carried a variety of goods, almost one of everything you could think of.

When I was growing up, the store had been a center point of the small community. But with time comes progress, and that included the inevitable invasion of the larger stores combined with town growth. One of those huge variety stores opened up near the interstate about twenty miles away. Since then, Martinson's had seen a slow but steady decline in business. The new store had everything under one roof, and folks liked its convenience and lower prices.

Mom gave me a lift into town since the walking boot made driving a pain in the ass. I had been going over the books again this morning and they weren't any better. We were bleeding money as our bills steadily ate our line of credit with the bank. Unless I could convince the bank to give us an extension or find another source of income, things were going to get bad, fast.

I was staring at my monitors when Mom stepped into the office. I had been so absorbed in the numbers that I had lost track of time, and it was almost noon.

"You go get some lunch and quit worrying about this," she chided, herding me to the front door. "I told you it will all work out, and it will. So, go. Get some lunch and gossip with Brianna. Wait, what do you girls say now? Spill the tea?"

"Please don't ever say that where anyone can hear you. We talked about you and slang. And I don't gossip! Brianna brings me up to date on the pulse of the town. This provides me invaluable insight as to current needs and wants so that I can anticipate what stock we need to meet the needs of our consumers."

I managed to get that out without choking on it. Mom raised one eyebrow in that patented 'Mom Look.'

"Fine," I huffed out. "I'll go gossip with Brianna." She just smiled and patted my cheek before sending me out the door. I felt like I was seven and heading off to school.

I stumped my way down the street to Brianna's place. Her and her husband ran Smith's Eats, a small diner nestled in the business district of our little town. I'm not sure how Brianna's grandparents had done it, but in their day, they managed to con the City Council into passing an ordinance banning eateries within a three-block radius around the courthouse. It also conveniently grandfathered in the Smith's since it was already in place. Thus, Smith's Eats had a monopoly on the lunch crowd for the businesses in the area.

The small bell above the door jingled as I entered. I paused for a moment to breathe in the place. The smells were almost as soothing to me as home was, which was not surprising considering how much time I spent here as a kid.

It was a classic, small-town diner. The counter ran down the right side of the room with the obligatory opening back to the kitchen. Round, padded stools with cracked vinyl tops were spaced out across the front of the counter. A pie carousel occupied one end of the counter, currently home to several of Brianna's famous pies.

A coffee pot and soda fountain occupied the back wall work area. The order window allowed you to see Brianna's husband, Brian, working in the kitchen. The ubiquitous order wheel hung in that opening, and a small silver bell sat under the wheel.

A jukebox sat on the back wall between the stools and the booths. Three booths were on the back left wall, and the back portion of the wall had some four-person tables, all supported by the jukebox.

Brianna looked up from wiping down the counter. "Hey, girl!" she cried. I took my normal spot in the booth at the far back corner, and Brianna arrived to set a glass of sweet tea in front of me.

Greg had gotten me hooked on the sugary drink when we were dating. When I first asked Brianna for it, she checked me for a fever. That prompted me to educate her on the proper method of making this Southern staple. Since then, she always kept some made up for me. I was proud to say that several others were now addicted to the beverage.

"Your lunch will be right up," she told me. "Your mom called and said to make sure you eat."

I thudded my head against the booth and started mentally listing the pros and cons of a retirement home for Mom while Brianna snorted and walked off. When she came back, she brought me my BLT—extra mayo, crispy bacon—and fries, my go-to lunch.

I grabbed the squeeze bottle from the little table caddy and made large ketchup circles on my fries. Satisfied with the application, I dug in and crunched through a couple before looking up at her, swallowing.

"You know, this whole foot thing is your fault!"

"*My fault?*" she exclaimed, bringing her hands to her chest in mock pain. "Whatever. I was just trying to get you out of that stuffy office and into some fresh air. Sorry for caring." She sniffed as if deeply hurt, but I wasn't buying it. She got a reprieve when the bell on the door jingled and Riley and Isabella came in. Riley was a teller at the bank and Isabella, or Izzy, as we called her, worked in the clerk's office at the courthouse.

Both voiced their hellos as they joined me at the booth. I was properly admonished for not telling them that I had been hurt. All three demanded I tell them how it had happened.

The four of us had been good friends in high school and had stayed in touch after moving on with life. Once I got back in town, we picked up where we left off. Riley was divorced, and Isabella married Bill, her high school sweetheart, and the two had never left town. They had two boys that gave Izzy hell.

Brianna came back a few minutes later with everyone's order, including a plate for herself. She pulled up an extra chair and settled in to eat.

"Okay, girl, spill it," Brianna said, waving one of her fries at me.

I shrugged. "First off, I still blame you. If you hadn't guilted me into taking that stupid hike, this wouldn't have happened!"

She threw a fry at me, hitting me in the nose. Luckily, she hadn't dunked it in her weird ketchup-mayo combination. "You're stalling," she retorted, picking up a replacement potato chunk.

As I ate, I told them what happened on Saturday. When I mentioned Jacob finding me, all three gasped and started speaking at once. I just laughed at them. "Damn, one at a time."

"You're telling me you woke up to that fine Jacob Berman bending over you?" asked Brianna, her eyes alight with excitement.

I looked at Brianna and just shook my head at the look of surprise on her face, and a bit of longing in her eyes. "Yeah. Had his hands almost on the girls. That's when I slugged him." Three cries of outrage bombarded me. I glared at them.

"Hey! You wake up to some strange guy ready to grab your tits and see how you handle it!"

"If it was Jacob, I'd have yanked that delicious mouth down to them," Riley said, grinning. There were murmurs of agreement, and I chose to ignore the fact that two of the hussies at the table were married.

Once the table had their hormones under control, I continued with the story. When I got to the exam part, I was interrupted again.

"Are you telling us that he ran his fingers through your hair and had his hands all over you?" asked Riley breathlessly.

"Yep."

"*Fuck ...*" breathed Riley, visibly flustered. Izzy just kinda sighed. Brianna stopped chewing. I reached over and shut her mouth. No one liked to see partially masticated fries dipped in, well, anything. I cast a questioning glance at them.

"What the hell's wrong with you three? What makes this guy so special?"

It was Riley who finally shook herself. "Are you seriously going to sit there and tell me that the hottest stud in three counties ran his hands all over you and you didn't start dripping? Fuck, I'd have soaked my jeans."

"Hottest stud? Seriously?"

The other three just looked shocked before Brianna chimed in, "Well, in fairness, girls, she's only been back about a month, and she's had her head buried in her mom's business. She's just not up to speed on the fineness that is Jacob Berman."

"Even so," said Riley, "How did you *not* notice how much of a hunk he was?"

I looked at her as if she had just spoken Latin. "Hello? Pain, injury, agony, unconsciousness." The murmuring continued. I took a couple bites of my sandwich while the estrogen levels lowered.

Brianna finally spoke up again, "You seriously expect us to believe that nothing about that man got you breathing hard? Hell, you should have reached between his legs and done an 'examination' all your own."

My mind snapped back to those cornflower blue eyes looking down at me and asking me to trust him. Eyes that looked like Greg's, the tone of his voice the same as when Greg would tell me he loved me, that same soft cadence. Someone at the table sighed deeply. Three barks of laughter clearly identified me as the sigh-er.

"Now we're talking!" cackled Izzy. "And just what part of him were you imagining just now? Hmmm? Spill the tea."

I just shook my head, smiled, and had another bite of my sandwich, prompting a serious round of fry-pelting. Score! More fries for me.

"Okay. Okay. How'd he get your skinny ass to the hospital? Weren't you shit deep in the woods?" asked Riley.

"He picked me up in his arms, forced me to cuddle up against his chest, and carried me for about a mile to get to his truck. Then he loaded me up and drove me to the ER."

Three faces looked at me with mouths hanging open. I don't think they were even blinking. Riley's hand crept up to the front of her blouse and began tugging it, fanning herself as she squirmed in her seat. Brianna had a fry halfway to her mouth and slowly tried to finish the trip, except it missed her mouth and smacked into the bottom of her nose, coating it in her weird mixture. She didn't even notice, just drug it down until it popped into her mouth. She bit and chewed, not even bothering to wipe off her new facial. Izzy drained her drink, pulled out her phone, and began texting.

Riley started to say something, but her voice caught. She took a couple of deep breaths before continuing. "He ... you ... in his arms ..." and her words faded away into a moan.

I nodded and took another bite of my sandwich. Riley drained her drink before looking at Izzy and Brianna in astonishment.

"I don't believe it," said Riley, waving her fingers at me as she looked at the others. "I've flirted with him *every* time he comes to the bank. Last time he got in line, I undid an extra button on my blouse so he could get a good look at my assets. Hell, I'd have gone heels up right there if he had asked. Nada. Zilch. Just smiled and asked me how my day was.

"*She* goes for a fucking walk in the woods and gets more action from him than any girl in this town has since he moved here. Lord knows we've tried." She pointed one finger at me, adding, "You're one lucky bitch. Good thing I love you or else I'd have to seriously kick your ass."

Izzy dropped some money on the table as she stood up, her sandwich half-eaten.

"Wait, where are you going, Iz? Lunch ain't over," Riley protested, confused, as Izzy started walking towards the door.

"Sent my boss a text that I wasn't feeling good and taking the rest of the day off," she said, not stopping. "Texted Bill our code for 'come have sex now' so I'm going home to jump my husband's bones." She was out the door before we could even say bye, the bell tinkling merrily.

Lunch wound down after that. As I hobbled back to the office, I started thinking that I needed to thank Jacob for his actions without being under the influence of pain. Yes, that's what I was gonna do. It was, after all, the polite thing to do.

I hadn't dated since Greg died. About a year after his death, our friends had started dropping subtle hints that it was time to move on, find someone else. 'Greg would have wanted it that way' was the biggest reason given.

But I hadn't felt like it. A big part of me had died, leaving me hollow inside. Kaylin was the only thing that kept me sane and not curled up into a ball of grief. How could any new man compete with what Greg and I had?

Then I fell, and Jacob came into the picture. I hadn't told the girls that Jacob had jump-started feelings that had been dead since Greg's passing. The three would have gone into full matchmaking mode, giving me all the best advice on the latest ways to get laid. Well, two of them might. Riley might have offered to demonstrate. That girl had always loved sex. It was best to let sleeping dogs lie.

Now I just had to figure out how to meet him again.

EIGHT

Jacob

My days were pretty much the same routine. I got up each morning at about six, did my workout and katas, then had breakfast. Each day of the week was a different workout, varying between cardio and strength. At least twice a week I donned a seventy-five-pound weight vest and did a thirty-minute forced-march through the forest around my work site.

Once my exercising was done, I would work on the house all day, stopping only for lunch. Dinner time found me back in the trailer, planning the next day's work, looking through the house budget, or monitoring my investments.

Kara and I had focused all my combat pay and any extra money we could generate into our investments. We wanted to retire when my military career was over so that we could focus on the next stage of life. We planned on three kids, which meant three college funds along with all the other needs that kids have. We also planned to travel the world and just enjoy life.

When she inherited the land around Lake Azton from a distant great aunt, one of our financial worries had been resolved. The 350 acres bordered the lake on the west and logging and timber land to the east.

Azton itself was perfect for us. With a population of just around 8,000, it had all the basic services we would need as well as a small modern hospital that served the region. Should more extensive care be needed, Spokane was only eighty miles to the south, a fairly short helicopter ride.

After Kara's death, I funneled the insurance money and the settlement money into our portfolio, causing a massive uptick in profit generation. When it hit $8 million, I had worked with my portfolio manager to start looking for capital investment opportunities. We looked at a multitude of possibilities but focused the lion share of our investing in veteran-owned businesses along with women and minority ownerships. I wanted to help those that needed a hand getting off the ground. Many times, these investments were grants and generated no profit back to me, which was fine.

It had taken me about a month after arriving in Azton to find a new portfolio manager in Seattle. I had deposited just under $100,000 in the local bank and made a few follow-up deposits as expenses built. No one in Azton knew of my wealth, and I intended to keep it that way. It had been my experience that once folks knew you had money, they treated you differently. For me, money was a tool, nothing more, nothing less.

One of Janey's nurses had a death in the family and would be out of town for a few days while another was out with a stomach virus. Janey emailed me and asked me if I could cover. I liked Janey and her quirky sense of humor and was always happy to help her. Thus, two weeks after the incident with Josie, I found myself back in Azton.

Four hours into the shift, I was sipping on a cup of coffee at the nurse's station while catching up on the patient charts. This was the only downside of modern medicine. Twenty minutes of care, two hours of paperwork. I was finishing the last chart update and pondering lunch when the click of heels on the tile floor echoed in the hallway. I looked up as Mrs. Martinson reached my station. I smiled as she stopped at the counter.

"Hello, Mrs. M. What brings you to the hospital today? Visiting someone?"

"Morning, Jacob!" she said brightly. "I *am* visiting someone today. You!"

I grinned at her. "You must be really bored. However, I'll gladly take a visit from someone as lovely as you!"

I liked Mrs. Martinson. Everyone in town raved about her and her husband before he passed. They were known as 'good people.'

She smiled at me, her cheeks all rosy. "Don't you flirt with *me, young man*. I'm a respectable woman." She tried to put her nose in the air and appear all haughty. It would have worked except she broke out in a giggle, causing me to laugh as well.

"What can I do for you today, Mrs. M?"

"First, please call me Flora. Secondly, I'd like to invite you to have dinner with me and my girls tonight. I owe you a big thank you, and this is how I wish to pay it." She smiled and waited expectantly.

"Now, far be it from me to turn down a home-cooked meal, but I'm not sure why you're thanking me."

She looked at me for a moment, appearing perplexed. After a few seconds, her eyes lit up and she began smiling. "Let's say it's for all the good things you've done for the town and all your help here at the hospital!"

I waited, but she didn't give me any more hints. "Well, like I said, I'll never turn down a good home-cooked meal. What time should I be there and what do I need to bring?"

"Just bring yourself and your appetite. It's lasagna night, so there will be plenty. Dinner is at six, so show up any time after five-thirty. Here's the address," she said, handing me a small slip of paper. With that, she wiggled her fingers at me and strolled back down the hallway towards the exit.

It wasn't till she was gone that I remembered the 'and girls' part. Janey had mentioned that Flora's daughter and granddaughter had come back to stay with her. If the daughter were anything like her mother, she would be a nice person to get to know.

I had enough time after shift to go home, shower, shave, and dress.

The downside of my small trailer was closet space. I didn't have much in the way of nice clothes. Most of my stuff was t-shirts, jeans, and work boots.

Still, Mama raised me a certain way. You dressed nice when someone invited you to dinner. I had two long-sleeve button-downs that were my sole non-t-shirt choices. One light blue, one forest green. Both were still inside dry-cleaning bags from when I moved my trailer here. I grabbed the blue one and hung it on the doorknob.

I had a pair of clean, fairly new jeans that I saved for times when I needed something other than work clothes. Those joined the shirt. Now for the shoes. I had two pairs of work boots and a pair of black Chucks. The work boots were worn and beat-up. The sneakers didn't feel right for tonight.

Coincidentally, I had taken a long lunch break yesterday and gone shopping for new shoes. Normally I'd just pick up a clean pair of work boots and be done with it. But for some reason, as I was shopping, I was struck with the desire to upgrade my wardrobe, including my shoes. About halfway down the last aisle of men's shoes, I found myself stopping at the cowboy boots.

I'd never been a fan of this footwear, but this one pair caught my attention. They were black with some nice tooling along the sides and uppers. I'd learned to trust my gut, so they left the store with me.

After getting dressed, I checked myself over in the small mirror hanging on the back of my bedroom door. I had to admit the boots looked good. Pinched a bit, but they were new and would stretch out. I chuckled to myself. I only needed a hat and one of those oversized buckles and I'd look like those cowboys my mom had liked to watch on TV.

On the way to Flora's, I stopped at the store for wine. Another one of Mom's life lessons was that you never showed up as a dinner guest without a nice bottle of wine.

Promptly at 5:45 p.m., I stood on Mrs. M's front porch and rang the doorbell. The door flew open, and I found myself looking down at a very cute young girl, one about six or seven years old, if I had to hazard a guess.

"Who are you?" she asked, giving me a wary glance. Before I could respond, another voice called out from inside the house. "Kaylin Maria Callison, how many times have I told you—Jacob?"

Surprised couldn't adequately describe what I felt when I saw Josie walk up to the door. This was a much different Josie than the other day. This was my first time seeing her standing up, and I was taken aback as I realized ... she was beautiful.

Auburn hair framed her face and fell in soft, lustrous waves across the front of her shoulders. She was about five foot eight and I could only guess at her weight, which was spread very nicely over her frame. She had kept herself in shape or had worked on it in the past because everything about her was nicely proportioned; very, *very* nicely proportioned.

She was wearing a lilac sundress that wasn't tight but still tight enough to display her curves. An opal pendant hung down to her chest.

But it was her eyes that captured me yet again. I knew that with just a little effort, I could become lost in them.

And it wasn't just the eyes. Her hair was the same color as Kara's, the only difference being that Josie's was longer. Displayed now with her hair down and brushed, it only further drove home the striking similarities between Josie and Kara. My heart ached with a longing for my wife and thumped hard at what I was seeing and feeling now.

I was so fixated on her that I couldn't speak, and I could barely breathe. It took my addled brain a moment to figure out that she was talking to me.

"Cat got your tongue?" she asked, smirking. I mentally shrugged, blinked, and glanced down at the little one and back at her. Holy cow, she was a mini-Josie. There was no doubt this was her daughter, right down to the hair and eyes.

"Momma, who is he?" mini-Josie asked, tugging at the sundress and glancing from me and back to her mother.

"Well, munchkin, maybe he will tell us once he remembers how to speak," she replied, raising one eyebrow at me. I shook myself mentally again and smiled.

"Berman—I mean, um, I'm Jacob. Jacob Berman. Mrs. M—I mean

Flora, came by the hospital today and invited me for dinner. She said with her girls—" but I was interrupted when the door opened a bit wider and Flora appeared wearing an apron and holding a wooden spoon.

"Oh, Jacob! You made it! Lord's sake, Josie," she scolded, pushing past them to get to me. "Where are your manners? You'd think I raised you better than to leave guests on the doorstep. Come in, come in, Jacob. Let him in, girls." She turned and shooed the pair back into the house while I followed.

Once inside with the door closed behind us, Flora turned to me and smiled that bright smile of hers.

"Welcome to our home, Jacob. I hope you brought an appetite because I made an extra-large pan of lasagna!" As if to back up her words, the wonderful scents of tomato and garlic wafted in from the kitchen.

I laughed politely and nodded before extending the wine to her.

"Thank you. You didn't have to do that. Let me take this into the kitchen. I'll open it a few minutes before dinner so it can breathe," she said, turning to Josie. "Josie, take Jacob in the front room and entertain him while I finish dinner. Kaylin sweetie, you come help me."

"Yes, Grandma," the young girl replied, giving me another quick glance before hurrying after her grandmother.

"Please come in and sit down," Josie said, waving me into the front room. It was nice as far as front rooms went. Fireplace on one wall, couch, several chairs, coffee table. The usual front room things. It had a nice, cozy feel to it. I liked it.

My eye was drawn to a large picture above the fireplace of a stately-looking man standing behind a younger version of Flora, who was seated in a small chair. His hand rested on her shoulder. I moved to get a closer look.

"Mom and Dad about eighteen years ago," said Josie quietly at my elbow. "He had it done for their anniversary."

"It's very good. I'm sorry I never got to know him very well. Everyone who's ever mentioned him has only great things to say about him."

"He was a character alright," she said. "He loved Mom deeply and doted on her incessantly. She always said that the one thing she loved about him most was that he always made her laugh. The practical jokes he played on her, the puns he'd spout ..."

I surveyed the other pictures on the mantle. Three appeared to be of Kaylin at various ages, one with Josie that seemed to be recent. There was also one with Josie and a man. Both were apparently at a ski resort, with trams and other skiers in the background. They were hugging and grinning at the camera.

"My husband. Greg," she said, her voice soft again, but it was tinged with an underlying hurt. I glanced down at her and could see that pain in her face, her eyes becoming shiny from unshed tears. I knew that look well because it looked back at me from my own mirror all the time.

"I'm so sorry. When?"

She blinked a couple of times before turning and heading back to the couch, taking a seat at one end. I chose the chair next to the couch. She took a deep, cleansing breath and gave me another wistful smile.

"A little over two years ago," she explained. "That picture was our last vacation before he died. We got a wild hair up our butt one day and decided to take a break from the bustle of life. We left Kaylin with one of our dearest friends who had a girl about Kaylin's age, and we headed to the slopes. It was a great weekend. Had I known what lay ahead, I don't think we would ever have left those slopes."

"How did it happen, if I may ask?"

"Massive heart attack out of the blue. He was healthy as a horse, or so we thought. We were always outdoors; hiking, biking, you name it. He was a forest ranger and passed his yearly physicals with flying colors. He was out with a crew checking one of the trails in our section of the national park, and he just keeled over. Autopsy showed a massive blockage of one artery. I heard someone refer to it as a 'widow-maker.' Guess it reached a tipping point that day."

I wanted to go to her on that couch and hold her, to tell her it was okay. As quickly as the feeling came over me, it was followed by one of surprise. I had just met this woman. How could I want to reach out and hold her like that so quickly? I wanted to hold her close and tight and take her pain away, to tell her it was all going to be okay. My pondering of these confusing thoughts was interrupted by the return of Kaylin.

"Grandma said it's time for dinner."

Josie smiled as she stood up and took her daughter's hand, following her towards the dining room with me bringing up the rear.

Dinner was excellent. Flora was a marvelous cook. The lasagna had just the right balance between the cheeses and the meats, complemented by the wine I had chosen. l had to smile when they gave Kaylin a wine glass of grape juice.

I sat there and listened as they laughed and joked about their day. Kaylin told Josie about some incident at daycare involving glue and glitter.

It was Flora who pulled me into the conversation, asking me about my day working at the hospital. I shared a few things, appropriate for small ears.

Laughter and good cheer. I basked in this family's love for each other, feeling almost embarrassed to be intruding.

As we were finishing dessert, probably one of the best apple cobblers I had ever eaten, Flora tapped her wine glass with her spoon. Josie rolled her eyes and her mom shot her 'The Mom Look' before raising her glass.

"I'd like to propose a toast of thanks to Jacob, a wonderful man who saved my daughter from a terrible demise and rescued her just like the knights do in those 'damsel in distress stories.' Thank you for saving my daughter."

"Wow," said Kaylin, "His face is all red. Is he okay, Mommy?"

Josie just laughed and told her I would be fine. Unfortunately, Kaylin wasn't finished.

She looked up at her mom. "Did he really save you?" she asked. I guess Josie hadn't told her what happened that day.

"Well, that might be a bit over the top," Josie replied, laughing. She gave Kaylin a brief rundown of those events. As Josie was telling her story, Kaylin kept glancing between me and Josie. When Josie finished, Kaylin was looking more at me than her mom. She seemed slightly awed at the events.

"Wow, Grandma is right. It's almost like a fairy tale," she said, still watching me. "She was attacked by the evil bunny and you saved her." Kaylin turned to her mom, gesturing for her to lean closer. She put her hand up next to Josie's ear and whispered something I couldn't hear. I saw Josie's eyes go wide, and then she began to smile. She looked down at Kaylin and nodded.

Kaylin slid out of her chair and walked around the table to where I sat. I looked at Josie and saw that her eyes looked wet. They weren't quite tears but close. She caught my inquisitive look and shrugged.

Kaylin stopped at my chair and paused, waiting for something. I turned in my seat to face her. When she kept waiting, I stood up, which put me towering over her. She looked up and smiled.

I knelt down, bringing myself eye-level with her. She then stepped forward and tentatively reached for me. I slowly raised my arms and opened them.

To my great surprise, she stepped in and hugged me. I hesitated for only a second before gently closing my arms around her, hugging her back. Once I did, she squeezed me tight, holding it for several breaths, then stepped back as I let her go. She let her hands rest on my arms as she captured my gaze.

"Thank you for saving Mommy. When Daddy had to go to heaven, Mommy got me a teddy bear and we named it Greg so I would never forget him. I'm gonna get another bear, and I'll name him Jacob so I won't forget you either."

I was speechless. I felt a lump rise in my throat, and it took several seconds before I could speak without my emotions overcoming me. I smiled and looked this wonderful young girl in the eye.

"You're very welcome. Tell you what, if it's okay with your mom, I'll stop by your grandmother's store in the next day or so and pick out a bear, and they can bring it to you."

We both looked over at Josie, who quickly wiped a small tear away.

I think that will be okay," she replied. Flora sniffed and quickly got up from the table, taking a dish into the kitchen.

"I think that'll be okay," said Kaylin.

Flora ignored my offer to help with the dishes and shooed me out of the dining room while she and Josie tackled cleanup. Kaylin took me into the front room and sat on the couch with me, keeping me company. She told me all about her friends and the things they had done while at daycare.

You hear the phrase 'Stream of Consciousness' at times, but until you have a young one tell you everything about her day all at once, you really have no concept. I loved it, soaking it up like a sponge. Deep down, a small part of my heart cried at the memory that I could never do this with my own daughter.

As she was telling me about some favorite movie, she paused.

"You know, Mr. Jacob, when the hero saves the princess, she's supposed to kiss him and then they live happily ever after. Kissing is yucky," she said, her face looking squeamish. It was right at that time that Josie and her Mom came into the room. "Mommy, aren't you supposed to kiss Mr. Jacob and live happily ever after? That's what all the other damsels do when the knight or prince rescues them."

I bit my cheek, as Josie looked like she had been poleaxed, and her mother was trying hard not to laugh but was losing the fight. I took pity on them both.

"I think on that note, it's time for me to say goodnight. I have an early shift in the morning, and all that good food is making me sleepy."

Flora, still trying not to laugh, told Kaylin it was bedtime. Kaylin gave me another hug goodnight, reminded me not to forget the bear, and took off with her grandmother. Josie walked me to the front door and paused before opening it.

"Jacob, I never did get to tell you thank you for helping me that day," she said.

"Really, Josie, it was no big deal. Just glad I was there to help."

She looked down at her hands.

"I also owe you an apology," she said quietly.

"No apology needed; kids will be kids. She didn't mean anything by it."

"No, what I owe you an apology for is the thing I said in the ER." She winced. "Ken told me what happened. I'm really sorry."

"Ah." I shifted, watching a pained look cross her face. "Look, it's okay. Really. You didn't know."

She remained quiet as she opened the door, following me out to my truck and waiting as I got in before stepping up to the open window.

"You know," she added, a light smile on her face. "We damsels in distress can't be beholden to princes and knights. Might set a bad precedent, and I wouldn't want people to think I was not grateful."

"Josie, really it's—" I started, but she held up a hand.

"Jacob, just so you don't get surprised and hit me, I'm going to kiss you on the cheek. Be prepared," she said, echoing my own words back at me. She leaned in and kissed me very softly on my cheek, the first woman to have ever kissed me in any fashion since Kara. I didn't realize I was leaning into it until she moved away, and I had to straighten back up.

She drew back out of the truck and nodded her head. "There, now I can tell Kaylin I've paid my debt. Night, Jacob." I watched her walk back to the house, slightly mesmerized. She paused at the door, gave me a little wave, and went inside, the door shutting gently behind her.

I started up the truck and backed out of the driveway. I woke up the next morning with no clear idea of making the drive home, undressing, or going to bed.

What the holy buckets was happening?

NINE

Josie

I was working the counter while Mom was out running some errands. With the boot off now, Mom had no grounds for me not returning to my normal work schedule.

It was a really slow morning, the store taking in a whopping $23 and some change. Mom just shook her head at my report when she came back and relieved me. I trundled back to my office to see if by some chance the numbers had changed since I had looked at them last.

I stared at the spreadsheets and accounts receivable paperwork, working back and forth between them, looking for corners to cut or billing errors that might be to our favor. I had been at it for a couple of hours when I took a break so my eyes would uncross. I rubbed them a few times before staring up at my vision board hanging above the desk.

A friend back in North Carolina turned me on to the idea of a vision board. It was really a simple concept. Take a board of any size or composition, cut out pictures or words to create an image of your wants and desires, then affix them to the board in no particular order or pattern. Each day, you focused on the board, concentrating on your images and imagining yourself obtaining them. You then waited for what believers called the law of attraction to bring you your dreams.

Right now, my vision board was filled with just one thing. A house. A beautiful house sitting well up on a hillside overlooking a lake. It was all I ever really wanted for our family.

Greg had not been much of a fan of my board. He thought I was just getting my hopes up and would be disappointed with any place we could afford. I told him it was okay to dream and that I would love any place where we were together.

My only guilt about the board was that I had saved money from the household budget Greg and I had set up and hired an architect to help me design the house. The yellow binder sitting to the side of my desk contained the floor plan with each of the rooms getting its own page. I picked out colors, tiles, flooring, everything.

I had the binder open when Mom came into the office.

"Aha! Caught you. Instead of working, you're wasting time with that silly vision watchma thingy," she chided, punching me lightly on the shoulder. Mom had never cared much for my vision board, but that's okay. She knew it was important to me, even if she joked about it now and then.

"Just taking a break, Mom. My eyes were starting to cross."

She glanced at the spreadsheets displayed across both of the monitors as I closed the binder and placed it back on its desk corner and took a deep breath.

"Well?" she asked. A simple question, but one that carried a lot of weight and anxiousness.

"I think three months."

Her small intake of breath was like an explosion in the office. She laid a hand on my shoulder and I covered it with mine.

"You sure?" she asked quietly.

"We've almost exhausted the line of credit from the bank. What we're taking in is barely covering utilities and payroll, and I mean barely. Any slip in sales and we don't even cover that. What's really killing us is the equity line Dad took out. What's left on the line of credit will pay that as well as its own payment.

"We're eating our own tail, Mom. In three months, we will exhaust that line, which will force us to miss that payment as well as the equity loan payment."

About two years before Dad died, there had been an electrical fire that destroyed two of the three main electrical panels for the store. Luckily, it had stayed confined to the closets. Unluckily, the panels were toast, literally, and had to be replaced.

Unfortunately, when Dad talked to the city codes department, they informed him that taking out the permit for the repairs and subsequent inspection would require him to bring the whole building up to code. Insurance wouldn't cover all of that.

Our family had owned the building outright for years. Dad decided that 'in for a penny, in for a pound' was the way to go. He talked to Uncle Frank and took out a $275,000 equity loan. He used that money to upgrade and renovate several areas of the building as well as do the needed electrical repairs. He also paid the staff for the missed hours while the store was closed.

This was on top of the $200,000 line of credit he already had with the bank to cover shortcomings in operational costs and other emergencies. What he had not factored into his plans was the Walmart that came in at the main interstate. He also didn't factor in his dying.

By the time I moved back home, Mom was already behind. It took me almost two weeks to get the books straight. Mom had tried her best, but she was always the face of the store, talking and gossiping with the customers, while Dad had been the bookkeeper and business manager.

"I have some savings and—" she started to say, but I stopped her.

"Mom, that's just a band-aid. We're going to need that to survive until I can find work. Fortunately, I also have what's left of Greg's life insurance. We can make it for a while."

"But that's for Kaylin's college. We can't use that," she protested. "We *have* to be able to do something else."

I pointed to several of the sheets on my desk. "Three of our suppliers have put us on a cash only basis due to our outstanding debt to them. Two have closed our accounts. We have a little over $75,000 in inventory that we have to cover, and I don't know where that money is coming from. Anything bad happens and we're finished."

"Well, now we know," she said softly. I could hear the sadness in her voice, and it hurt.

"Keep the faith, oh Mom of mine. I'm going to go talk to Uncle Frank tomorrow and see what magic we can work."

She patted me on the shoulder and went back out to the front of the store.

I walked into the Azton National Bank at 10 a.m. sharp the next morning. Frank Barklen and Dad grew up together in Azton. Frank went off to school in Seattle, and Dad stayed in town, married Mom, and jumped into the emporium business with Grandpa. After sowing some wild oats in Seattle, Frank came back, got a job at the bank, and was now the manager. While he and Dad were not related, they were brothers in every other sense of the word. Frank had been Uncle Frank to me my entire life as well as being my godfather.

Uncle Frank was standing outside his office talking to another employee when he saw me. Smiling, he waved me over and ushered me into his office.

I liked his office. It was a bastion of old-world charm. Soft leathers, dark wood paneling, cherry desk. The only nod to modern technology was the office phone on his desk corner and the computer.

He happily accepted the hug I offered. I inhaled the fresh scent of his cologne, laughing to myself. Uncle Frank had not changed colognes for as long as I had known him. I released him, and we both took our seats.

"Thanks for seeing me, Uncle Frank."

"Always time for you in my day, Josie. How's Kaylin?" he asked.

"Growing like a weed. Seems like I just bought her new clothes last week and she has already outgrown them. Lord, don't get me started on the attitude." He started chuckling and shaking his head. He had three grown daughters, so he knew what I was talking about.

"Sounds like another little girl I knew. All sass and spit to her parents," he said, grinning at me. I sniffed in mock disdain.

"I'm sure I have *no* idea what you're talking about."

He held my gaze until I giggled. HIs smile gave way to a more serious look as he turned to his computer. He tapped a few times on his keyboard. I couldn't see the monitor very well, but I assumed he had just called up my accounts.

Steeling myself, I addressed the elephant that had wandered into the room.

"What are our options, Uncle Frank?"

He glanced at the desktop, and I could see the flickers of emotion on his face. Raising his eyes, he brought his hands up to steeple his fingers together, looking at me over them.

"I'm very sorry, Josie. I spent all afternoon yesterday and this morning reviewing the information and your financials. I can't extend your line of credit any further, nor can I restructure the equity loan your Dad took out."

I played my last ace. "Mom and I are willing to mortgage the house to provide collateral if needed."

He shook his head and sighed lightly.

"That would be a suicide option for both of you. The house is paid off. Given your debts, even if you got full price, the money would provide nothing more than a brief respite. When the inevitable occurs, you would lose the store *and* your home. Right now, the business is held under the LLC your father established years ago to protect him and your mother from just this very scenario. My advice would be to keep it that way."

I dropped my gaze to my lap as I felt the acid in my stomach erupt like a volcano and the tears threatened to start flowing. I had pinned my hopes of saving my family's store on this visit. Hearing the words that meant the death of those hopes was heart wrenching. I blinked a few times to clear my eyes and took a few deep breaths before looking up at Uncle Frank. He gave me a sympathetic look as he continued.

"Josie, I really wish there was something more I could do for you. I increased the credit line for your mom right after your dad passed, and I shouldn't have done that, but she needed the breathing room."

I met his gaze now, looking for any hope in those warm, familiar eyes, but all I found was unhappiness and a touch of embarrassment. The sigh escaped before I could control it.

"So, there's no hope then?"

He simply shook his head. "Short of a miracle source of funding? No, there is nothing more that we can do. I have feelers out looking for any kind of venture capital or investment seekers. Maybe something will turn up."

I harrumphed at that. "Yeah, I'm sure there are tons of folks out there willing to invest in a losing business." I stood up, and Uncle Frank came from around the desk to give me another hug. He walked me to his office door and opened it. But before I could walk through the door, he lightly touched my arm, stopping me from leaving.

"I'm really sorry, Josie. I love your mom to pieces and if there was *anything* I could do, I would, but my hands are tied on this one," he said softly, for my ears alone.

I patted his hand and smiled before I turned for the door. I needed to get out of the office before I started to cry. I went out the front door and into the fresh morning air. Taking a deep breath, I turned and headed down the sidewalk at a brisk pace. This level of bad news called for pie, and there was only one place to get it.

TEN

Josie

Twenty minutes later, I was ensconced in my booth at Smith's Eats with a slice of Brianna's deep-dish apple pie, topped with a scoop of strawberry ice cream and a large dollop of real whipped cream. I took the first big bite and closed my eyes, feeling the tension from my meeting start to flow away. I moaned softly at the fruity, delectable creation that was melting in my mouth. I sat there and chewed, letting the tastes wash over my tongue and my worries flow away.

"Do you and your pie need a moment?"

My eyes shot open to see Jacob standing at the booth, grinning down at me. I swallowed the bite and started scooping another.

"Jealous?"

He laughed and shook his head. "Not *me*, but I think the other pies are feeling very inadequate right now." He waved his hand down at the opposite side of the booth. I nodded, and he slid in as Brianna sauntered over.

"Hello, good looking. The usual?" she asked.

"Please," he replied. She turned to me, and I nodded as well.

Brianna shook her head and smirked, looking for all the world like she knew a secret and headed back to the kitchen.

"Shouldn't you be up at the hospital?" The second bite was as good as the first, and I worked hard to not moan again. Jacob knew it too, given the way he smiled knowingly before offering a shrug.

"Slow day today. They told me to take a long lunch. You can only clean and prep the exam and triage rooms so many times."

I chewed another bite as he smiled at me. I tried not to focus on his eyes but failed miserably. His eyes twinkled with that smile, and I seriously wanted to plop some whipped cream on the tip of his nose.

When he had stood at our front door the other night, and during dinner, I took notice as to just how good Jacob looked. With him standing before me again, I could definitely see what the girls were talking about, and I had to agree with them. Jacob was a hunk. He had on a black t-shirt today that left no doubt he worked out. Biceps stretched the sleeves out every time he bent his arms, threatening to rip those sleeves like the Hulk.

He looked to be about six feet tall, somewhere in the area of 200 pounds. He had sandy-blond hair that he kept short, but not skin close like the sheriff wore. There was enough there to run your fingers through. He also had blue jean encased legs that I knew were well muscled. I hadn't seen him enter, but I was pretty sure I'd like watching him leave.

He was fit, but not muscle-bound. His hands examining me that Saturday had been nice. Calloused, but not too hard or scratchy. His touch had been gentle and firm. A rugged chin and great eyes topped off the package. The girls had called him the most eligible stud in three counties. They weren't kidding.

I flashed back to dinner and him standing at the door. He had looked hot. The shirt was fitted, and it had *fit*. That color made his eyes pop. The jeans were nice, and then I'd seen the boots. Black cowboy boots. All he needed was a hat to complete the picture. A black cowboy hat. The image of him in that black hat had parts of me heating up that I didn't need heating up at the moment. Fuck, where was this coming from?

But it was his eyes that really drew me in. They had scared me when I first saw them. It was as if I had been looking up at Greg. But Jacob *wasn't* Greg, and that was okay, too.

There was also a small white scar that stretched from just under his left eye and moved backwards towards his ear for about two inches. It gave him a bit of intrigue. I found myself really liking the overall package and had a sudden desire to get to know this man. I also found myself wondering what he would look like with his clothes off, naked and sweaty.

These reactions were surprising and immensely confusing. I hadn't wanted to date following Greg's death. What Greg and I'd had was perfection. I knew that anyone else would be a disappointment because I would use Greg as a yardstick to measure them by. That would have been an unfair expectation to take into a relationship, so I did the easy thing and just avoided looking for anyone.

But here I was, after only just meeting Jacob, finding that I wanted to get to know another man and thinking about him naked. It was unnerving. It was exciting.

My contemplation was broken by the arrival of Brianna and our lunch. She transferred the contents of her tray to our table. Once finished, she looked between us expectantly as she waited.

I reached for my sandwich and stopped, staring across the table at Jacob's plate. Its contents were identical to mine. Sitting next to it was a glass of light brown liquid. I looked up at him just as he looked up at me.

"Extra mayo?" he asked, pointing at my sandwich.

I slowly nodded and pointed at his. "Crispy bacon?" He nodded, that grin back on his face. I pointed at the glass. "Sweet tea?"

He nodded again.

I laughed. "I can't believe you drink sweet tea."

He shrugged his shoulders. "I was born and raised in Tennessee. I'm pretty sure my first bottles had sweet tea in them. I think it's a state law that you have to like it. Where did *you* pick up the habit?" he asked, biting into his sandwich. A small bit of mayo stayed at the corner of his mouth and I found myself wanting to lean across the table and lick that spot off.

Where the hell was *that* coming from?

I realized he was looking at me, waiting for an answer. *Focus, Josie. He asked you a question.* "I Attended school and lived in North Carolina for several years. Greg drank it by the gallons during the summer." I glanced at the sandwich in his hand.

"The BLT?"

He chewed quickly, nodding his head as he tried to hurry the process. Swallowing, he wiped the mayo off of his mouth before speaking. Damn.

"It was a quick, easy meal that even a kid could make using a microwave and a toaster. Mom's the one that got me hooked on the extra mayo. Comfort food."

I picked up my tea glass and raised it. "To comfort food." He laughed and raised his own, clanking it against mine.

We talked easily as we ate our meal. Local gossip, happenings with Kaylin, his work with the hospital. Nothing heavy, just the day-to-day happenings in our lives.

We talked like we'd been friends for years. It felt good. Scary good. Good enough that I found myself not wanting it to end, which again shocked the shit out of me.

An alarm on Jacob's phone brought our conversation to an end. He silenced it, and I could swear a look of disappointment crossed his face. He glanced over at me.

"Well, lunch time comes to an end. Time to head back and finish out the shift. Gotta count the specimen bottles we inventoried last week. Yay me." He drained his tea and stood up, wiping some crumbs off his lap. He looked down at me, smiling. "Thanks for letting me share the booth. I really enjoyed it. Sorry to have interrupted your pie time," he said, grinning at that last.

"That's true, you *did* cause my ice cream to melt. I think you owe me now, don't you?" I replied, and he raised an eyebrow in question. I rushed on before I lost my nerve. I pointed down at my leg. "I got the boot off yesterday and Kaylin has been bugging me to take her out for pizza. If you're not doing anything Friday night, want to join us at Gordo's?"

There, I had put it out there. Damn. I was like a teenager waiting for Billy to text me because Brianna's friend Sally's sister Jane's friend Emily said Billy liked me.

"That the place with all the games?" he asked.

I nodded, waiting for his answer.

"Well, I *was* supposed to meet the governor for dinner. But the chance to spend time around a bunch of screaming kids hopped up on pepperoni and soda? How can I possibly refuse? I'll let the governor know to reschedule. What time?" he asked, his eyes glittering with amusement.

Holy shit! He said yes. Deep breath, Josie. "Is six okay?"

"Perfect," he said. "It's a date."

We exchanged numbers so that we could call or text if anything changed. He waved his fingers at me and headed up to the register. I watched him chat with Brianna as he paid, saying something that made her blush and slap at him before he headed out the door, bell tingling. Yep. His ass filled out those jeans just as I had imagined. Brianna came and sat down at my booth.

"Well, *you* two seemed to have a stimulating lunch," she observed, her eyes twinkling. "Did he ask you out?"

"Brianna, it was just lunch. Don't plan the wedding just yet." I looked back down at my fries, feeling my face starting to get flush.

Brianna cackled. "Ha! He *did* ask you out! You're blushing! Spill it girl. I need deets."

"Deets?"

"Details. *Some* of us keep up with the current slang," she retorted with a wave of her hand. "You're not getting off that easily. Give." She was like a stalker when she was after something, always had been.

I raised my empty tea glass, shaking the ice. She rolled her eyes in exasperation before getting up and fetching the tea pitcher. She filled my glass and plopped the pitcher down on the table. She then cradled her head in her hands and gazed at me.

"Well, to burst your bubble, he didn't ask me out." It was hard to hold a straight face as Brianna's mouth opened and closed a couple of times.

"I don't understand," she said, looking back at the door and back to me. "He bought your lunch and you're blushing and fidgeting."

I stopped fidgeting. The blush was on its own.

"Just telling you, he didn't ask me out." I let her hang there for a few more moments before I put her out of her misery. "I asked *him* out." I grinned as she stared at me, her face slowly breaking into a smile as she caught up with what I had said.

"You go girl!" she exclaimed, holding her fist out for me to bump as I told her what Jacob and I had made plans to do. "Wait a minute, you're going to take *Kaylin*? On a date with studly? Where the hell is the romance in that? What if he doesn't like her? What if he wants to let your tongue meet his?" she demanded, all her questions coming out in a rush as one long sentence.

"He likes Kaylin, and she likes him. She thinks he's a hero and will love playing games with him."

"A hero?" she asked. "How the hell can she think that since she hasn't …" I giggled as I watched her process the statement. You could almost smell the synapses in her brain burning.

She gave me the evil eye, one eyebrow raised.

"And just *when* exactly did Kaylin meet Jacob?" she asked sweetly.

"Mom invited him for dinner the other night—without telling me, by the way. Imagine my surprise when the doorbell rang and there stood Jacob. We had dinner, talked a bit, and I told Kaylin about him helping me. She got excited and told him he was like a knight saving a damsel."

I relayed Kaylin's conversation about Greg and the bear, and Jacob's response. Brianna's hand covered her mouth as she gasped a little. I told her about Kaylin sitting on the couch with him, telling her all about her day. I finished by telling her about asking him to join Kaylin and me for pizza on Friday.

I chuckled as Brianna shook her head and sighed. She whipped out her cell phone and began texting.

"Um, Brianna? What are you doing and why am I suddenly filled with dread?"

"Just texting Riley, Izzy, and a few others." Mentioning those two did *not* help the bad feeling in the pit of my stomach.

"Why?"

She looked up at me like I had uttered the dumbest phrase known to man.

"I'm putting the word out that Jacob is off the market. I think Riley may either claw your eyes out or not speak to you. Maybe both. It's a toss-up. She *really* had her sights set on Jacob."

"Would you just stop! We haven't even been on a date yet. It's just pizza, and Kaylin will be with us. You're going to get us both in trouble."

She held up one finger. "He rescued you in the woods." A second finger joined the first. "Dinner with Mom and Kaylin. He's met the 'rents." A third finger appeared. "Night out with Kaylin, at a place geared towards her." She just laughed, glancing down as her phone started blowing up with incoming texts.

She looked back up at me, grinning.

"Three dates, your Mom likes him, Kaylin likes him. No other woman in this town has managed to get *one* date with him, much less three. Face it, you're *dating* and he's off the market." She turned back to her texting.

I let my head thump back against the booth and just stared at the ceiling. I really did want the first date to lead to more. And, if I was being totally honest with myself, it felt good that he had said yes to me and not anyone else.

ELEVEN

Jacob

I parked my car and headed back into the ER, still trying to figure out what had happened at lunch and yet, at the same time, knowing *exactly* what had happened.

I had a date. Something that hadn't happened since Kara died. After pulling myself out of the dark pit that the death of my wife and unborn child had dumped me into, I swore that I'd never put myself in the position to feel that level of pain again. It was easy at first, since the hurt was so fresh and I was still working on getting out of the Army, not to mention all the crap that had ensued with Kara's parents. Dating at the time was the *last* thing on my mind.

After my move to Azton, I kept myself busy and stayed out at my trailer, only coming into town to get food and other essentials, along with working the occasional shift at the hospital. I did my best to stay under the radar.

I had worked out a deal with the hospital administrator to keep my skills up to speed. That had taken some doing with state health boards and the lawyers for the hospital, but in the end, I was allowed to fill a nursing position on an as-needed basis, a win-win for all involved.

When I met the sheriff, he immediately enlisted my aid for when occasional search and rescue efforts were needed. We always had some kid wandering off or a tourist getting lost on a trek. Either way, I was kept busy.

But you just can't escape the closeness of a small town. While the population may have been around 20,000 for the county, with about 8,000 living inside the city limits, it was small. Everyone still knew each other. And you don't drop a new single man into a small town of single women without word rapidly getting around.

I was flattered with the flirting, but I just wasn't interested. They were all nice enough women; some were actually attractive. Under any other circumstances, I would have gladly dived back into the dating pool.

My 'no dating' rule was working well until that Saturday with Josie. From the minute I found her in the woods, I just couldn't shake her out of my head. At night before going to sleep, or any other quiet time, I found myself recalling her laugh, her smile, her eyes. Eyes that consumed me every time I thought about them, about her.

The shock of seeing her at her mother's front door, really seeing her for the first time, caused me no end of confusion. Her resemblance to my dead wife was undeniable, yet, at the same time, she wasn't Kara. She was different, and I liked those differences.

Lunch had been the best time I could remember having since Kara's death. Common interests had led to an amazing lunch conversation. My alarm going off had startled me at first, but then it bummed me out. I realized I hadn't wanted lunch to end. Then she asked me to have pizza with her and Kaylin, and I leapt at the chance, even calling it a date.

Now I had a *date*.

That thought was still doing laps in my head when I walked back into the ER. A few moments in the on-call room to store my stuff and I was back out to the nurse's station.

Over the next few hours, we had a few patients. Nothing major.

An aspiring logger managed to slice open his forearm when he mishandled a double-bladed axe. Luckily, he missed the major arteries. Twenty-five stitches and a tetanus shot saw him whole and reasonably healthy again.

We had one broken wrist resulting from a failed 360-degree toe flip by an aspiring skateboarder. A pink cast was applied and, in a few weeks, she'd be back in the halfpipes trying again.

But the winner for the afternoon was the nice older gentleman who was allergic to shellfish. We tried to tell him that even though you peeled the shrimp out of their shells, they were still shellfish. Nothing a few cc's of epinephrine and a lecture on the definition of shellfish hadn't fixed. Something told me we would see him again.

I was finishing up the paperwork on Mr. Shellfish when Janey walked up to the counter and leaned on it, watching me type. I ignored her, hoping she would wander away when she saw I was busy. Apparently, she didn't care about my busy state. I gave her a sideways glance.

"Bored, Janey? Don't you have some wedding plans to finalize?" I asked. Janey and Ken's wedding was coming up very soon.

"Nope," she replied with a shrug. "We're all good. Thanks again for covering for me while we honeymoon."

"Least I could do. We nurses have to stick together."

"Hopefully no emergencies pop up and you can make the wedding," she said, picking at something on the countertop.

"Back to the original question, oh engaged-one. Bored?"

"Nope, just curious." She began to twirl a pen on the countertop. I tilted my head towards her, showing her I was listening, but I kept typing.

"And might one ask, especially one who is as busy as I am, what has piqued your curiosity this day?"

"Well, we're friends, right?" she asked. I paused in my shellfish chronicling to peer up at her. All of my male danger warnings were going off. No good could come of that tone and that question from a female.

"Covering for you to go off and spend a week doing unspeakable things with Ken on a beach? Yeah, I think that makes us friends. Why?"

She nodded. "Well, I thought that was the case, but I just couldn't figure out why you didn't tell me."

"Tell you what?" *Warning, warning, danger, danger!* These signals were screaming through my head, setting me on edge.

"That you and Josie Callison were dating."

I must have looked like the proverbial deer-in-the-headlights because she started laughing. *Abort mission. Abort mission. Evade. Escape.* I glanced at the exits. Maybe I could distract her and slip out the back.

"We're not dating." There, simple denial. Simple was always best.

She just cocked her head at me, eyes twinkling.

"Really?" she asked. "Not what I'm hearing. You did have lunch with her today, right?"

I broke eye contact and shuffled some papers around in my work area. One part of my brain was rapidly thinking of a response that would get me out of her sights. Another part was amazed at the speed of the rumor mill in this town.

"Someone's lying to you, J. I told you, no dating. Any evidence is a fabrication and easily refutable in court. As to lunch, she was already there eating when I got there. We just shared a table." This was not a conversation I wanted to have at this time. I needed an exit strategy in a bad way.

"Gotcha. Oh, just one small question, if I may be so bold?" she asked, looking all innocent. The hairs rose on the back of my neck.

"Didn't you have dinner with Josie, Kaylin, and Flora the other night?"

Well … shit. I was up against an enemy that had superior intel. It always sucked when the enemy was well prepared. More plans got shot to hell that way.

"Yes, I did, but it wasn't a date. Flora wanted to thank me for helping Josie that day in the woods."

"Wow," exclaimed Janey, oozing amazement. "Josie moves fast. Took you home to meet the parents on the first date."

I threw my hands up in exasperation. "It *wasn't* a *date*. I didn't know Josie was her daughter."

"Uh huh," Janey said. "One final question, if I may?"

I was seriously beginning to wonder how many crime shows Janey had been watching. I stared at her, giving her neither a 'yes' nor 'no' scowl. She was unfazed by my stoic expression.

"You doing anything special this Friday night?" she asked, slamming her trap shut.

When faced with an overwhelming superior force, retreat is an honorable option. Unless, of course, the enemy has you surrounded and knows you can't leave because it's not the end of your shift. It didn't help that Janey had access to a gossip network that rivals the NSA on intelligence gathering.

"Nosy busybodies" I mumbled as I shuffled my papers again.

"Sorry, what was that, Jacob?" the shark asked the minnow.

"I'm going to Gordo's for pizza." There, a truth, just not the whole truth. It was a desperate attempt. I knew I was doomed, but sometimes you just had to keep fighting till the end.

"Oh, great place, good pizza. I hear it's all the rage with the twenty-five to forty crowd. I've been meaning to check it out myself," she said in her best food critic voice.

"By all means, you should. Well, if you'll excuse me, I have some paperwork to finish up. Nice talking with you, Janey." I turned to my computer screen and began clicking away with the mouse. Unfortunately, once she smelled blood, the shark was not to be deterred.

"Oh sure, I understand. Who ya meeting at Gordo's, Jacob?" she asked smugly since she apparently already knew the answer. Shark-bite right to the ass. Fuck. Game over. I rolled my eyes in defeat.

"*Fine*. I'm meeting Josie and Kaylin, as if you didn't already know." She broke out in a rich belly laugh. I could hear the underlying tone of mockery.

"And I suppose you are going to tell me that 'it's not a date'?"

Discretion being the better part of valor, I kept mum. Janey just kept laughing as she headed back to wherever it is that lawyer sharks go after devouring a witness. I turned back to my work, glad it was over. How wrong I was. As Janey walked away, she began singing.

"Josie and Jacob sitting in a tree …"

I once again questioned my sanity for working in a hospital where virtually the entire nursing staff was female and apparently still in grade school.

TWELVE

Josie

I walked into the house and was immediately treated to the smell of
Mom's meatloaf. I loved her meatloaf. It was my favorite thing to
eat growing up. Luckily for me, it was Dad's favorite meal, too. She
always made a huge pan on Friday nights so that Dad and I could eat
meatloaf sandwiches for lunch on the weekends.

After dropping my purse and keys on the hallway bench, I strolled
over to the dining room where Kaylin was putting silverware on the
table. She saw me and darted around the table to wrap me in a hug.

"We're having meatloaf, and Grandma let me help!" she exclaimed
as she pulled out of the hug. "Come see!"

Grabbing my hand, she tugged me into the kitchen island where a
meatloaf sat on a cooling rack. She let go of my hand and clambered
up on a stool.

"See? It's good, huh?" She turned her shining eyes up to me. I
crossed one arm over my waist and cocked the other arm up so that I
could tap my lips with one finger. I walked around the island as I
examined the culinary effort.

Kaylin tracked my movements. I wasn't sure she was even

breathing as I did my once over. Coming back to stand next to her, I glanced down and adopted my best haughty face.

"Madame, ze meatloaf, she is magnifique! It iz, how you say, too good to eat!" I gave a chef's fingertip kiss, which caused both of us to break out in giggles as she hugged me again.

The three of us had an amazing dinner together. Kaylin caught me up on all the plans she and her playmates were making for the upcoming school year, which would start in a few weeks. Boys were still yucky, of which I was most grateful. Mom talked about a craft fair in Spokane that she and some of her friends were attending this weekend.

Mom was an avid quilter and was sorely disappointed in my utter lack of interest or ability to sew a stitch. I grew up a tomboy, spending my childhood with Dad in the store or outdoors. Kaylin, on the other hand, loved sewing with Grandma, so Mom had someone to pass on her knowledge to.

For dessert, Mom made an apple cobbler. She tried to make one dessert a week and we would usually eat sparingly of it. But in this case, Mom knew the cobbler's life span would be about two days. If there was anything I liked better than her meatloaf, it was her apple cobbler, warm and fresh from the oven.

Kaylin was scraping her fork across her plate to get any stray cobbler when I decided to broach Friday night.

"So, munchkin, got any big plans for Friday night? Any hot dates with a boy? Going shopping with the girls?"

"Moooommmm. I told you, boys are yucky," she said, rolling her eyes. *Wait, when did the eye thing start?* Mom snickered. She may have muttered something about karma under her breath, but I'm *sure* I misheard.

"Well, if you have no plans, I thought we might head over to Gordo's."

Kaylin's face lit up like a Christmas tree. "Gordo's? Really?"

I nodded. "Yep."

She jumped up from the table and began a happy dance. Taking in a nervous breath, I laid out the other part.

"Kaylin?" She paused in mid-twirl and stared at me expectantly.

"If it's okay with you, I thought Mr. Jacob could go with us." I worried at my lower lip as I watched her closely. She barely even blinked.

"Sure! I like Mr. Jacob. I bet he would play skee-ball with me and win me lots of tickets!" she exclaimed before dashing off to her room.

"Hey, not so fast. You still have to clear off your plate." She slid a few feet down the hallway on her sock feet, turned, and ran back to the table to grab up her dishes. Mom gave me one of her patented Mom-appraisal looks as Kaylin disappeared to her room.

"What?" I met her gaze with one of my own.

"So, pizza with Jacob?" she asked. The tone of her voice sounded exactly like the one I would get when I was in high school getting interrogated about a boy's intentions.

I shrugged. "I asked him at lunch today, and he said yes."

Mom took a sip of her coffee as she surveyed me, eyes twinkling.

"You and Jacob met for lunch?" Her words were all innocent-like, which I didn't buy for one minute. Mom was part of Brianna's text-based alerting system.

"No, we didn't *meet for lunch*. I was having some pie after my meeting with Uncle Frank and Jacob showed up. He asked if he could sit with me and I didn't mind, so he did, and we had lunch. No big deal."

Mom's face grew pensive. She had needed to run some errands while I was at lunch and never made it back to the store. "So, anything from Uncle Frank?"

I shook my head, unable to keep the sadness from creeping into my voice.

"No, nothing different from the last time I talked to him. He'll keep looking, but he can't help us anymore."

She nodded, taking another sip of coffee and staring into her cup. I could tell she wanted to say more, so I waited. Sometimes saying nothing was the right thing to do instead of filling the silence with mindless chatter.

"I was worried about you after Greg died," she said quietly. "You held yourself together for Kaylin, but I watched you draw in and away from everyone. Since you've moved back here, you've still maintained that wall, to some extent."

She smiled at me through the steam rising up from her cup, the smile not quite reaching her eyes.

"Oh, you hide it well, but you've not let anyone in, Josie. While I *am* happy to see you dating, you have Kaylin to worry about now, and you have to know how dating someone will affect her."

"I didn't mean to worry you ..." I started to say, but she raised a finger to stop me.

"No parent wants to see their child go through that pain you did when Greg died. I wanted to make it all better for you, and it hurt when I couldn't."

She took another sip of her coffee and contemplated me for a moment.

"Why Jacob?" she asked. "You've turned down several dates since you came back. Yet here you go and ask someone out after basically just meeting them. Don't get me wrong, Jacob is a great guy, and lord knows the single women in this town have been after him since he got here. But why *him*?"

I looked down at my plate, using my fork to make small doodles among the cobbler remains, pondering my answer.

"I like him, Mom. He's the first guy since Greg that I've been attracted to, and I don't mean in a 'oh wow, he's hot' kind of way either."

Mom gave me *that* look again. I sighed, stopping my own eye roll before it finished.

"Okay, him being hot doesn't hurt, but it's more than that," I paused and met her soft, worried gaze. "We talked at lunch today. Really talked. It was as if we had known each other all our lives. We just ... connected."

I heard her slight intake of breath and knew what she was about to say.

"No, Mom. No love-at-first-sight stuff. I looked across that table and looked him in the eye, and he looked right back. He didn't leer at me, he wasn't measuring me up, he looked at *me*. He talked to *me*. He was attentive, joking, and confident. I found myself not wanting the lunch to end. Does that make sense?"

A small ghost of a smile appeared on Mom's face. "Yes, it does. We women are creatures of attention. We want to be noticed and told we're special."

Before I could speak, she pressed on.

"What do you know about him?" she asked.

"Not much. I've seen him around town before but never really noticed him until I woke up with him leaning over me, looking down at me with eyes like Gr—" I caught myself before finishing that sentence, but Mom knew what I was about to say.

"Eyes like Greg," she finished for me. "He has Greg's eyes, hair color, and some of his mannerisms. Josie, he is not Greg. And it's unfair to put that on him."

"I know that Mom, I really do, but I'm not blind to the fact that he is like Greg in some ways."

"Josie, this man is vastly different from Greg in many ways," she chided. "Greg was a great guy, gentle as a lamb, wouldn't hurt a fly. Jacob has a past, one you need to be aware of."

"Ken told me about the Branson girls before he brought me home from the hospital. That's why we were late getting home."

"So, you know that Jacob was in the military, that he's fought and more than likely killed people?" she pressed.

"Yeah, Ken mentioned all of that. He also told me that he was a medic person of some type. That's why he works at the hospital sometimes."

"All I'm saying is that you need to take your time with Jacob and get to know him better. There is a pain in him, Josie. Call it a mother's intuition if you want, but he has a hurt that he holds close. Given what's in his past, you need to make sure that he is not someone who might hurt you or worse, Kaylin."

I shook my head, frowning. "I can't see Jacob doing that, Mom. You saw him with Kaylin. She took right to him, and she never does well with strangers. I think he'd die before he hurt her. Call it my *own* mother's intuition."

"Maybe," she allowed. "I'm happy you're taking the leap, Josie. I just don't want you or Kaylin hurt. You're a young, intelligent, attractive woman, and I hope you do find someone to spend your life with, someone who will love both Kaylin and you. Just be careful, okay?"

I covered her hand with mine and gave it a gentle squeeze. "I will, Mom, I promise."

Lying in bed that night, Mom's words swirled in my head like wisps of clouds. I knew she was worried, and I would be too, if I were in her shoes. But I also knew my own feelings. I had things to learn about him, no doubt. I was looking forward to Friday night and starting to learn more about one Jacob Berman.

THIRTEEN

Josie

After trying on my fifth outfit, I was ready to scream. I had nothing to wear. I spent an hour going through my closet while Mom stood in the doorway, laughing.

"Josie, stop. Just stop," she said, still laughing.

"What? I don't know what to wear."

She shook her head, still laughing at me. I was glad I was able to make someone happy. "Tell me something. If it was just you and Kaylin going, what would you wear?" she asked.

"Mom, I want him to be—"

"Stop."

I paused, waiting for her to continue as she walked into my room, took my chin, and looked me in the eye. Tall women ran in our family, and she had me by about an inch. Kaylin was already giving hints that she would be as tall or taller than me.

"You're not going out for a candlelit dinner for two. You're going to a kid's pizza parlor. If it was just you and Kaylin, you know good and well you'd be in the ball pit playing. Right?" she asked.

I could only nod as she continued.

"He agreed to go out with you *and* Kaylin. To Gordo's. My suggestion to you is that you dress accordingly. Now, given that, what would you wear? Don't tell me, show me."

In a few moments, I had on my favorite jeans, complete with small holes in the knees. They hugged my ass nicely without looking painted on. Socks and my black Chucks went on my feet. I finished off the look with my favorite football jersey that Greg bought me when we attended a pro game in North Carolina.

Next was mascara, a little blush, and some colored lip balm. As an afterthought, I added a small touch of my favorite perfume behind each ear and at the wrists. I looked to Mom for confirmation.

"Better, much better. What about your hair?"

I looked at the mirror, teasing my hair in several styles. Mom just tutted at me again.

"Pizza parlor, Josie."

I grabbed my brush and pulled my hair back into a ponytail, wrapping it through a couple twists of a scrunchy. I glanced back at Mom, raising a brow. She gave me a quick once over and smiled before turning and heading back to the front of the house.

It was five minutes 'til six when I pulled into a parking spot outside of Gordo's. The parking lot was moderately crowded, which promised a very noisy night. The car barely made it into park before Kaylin was trying to get her seatbelt off.

"Come on, Mommy! Hurry up!"

"Hold your horses, little girl. Gordo's isn't going anywhere!" I turned the car off and got out to open her door, helping her untangle from her seat belt as she slithered down from her booster seat. She straightened her shirt and started for the restaurant.

"Wait for me—and don't you run away from the car!" That girl was going to be the death of me, but I was happy to see her so excited. It had been a rough couple of years for both of us.

Kaylin grabbed my hand and hauled me to the front door. I think if she could have picked me up and carried me, she would have.

"*Hurry*, Mommy! Suzie and Bethy both said they might be here!" she said excitedly.

We opened the restaurant doors and were instantly assailed with the sounds of electronic games, music, and the laughter and yells of kids having unabashed fun.

Gordo's had been around for a few years. Gordo Jergen, the guy who ran it, was another of my high school acquaintances. He left for Spokane right after high school to escape the small-town life. Mom said he and his new wife moved back about eight years ago. They wanted kids, but apparently they couldn't have them on their own. I knew that must have hurt Gordo. He came from a big family and always wanted a big family.

He and his wife decided to foster, which led to adoption. By the last count they had five kids between the ages of eight and thirteen. It always amazed me to think of raising that many kids, and I admired them for taking it on. I had trouble with just one.

So, it was only natural that Gordo created a place that would put him around lots of kids. He had taken an old warehouse and turned it into a kid's paradise. Every electronic kid's game you could think of was scattered around the building, including a line of skee-ball machines. All of the machines rewarded tickets that could be redeemed for prizes.

But his biggest draw was the ball pits that took up the back third of the warehouse. The small one was like a kiddie pool. It had black netting to prevent balls from getting out and was only about a foot deep. Perfect for toddlers.

It was the big one that drew the crowds. It was huge and took up almost the entire back seating area. Along with thousands of plastic balls, there were padded boxes of various sizes and shapes spread throughout the pit for kids to climb on and leap off. Unlike the kiddie pit, this one had no netting to keep balls inside. It was a war zone for kids, and they ate it up.

Not just the kids either. The occasional parent could be seen cutting loose, tossing kids around, and generally letting their own inner child out. It was an unwritten rule among the adults: *What happens in the ball pit stays in the ball pit.*

Gordo wisely placed a line of booths and tables around the pits so that parents could keep an eye on their ball-flinging maniacs. It also gave the kids a place to quickly dash out for refueling before jumping back into the fray.

Combine all of that with pizza, burgers, hotdogs, and soda and you had the ultimate kid paradise.

"I see you made it."

I whipped my head to the prize area and saw Jacob with his arms crossed, leaning against the wall. He was wearing those same jeans from the dinner at Mom's, a pair of black Chucks just like mine, and a football jersey depicting the pro team from Tennessee. He looked good, really good. A quick image of me peeling that shirt off and running my hand across his chest popped in my head. I grinned at him.

"We're early, actually. Nice shirt. Couldn't find one for a real team?"

He laughed as he tugged at the hem. "High school buddy sent it to me a few years back for Christmas. She's a football fanatic. I'm not much of a sports fan, but it's comfortable," he said.

Kaylin ran over to give him a hug.

"Come on, Mr. Jacob, you have to play skee-ball with me. Mommy stinks at it," she said, tugging on his hand.

"Hey, now. I do *not*." My daughter rolled her eyes again and looked at Jacob, who just raised one eyebrow. I was outnumbered.

It took us a few moments to get a food order in and to acquire a king's fortune in tokens for the games. Kaylin pulled us over to the tables next to the big ball pit. We lucked out and got a booth that someone had just left.

We deposited our drinks, and Kaylin quickly led Jacob over to the skee-ball machines. Much to my daughter's delight, Jacob proved exceptionally adept at flicking those wooden balls into the higher scoring holes. Streams of tickets flowed into my daughter's greedy little hands.

They called out our food number, and we headed back to our table to eat. Kaylin wolfed down two pieces of pizza and several slurps of soda before her two friends found her. Amongst numerous squeals of delight and promises to be good, the three amigos loaded up on tokens and headed off to do more ticket damage.

"She's a bundle of energy," Jacob observed, watching her scamper away with her friends. "Is it safe to let her roam out there?"

"Yes and yes. Gordo has a couple of staff who roam the floor, always watching and making sure the kids are safe. It's a small town, and strangers stand out." I was warmed that he was concerned for her safety. "Besides, she'll wear herself out tonight and will probably be asleep before I get her home and to bed. She might even sleep in a bit tomorrow morning, thus letting *me* sleep in."

"Early riser?" he asked.

"Me? No. Her? God, yes. I don't need an alarm clock with her around. She's up bright and early, raring to go around six every flipping day. Mom and I trade off on weekends so one of us gets to sleep in." That prompted another laugh from him. He probably slept in every weekend and was rubbing it in. Bastard.

For the next hour, we tried to have a conversation over the din, but it was difficult. Kaylin made repeated pit stops to dump her tickets, fuel up on soda, and occasionally getting Jacob to go win more skee-ball tickets. On her last trip, she and her two friends headed into the ball pit where I quickly lost them amongst the others.

Kids were jumping off the structures and balls were flying. Luckily, they were a spongy plastic and couldn't hurt you, even at short range. As we watched, the occasional ball came flying out towards the tables. Laughing parents just tossed them back in.

I turned to ask Jacob a question when it happened.

Thwack. A plastic ball hit me on the shoulder. I glanced at the pit and turned back to attempt my question again.

Thwack. I gave the pit another glance and still didn't see anyone looking at me. I turned back to Jacob, but he was grinning. He mouthed "Kaylin." I nodded slightly.

Thwack. This time when I looked over, Kaylin was standing at the pit edge with her two friends. The expression on her face was one of dare, excitement, and pure innocence. I shook a finger at her and turned back to Jacob just in time to see his eyes suddenly go wide open.

The first ball took me in the shoulder, the second hit him on the head, and the third fell short of the table.

The gauntlet had been thrown down.

I locked eyes with Jacob, and I could have sworn we read each other's minds. We exploded out of the table, heading for the pit as all three girls screamed and took off. Jacob and I vaulted the pit wall and threw ourselves into the fray.

The battle quickly consumed all the kids in the pit. Parents were laughing as balls flew like bullets. Jacob was tossing kids left and right as they jumped on him from perches they climbed up on. He made sure that where he tossed someone, no other kid was near the landing, and he didn't throw anyone too hard. The kids were eating it up.

I jumped up on one of the boxes.

"TIMMMMEEEE OUTTTTT!" I bellowed.

All the eyes in the pit snapped to me and maybe even a few kids in the game area. I counted noses, and the numbers put the girls a couple bodies ahead.

"Last battle of the night, you vicious savages! Boys at that end of the pit, girls at this end. Last one standing is the winner. You get hit by a ball, you're out."

"But there are more girls than us," said one little male whiner.

His friend bopped him on the shoulder. "They're girls, *stupid*. We can beat them easy." I instantly marked him as my first victim.

"Rules?" asked Jacob, grinning at me.

"We don't need no stinkin rules, you boy you." With that, I yelled "GOOOOOO" and jumped down into the pit.

Thus began what historians would later refer to as "The Great Gordo Battle Royale". Balls and bodies were flying. Taunts and yells of encouragement were drowning out the sounds from the rest of the games. Cries of "CHEATER" and "I GOT YOU" flew through the air, along with a lot of balls.

An audience gathered around the pit. Parents and kids were cheering on the players, yelling out advice. Occasionally, some of them were collateral damage. No one filed a Geneva Convention violation, so the battle raged on.

Players exited the battlefield in a steady stream until we were down to the final three. Jacob was hunkered down behind a big cylinder at his end while Kaylin and I were gathered behind a large box about halfway to him.

We were in a stalemate for several minutes before I devised a solution. I pulled Kaylin over to me and whispered in her ear. She started nodding and grinning, then fist-bumped me. I used my fingers to count down from three and we exploded out from behind our box, me going right and Kaylin going left.

Jacob charged out to meet us and paused for a second when he saw that we weren't together. Kaylin almost got him with a quick throw, forcing him to dodge and face her. I kept moving away from him as she rushed closer. He finally plinked her with a ball, and she fell down screaming, grabbing her knee.

"It *hurts* ... Mommy ... it HURTS." My little drama queen was selling it for all she was worth. Tears were flowing down her cheeks. It was an Oscar-worthy performance. Parents went quiet on the walls as the kids stopped cheering, sensing one of their own was hurt.

Jacob, true to my expectations, immediately dropped the balls he was holding and waded over to Kaylin, turning his back to me and leaning down next to her. It was then the trap snapped shut.

"Sucker!" Kaylin yelled, grinning up at him as she scrambled away. Jacob spun around, but it was too late.

While screaming 'BANZAAAII' I leapt from the box towards Jacob, becoming airborne for a few moments. I flung a handful of balls at him even as I was falling. He dodged one, but two others took him square in the chest. He had just enough time to get his arms open before I landed in them, smashing us flat.

I scrambled to sit up on top of him, my arms raised in victory and a superior gloat on my face. I yelped as he suddenly tossed me off and rolled away from me, coming up on his knees. At first his expression was odd, as if he were bothered, but it quickly melted into a grin that made him look like a kid.

"You cheated!" he growled. "You used your daughter to trick me. And she *helped!*" Kaylin was laughing with unabashed glee. I just grinned and pointed two fingers at him.

"Booyah, loser! Girls rule, boys drool!"

He laughed again and dove for me. I screamed and rushed my way through the pit. I began highfiving with Kaylin and the other girls. They began chanting "Girls rule, boys drool" as we exited the pit to the cheers and applause of our adoring fans.

After the parents finished thanking us for entertaining both them and their kids, it was time to go. Gathering up Kaylin's tickets, we headed up to the prize area so she could redeem them for the bounty of cheap stuff available. She gave her friends big hugs as we all made it out the door, then out into the cool air and shocking quiet of the parking lot.

As we reached our car, Jacob told us to wait and headed over to his truck. He came back, hands behind his back. Kneeling down, he looked at Kaylin.

"Remember I told you about getting a bear?" he asked.

She nodded, moving her head to try to see around his back. He laughed and brought forth a small bear about fourteen inches tall. It was dressed in Army camouflage clothes, and it had little black boots on and a green beret on its head.

"I was in the Army and I found this bear at one of the posts I lived on. I was going to give this to someone else, but I think they would rather you have it," he told her, handing her the bear. Her eyes lit up as she took the stuffed animal, looked at it, and looked back at him before leaping on him to wrap her arms around him.

"Thankyouthankyou, Mr. Jacob. I'll call him Mr. J., and he can sleep with me too!"

I watched with a catch in my throat at the thoughtfulness that this man showed my daughter. Hell, I was almost an afterthought tonight as he paid her all the attention she could handle. It took me a second to get my voice.

"Tell Mr. Jacob goodnight, Kaylin," I said. She hugged him again and told him good night. He took her hand and made a big smooching kiss on her knuckles.

"Good night, Princess Kaylin," he said grandly.

She giggled and climbed up into the car. I got her strapped into her booster seat and turned around to find Jacob staring at me intently. I could have sworn there was a flash of hunger in his eyes, and as quickly as it appeared, it was gone.

"I had a great time tonight, Josie. Thank you for inviting me," he said, moving closer to me. Was he going to try to kiss me? Were my lips too dry? What would Kaylin say?

"Me, too. It was really nice to see Kaylin having fun. Of course, beating you in the ball pit was just icing on the cake!"

He laughed heartily. "So, I was wondering …"

I realized I was holding my breath. "Yes?"

"If you're not doing anything Wednesday, I thought we could have dinner?"

Holy shit. Did he just ask me out? Yes, he did. Give him an answer, girl.

Calmly, speaking as though my insides weren't flipping over and over, I replied, "Wednesday? I don't think I have anything planned."

He cocked his head, a pleased expression crossing his face. "I can pick you up at your Mom's at six?"

"Sure. Six. Six would be good. Sure. That works." *Babble much, girl? Sheesh.*

He smiled and reached down to take my hand. Not breaking eye contact, he brought my knuckles up to his lips. His very warm, *soft* lips. The light kiss he gave them with an ever so slight touch of his tongue to one knuckle sent an immediate zing to the girls and other zing-prone areas.

"Good night, Princess Josie," he said softly, slowly lowering my hand and letting it go all too soon.

"Nirgg … I mean … goodnight, Jacob."

"Wow! He called you a princess, too, Mommy!" said the cheerful little voice from the back seat. I could only nod, still looking at him.

Jacob smiled and turned towards his truck, and I again noticed how well he filled out those jeans. I sighed and climbed into my car, starting the engine and pulling out of the parking lot towards home. I wondered what it would have been like to have my lips kissed instead of my knuckles. Damn. It was going to be a long trip home with achy nipples and damp panties. Visions of his lips and those jeans carried me into sleep that night.

FOURTEEN

Jacob

I woke up Saturday morning and did my best to figure out what the hell was going on with my life.

In the short span of a week, I went from never wanting to date anyone to having dinner with Josie, lunch, and now a pizza free for all. To cap off the madness, I asked her out for Wednesday. I'd watched myself ask her out, heard myself ask her out, but still couldn't believe I'd asked her out.

When she said yes, it sent a shiver up my spine. The smile on her face and the look in her eyes caused some stirrings within me that had not stirred in a long time.

The whole drive home, two thoughts ran through my head. 'She said yes' along with 'what the hell was I thinking?' My whole 'not dating again' rule hadn't just flown out the window; I'd used an air cannon to hurl it across the lake.

I spent the morning working on my project. Working at the hospital always put me behind, but since I wasn't under any schedule but my own, it was easy to make adjustments.

Around 5 p.m., I called it quits for the day and cleaned up. After a quick shower and change of clothes, I headed into town to meet Rick for dinner. I helped him with some equipment purchases a few days ago, so he was treating me to beer and burgers as a payment. I wasn't one to turn down free food and beer, especially if Rick was buying.

I pulled up to Danny's around six. Danny's was a decent bar and grill and did a fairly good business. The drinks were always cold, the staff was always friendly, and since Rick and his deputies were known to stop in for dinner, the crowd was always under control. A good place to have a drink, listen to some music, play pool or darts, and eat a burger.

Rick was already at a table in the back and waved at me as I came in the door. Johnny Cash was belting out of the jukebox. Rick loved Cash and anytime he came to the bar, he dropped enough money into the machine to play Cash for almost an hour, much to the dismay of the more modern country-western fans in residence.

I liked Rick. He had been Sheriff here for about eighteen years after spending twelve years in the Marine Corps. People liked him and liked the job he did, so they kept reelecting him. On the flip side, Rick loved this town and its people and there was nothing he wouldn't do to protect them.

As a Marine, he spent almost all of his time in Recon and shared similar experiences as me, just from different time frames. We both spent more time on the pointy end of the spear than either of us cared to admit.

Like most Marines I knew, he still wore his hair shorn close to the scalp and kept himself reasonably fit. He stood about an inch taller than me and probably had me by about fifteen pounds. I kidded him about getting flabby sitting behind that desk and steering wheel. He kept telling me that anytime I wanted to test that theory just meet him at the gym.

He and I were always competing with each other at the local shooting tournaments. He clobbered me with a long gun, but I always beat him out with pistols and assault rifles. What really got his goat was that I was ambidextrous. My scores in shooting from right or left-handed were virtually identical. As much as he tried to change, he was and would always be a right-handed shooter.

"Bout time you got here grunt," he said, taking a swig from his beer.

"Some of us work for a living, jarhead," I replied with a shrug, waving at the waitress as I sat down at the table. "Couldn't you just for once play something other than Cash? There are other singers out there, you know."

He just grunted, setting his beer back on the table. The waitress dropped a long neck at my spot and pulled out her order pad.

"What's it gonna be tonight, guys?" she asked, popping some gum. Rick smiled up at her.

"Don't think I've seen you here before," he observed, sensing a new prospect.

"Just started last week. Names Lynn." she told us, smiling and still working her gum.

"Well, Lynn, who's cooking tonight?" he asked.

She waved her hand back towards the kitchen area. "Jimmy's on the grill tonight."

"Well then, darling, I want the All-American burger with cheese and bacon. Throw on some onions, ketchup, and a bit of mustard along with a double side of onion rings. You tell Jimmy I want that burger medium. Not medium rare, and not medium well. Medium or else I'm gonna lock him up until he's fifty."

She scribbled down the order without even blinking at Rick's threat and looked at me.

"Give me half a rack of ribs, dry rub only. Baked potato, loaded, fixings on the side, and if the lettuce isn't too wilted, throw me a house salad together, please."

She smacked her gum some more, scribbled and turned back towards the kitchen. Rick kept his eyes glued to her ass, which was encased in jeans that appeared to be painted on. He turned back to me, grinning, and I shook my head.

"Hey, she's got a nice ass. Sue me," he said, taking another pull from his beer.

"Surprised it didn't burst into flames the way you were glaring at it. You know she can't be more than twenty-three, twenty-four?"

"Just because you're not interested in figuring out what color her bush is don't mean I'm not. I'm betting she shaves it," he said before sipping his beer.

Rick was the only person in town that knew about Kara. Near the end of his career, he lost his wife to cancer. He had been able to work an assignment to the DC area that gave his wife access to Bethesda Naval Hospital. Unfortunately, there had been nothing they could do to stop the aggressive form of breast cancer that she had been diagnosed with and she died within a year of their move.

Unlike me, though, he had no problem chasing women afterwards. He grieved for his wife, mourned her loss, and then decided to get on with life. His one rule was that any girl he went after had to be over twenty and unmarried. "Not doing teenagers or hanging horns on another man," he'd told me.

I'd learned his dating rules, and more than I really wanted to know about some of his conquests, over a long weekend about a year ago. He invited me out to his place to do some shooting on his range. When I got there, we barely shot a hundred or so rounds each when he decided he'd done enough and retreated to his fire pit and cooler.

For the rest of the night, we sat and drank, swapping stories. A couple hours and a lot of beer later, he told me about his wife. Seems that night was the anniversary of her death. It was the one night he allowed himself to remember and reminisce. Him trusting me enough to tell me about her gave me the strength to tell him about Kara.

He hadn't judged or even voiced any opinion when I told him about never dating again. We drank a lot more beer and crashed right beside the fire pit, neither one of us strangers to sleeping under the stars.

Lynn brought over two more beers and our food. Rick stopped her by touching her arm.

"So, sweet cheeks, what are you doing after your shift?" he asked, turning on the charm.

"Oh, thought I might go home, take a nice long, hot, soapy shower," she replied, stepping back so that her leg was just out of reach of Rick's hand.

"I'll bet that's relaxing," he said. "Even better if someone can help you clean those hard-to-reach places." I mentally groaned at that one. His lines were corny, but they usually worked for him.

"*Oh*, sweetheart, I couldn't agree with you more," she purred back at him. "My husband is great at getting into all my hard-to-reach places, multiple times."

"Lucky man," Rick retorted, still smiling and acknowledging the hit. It didn't stop him from staring at her ass again as she walked away.

He and I had both seen our share of marriages and relationships broken by cheating. Unfortunately, the 'Dear John/Jane' letters were a part of life when you were deployed away from your spouse for months at a time. As a result, we both developed a serious hatred for cheaters.

"You look like shit tonight, Rick. For a beat-up old Marine, that's saying a lot."

Rick rolled his head, and his neck popped like bubble wrap. "Been a busy few days. Someone's been breaking into some of the lake houses and boats at the marina. Looting, mostly. Camping supplies, food, that kind of shit," he said, taking a pull from his beer.

"Any ideas?"

"Not really. We get weirdos and asswipes every so often that want to go live off the grid. They head off into the deep woods and set up camp, hug a few trees," he explained. "Normally pretty harmless. Now and again, we get some dickheads that steal rather than buy. Best keep an eye out your way, or else they might decide you're easy pickings."

I nodded, taking a swig and starting on my food. I had just bitten into a rib when he spoke up again.

"So, you and Josie?"

I rolled my eyes as I finished chewing a hunk of rib meat, washing it down with a drink. "Damn, even you? Is there like a gossip website or message service that has everyone on a mailing list or something?"

"Nope, we all know Brianna in one way or another. That woman knows damn near everyone in town. Shit, she's the root of the fucking grapevine. She puts out a word to a few of her key folks and those folks spread it on out. Best damn pyramid communications setup you've ever seen." He laughed. "Hell, I have her in my files as an emergency notification system if I need one. Now, quit sidestepping the question, grunt."

I wiped my fingers and thanked Lynn for the new beer she placed on the table. She nodded and grabbed the empty one before leaving. I liked an attentive waitress, and her tip was climbing.

"Flora invited me over for dinner the other night. I swear I didn't know she was Josie's mom. Then I saw Josie at Brianna's Tuesday, and we sat at the same booth for lunch. Josie invited me to have pizza with her and Kaylin Friday night, and I asked her out for Wednesday. See? Nothing major."

Rick studied me as Johnny Cash started wailing about prison in the background. I could hear the crack of the pool balls over in the corner and the cook yelling out about some order. I picked at another rib before the silence got to me.

"Well, you gonna say something?"

"Nothing major, huh? You haven't chased a single skirt in this town since you got here. If you'd managed to lay any pipe, Brianna would have been burning up her phone telling everyone about who finally bagged the new stud."

He took another sip of his beer before continuing.

"You've had three dates, or whatever *you* want to call them, with Josie in what? A week? And we sure as hell can't forget the whole hiking shit that started this train. Hell, some would say you're off the market."

He used an onion ring to mop up some ketchup and mustard that leaked from his burger and popped it in his mouth. I wasn't even sure he chewed it more than twice before swallowing it down, followed by a slug of beer.

"Look, I know you've had a rough patch in life. Lost a good woman. I get how that can shut a man down. Thing is, you're a good man. It's been five years since ya lost Kara. I can't count the number of times I've told you to get your shit together and move on," he added, giving me another hard stare. "I knew Josie before she blew out of here for college, and I've watched her since she got back. She's a good person and a damn fine woman. She has a daughter, meaning whoever hooks up with her has to be ready to love that kid as if she was their own. I'm thinking that's not an issue for you?"

I just shook my head.

"Figured so. I met that husband of hers a time or two when they'd come back to visit. Good man; loved Josie to pieces." He polished off his beer and signaled Lynn for another. I sipped my longneck and waited, knowing he had more to say. "I think you'd both be good for each other. You're better for her than anyone else in this town. Time to bust down that fucking wall you've built and let someone in. If it's Josie, all the better."

He smiled up at Lynn as she set another bottle on the table and took away the empties, giving her ass another leer as she left. He turned his gaze back on me, and I blinked at the sudden change I saw in his face. Gone was the sheriff and my friend Rick. The guy looking at me now was pure death and soulless eyes.

I knew that look all too well.

"You know me, grunt, what I was, and what I am. You fucking hurt that woman or that little girl in any way, and you'll never hear the shot," he snapped, his voice ice cold.

I met that stare without blinking and drained my beer. "If that happens, I'll dig the hole for you."

He nodded, and just as quickly the mood at the table shifted back to one of alcohol contemplation and the intricacies of Johnny Cash's contribution to mankind.

FIFTEEN

Josie

M onday rolled around like it always did and I again found myself at Brianna's for lunch. I knew she would waylay me as soon as I walked in. What I didn't expect was The Tribunal.

My booth was occupied by Alexis Patterson and her new baby boy. Alexis worked at the courthouse with Izzy.

It was the table in front of the jukebox that pulled my attention. Riley, Izzy, and Brianna were already seated at the table, glasses of drinks in front of them. Three sets of eyes latched onto me. I gave a big sigh and marched to the table like a condemned man heading to his hanging. The bitch court was now in session.

I sat down, sipped at the glass of iced tea that was already at my place, and looked at each of the other three. I'd be damned if I cracked first. Brianna must have been the spokesperson.

"Well?" she asked.

I raised an eyebrow at the single-word question. "Yes, I'm well. You?"

Izzy rolled her eyes before speaking. "Give, Josie. We know you had a date with Jacob, and we want to know what happened. *Everything.*"

Three pairs of hands clasped together and laid on the table in front of their respective owners, all proper like. Since I couldn't get away from this, maybe I could have a bit of fun with it.

"It was the most erotic night I've ever had. He followed me into the women's bathroom at Gordo's and took me from behind in a stall. Bent me over the toilet and pounded me like a jackhammer. I think I came four times before he flooded me. I had both of us running down my thighs like milk. Best damn sex ever." I took another sip of tea. Take that, girls.

Riley's eyes narrowed to slits, and her lips compressed to thin bloodless lines. Brianna's mouth was hanging open. Izzy just rolled her eyes again before chuckling.

"And he was hung like a horse, I'm sure," said Izzy. "Now that you've given us the night's whore report, take pity on Riley and give us the *real* scoop."

I looked over at Riley. "Why am I taking pity on you?"

"You knew I liked him, and you asked him out anyway," she replied with just a hint of anger. Oh hell no. I'm feeling the best I have since Greg, and I'm not letting Riley pull me down.

"So, let me see if I understand correctly. And Riley, you just tell me if I'm wrong. He's been in town, what, three years? And during that time, if I believe what you're saying, you've been lusting after him like one of those hunky studs on the covers of those trashy romance books you read?"

I swept my gaze across each of them. Brianna and Izzy nodded. Riley looked pissed.

"Dammit, Josie," she hissed. "I told you last week I was after him. You know the fucking rules. You should have backed off and kept your tits to yourself."

"Riley, wasn't it *you* that sat here the other day and whined about him not being interested in you?"

Riley just crossed her arms and glared at me. She and I had history when it came to boys. She'd slipped behind my back once in high school, getting my then-boyfriend at the time, Jarret Bonner, very drunk and hauled him into the back seat of his car like a skank. She had been pissed that he wouldn't give her the time of day while he was with me. Riley didn't like to be told no.

When I found out about it, I kicked Jarret in the balls and then went to find Riley. She saw me coming and just smiled at me with that *'yeah, I fucked your boyfriend, what are you gonna do about it'* look.

What I did about it was to scream and leap onto her, driving her into the floor and tearing into her like a tornado. It took four teachers to pull us apart, and one of them got an elbow to the groin. They gave us both five days of suspension and two weeks of follow-on detention.

It took Bri and Izzy a month to get us to even speak to each other again and another month before we apologized and moved on.

But this wasn't high school.

"Riley?"

"Fine. Yes, that's what I told you," she said. *"That's* why you should have kept your damn hands off him."

Narrowing my eyes at her, I decided it was time to bring this to an end.

"So, Riley, since Jacob was all yours, when did you two last go out?"

Now it was Riley rolling her eyes. "I just told you—" she began, but I cut her off.

"I said out. Flirting, giggles, and tit-shots don't count. When did you last go up to him and say 'Jacob, what say you and I hook up this weekend?"

Riley just glared at me, saying nothing. Nope, we weren't playing that game today.

"Well?"

"I haven't asked him out," she spat. "There. Happy?"

"You snooze, you lose. Next time, put on your big girl panties and be a big girl."

Riley sat back in a huff while Brianna shook her head sadly. Izzy picked up where she left off.

"The date. Details, please. *Real* details, not fantasy bathroom hookups," she said.

Knowing I would get no respite—or lunch—until I told them, I relayed the night's events, including Jacob giving Kaylin the bear, which caused all four women to go 'aww' as a group. I concluded with Jacob kissing our hands and wishing the two princesses' good night.

"Wait a damn sec," demanded Riley, leaning forward and tapping the table with one fake, acrylic fingernail. "You mean to tell me you two played stupid kids games all night, ate crappy pizza, and only let him kiss your hand? No groping? Did you even cop a feel?"

"Yep. That's all. That's how you do it, Riley. Didn't have to flash my tits or stick my panties in his back pocket. Just asked him out."

Brianna finally chimed in, "Did you ask him out again?" Four sets of eyeballs laser-focused on me.

"No, I didn't ask him out again."

"Good. Stay away from him," huffed Riley. "I'll ask him out and show him what a real woman can do. Once I get him between my legs, he won't remember his name."

"He asked me out for Wednesday, and I said yes."

Riley choked on the drink she had just taken, sputtering and coughing. Brianna and Izzy determined that the inquisition was over. Izzy mentioned getting back to work as they helped Riley to the door. Riley glared at me all the way to the exit.

I smirked as Brianna sat back down at the table. "You enjoyed that, didn't you?" she asked.

"Hey, it's not my fault. She had plenty of time before I got here to ask Jacob out. This wasn't a 'Ho's before Bros' situation.' Jacob was fair game."

"Girl, there are times when you can be a real evil woman," said Brianna, shaking her head.

"I hope I never get you mad at me," chimed in Alexis as she patted her baby for his post-suckle burp. I laughed again and looked at the baby a little more closely. A thought began to tickle through my brain. An evil thought, one that reeked of revenge and filled my heart with cackling glee.

Brianna's phone dinged with an incoming text. She read it and grinned at me.

I raised a brow. "What?"

"Seems Jacob is heading this way for a quick cup of coffee."

"Not even going to ask why your spy network gives out movement reports on Jacob. But since he's heading this way, how does he take his coffee?"

"Usually just cream, why?" she asked.

I laughed evilly and motioned her over to me and Alexis. I began quietly explaining my plan. Alexis's hand flew to her mouth and she blushed as I explained what I wanted her to do. She agreed, still blushing. Brianna snorted but she had that wicked gleam in her eyes. Two seals of approval. Alexis quickly pulled out her pump from the diaper bag and we quietly begin preparations for some payback.

Brianna had just finished her part of my plan when Jacob came through the door. Seeing me, he came and sat down across from me.

"Hi," he said, smiling. That smile just melted me.

"Hey yourself. Recovered from all your battle wounds?"

"Oh yeah, all is good. Any problems with Kaylin going to sleep?" he asked.

"Nope, she was out like a light. You don't really know frustration until you try to put a little girl into her PJs while she is dead asleep and has a death grip on a bear. Took Mom and me both to get her dressed. Oh, where are my manners? Jacob, do you know Alexis? She works with Izzy over at the courthouse."

"No, I don't. Hi, Alexis. That looks like a brand spanking new model you have there on your shoulder!" he exclaimed warmly.

"Hey, Jacob. Right off the factory line, so to speak. This is Michael, and he's about eight weeks old," Alexis replied, lightly caressing her son's cheek.

Brianna showed up before Jacob could respond and sat a cup of coffee and a creamer cup on the table. I looked up and she nodded ever so slightly.

"Anything to eat Jacob?" she asked.

"Nope, just coffee," he said. "Sheriff wants me to go to Spokane with him to inspect some more equipment the county wants to buy. Told him I'd help him give it a once over."

We all watched as he poured a good dose of cream into his coffee and stirred it around. I took a sip of my tea to hide the grin on my face.

Tapping the spoon on his cup before setting it down, he raised it and blew on it before taking a sip. I was biting the inside of my cheek to keep from laughing. You could see him pause, work his lips a bit as if trying out a new unidentified taste, before taking another sip of his coffee.

He looked up to Brianna. "You using a new coffee?"

"No, why?" she asked with a straight face. Never play poker with Brianna.

"Coffee tastes a bit different today," he said as he sipped his drink again. I could tell he was rolling that sip around in his mouth.

"No, same coffee. Oh, but we are trying a different creamer. Locally sourced. Doing our bit to help out our farmers," she said, beaming proudly. She'd make a killing at Vegas.

"That's what it is," he said. "There's a sweeter taste to the coffee." He poured a small measure of cream into his spoon and slurped it down. I almost pissed my pants right there. Alexis turned a laugh into a cough and started rocking her sleeping son. Brianna gave no outward sign of her amusement other than gripping her apron tightly in her right hand.

"Hey, that's not too bad. I like it!" he exclaimed, smacking his lips as he quickly poured and sipped another spoonful. "Who did you get it from? I might want to get some for myself."

"Oh, you need to talk to Jimmy Patterson, Alexis's husband, about that," said Brianna, never even cracking a smile. "But it's a small amount and for a limited time only."

Jacob looked back to Alexis, who laid the now-sleeping infant down into his small baby carrier.

"So, can you talk to your husband for me?" he asked. Her eyes flipped to mine, and I nodded my head ever so slightly. She turned back to Jacob.

"Well, I could, but I'm not sure he's gonna want to share it. But as long as we don't tell him, I guess I could sneak you some now that might last you a few days."

"Sneak?" asked Jacob, looking confused. I was biting the inside of my jaw, doing everything I could not to explode.

Blushing, Alexis grabbed the buttons of her shirt. "You might say I have it with me all the time. I can get you some now. It would just take a sec."

Jacob again looked at her strangely for a few seconds and you could tell he was trying to figure out what was going on. He glanced at his cup, then back to Alexis, who was blushing even more. As I watched, his eyes flew wide open, and his face started glowing a nice shade of pink.

That's when Brianna blurted out a stripper tune and I almost fell out of my chair laughing. Alexis sold us out immediately.

"She made me do it! Said she owed you!" she exclaimed, pointing at me.

Brianna and I had tears rolling down our faces. I'm pretty sure I peed myself a little. Jacob was silent for long enough that I began to think my joke may have backfired. I was trying to figure out my apology when he began to laugh and shake his head. He stood up and moved around the table to take Alexis's hand. "My compliments to the chef," he said softly. She lit up like a neon sign. He turned his gaze on me.

"We're still on for tomorrow night?" he asked. I nodded, trying and failing to hold back the laughter. He gave me a two-finger salute and walked away to the sounds of hens cackling.

SIXTEEN

Jacob

It was a nice night. This far out from town, I didn't have any light pollution, so the stars stood out bright. Standing here, looking out over the lake, I am reminded of the beauty of nature. The light from the stars, a crisp clear sky, and the sounds of the woods at night all combined to provide me a sense of peace.

Using a tongue depressor, I stirred my newly poured cup of coffee, one with non-Alexis creamer. Blowing across the top of the cup, I took a sip and sighed with satisfaction before chuckling quietly. Josie got me good today. I would have to remember that for the future. She might get mad, but she got even too. She was intelligent and had a wicked streak in her that would keep a man on his toes.

Yet I was still drawn back to the diner and that slice of pie.

Sitting there, eyes closed, a look of pure bliss on her face as she ate that pie was enough to cause a stirring of feelings I had not felt in quite some time. Then she moaned.

The throatiness of that moan reached deep inside me and grabbed ahold of those feelings I had been suppressing and pulled them straight out of me through my dick. How I hadn't busted out the front of my jeans, I didn't know. That she didn't notice my condition was a miracle in and of itself.

Jealous? she had asked. As a man, my ego would explode out my head if I could ever do anything to a woman that gave her so much pleasure that she made that sound in that way. Hell yeah I was jealous.

I sipped my coffee again and listened to the sounds of the night. Some squirrels were scampering off to my right through fallen leaves, the crinkling and chittering marking their passage. A shadow flitted through the bright moonlight as an owl floated across the side yard, searching for its next meal.

It's been five years since Kara died and almost six since I'd had sex. I could still recall that last night with Kara before I left for deployment. She'd worn me out, let me sleep for a couple hours, then wore me out more. It was as if she had been trying to create and store enough memories to last until I got home. I still couldn't recall getting on the plane. The one thing I remembered was that more than a few of the guys, married or single, looked to be in the same shape as me.

When Kara died, I lost all interest in women. She had been perfect. No one could have measured up to her, so why bother looking? Not long after moving here I noticed the attention I started to receive from the women in the town. The subtle hints, the touches. I had almost been embarrassed on my last visit to the bank. Riley, the teller who helped me, had enough buttons undone on her shirt to leave no doubt as to the message she was sending.

While I had been flattered by the attention, I simply hadn't been interested.

Until now.

The first time I looked into Josie's emerald eyes, I felt an instant spark of attraction. It didn't matter that she was lying in a dust heap with twigs in her hair. She was a stunningly beautiful woman, at least to me.

And those eyes. Kara's eyes. The same coloring, shape … everything. I'd felt my own heart catch for a moment and had almost blurted out my dead wife's name on that eventful day. Then, seeing her at her mom's had been unnerving and exciting all at the same time.

I sipped my coffee and stared out at the lake. I knew it was always a possibility that at some point in time, after the pain dulled enough, that I might date again, maybe even find love. I pictured it happening years from now. Unfortunately, they don't make an instruction book for grief with a chart that tells you how long the proper time of mourning is.

Josie and I had tried to talk at the pizza parlor, but it was too loud to really hear ourselves. Kaylin had been so excited that I couldn't help but be caught up in her good mood. She dragged me and Josie around to game after game to win her tickets.

Josie had looked amazing. Nice fitting jeans, jersey, and a ponytail. Her shirt was just tight enough that I could tell she was nicely endowed. Her jeans emphasized shapely legs and a very nice ass.

The whole package screamed "I'm a vibrant woman who doesn't need to be a Barbie doll" and I responded to that, and to her. Josie was neither fat nor thin. She was just ... fucking amazing. It definitely didn't hurt that she was tall, only about four inches shorter than me.

Those green eyes and that ponytail. She'd hit my two biggest triggers, and my blood began to pump faster, my pulse escalating. Josie was a completely perfect package and in that ball pit, that perfect package jumped straight into my arms and sat on me.

While her flight through the air had only been mere seconds, it was an image I would remember to my dying day. The excitement of the moment had brought a blush to her cheeks and a smile to her face. The term 'goddess' had immediately sprung to mind as she landed on me.

She hadn't been upset when I tossed her off me, assuming it was all just part of the fun. What she hadn't known was that I'd needed to get her off me before she felt the instant erection I got the moment she sat on me. Even now, the memory of her was still making me excited and hard. If she had ground even once, I would have exploded in my pants.

I took another sip of my coffee, working my thoughts away from Josie and onto the other half of the one-two punch that were the Callison women. Kaylin.

My heart ached at what could have been had Kara and Karen survived. Karen would have been just about the same age as Kaylin. I would never get to do with my daughter the things I had already done with Kaylin.

And I gave her Karen's bear.

I still remember going to the PX and buying it when Kara finally let me know she was pregnant. Since my vacation in the sand, courtesy of the Army, had just been starting, it would have been months before I could have given it to her. Regardless, I had wanted it right away. Not only to give to my daughter when she was born but to have as a symbol for what was waiting for me back home. Now I had given it away.

I thought about the dinner at Josie's mom's and that adorable little girl. She floored me when she talked about the bear and her daddy. How does a mere mortal such as myself compete with a memory that strong?

Simple answer was that I couldn't and more importantly, wouldn't. If by some weird chance of fate I were ever in a situation where Kaylin was part of my future, it was on me to make sure she understood that I was never a replacement for her daddy, just someone else who would love her as his own.

As if imagining a future with her mother was not scary enough, was I ready to be a father to an 8-year-old? No chance to grow up with her, just step in the door and be in her life. Pizza and bears were the fun part, but what about bedtimes, teeth brushing, and the multitude of other areas where conflict could arise? How would Josie feel about it or how would she define my role?

More importantly, how would Kaylin see this? So far, I was just Mr. Jacob, champion skee-ball player and fun guy to hang with. How would she react to me being there all the time? Would she be scared or worried?

I wasn't afraid of being a father. When Kara told me she was pregnant, I freaked out half the camp when I danced across the compound. I loved kids and told her I wanted at least a dozen. She told me I was insane and countered with two and a promise to talk about more.

These thoughts made me really question the speed at which Josie and I were moving. But I had always looked to the future when planning, looked at best- and worst-case scenarios. Some might call me stupid for already thinking the way I was about Kaylin, but I didn't see it that way.

I stared out over the lake, gut churning. What was I doing? Kara was the love of my life. I'd never even looked at another woman once we were together. She had been my everything. The day she stood up to her parents and told them we were getting married, I fell for her all over again.

Then she was taken away, leaving me with just memories and what might have been.

Was I being unfaithful? If Kara meant so much to me, how could I be thinking of Josie so much? She was invading my head constantly. I ached to hold Josie, hear her laugh. What would it be like waking up next to her? Could I make her moan like she had when eating pie? Fuck, what was I gonna do?

As I flipped the contents of my coffee cup out on the ground below, the sound of a motor reached my ears.

I cast my gaze out over the lake and let it drift along its surface. Movement to my right drew my attention to where several dark shapes were moving on the water's surface. Boats were unusual for this time of the night, and it was even more unusual to have boats running without lights. As I watched, they moved off to the far end of the lake.

There were three boats in all. Probably a bunch of teenagers heading up to the north end of the lake to have a party, as far from the marina and others as you could get. I found party remains a couple of times when I was hiking around that end of my land. Nothing major, just burnt wood in fire pits and a few beer cans and bottles. Hopefully, none of them would get too stupid up there.

I took the Gator back down to my trailer. I cleaned up and laid down on my bed, slipping between the cool sheets. I stared up into the darkness at the ceiling, trying to calm my racing mind. My life had been so damn easy until that fateful Saturday when Josie literally fell into my life, blowing my serenity away.

Sleep was a long time coming.

SEVENTEEN

Josie

"You look pretty, Mommy."

"Aww. Thank you, pumpkin."

Kaylin was sitting on the end of my bed, watching me get ready for my date with Jacob and asking all kinds of questions about makeup. Her infectious curiosity helped calm my nerves.

Boy, did they need calming. I was about forty-five minutes from having my first real date in over two years, and I had eagles flying around in my stomach. I don't think my 24-hour deodorant was going to last thirty minutes, and I was pretty sure I wanted to throw up.

"Mommy?"

"Yes, pumpkin?"

"Is Mr. Jacob gonna be my new daddy?"

The small makeup brush fell to the dresser vanity top as I kept myself from whirling around. Taking a deep, calming breath, I padded over to my bed in stocking feet and sat down next to Kaylin.

"Why do you ask that?"

"Well, Bethy's got a new daddy, and she said her mommy went on dates with him. So, since you are going on dates with Mr. Jacob, does that mean he's gonna be my new daddy, too?"

God bless six-year-old logic. I wrapped my arms around her and hugged her tight before pulling her up into my lap and brushing her cheek with my finger.

"No, pumpkin. He's not going to be your new daddy. Mr. Jacob and I are just going out to dinner."

"What is dating?" she asked, reaching out to play with the small pendant I was wearing.

"Well, dating is what two people do who think they might like each other. They go out on dates, and they talk and get to know each other. Sometimes they find they don't really like each other, and then they don't go on any more dates. Sometimes they do like each other, and then they go on more dates. If they like each other enough, they may even find out they love each other."

"Do you like Mr. Jacob?

"I think I do, baby. That's why I want to go on a date with him. I think he likes me too because he asked me. Do you like him?"

"Oh yeah, lots. He gave me a bear, and he played skee-ball and won me all those tickets. He's lots of fun."

Kaylin reached up one small finger and brushed my lips.

"Are you going to kiss Mr. Jacob on the lips?"

Dear god, not this talk, not now.

"Baby, who have you been talking to about kissing?"

"Well, Bethy says she saw her mommy kissing her new daddy after dates and it looked all gross. Now Bethy is gonna have a new baby brother. I don't want any yucky brother."

I laughed and hugged her again.

"I promise you, no new baby brother. Look, pumpkin, Mr. Jacob and I are going on a date. We will have dinner, and we will talk and get to know each other. We might kiss, we might not. Right now, it's yucky to you, but someday, oh say in about eight or nine years, you might not find it so yucky."

"Can I go watch TV?" she asked, patience with this subject gone. I hugged her again and kissed her forehead.

"Sure."

She hopped down and trotted off to the living room. Lord, she was growing up way too fast. I'm sure somewhere Mom and karma were enjoying a good laugh. I made a mental note to keep an eye on Ms. Bethy. Time to finish getting ready.

I was stepping into my dress when Mom ran to the doorway.

"Josie, we have a problem at the store!" she said in a panic. "Jerry just called and said there's a busted water pipe flooding the storeroom."

"Shit!" I dropped the dress and grabbed my jeans, yanking them on my legs.

"I had Jerry doing some cleanup after the store closed. He was getting some stock from the storeroom and stepped in water. Said it was spraying from several pipes on the ceiling."

"Did he shut the water off?"

"He didn't know how," she explained with a sigh. "What are we going to do? We can't lose that stock."

I yanked my shirt on, grabbed my shoes and purse, and ran for the front door. "Stay here with Kaylin." I threw open the door and ran smack into Jacob. We both stumbled as he grabbed hold of me, steadying us both.

"Glad to see you so eager for our date." he quipped.

Fuck. Jacob. Date. Why did the gods hate me?

"I need to get to the store. Busted water pipe. Sorry." I disentangled from him, trying to get around him and to my car. Bless him, he didn't ask questions. He ran to his truck, yelling for me to get in. I barely had the door closed before he was backing out of the driveway.

I had Jacob park in the alleyway near our small loading dock. I hopped out of the truck and rushed to the back door. Jerry slammed it open, waving at me. I ran up the stairs and into the back storeroom and splashed right into a flooded floor.

A glance up to the open ceiling showed water coming from several spots along three of the overhead pipes, spraying down into one corner of the storeroom. The two shelves in that area were soaked, and there looked to be about two inches of water on the floor.

"Where's the cutoff?" Jacob asked as he surveyed the indoor monsoon.

I ran to the mechanical room with him trailing right behind. Slamming open the beat-up metal door, I rushed in and to the left where the city water came in. Grabbing the valve, I rotated it 180 degrees, shutting off the water to the building. Out in the room we could hear the spraying sounds fade out.

Jacob followed me as we waded back to the busted pipes. Small drips and sprays were still coming out as the pressure in the pipes slowly bled away.

I sloshed over to the storage racks and almost sobbed. This area contained almost $20,000 in soft goods. Clothes, boxes of greeting cards, stationery, and other paper or cloth-based products, all of it which was now soaked and virtually ruined.

Dad had not believed in carrying a lot of insurance. While the building was protected for fire, it wasn't covered for water damage, nor was our inventory, a chunk of which was now virtually lost. If I were lucky, I might be able to sell most of the clothing at a 'damage sale' but that would only get me pennies on the dollar.

Of course, that didn't even cover the plumbing. I walked over to Jacob, who was surveying the pipes. He turned his head to me as I waded over.

"Sorry, Jacob, not quite the date you probably imagined."

He shrugged. "Not like you planned this," he replied. Then he peered at me suspiciously. "Unless of course, you *did* plan this to avoid dinner? In which case, it's a bit extreme don't you think? A simple no would have saved you tons on your water bill."

I rolled my eyes. "Damn, you caught me, figured out my diabolical plan."

He laughed and returned to surveying the pipes.

I sighed, looking up as well. "Just one more damn expense I didn't need."

"Insurance?" he asked.

"Not for water. Dad was only scared of fire, thinking we could handle anything else. I know it makes no sense, but Dad was really weird about insurance."

"Ouch," he said. "So, the inventory?"

"Won't know till I figure out the full damage. On top of which now I have to call the plumber to make an after-hours service call. I can probably open the store tomorrow without water, but it will be a pain in the ass."

"You got a ladder anywhere?" he asked.

"Yes." We both sloshed back to the mechanical room. Luckily, the ladder was tall enough for whatever he wanted. Grabbing it, he headed back to the pipes.

I watched as he set up the ladder and began climbing up. Damn that man had a nice ass.

Shit, girl. You're standing in water that could destroy your store, and you're looking at his ass?

Shaking those thoughts away, I moved around to the front of the ladder.

"What are you doing?"

"Figuring out what needs to be fixed," he said absently, examining the pipes.

"I didn't know being a nurse qualified you as a plumber."

"I am a man of many talents," he said, climbing back down.

"Uh huh, sure you are."

"You want the good news or the bad news?" he asked, grinning at me while he leaned on the ladder.

I smacked him on the arm, not willing to play that game again.

"Ouch, such violence. You don't need a plumber. I can have this fixed in about an hour, two tops," he said proudly.

I glared at him. "Don't mess with me, Jacob. It's not a good time."

He crossed his heart. "All true, I swear."

"How much is this gonna cost? My budget is a bit thin."

"Probably less than fifty dollars. Couple pieces of pipe, some fittings. Depends on the cost of the parts. I got my tools in the truck."

I stared at him like he was speaking Greek. "Fifty dollars? You can fix this for that little? Hell, the plumber would probably charge me five times that just for coming out at night to tell me how much he was going to charge me to fix it."

He shrugged. "Well, I'm here already, and this is an easy fix. If I mess it up, I'll pay for the plumber. Your call."

"Are you sure you can fix this?" I pressed. He stepped up close and put a hand on each of my shoulders, looking me in the eye.

"Josie, trust me. This is easy."

Trust him. Shit, he smelled good. A hint of soap, but I couldn't place the cologne. Didn't care either. I may have inhaled deeply. I felt myself starting to lean …

"Earth to Josie?"

I snapped back to reality, staring at him. "Well, what do you want to do?" he asked.

"Sure. Yeah. Go ahead. Sorry, was thinking about lost inventory."

He popped out his phone and dialed. "Ben, Jacob, can you stay open for a bit? Small emergency and I need three 10x1-inch copper pipes and about six of those push-connect fittings. Type? Um, M or K should do. Repairing a water supply line. You can? Great. Be right there."

He stuffed his phone back in his pocket and dug out his truck keys.

"Okay, I gotta run over to Ben's store. Got any mops or a shop vac?"

"Yeah. Jerry and I will mop while you're gone." He laughed, leaving out the back door as I yelled for Jerry to grab the mops.

Jacob was back in about twenty-five minutes with his supplies. Jerry and I had made a pretty decent dent in cleanup and were probably down to our last ten or so buckets.

We kept mopping while Jacob started working. He climbed up the ladder and marked off a section on each of the three busted pipes. I kept glancing at him as he cut out the damaged sections of the old pipes, measured and cut replacement pieces, then used some weird brush to scour the pipe ends for some reason.

By 8:30 p.m., Jacob finished the repairs and had me turn the water back on. He bowed to me when the water flowed again without escaping the pipes.

Without really thinking about it, I gave him a hug. He froze for a moment before returning it. Fuck, he felt good. I inhaled deeply, filling up on him again. I let myself enjoy it for a few seconds before reluctantly releasing him, blushing.

"Sorry. Um, thanks for this."

"You're most welcome," he said, smiling.

Jacob picked up his tools while I put the ladder away. We then all stepped out on the back dock, and I locked up the shop. Jerry left for home, and Jacob and I walked to his truck. I called Mom to update her on the situation.

"Hey. We got the water stopped and fixed."

"Fixed? You already had the plumber there? Oh lord, how much is that going to cost us? What about all that water? Did you get it cleaned up?"

"I didn't need to call a plumber. Jacob actually fixed the problem and it only cost us about $50 in parts. While he was doing that, Jerry and I got the water all mopped up."

"Seriously? Jacob fixed it? For $50? How?"

"Cut out the damaged pieces of pipe, fitted in some new pieces. By the time Jerry and I were finished cleaning, Jacob was done. Water's back on and no leaks."

"Oh that's great news. But, what about our stock? How bad is it?"

"That's the bad part. We lost those back two racks of soft goods. Pretty much a total loss. We might be able to sell some of it discounted, but not enough to really make a difference in the loss. Look, we can talk about it more when I get home. Jacob can drop me back off and we can figure out what we're going to do."

"Well, nothing we can do about that now. Oh, Josie ... your date. I'm so sorry. Would he like to come over and have pizza? I ordered some for Kaylin and me. There is still plenty. It's the least we can do."

"Um, I don't know. I'll ask." I turned to Jacob, biting my lip. "Mom ordered pizza for her and Kaylin. Says there is plenty left if you want to come eat."

"Sure. Gives me a chance to dry out my boots and socks," he said.

I grin. "Hear that, Mom?"

"*Yes. I'll whip up some salads to go with the pizza.*"

"Okay, see you in a few. Bye."

We loaded back up in Jacob's truck for the drive back home at a more sedated pace than the previous trip. Mom met us at the door. She showed Jacob where to put his wet footwear while I went to check on Kaylin. She was sound asleep holding both her bears. I gently smoothed the hair from her forehead and kissed her lightly. I quietly closed her bedroom door on my way back out to the kitchen.

Mom and Jacob set two plates at the breakfast nook and had the pizza reheating. She threw together a couple of small salads and placed them and a pitcher of tea on the table.

"Well, I think I'll turn in now," she said, yawning. She hugged Jacob. "Thank you for all your help tonight. Sorry about your date."

"No worries. Glad I could be of help," he replied with a small smile. She patted his arm and then hugged me. "Not too late, young lady. You have school tomorrow." She laughed as I rolled my eyes, then she kissed the top of my head and headed back to her room, leaving me alone with Jacob.

Before I could say anything, the oven timer binged. I pulled the pizza out of the oven, placing it on a potholder Mom had put on the table.

Jacob sniffed appreciatively. "Pepperoni. My favorite," he said. He deftly slid two pieces onto his plate, wincing at how hot they were and blowing on his fingers.

I chuckled, using the pizza cutter to lift my slices so I didn't burn myself. "It's okay, but I prefer pineapple and sausage."

He paused to glare at me. "Don't tell me that you're one of *those* pizza eaters."

"Those?" I raised a brow.

"Yes, one of those. The kind that ruins a perfectly good pizza by putting fruit on it," he said with mock indignation.

I shrugged and grinned at him. "I like what I like."

"Whatever," he harrumphed before biting into his pizza. I drizzled some French dressing on my salad and stirred it around. Jacob mirrored me, using his fork to mix in the dressing. We ate quietly for a few moments before I spoke.

"Sorry our date got ruined. I was really looking forward to it."

He paused with a bite of salad almost to his mouth. "Why do you say it's ruined?"

"Most dates don't usually involve a flooded storeroom and plumbing repairs."

"Ah. Well, that might be true if you looked at the date in specifics, but not in general." He ate his bite of salad, chewing quietly while watching me digest that tidbit.

"That's the kind of analytical talk every girl wants to hear on a date. Really gets her all hot and bothered."

Jacob chuckled and wiped his mouth, reaching for a slice of pizza. "Josie, what was the plan tonight had we not had the aforementioned plumbing emergency?"

"No idea. I assumed we might do dinner, maybe a movie, walk in the park, a trip up to lovers' lane for some passionate window fogging."

He sputtered and almost spit out the tea he had just drank, and I covered my mouth, trying not to laugh too hard. Once he had wiped off his chin and the front of his shirt, he gave me the stink eye.

"Are you trying to kill me, woman?"

I gave him my best innocent angle pose. He cocked one eyebrow at me. Not sure he was buying it.

"Uh huh," he said, taking a bite of pizza and chewing for a few moments, before swallowing and wiping his mouth

"Anyway, you are generally correct. I was planning on dinner—Italian, by the way. After that, maybe a movie or coffee somewhere quiet so we could talk."

"Still not seeing how fixing my pipes didn't ruin the plan, Professor."

Jacob choked on his food as I realized what I said. Shit, I killed him. He held up his hand as I slid my chair back, ready to come help him. Coughing a few more times, he took a drink and stared at me.

"You are ... unbelievable, you know that?" he asked, his eyes boring into me.

"Sorry not sorry. Didn't answer the question."

I took a bite of my pizza while awaiting his next explanation. He sipped some more tea, keeping a wary eye on me as he swallowed. He made it so easy, but I took pity on him. This time.

"It's been my experience that dates generally follow the same plan," he began. "One, an activity that two can do, such as movies, dancing, etc. Two, a meal together. Three, companionship, which can take many forms. Now, one and two can be interchangeable. Some dates might just be two and three. All depends."

I chortled. "Are you always this formal and all analytic? Almost sounds like one of my old college professors talking. Must make for some boring dinner talk." I paused, then dropped the next line on him. "So, you think our date is going swimmingly?"

He broke out laughing, then clamped his hand over his mouth, remembering the others that were asleep. Those eyes of his danced with amusement as he dropped his hand, grinning.

"Swimmingly ... flood. Good one," he said, shaking his head. He lifted his tea glass in toast to my obvious comic genius. After he took another swig, he continued his explanation. "We did our activity, and we are having dinner—even Italian, and we're talking. So, yes, I think it's going quite well."

We ate quietly for a few moments. I was famished, and the conversation lulled as we both polished off the pizza and salad. Jacob helped me clear the dishes, and we came back to sit at the table. I refilled our glasses, then asked what had been working at the back of my mind since the Tribunal grilled me.

"Jacob, could you answer a question for me?"

"Depends on the question," he replied. He leaned forward, giving me his full attention, his eyes meeting mine. I liked that. He made me the focus of his attention, and that made my heart go thump for a beat or two.

"Why me?"

"Excuse me?" he asked.

I gave him a rundown of the Tribunal's response to me asking him out for pizza, forgoing Riley's plans for him. He drank some more tea as he looked thoughtful. I figured that had been the last question he was expecting. I rushed on before he could answer.

"You said yes when I asked you out for pizza, and you asked me out for tonight. According to the girls, you haven't dated or hooked up with anyone since you got here. Humor me. Why me?"

He stared down into his glass, swirling the ice a bit. When he answered, it was quiet, and he kept his gaze on the glass in his hand.

"You're an intelligent, beautiful woman, and any man would be lucky to spend time with you. At dinner here the other night, I also saw that you were a wonderful mother who loves her daughter. You're the first woman I've felt a spark of interest in since ..."

He paused and took another drink and I could see his jaw muscles working while he struggled with whatever decision he was trying to make. He inhaled deeply and then met my gaze. I could see that hurt in his eyes that mom mentioned.

"You're the first woman I've been attracted to since I lost my wife and daughter. Of all those women your friends referred to, you alone can understand the pain and the hesitation to expose oneself to that possible hurt again. I haven't dated anyone, or had an interest in anyone, since the day they died."

I sat back in my chair, floored. Of all the answers he could have hit me with, that one wasn't even on the radar. He had been married before; he had been a *father*. No one, not even Brianna and her gossip network, had ever mentioned that.

"When?"

"Almost five years ago," he said quietly. "They were killed in an auto accident while I was deployed overseas. I didn't even make it home for the funeral."

"I'm so sorry."

Without thinking I reached across the table and took his hand. He grasped mine, and I gave it a small squeeze. Nothing was said for a few moments as we were both lost in our own pain and memories. His grip loosened, so I reluctantly withdrew my hand.

"Thank you for telling me. Can I ask her name?"

"Kara. When she died, she was eight months pregnant with our daughter, Karen."

I felt the first tear slide down my cheek. I could only begin to imagine his grief. When Greg died, I at least had Kaylin to help me get by, a piece of him that I would always have. But Jacob had only the memory of that future and the pain associated with it.

He handed me a napkin, and I wiped the tears away. "Why haven't you told anyone in town?"

"The sheriff knows."

"Why only him?"

"I came here to separate from her family and all the pain and bad memories, to start over and to honor the plan she and I had made," he said softly. "We were going to live and raise our kids here, far away from as much of the craziness of her family and the world as we could escape."

"Azton is a great place, and I'm not biased because I grew up here. Greg and I were going to do the same thing. I don't think it was as appealing to him as it was to me, but we're close enough to the national forest that he could have gotten work. He was a forest ranger."

"Turn the tables," he replied. "Why me?" Well, I guess fair was fair

"Pretty much the same reason. You're the first man since Greg that I felt an attraction to. The fact that you saved my bacon on the hike *and* that you're good looking doesn't hurt either. To put the icing on the cake, my daughter likes you."

I sipped my tea, collecting my thoughts before speaking again.

"Losing Greg was tough on me and Kaylin. Maybe the fact I was able to be there for the burial helped me with closure. Of course, having Kaylin meant I would always have a piece of him near me. Kaylin is something I always have to be concerned about if I date. She and I are a package deal."

I cocked my head to the side and gazed at him, reading his face for any bad reactions and seeing none. Good.

"But I get the feeling from you that Kaylin wouldn't be an issue," I added.

Jacob smiled. "She's a great kid from what I've seen of her so far. And no, she's not an issue, far from it."

I grinned back. Slowly, cautiously, we got to know one another. We exchanged stories on meeting our spouses, dating them, and a minutia of life experiences. I asked him about the Army, but he deflected by asking me about Kaylin's birth. I made a mental note to broach that subject again later.

I loved that we could both share about our spouses without making it awkward. Neither of us shied away from talking about them. Maybe it was because we both loved and lost, and that commonality made it so comfortable. Our spouses were a part of who we were, and we both understood.

Somewhere in the process, our hands met again. When they did, a small zing coursed up my arm. His hand felt good. Calloused, but not too rough, and at some level I could sense that they could be gentle when touching.

When he lightly brushed his thumb across my knuckles it sent little tingles to all my tingle-prone places. I didn't think he was consciously doing it, but I liked it a lot, and I felt a delicious heat starting to build in my core. An excitement at the connection that was happening.

"Is your store in trouble?" he asked.

I started to reply but stopped. Mom and I hadn't discussed the store with anyone but Uncle Frank. Should I tell him this? But he trusted me with Kara, and I knew I could trust him with this.

Sighing, I nodded.

"Sales have fallen way off. Mom and Pop general stores aren't surviving in this world of online shopping and next-day delivery. We don't have the deep pockets to cover the overhead. A Walmart opened up near the interstate, and that hasn't helped.

"A few years ago, we had a small electrical fire. Dad took out an equity loan to do the repairs and some other upgrades he had been putting off. At the time, sales were covering it just fine. Now that loan is killing us. We have a small operating line of credit with the bank, but we're using it to cover the equity line payment, and sales barely cover costs, which includes payment on the line of credit. We're eating our tail. I think we have about three months, but that was before I lost that stock tonight."

"Are you going to close? Can't the bank help you?"

I updated him on my trip to the bank and my discussion of the numbers with Mom.

"What are you going to do if it closes?"

I shrugged. "Get a job. The bank will get the building, and the store will declare bankruptcy. The house is paid for, and Mom has her Social Security and what's left of the life insurance policy she had on Dad. Greg's life insurance was enough to set up a small college fund for Kaylin and give me some padding. Moving back in with Mom reduced my costs and stretched out that safety net. We'll be okay until I can find work."

"I have money that I can—" he started to say, but I squeezed his hand to stop him.

"I appreciate the thought, really, but the amounts I need are not small. Like I told Mom, any small savings or such thrown in is just wasted money."

He nodded, his eyes thoughtful.

My phone pinged with an incoming text message. Who could be texting me this late?

"It's late, young lady. Work tomorrow."

I looked at the time and was shocked. It was after one in the morning. We had been talking for over four hours, and it felt like no time had passed at all. I shook my head and showed Jacob Mom's message. He started grinning.

"Guess I need to go. Don't want your mom to ground you," he said, rising. He started to clean up the dishes, but I stopped him.

"Leave them, I'll get them later."

He grabbed his socks from the back of the chair and pulled them and his boots back on. Properly dressed again, he made his way to the front door, and we stepped out on the porch. I had butterflies in my stomach, and I could see he was just as nervous as I was. It was high school all over again.

We did the awkward date shuffle at the door, neither of us knowing how to end the night but both of us knowing how we wanted it to end.

Jacob stepped a bit closer and took my hand. My pulse began to race at his touch, anticipation at what might be happening next.

"I really had a nice time, Josie. Nicest I've had in, well, awhile."

"Sorry it wasn't quite what you planned."

He shook his head, smiling. "It was a great time, and I hope we can do it again."

I grinned back and nodded in agreement.

I couldn't tell you which of us moved first.

The minute our lips touched, that heat exploded inside me like an erupting volcano. I didn't hear anything, my awareness seeming to center on Jacob. For a few seconds, neither of us moved.

I remember my first kiss with Greg. This one left that memory in the dust.

It wasn't a kiss of passion; it was a kiss of connection, as if two halves snapped together to become a whole. It felt like something wrapped around and hugged my soul.

Jacob brought his arms around me, and my hands worked up his back to his shoulders. We didn't mold to each other, but we connected at almost every point.

His tongue teased my lips, and I let him in. It was a gentle but insistent ballet as we explored each other. I took a moment to capture his tongue and lightly suck on it. He groaned and tightened his hug to the point that I could feel all of him pressed against me, including a very nice hardness.

When he attempted to back it away from me, I dropped one hand to his waist, holding him in place. I wouldn't grind, but I wanted the contact and wanted him to not be afraid to let me feel it, especially since it felt really, really good.

At some point, air became a necessity, and our lips parted, but we kept holding each other close.

"Josie ... I never ... can I ..."

"Oh god, yes," was all I said before meeting his lips again. There was no hesitancy this time as our tongues met immediately and picked up where they had left off. Again, the dance was a ballet of heat and passion, but tempered. I never felt anything like this before, and I never wanted it to stop.

One moment, his tongue danced with mine, and the next, he pulled back, capturing my lower lip between his teeth and tugging and sucking. I swear I had a small orgasm. Pulling him tight to me, I dove back into his lips.

Once again, our inability to breathe and kiss at the same time forced us apart. Jacob leaned his forehead against mine, and we both took several deep breaths, trying to bring down our heart rates.

"Jacob ... I ... you ... wow ..."

"Josie, I ... really need to go," he said haltingly.

"No... Please, don't."

"I don't want to Josie, but I *really* need to," he replied, his voice holding a hint of desperation.

I ached as he slowly pulled back away from me, forcing my arms from around him so that we ended up holding hands again. His eyes were focused on me, and there was no mistaking the intense hunger reflected in them. If what he was feeling was as strong as what I was, we needed to stop now before clothes began dropping on the front porch or I dragged him back to my room.

"Lunch tomorrow?"

"I can't," he said, and I could hear the regret in his voice. "I have to go to Seattle tomorrow or rather, today. Won't be back till late Friday"

"Saturday?"

"Sure. Something with Kaylin?"

"Sure."

Jacob gave me another quick kiss before stepping away from me. Our arms stretched out until our fingertips slipped past each other and he turned for his truck. I gave him a small wave as he backed out, and he waved back. I stepped back in the house and closed the door quietly.

I crawled into bed and tried to sort out my swirling emotions. Emotions that died with Greg were now shouting in my head and my heart. I told Mom about this not being love at first sight. I never said anything about love at first kiss.

As I recalled those kisses in their fullness, and the feel of his hard length pressing into me, I did something I hadn't done in a long time. I let my hand drift its way into my pajama bottoms. I knew that sleep would come, but not before I did.

EIGHTEEN

Josie

I stared at the refrigerator, elbows on the table, holding my coffee cup in both hands as I sipped it. Sunlight from the kitchen window washed over me, warming and caressing me. I felt good this morning, almost revitalized. Last night's sleep had been the best I'd had in longer than I can remember. Having a couple of really good orgasms tends to make a lot of things seem better.

"Mommy, are you okay?"

Kaylin's voice pulled me back from my recollections. She was working on a bowl of cereal for her breakfast.

"What, pumpkin?"

"Are you okay? I was asking a question, and you didn't answer me. Does your tummy hurt? Maybe you need to not go to work. I don't like going to school with a tummy ache. *Oh*, I could stay home with you and take care of you like you and Grandma do for me!"

I laughed and rubbed her cheek. "No, my tummy's fine. Sorry, I was just thinking. What were you asking?"

"Did you kiss Mr. Jacob?"

"Yes, I did." Hell yeah, I did.

Kaylin's face scrunched up like she'd smelled a dead fish. "*Eww.* I'm never gonna kiss any yucky boy. They have cooties," she retorted with all-knowing feminine authority. I merely smiled. "Mommy?"

I was never going to finish this cup of coffee which, of course, was cold now. I got up to pour it out and refill my cup.

"Yes?"

"Are you and Mr. Jacob gonna do more dates?"

"Yes, I think we are. In fact, he wants to do something with the both of us this Saturday. What do you think about that?"

She clapped her hands with glee. "Can we go back to Gordo's and play more skee-ball?"

"Well, let's think of something else. We can do Gordo's another time."

"What about putt-putt? Can we go there? Can I ask Bethy to go with us? Can she spend the night?" she asked excitedly, cereal now forgotten.

So much for more alone time with Jacob. Well, this was probably going to be the norm when dating with a child in the mix.

"I suppose that'll be okay. I'll call Bethy's mom today and we can get it worked out. Now, finish your breakfast." I gave her a serious look.

Kaylin began shoveling in her cereal, her excitement bubbling over.

"Slow down before you choke, young lady." Her intake reduced to a slower blur.

Breakfast finished, teeth brushed, backpack ready, we headed to the door for our quick drive to daycare where we joined the line of cars dropping off the future leaders of the free world.

"Mommy, am I dating Mr. Jacob too?"

Good lord, was she *trying* to give me a stroke? Deep breaths, Josie, deep breaths.

"Well, I guess in a way you are. We Callison girls are a package deal. If Mr. Jacob likes me, he has to like you."

"Oh," she said quietly.

I glanced at her, and I could see her little mind racing. "Everything okay?"

"Um … does this mean I have to kiss Mr. Jacob on the lips, too?"

I really wanted to break out in laughter but the tone of her voice told me this was really bothering her.

"Oh, no sweetie. Not at all. You leave the kissing to Mommy and you worry about skee-ball and those kinds of things. But I tell you what, if you want to thank him some time, you can give him a little kiss on the cheek. I'd bet he'd like that."

"Okay, Mommy, I can do that. He's really, really good at skee-ball." What is it about skee-ball? We got to the drop-off point, and I handed her off to the daycare staff.

It took all morning to sort through the mess in the storage room. Most of the damaged stock was a complete write-off. The clothes could probably be sold at a huge discount but would still cost us in the long run. The paper and dry goods were a total loss.

I spent more time on the phone with our suppliers. They were sorry about our losses but were unwilling to cut me any breaks on slowing or altering the payment due on the goods. They were puzzled as to why our insurance would not cover these things.

It was almost lunch time when Mom stuck her head in the door.

"Got a minute?" she asked.

"Sure, whatcha need?"

She settled into the chair next to my desk and closed the door. I looked at her curiously, waiting to hear what she had to say.

She put her hands in her lap and looked at me. "So, it's been a while since you've tried to swallow a boy's tongue on the front porch, young lady," she began with a slight smirk. I guess I started blushing and my eyes bugged out a little because she just laughed. "You didn't close the door," she added. "And between the porchlight and street-light, you were very visible."

"Sorry." I was *so* not sorry.

"Yes, well, you seemed to be enjoying yourself," she observed dryly.

Is it possible to blush on top of a blush? I could have sworn my face felt like a furnace.

Mom simply laughed and patted my hand.

"Josie, talk to me. That wasn't a first date kiss. What's going on?"

I took a moment to collect myself. Mom and I always had a close relationship and could talk about anything, even more so once Dad passed. I took a couple of deep breaths before proceeding.

"Mom, do you remember me telling you about my first kiss with Greg?"

"I do. You said it was the best kiss you ever had and how you knew he was the one. Oh. Oh Josie, Josie. We talked about this," she said, worry creeping into her words.

"Mom, kissing Jacob was a hundred—no, a *thousand* times beyond that first kiss with Greg." I almost laughed when Mom's eyebrows shot up. "Look, I'm just telling you that I haven't felt this way since Greg died. I loved Greg, Mom, loved him to pieces. But when Jacob kissed me, I've never felt more whole and complete in my life."

I looked down at the desk, tracing the lines in the faded top before looking back up at mom.

"I know I should feel guilty about that comparison. It's been in the back of my brain all day. But mom, I … I don't feel that guilty. I've thought about it and tried looking at it from all angles, but I still come up with the same answer. I … I just don't feel guilty."

Mom stared at me, her eyes studying me intently. "Josie, how do you know it's not just that way because it's been so long?" she asked.

"Trust me. I've spent most of this morning waging that argument in my head. But Mom, the zing was there immediately. Feelings and, well, urges, awoke in me that have been gone since Greg."

Mom sat quietly, studying her hands. After several moments, she stood up and walked back to the doorway. Pausing, she turned back to me, smiling softly.

"I want you to be happy," she said. "If Jacob makes you happy, then I'm all for it. I just don't want to see you hurt again."

"Love you Mom, and thanks." She nodded and made her way back to the front.

Lunch time came, and I headed off to Brianna's. She looked up from the counter as I came in and waved. I seated myself in my normal spot and began reliving that kiss. She came over with a glass of tea.

"Hello, girl. I suppose—" She paused in mid-sentence, staring at me.

"What? Is there something stuck in my teeth?" I asked, beginning checking my teeth with my tongue.

She plopped herself down in the booth across from me.

"Spill it," she ordered.

"What are you talking about?"

"Girl, don't make me hit you with this order pad. What happened with you and Jacob? Did you clap cheeks? Play sheet twister? Did he make you scream and pass out?"

"Damn, Brianna! Calm your tits. Nothing happened!"

"Don't you lie to me, you little hussy. You haven't stopped grinning since you sat down. Now, get busy *spilling*. Why *exactly* do you look as if you're about to get hot and heavy? Describe it to me—in many details, leaving nothing out. I'm living vicariously through you."

I gave her a brief rundown of the night.

"Well, not your typical first date I'll grant you. Still waiting on the good stuff."

I told her about the kiss, its effect on me, how it was the greatest kiss I'd ever had, even better than Greg. I even added how my night ended before going to sleep. She whooped and grabbed my arm.

"Damn girl, you don't mess around, do you? When's the wedding?" she asked.

I flushed. "Would you calm the hell down? It was one date, one kiss. A really, really, really good kiss, but still one."

"At the speed you're going, you'll be married and pregnant by the end of the week," she retorted smugly, tapping the table with her finger.

"Would you just bring me my lunch, Ms. Wedding Planner?"

She laughed all the way back to the kitchen. Luckily, the lunch crowd picked up and she had less chances to pick on me.

The afternoon in my office was dragging and to be honest, I was not getting a lot of work done. My mind kept drifting to my conversation with Jacob and that wonderful kiss. I swear I still could feel his lips on mine.

I also could not stop thinking about Brianna's prediction. Marriage. Pregnant. Two words that haven't been anywhere in my vocabulary in a long time. Greg and I planned to have more kids but even with vigorous amounts of practice, nothing seemed to happen after Kaylin. When Greg died, those dreams died with him. Or so I thought.

Now Brianna's words brought those dreams back to life. Well, that and Jacob. The feelings I knew were growing for Jacob provided fertile ground for Brianna's words to take root. I could see it, imagine it, and surprisingly, it didn't feel wrong.

The phone ringing broke me out of my daydreaming.

"Martinson's. How may I help you?"

"*You never call, JC. It's like you don't love me anymore.*"

"GARY! Now you know that's not true. I never loved you in the first place."

"*Now JC, that's just mean. I'm hurt. Wounded deeply.*"

I broke out laughing. "How are you doing? Where are you? Can you come visit?"

"*Sorry, love. I'm at LAX on my way to Boston for a merger meeting. Hadn't talked to you in ages, so I wanted to touch base. Will be in Boston for a week or more. Maybe when I get that wrapped up, I can come out to the boonies for a few days.*"

"Oh, that would be great. Kaylin and Mom would love to see you and we could catch up on everything. We can show you our brand-new indoor plumbing. I hear it's all the rage in the non-boonies world."

"*Ohh, aren't we catty today? Look, that sounds good. Oops, calling my boarding zone. Talk to ya soon, JC. Love ya. Kisses to Kaylin.*"

"Love you. Be safe."

Gary Preston had been Greg's best friend for almost forever. He was a corporate lawyer who grew up next door to Greg, and the two had been thick as thieves. Gary, along with his younger sister Melinda, would always drop in to see us, especially in the winter. We all loved to ski, so we explored all of the major ski slopes within a four-hour drive of our home. Melinda became the sister I never had. The two of them were family as far as Greg and I were concerned.

When Greg died, they both dropped everything to come help me. Gary took care of all the funeral arrangements and ensured that the legalities of Greg's estate were addressed. Melinda had been my constant shadow, giving me a shoulder to cry on or scream into when the pain was too much to handle.

Later that evening, I was sitting on the couch with Mom, enjoying a glass of wine. Mom was telling me about some trips her group was planning when I remembered the earlier call.

"Oh, guess who I heard from today? Gary."

Mom's face lit up. "Oh, how is Gary? Who was that he married? Oh yes, Jeremy. How's he doing? Are they and Melinda coming to visit?" she asked.

Mom bonded with Gary and Melinda the first time we brought them to Azton. Dad was gone on a fishing trip with Uncle Frank and a couple of other buddies when we dropped in on Mom. Gary had a ton of frequent flyer miles and cashed them in to get us all discounted tickets.

"He's doing good. He was on his way to Boston but said if he got wrapped up early, he would stop by on his way back to L.A."

"Oh, I do hope he can visit," Mom replied. "He so loves my apple cobbler."

I had to laugh at that one. Everyone loved Mom's apple cobbler.

Mom topped off our glasses and we sat in contemplation for a bit, just enjoying the quiet. I found myself thinking about Jacob, especially about what he shared about Kara. I'd been thinking about him quite often during the day. I was staring at the fireplace, lost in my thoughts. Mom must have sensed it. Her voice startled me from my trance.

"Penny for your thoughts, as if I didn't know what they were," Mom remarked, raising a brow. "Jacob?"

I looked at the wine in my glass, swirling it gently, smiling softly.

"Am I that transparent?"

Mom arranged herself on the couch to face me better. "You're my daughter. I'd like to think I can read you pretty well."

Taking a sip of my wine, I sat my glass down on the coffee table before turning to face Mom, letting my head lay on the back of the couch.

"Do you remember telling me you saw something in him, a pain?" I asked, and she nodded. "He told me about it when we were eating last night, along with other things. Something only the sheriff knows." For a moment, I remembered that pain of loss and the emotion he fought telling me. My eyes teared up, and I felt a tightness in my chest and heart. Mom scooted closer, placing her hand on my leg.

"Josie?"

I cleared my throat. "He was married. She died, along with their unborn daughter, in an accident not too long before Greg. He ... he understands, Mom. He knows exactly what I've gone through—*am* going through."

The first tear slid down my face. I hadn't cried for Greg in some time. But this time, I wasn't crying for him but for Jacob. Mom pulled me into a hug.

We sat there for a few moments as she stroked my hair. I finally got myself together and sat up, Mom staying close.

"He told me that's why he didn't date any of the women around town. Just like I did with Greg, he lost all interest in dating when Kara, his wife, died. "

Mom looked over at Dad's picture above the fireplace for a few moments. I could only imagine the memories she was recalling. Then she turned back to me

"But now there is you," she said softly.

"Yep, me. The first woman he's been attracted to since her. Call it what you want, Mom. Fate, kismet, whatever. Two people who've had similar losses, who drew in on themselves, both of us living in this small town and then finding each other. I know we've only seen each other for a short time, Mom, but I can't deny what I'm feeling. I'm attracted to him. Very attracted."

"Well," she said with a sigh. "I hope it works out for the both of you and Kaylin."

We sat for a few more moments, just enjoying the quiet. At some point, Mom patted my leg and took herself off to bed, leaving me with my thoughts.

I thought about Greg. Our time together, the memories we built, the little girl we made out of our love. It had only been two years. I told Mom that Jacobs' kiss was so much better than Greg's. How the hell could I say that if I had been so in love with Greg?

A few weeks before I moved back to Azton, Melinda had dropped in for a visit. She was all for me moving, getting away from where my life with Greg had been. She also told me that I deserved to find someone else to love and to be with. She told me Greg would have wanted it. She said that I didn't need to go looking for it, that it would find me. The universe would guide me, much like the vision board.

Had the universe brought Jacob to me? I wish I knew. What I did know for certain was that I felt more alive right at this moment than I had in months. And there was no doubt that it was due to Jacob. Hunky, drop-dead sexy Jacob.

Sighing, I glanced at my phone. It was late, and I was thinking about either bed or another glass of wine when my phone chirped with an incoming text.

NINETEEN

Jacob

When I finally parked my car at Arnie's office in Bellevue, I was beat both physically and mentally. It was a little after three, and it had been a long drive after a very short sleep.

Normally, I got a good night's sleep before driving to Seattle. The drive gave me plenty of time to review what I needed to discuss with my accountant and to enjoy the scenery that was western Washington State. It was about a six-hour drive from Azton, and I normally left at 5 a.m. and arrived early enough for a shower and a nap before meeting Arnie. This time, I overslept and didn't get on the road until almost eight.

I found myself unable to sleep this morning after getting home from Josie's. Mainly because I couldn't stop thinking about how fast I was falling for her, not to mention the kiss.

That kiss had broken open something inside of me that had been sealed shut since Kara. I hadn't felt that whole, or that good, in a long time. Kissing Josie and holding her in my arms, feeling her pressed up against me felt … right.

I loved Kara completely, but my first time kissing her was nothing like it had been with Josie. It didn't even come close in comparison.

Dating Kara had been slow due to her initial dislike of me being in the Army, for which I blamed her parents. I asked her out for three months before she finally agreed to go on our first date.

In a week and two dates, I was just as comfortable with Josie as I had been with Kara. I felt I could tell Josie anything, even if I hadn't answered her question on why I joined the Army. That was a darker subject, and it wasn't first date material. All of this and more made my sleep uneasy and my drive feel much longer than it actually was.

I rode the elevator up to Arnie's office suite and checked in with Jill, his receptionist, who waved me right into his office.

Arnie Frankton had been suggested to me by my previous lawyer when I told her I was moving to Washington and wanted a local area financial person. He was a no-nonsense advisor who didn't stand on a lot of formalities. I could count on one hand the number of times I had ever seen him in a suit.

I quickly learned not to judge Arnie by his appearance. He had all of the essential degrees and certifications you would expect from an investment manager. What you didn't expect was his ability to sniff out a profitable fund from the weeds and chaff that littered the investment market. Several times he recommended investments to me that made absolutely no sense on the surface. When those investments started returning high profits, I knew to trust him, and had so, for the last three years.

Even still, what sold me on him was his priorities in life. He could be making millions at other brokerage houses or taking on higher-profile clients. When I asked him about it during our initial meeting, he told me that his family came first, second, and always. Which in hindsight was driven home to me considering our first meeting was at a BBQ he was holding at his house.

Arnie lived for his family and made enough money to ensure that he could devote the maximum time to them. He had all the money and things he needed and saw no need to pile on the high-stress and family-time consuming environment that came with working in the upper levels of his world. I hired him that day over a plate of ribs and began my quarterly drive to Seattle for our review.

"Jacob! Good to see you, man. How was the drive in?" he asked, coming out from behind his desk to meet me in his usual office attire of polo shirt, jeans, and deck shoes.

"About the same. How's Peggy and William?" He steered me to a couple of chairs and a coffee table where he had iced tea and coffee available. I knew that tea would be sweet because Arnie didn't miss details like that.

"Oh, just fine, fine," he said, smiling. "Peggy said to tell you hi. William is chugging along over at UW. He still hasn't decided on a major. He's just focusing on core courses till he can make up his mind. That and chasing girls, like any normal college boy."

He poured us drinks while he was catching me up.

"Peggy also said you'd better be coming to our place for dinner, or else she'll hunt you down," he added, settling back in his chair.

"Let me guess, she has a new matchmaking target?"

Peggy made it her life mission to get me married, making sure to have a new candidate handy each time I came up. They were all intelligent and attractive, but I just had no interest.

He chuckled. "Yep. It's her sister Marissa, the psychiatrist. She's been divorced a little over a year, and Peggy thinks it's time she meets someone new. I keep telling her that you're not interested in dating, but does she listen? No. Not to mention the fact her sister's practice is in Seattle and you live on the other side of the state."

Moment of truth. I swirled the ice in the glass before setting it on the table.

"Tell Peggy that I would love nothing more than to come feast on her world-famous mashed potatoes, but I don't think the woman I'm seeing would appreciate me hooking up with Peggy's sister."

Arnie's cup stopped halfway to his mouth. He started to raise it again, paused, and finally lowered it to the table. As I watched, he pulled out his phone and fired off a text. He waited, grinning at me. His phone dinged with what I assumed was an incoming text. Reading it, he grinned and put his phone on the table.

"You just made me $500 richer. Oh, and Peggy says she now hates you," he announced, laughing hard for a moment.

I raised an eyebrow at him, crossing my arms.

"Peggy bet me $500 that she could get you fixed up with her sister," he explained. "I told her she was full of shit and took her up on the bet. Fair warning, expect to be grilled at dinner about this new woman."

"Been grilled by worse."

Arnie shrugged. "Well, let's get to business," he replied.

He rose, moving over to his desk to grab two small black binders. Sitting back down, he handed me one and turned to the first page in his.

"Overall, the fund is up about 12 percent year to date," he began. "Your portfolio, after fees and commissions, is now over $6.5 million. I've moved some of the short-term holdings into your risk pool. Several of the ventures we were playing with paid off, and I've moved them to your long-term and short-term sections. That depleted the risk pool a bit, so I wanted a bit more beef in that area in case I find something interesting."

Arnie continued giving me an overview for each of my investment areas. We spent the next hour looking at his projections and getting a feel for where the markets were trending and what adjustments we might have to make. I didn't understand all the intricacies like he did, but I enjoyed the risk analysis and strategizing. Reminded me of mission prep back in the day.

"So," he said, closing the binder, "Unless you have any questions, I think that should finish us up."

"I do have a question, actually. Are we still good for the Branson's?"

He nodded. "The trust we set up is still well funded. They've drawn on it at the rate close to what we predicted. Largest pulls are still for medical, and the girls' education. I can get you a full transaction list if you need it. Based on the PI reports, the girls are settled north of the campus and are doing well."

I was glad to hear that. When we left the courtroom the day of Mad

Dog's sentencing, I gave Arnie's card to Mr. Branson, telling him to contact Arnie when they got to Seattle. I already spoke to Arnie, explained the situation, and had him set up a trust to pay for Alice and Jenny's medical and educational needs as well as the family's relocation costs. I made only one request to the Branson's and Arnie. The girls were not to be told that I was the source of the money their parents were using. Mr. Branson could make up any story he wanted, just not the truth.

Money really didn't mean much to me, but in this case, it did let me counter some injustice. Those girls deserved some good in their lives after what they had been through.

"I want to do something else that's not an investment. In fact, you're not going to like it at all," I told Arnie.

He crossed his legs and folded his hands over his knee. "You've got my attention."

I proceeded to fill him in on Josie, who she was to me, and the situation she was facing at the store. He sat quietly, asking no questions until I was finished.

"Okay, what do you want to do?" he asked. "And yes, I am probably going to advise you against it, whatever it is. I should point out that most boyfriends buy their women jewelry, not bail them out of large debts."

"I want you to set up a liquid line of credit with the bank here in Seattle. Sell off enough of long-term and short-term options, a 70/30 split, to fund a secured credit line for $850,000. You and I are going to call the manager, Frank Barklen, at the Azton National Bank and tell him that he has found an investor that helps women-owned businesses who are struggling. I want to pay off all of the store's outstanding credit lines. I can't see it being more than about half of what I am setting up for. The investor wishes to remain anonymous. Frank will not tell Josie until you have arranged all the paperwork and give him an account to pull against."

Finished with my request, I sat back and waited. Arnie stared at me for about two minutes before he dropped his leg down and slapped his knees.

"You're right, I don't like it. You'll take a large hit in fees and taxes on the sell-off. But," he said, his eyes boring into mine, "it's your money. You've followed my plans for your finances religiously and indulged my chance to play and make us both a lot of money. Pretty much been the ideal client. Every customer usually makes a big splurge. I thought the Bransons were it, but that's the way it is. Be back at the office tomorrow morning at eight, and we'll get the ball rolling."

Business concluded, we said our goodbyes until tonight. I headed back to the hotel to take a shower and get cleaned up before dinner.

Arnie lived in a very nice neighborhood called Somerset. The times I had been there during the day provided some beautiful views of Lake Washington and the Olympic mountains. I stopped along the way and picked up a bottle each of a nice white and red wine that I noticed in their wine rack the last time I was at their house.

Peggy answered the door when I rang the bell.

"Jacob! It's so good to see you," she exclaimed, giving me a big hug and a peck on the cheek before ushering me into the house.

Once inside I handed her the bottles of wine. "I think these are some you like?"

She gave me a wry look. "You didn't have to do that, you goof, and yes, these are two of my favorites! Let me put them up. Arnie's in the game room watching some sport thing. Arnie? Jacob's here!" she shouted towards the other part of the house before heading to the kitchen.

I wandered into their game room and found Arnie watching a college football game. He popped up as I came in.

"Glad you made it. Can I get you a beer or something harder?" he asked.

"Beer's good."

He went over to the small bar in the corner and pulled a Sam Adams out of the fridge before popping the top for me. We settled back and began watching football. I'm not a huge sports fan, but Arnie took his football seriously, so there was no chit-chat, just yelling at the game. We had watched twenty minutes or so before we were interrupted.

"Arnie, Peggy said dinner is ready," said a soft voice behind us.

I stood up, turning to face who I assumed was Peggy's sister. She was about five three, with brown hair that was styled in a page cut and brown eyes. Not overly slim, but not overweight either. Closer to what some would call voluptuous. Arnie was at my elbow and made introductions.

"Jacob, this is Marissa, Peggy's sister. Marissa, Jacob, one of my friends who just happens to be a client that makes me good money."

She laughed, a pleasant sound, and her eyes twinkled.

"Yes, I understand that you made Arnie $500 just this afternoon. Peggy was very disappointed." She held out her hand, and I shook it lightly before we followed her back to the dining room.

Dinner was pleasant. Peggy had indeed made her world-famous mashed potatoes. It was an old family recipe that had to have included a full stick of butter. She had also made a white gravy to pair up with the potatoes. Steamed broccoli along with fresh sweet corn rounded out the vegetables. A napkin covered serving basket contained fresh croissants. For the entree, Peggy had prepared a rack of four lamb chops with a brown sugar glaze.

The conversation flowed freely, with the two sisters dishing dirt on each other, keeping me and Arnie laughing. While we talked, I realized that I never really shared much of my past with Peggy and Arnie. I came to their house every time I came to Seattle, but I hadn't really opened up much. Maybe it was time to correct that.

It was Marissa who actually asked the question that gave me my opening.

"So, what do you do for a living, Jacob?"

"Actually, not much since I got out of the Army. I mostly work on building my house. I help out at the hospital and the local sheriff's department as they need it, mostly search and rescue, lost hikers, things like that."

"I don't think you ever mentioned the Army before," Arnie remarked.

"I was in for almost fourteen years. I got out not long after my wife

Kara died." For the first time outside of the sheriff and Josie, I brought up Kara.

Both ladies' forks clinked back down on their plates as they turned to me.

"When did she pass?" Marissa asked me quietly.

"It was five years ago, this November. We got married in April of the same year, about three weeks before I deployed to Afghanistan."

I paused and took a pull from my beer. It still hurt to bring it up, but it was bearable. It was Marissa's hand on my arm that pulled me back from my thoughts.

"I'm sorry for your loss," she murmured.

"Thanks. It still hurts, but lately I've taken to speaking about it more."

"If we can ask, how did she die?" asked Peggy.

"A stupid accident. She was heading home from visiting her parents, and a semi crossed the middle line. Seems the driver had been driving for almost twenty-two hours and fell asleep at the wheel. He worked for a major shipping company, and the investigation found that not only had he been falsifying his logbook, but he was on amphetamines at the time of the wreck."

I paused for a moment to collect myself. This would hurt even more.

"She was killed instantly, along with our unborn daughter."

The silence at the table was almost unbearable. Both ladies looked like they were going to tear up. It was Arnie that broke the tension.

"I hope the bastards paid for that," he growled.

I nodded. "It's pretty much the basis of my investment fund, Arnie. Between the life insurance and the settlement, I came into a very large windfall."

"Is that why you're not in the Army anymore?" Peggy asked.

"Yes and no. Her death hit me pretty hard. I wasn't in a good place mentally, definitely not someone who needed to be out doing missions and being responsible for the lives of others."

Marissa nodded her head in agreement.

I continued, "The Army treated me right. I got to talk to some good therapists. My commander worked with his superiors to grant me an honorable discharge due to 'major lifestyle change.' I spent my last few months filling in odd posts at my unit. My commander gave me free control of my time and let me work through things without interference until I was separated."

I finished my beer and looked around at the concerned faces and sad eyes watching me.

"Sorry, I didn't mean to be a downer. I think that's the first time I've talked about that whole situation since moving to Azton." Marissa kept her hand on my arm but withdrew it once I was done talking. "So, how about the Seahawks?" I asked. That's all Arnie needed to begin his prospectus on how the team was shaping up for the new year. Both women looked at each and rolled their eyes.

When we finished eating, Peggy roped her husband into helping her clean up and ushered Marissa and I into the front room 'since we were guests'. Apparently, she wasn't giving up that $500 easily.

I said to Marissa, "Arnie tells me you're a psychiatrist. Do you specialize in any particular field?"

She nodded and set the glass on a side table. "I've got a partnership with several other doctors, and we work on trauma victims. We have a practice here in Seattle," she explained.

"Trauma?"

"Yes. We focus on helping those who have suffered some tragic event such as spousal abuse, rape, family violence, etc. Most of our clientele is female, but we do get the occasional guy."

I had a momentary flashback to the Branson sisters and hoped that they were getting good care.

"Do you ever treat veterans or others suffering from PTSD?"

She nodded as she took another drink of wine. "Absolutely. We work with law enforcement in and around Seattle. We provide assistance to the military hospitals when more advanced care is needed."

I cleared my throat. "Well, as someone who has seen PTSD suffering up close, thank you for your efforts. I know your patients appreciate it."

"You don't suffer from it?" she asked curiously.

"Not yet at least. I did a lot of talking with the Army therapists, and we determined that I was one of the lucky ones that could safely rationalize and deal with the traumas and atrocities I witnessed. Something about how my brain processes it."

She started to ask me something else when Arnie and Peggy came in from the kitchen. Arnie plopped into his chair, and Peggy took a seat next to Marissa. Peggy brought the wine with her and topped off Marissa's glass before setting the bottle on the end table.

"Well," said Peggy. "You two finding lots to talk about?" She started taking a sip when Marissa glanced at me and winked.

"We were just deciding which hotel to use when we leave here and what sex position I liked best."

Arnie barked a laugh, and Peggy choked on her wine. Marissa rescued the glass before Peggy could drop it while Arnie began patting Peggy lightly on the back. Once she was under control again, Peggy glared at her sister, who gave her back a look of pure innocence.

"You're sooo gonna pay for that one, sis," Peggy snapped. Marissa merely laughed and handed her wine back to her.

"Consider it payback for setting me up for another blind date." She gave me an appraising look. "Although, I think I would have very much enjoyed seeing Jacob had the circumstances been different."

"Too bad he's taken. Speaking of which, where's my money honey?" Arnie asked.

Peggy ignored him and turned to me. "Jacob, tell us about this young lady you're seeing. Is it serious? How did you meet? Did my baby sister have a chance to show you the little tattoo she has over her—"

"PEGGY!" Marissa shrieked, turning two shades of red. Peggy burst out laughing.

"Payback's a bitch, huh?" she said, grinning at her sister.

I waited to see if Marissa decided her sister needed to die. When it appeared that no bloodshed was going to occur, I told them about Josie.

"Her name is Josie Callison. She and her mom run a general store in Azton. She has a little girl, Kaylin, who is adorable. She was married before, but her husband died suddenly a few years back. I actually met her while out hiking about a month ago."

"Ahh, found her wandering the trails?" asked Arnie.

"No, actually, I found her unconscious from a fall. She punched me in the jaw when she came to and found me squeezing her chest."

Three sets of eyes stared at me. It was Marissa who broke the silence, her tone cold. "Do you normally molest unconscious women?" she asked, her words clipped. I turned to the good doctor and could see the cold anger in her glare.

"Quick to judge? As it happens, that's pretty much what Josie thought as well, thus the aforementioned punch to the jaw. She's got a decent right cross." I absently rubbed my jaw where she slugged me. I took another pull from my beer, keeping eye contact with Marissa. "Actually, I was performing field triage, checking her ribs for breaks. I didn't see any frothing pink foam, so I was fairly confident she didn't have a lung puncture from a broken rib. She came too as I was feeling her ribs right under her ... well, you get the picture."

Marissa had the decency to blush. "Triage? You're a doctor?"

"Nope, I trained as a medic in the Army. Same basic level as an EMT. Josie had fallen down an embankment, screaming as she went. She smacked a tree and a few rocks when she made it to the bottom. Luckily, I happened to be in the area and was able to get to her fairly quickly. Considering we were deep in the woods and miles from anyone, it all worked out for the best."

Arnie and Peggy stared at me, but Marissa actually ducked her eyes for a moment.

"Forgive me for—" she started to say but I cut her off.

"It's okay, really. I appreciate your passion for protecting those who are victims and I'm sure your patients benefit from that."

She smiled slightly at my praise. "Thank you. Now, tell us more about this damsel you rescued."

I spent the next few minutes outlining the highlights of my few dates with Josie and her daughter. They all got a good laugh about the ball pit as well as the plumbing incident. During a lull in the conversation, Marissa gave me another one of those sideways looks.

"You're from Azton. You never told me your last name," she said.

"Berman."

Her eyes widened slightly, but she gave no other outward indication that she knew me. Perhaps it was time to call it a night.

"Well, folks, I think it's time for me to head back to the hotel. I've got Arnie's early meeting followed by a long drive back home. Peggy, wonderful cooking as usual." I stood and made my way to the front door.

"I think I'll go as well," Marissa added, rising to follow me. "I go on-call early, so I need to get some sleep before the phone starts ringing."

Taking her light wrap and small clutch from the stand next to the door, she hugged Arnie and Peggy good night, promising Peggy she would call her tomorrow. Arnie slapped me on the back and said he would see me in the morning.

"Jacob, a moment please?" Marissa asked once we got to her car. I was parked beside her. I had my back to the house, and she leaned against her car door.

"Are you going to tell me where you know me from?" I asked.

She stared at me before smiling. "What gave me away?"

"Eyes. Very slight widening, but other than that, no other reaction to my last name."

She put her wrap on and tapped her crossed arms with her fingers while she glanced off down the road. She appeared to be mulling something over. She apparently reached a decision about whatever was bothering her because she turned back to stare at me.

"If anyone ever asks, we never had this conversation, okay? What I'm about to tell you violates enough federal laws to end my career and send me to jail. Laws you're probably familiar with."

"You have my word that nothing was said here."

"Does the name Branson ring any bells?" she asked.

My jaw clenched and my blood began to chill.

She smirked. "Ahh, I can see it does. It's okay, really. I'm the girls' doctor."

Relief flooded through me, and my jaw unclenched.

"How ... how are they?"

She laid a hand on my arm. "They're doing good, really. It took our team about eight months to get Jenny to the point she could talk about that night, but now she's making real progress in dealing with what happened. She's had several plastic surgeries, and most of the physical reminders are repaired. Alice's wounds healed quickly, and we've been working through her survivor's guilt."

She tilted her head, looking at the house and then back at me.

"You're the one who's been paying for their care." This woman must be a hell of a therapist. Her mind was sharp, having pulled that out of a few clues.

I shrugged. "Yeah. I gave them Arnie's number the day before they left Azton. I asked them not to tell the girls about the money coming from me. I'm not sure what story they made up."

"I think the girls believe their parents have taken out a loan," she said.

I replied, "I wanted them to have a clean break from Azton. The girls didn't deserve what happened to them, nor did that family. It's just money, and I have more than enough. Please, don't mention to them that you met me. I don't want them thinking of me and having flash-backs of what happened."

Marissa took a deep breath and looked at me again, before shaking her head.

"What?"

"Peggy tried to get me to come to dinner the last time you were in town, and I turned her down. I wasn't ready to date. For once, I should have listened to my sister. My loss." She moved in and stood on her toes, kissing me on one cheek. "That's for Alice," she said, then kissed me on the other cheek. "That's for Jenny." And then she kissed me lightly on the lips, lingering for just a second. "That's for you, for what you've done for those girls."

She grinned at me as she stepped back.

"And maybe just a little for me."

She reached into her clutch and handed me a business card.

"If you find yourself unattached again, please call me. My private cell is on the card." She got into her car and started it, rolling down the window. "Do me a favor and tell Josie that she's one lucky girl and I wish you both the best."

"I think I'm the lucky one."

She smiled a tiny smile and just held my gaze for a moment. Shaking her head, she backed out of the driveway and drove off into the night.

It was almost 10:30 p.m. before I got back to my hotel and was able to stretch out in my bed. Taking a chance, I grabbed my phone and tapped out a message to Josie.

"Hey, you still up?"

A few seconds later, my phone beeped.

"*Yes. Relaxing a bit. Was talking with Mom, but she just went to bed. No big parties tonight?*"

"No, just dinner with some friends. Just getting back to the room."

"*Good dinner?*"

"Yeah, but I wish you'd been there."

"*Aww, miss me already?*"

"Yes, I do. It's a bit scary, actually."

"*I know what you mean. I've spent a lot of my day thinking about you and not my work. Mom caught me daydreaming a couple of times. She's worried.*"

"About what?"

"*That we're moving too fast. She saw us kiss and said it wasn't a 'first date kiss'*"

"Are we moving too fast? That's part of what's scary to me. I've been by myself for so long, but I find myself ..."

"*What?*"

"I find myself wanting to be with you more. You and Kaylin."

"*Jacob, I feel the same way. I know Mom's worried, but it feels right, you know? Like ... very, very right.*"

"I know."

"*I told Kaylin we would take her and her friends to putt-putt, if that's okay?*"

"Works for me. I'll just have to display my badass putt-putt skills."

"Is that a challenge?"

I grinned as I read her message. After the ball pit, I knew there was a major competitive streak buried inside her.

"Oh, most definitely. But since I'm a superior putt-putt putter, it probably won't be much of a challenge."

"I am so kicking your ass!"

"I am so not scared."

"Much as I want to keep chatting with you, the wine is kicking in, and Kaylin will be up early."

"I need to be up early too so I can finish up my business and get back home."

"Come see me when you get back, please. Text me when you're almost home, regardless of the time. Please?"

"Okay, I will. Night, Josie."

"Night, honey. Sweet dreams."

Honey. I liked it.

I rolled over and stared at the ceiling. How could I be falling for this woman so fast? My head was screaming at me to slow down, but my heart, if I was honest, kept saying speed up.

For the first time since Kara, I could imagine a future with someone. As sleep took me, that last thought should have scared me, but all I felt was ... anticipation.

TWENTY

Jacob

I walked back into Arnie's office at nine the next morning. Arnie had laid in some donuts and coffee. Having eaten breakfast at the hotel, I limited myself to a single maple-iced circle of goodness. Arnie topped off my coffee and laid out some papers on his desk.

"Okay, I've got the line of credit established with your bank here in Seattle. I actually had some CDs there, so I cashed them in and used that to partially fund the credit line. I've issued sell orders on the stocks I've earmarked and I've moved some liquidity from your other accounts. Once the transfers finish, we should be at just over $600,000. Stock sale will probably take about three days. I estimate a week for us to be able to fully secure the line. Once we have our conversation with Mr. Barklen, I'll pass him the account and routing numbers. Good?"

"Awesome. Thanks."

He leaned back and gave me a smirk. "So, you and Marissa seemed to get a bit friendly after you left. Thought you had a girl? I've already spent that $500."

"I do, and she's a woman, not a girl. As to Marissa, your sister-in-law is a very smart woman. She put together some clues and figured out something about me."

"That you like long moonlight walks on the beach and quick smooches in driveways?" He quipped before busting up laughing. I let him get it out of his system. It would be easier and faster in the long run. I waited for the chortles to die out.

"Feel better?"

He nodded, wiping at the tear on his cheek.

"She's the doctor treating the Branson girls."

That sobered him up. "Damn. Once I set up the secured bank account and gave the information to Mr. Branson, I never really paid that close attention to the payees. Shit, I'm getting old." He drank his coffee and chewed a bite of donut. "I apologize, Jacob. I should have caught that detail. That was sloppy of me. Is this going to be an issue?"

I shook my head. "Nope, don't think so. Marissa isn't going to say anything to the Bransons. What you saw through the window was her thanking me for what I had done for the girls." I didn't think it was necessary to tell him about the rest of the conversation, or the card. Peggy didn't need any more ammunition to use against me or her sister.

"Good. Ready to call your banker?"

"Yep. I'm gonna call his cell. I'll tell him to expect a call from you in his office."

He raised his eyebrows a bit. "Is the banker a friend of yours?" he asked.

"Well, I'm a valued customer who just happens to have a hundred thousand dollars in his bank. That tends to get you his personal attention." Arnie merely laughed and nodded.

I found Frank's number in my contacts and hit dial. Four rings later, he picked up.

"Jacob, my boy. A pleasure hearing from you, young man. How can I be of assistance today?"

"Are you in your office by chance?"

"I will be in a moment. Just checking the vault. Is something wrong?"

"Nope, nothing's wrong. Frank, when you get to your office, you're going to get a call from Arnie Frankton with Frankton Securities. Take that call, please."

Even over the phone I could hear the gears turning.

"Very well, Jacob. Anything you need to tell me? Are you being kidnapped? Do I need to call the police?" he asked. I laughed quickly.

"No, Frank, it's all good. Just take the call, please."

"Okay. Give me about five minutes." He hung up, and I put my cell away.

Ten minutes later, Arnie called the bank, placing his phone on speaker mode.

"Azton National Bank, how may I help you?"

"Good morning. Arnie Frankton here, Frankton Securities. Who am I speaking to please?" asked Arnie, ever the polite one when it came to business.

"I'm Laura, the bank receptionist, Mr. Frankton. How may I direct your call?"

"Mr. Barklen, please."

"One moment, sir."

We waited about thirty seconds or so before Frank came on the line.

"Frank Barklen."

"Good morning, Mr. Barklen. Arnie Frankton, Frankton Securities."

"Hello, Mr. Frankton. Jacob Berman said you would be calling. How may I help you?" Arnie looked at me and nodded his head towards the phone.

"Frank, Jacob here. Thanks for taking the call."

"Jacob? Okay, color me confused here. Care to explain what's going on?"

"Happy to, Frank. Before we get started, I need you to understand that everything we are going to discuss is confidential. Not even to Mary, understand?"

Arnie looked at me and I mouthed 'wife.' He nodded.

"Jacob, perhaps if you explained to me what is going on—" Frank began, but I cut him off.

"Frank, I need you to trust me on this. Once I do explain, it will make perfect sense. Nothing we are going to talk about is illegal or will get you, me, or the bank in any trouble. Only three people will know of our talk, and all three are on the phone right now. You have my word, Frank."

Both Arnie and I waited while the line stayed silent. I thought for a second that we might have been disconnected, but Arnie held up one finger. A few seconds later, Frank spoke again.

"Very well, Jacob. Your word is good with me. May I ask what this is about?"

"Josie and her mom's store."

"Jacob, I can't really discuss any details of the bank's dealings regarding Flora and Josie. That is not public information at this time." I liked Frank, liked the fact he was protective of Josie and her mom. Even if it were legal, I knew he wouldn't violate their confidence.

"I understand completely. I know they are close to going under and you're not extending any more credit. I also know you have feelers out trying to find help for them." I paused to let those words sink in. Arnie and I waited patiently through another lengthy pause.

Frank replied, "You're very well-informed, Jacob. I can only assume that since you are dating Josie that she's told you about their situation. Oh, and if you hurt my goddaughter in any way, well, I may not be much of a fighter, but I can—"

My laughter cut him off. "Ricks already made the same threat, Frank. I know he can carry it out. I have no plans for hurting Josie. In fact, today's call is about helping her and her mom."

"Very well, I'm listening."

"Excellent. How much would it take to pay off the equity line and the operating line that they have with you?"

"That's very nice of you, Jacob, but even if you emptied your account with me, while substantial, it would not clear them completely. It would, however, help them greatly. Is that what you want to do?"

"Yes and no. How much to clear their accounts?"

"Let me check." I heard him tapping on his keyboard for a few seconds. "Taking out their payments, which we'll pull tonight, they will owe $293,472.27."

I looked at Arnie who scribbled that down and started typing quietly.

"Perfect Frank. Okay, here is why I asked and why I need you to keep this strictly between us. Arnie is my accountant. Once I get done talking, Arnie is going to jump on and take care of the legal and financial aspects of this call."

Taking a moment, I prepared to yet again share something about myself.

"Frank, I've asked Arnie to set up a secured line of funding to the tune of $850,000. You will use this funding to pay off all of the store's debts. That includes any outstanding debts they owe to their suppliers. I want them to be totally debt-free."

"$800 ... Did you say $850,000?" Frank sputtered.

"Yes, that's what I said, Frank."

"Dear lord. Jacob, how ... I mean ... why? How can you afford to take out a loan ... I mean ..." Frank's response tapered off and the line grew quiet. I waited a few moments so he could process.

"Still with us, Frank?"

Yes ... I'm ... um ..."

I started laughing. "Breathe, Frank. Don't pass out on me."

"Very funny," he retorted. I heard him take a deep breath. "Okay. I'm good. Now, as I was saying, how can you afford a loan of this magnitude? I can't in good conscience let you take on a debt just to help out Josie. I want her and her mom to succeed, but not at your expense."

"Frank?"

"Yes?"

"There is no loan. I am going to fund this out of my own assets. And before you ask, yes, I can afford it. Easily. Right, Arnie?"

Arnie leaned towards the phone. "Mr. Barklen, let me assure you that Jacob is quite serious. I've been his accountant for just over three years, and he already had a sizable portfolio when I picked him up as a client. While the size of this line is not insubstantial, his portfolio will probably recoup 30 percent of that amount within the next twelve months. Please trust me that he is quite serious. I should have the rest of the line funded within the next week. But there is immediate funding available right now to easily cover the amount you indicated."

A very quiet "*dear god*" came through the line.

"Frank? You okay?"

"Ye—I mean yes. Yes, Jacob. I can't believe—My god, this will be a great help to Josie and Flora. When will you tell them?"

"That's where the confidential part comes in, Frank. We never had this call. You're not to mention me at all. You're going to tell Josie that you found an anonymous investor who believes in helping out women- and minority-owned businesses who are having troubles. It's not a loan; it's more like a grant. The investor contacted you. Josie said you were putting out feelers. Well, one of them got you something."

"Jacob, I'm sure that Josie would love to know that you've helped her. Are you sure about this?"

"Very sure. You talked to the investor via Arnie. The investor was once in the same boat as Josie and knows how hard it can be to recover. Now that the investor is successful, they like to help others. Oh, and you also know nothing about me or my finances. Like I said, Frank, we three are the only ones who know the truth behind this. I'm counting on you."

"Very well. If that's the way you want it, I'll abide by your wishes. Thank you, Jacob, for what you are doing for Josie and Flora. I just hope that the time will come when they can know what you've done for them."

"One other thing, Frank," I continued, "I know they have some other small issues with inventory control after the plumbing issue the other night. After you clear up all their debts, I want you to extend them $50,000 in liquid cash as an operations fund. I don't want them to start tapping that line of credit with you. If they burn through that, it will be time for a different conversation. Any questions?"

I got nothing from either of them.

Grinning, I added, "Good. I'll leave the two of you to finish up the details. Time for me to head home. Going to put you on hold for a second, Frank. Don't go anywhere." I nodded to Arnie, and he muted the call.

"You still want to fund this fully?" he asked. "Sounds like we have more than enough to do what you wanted."

I nodded. "Go ahead. If we end up not using it for anything, we can always reinvest it." Arnie nodded and rose with me, coming around to slap me on the shoulder.

"Good seeing you, Jacob. Always a pleasure doing business with my favorite client. Maybe you can bring Josie next time."

"Maybe. Let me know if you have any issues."

"Sure thing."

I closed his office door, leaving him to talk routing numbers and other such banking things with Frank. It was time to get back home.

What should have been an easy drive back with enough time to have dinner with Josie, turned out to be the drive from Hell. Two hours outside of Spokane, a semi blew several tires and decided to mate with a partner semi in the next lane. It took them hours to untangle the two metal lovers and open the road back up. It was almost 8:30 p.m. by the time I was able to turn north from Spokane towards Azton. Stopping for gas and a potty break, I sent a quick text.

"You still up?"

She answered within a few seconds.

"Hi. Yep, just folding some laundry. Where are you?"

"Grabbing gas just north of Spokane. Big accident on the interstate."

"Sorry, but that means you're almost home. I can't wait."

"You still want me to come over? Not too late?"

"You driving yet?"

"Um … no, I'm texting you."

"Quit texting and get your butt on the road. My lips ain't gonna kiss themselves."

I flashbacked to that kiss. I sure hoped any deputies along the way were napping.

TWENTY-ONE

Jacob

I t was almost an hour after sunrise Saturday by the time I let myself into my trailer. I began my coffee-making ritual, and the coffee pot was soon gurgling happily. I didn't wait for it to finish, merely stuck my cup under the downpour. Once my cup was filled, I swapped the pot for my cup, never spilling any of the life-giving juice. I doctored it up nicely and stepped back outside.

I sipped my nectar, my mind lost to the memories from last night.

Josie met me at the door in her pajamas, and I decided that flannel was a good look on her. The kiss she laid on me as soon as I stepped inside woke up every part of me.

"Is it wrong to have missed you so much even though you've only been gone a couple days?" she murmured, breathless.

I shook my head and kissed her again before we made it inside enough to close the front door.

"Hungry?" she asked. I nodded, following her to the kitchen after she peeled herself off of me, much to my dislike. She warmed up some leftovers and sat with me at the table while I ate, catching me up on her day.

Once I finished, we moved to the couch and sat down. I didn't get a chance to ask about Kaylin before she pulled my head down to hers and devoured me. It was like being back in high school.

Josie was doing her level best to check all my teeth for cavities using just her tongue as I moaned into her mouth. I'm not sure when we moved, or how it happened, but we were soon laying down with my back to the couch and facing Josie, my hand on her hip and hers in my hair.

We pulled apart, panting.

"Shit, Josie, what are you doing to me?"

She ran her hand down to my chest and pressed her face into my neck, kissing it lightly and sending shivers across my stomach.

"What am I doing to you? My mother and daughter are down the hall and all I can think about is stripping our clothes off and pulling you on top of me so you can bury yourself inside me."

I groaned and devoured her lips until I needed to breathe again.

I growled, "Dammit, Josie, you can't tell a guy things like that when he can't do anything about it."

"It's been a long time for both of us, honey. I wanted to make sure you fully understand my position on the subject. Now shut up and kiss me."

I started kissing her again, easier, softer. I wanted to show her how I felt, how good she felt to me. Our kisses gradually deepened, our tongues dancing together. Mentally taking a deep breath, I let my hand slide up her waist, pushing up under her pajama top until my hand was resting on her bare skin. She stiffened for a second as she held her breath, never breaking the kiss. I froze. Fuck, too fast. I had been too eager to touch her. Stupid. Stupid. Stupid. She pulled back from our kiss, panting slightly.

"Jacob, honey, what's wrong? Why'd you stop?" Josie whispered.

"You—you froze. I'm sorry, I didn't mean—" She lightly kissed me again.

"You're the first man who's touched me since Greg. Sorry, it scared me for a second. I didn't mean for you to stop."

"Maybe this is too fast." I started to pull my hand away.

She pulled me in tighter, trapping my hand between us, kissing me deeply. Moving her hand to join mine under her shirt, she grasped mine tightly and pulled my hand up until it was laying on her ribcage just under her braless breasts. She dropped her hand away and leaned forward to lightly nip my jaw.

"Jacob, I like you touching me. I want *you to touch me," she said breathlessly.*

I raised a brow. "Last time my hand was here, you punched me."

She laughed quietly before she pulled my head to hers and blew lightly in my ear, her lips grazing my earlobe. I moaned and felt my toes curl.

"Jacob?" she whispered.

"Ye—yes?"

"I think my doctor should examine me again. Fully."

Fuck. I thought I had been hard before. Now I was like steel.

I began kissing her again, my hand moving higher until I was gently cupping her breast. I gave it a light squeeze, and she gasped into my mouth.

I let my thumb brush lightly across her nipple, which was already stiff.

"Yess ..." she gasped, pushing harder against my hand. Somewhere in the back of my head, I made note of this reaction for future reference.

I kissed her jaw and neck as I was kneading her breast and lightly brushing my thumb in small circles on the top of her nipple.

As I nipped the juncture of her neck and shoulder, I pinched her nipple and rolled it between my thumb and finger.

"Oh god yes, baby," she moaned. "Like that. More ..."

I cupped her breast fully. Gods, she felt perfect. I began to knead a bit harder, taking my cue from her. She grabbed my hair and pulled my mouth to hers, her tongue spearing mine as she breathed loudly through her nose. She pulled her lips from mine.

"Other ... other one ... please," she gasped out before kissing me again.

We weren't teenagers, and the couch was not that big. I pushed against her until she leaned away from enough that I could drop my hand to her other breast. Unfortunately, I could only use one hand, my other hand and arm being underneath and around her.

I moved between her breasts, kneading, pinching, pulling. She kept her lips mashed to mine, moaning and gasping into my mouth.

She reached under her top and grabbed my hand beginning to push it towards her pajama bottoms. My heart rate found a new gear when she shoved it inside. Even without being there, I could feel the heat of her.

Just as my fingers grazed the first of her wetness, a door opened. Josie and I froze as we heard feet shuffle in the hallway. Small, tiny feet.

It is amazing how sound carries in a quiet house. We heard the water in what could only be a bathroom sink come on, followed by a glass filling. A slurping sound and then the plastic clink of a glass being put back on the counter. Small feet shuffled back down the hallway and a door closed.

I'd been in combat, known the fear of enemy fire all around me, hand-to-hand, fighting-for-my-life fear. None of that compared to what I was feeling right now. My heart was tripping like three pile drivers. How would I have explained to Kaylin why Mr. Jacob's hand was in Mommy's pants and Mommy was making funny noises?

I was willing my heart to slow down as I quickly yanked my wandering hand out of Josie's pajamas and put it around her, pulling her closer. She began to tremble.

"Josie, honey, what's wrong? Talk to me." Hell. I broke her. We went too fast, I screwed up. What was I thinking?

She began to wheeze like a tire with a leak that someone kept squeezing. It took me a moment to realize she was trying to hold back laughter.

She found this funny? Her daughter almost caught us making out like two hormone-crazed teenagers in heat and she thought it was funny? Then it dawned on me that we were on a couch making out like two teenagers in heat. I began to wheeze myself.

After a few minutes of mutual wheezing, Josie leaned in and kissed me lightly.

"Guess we got a bit carried away," she said, stroking my cheek.

"You are a wild woman."

She took one finger and bopped the end of my nose.

"I am, and don't forget it. Jacob?" she asked.

"Hmmm?"

"Can you just hold me for a bit, please? Don't worry if you fall asleep. I'll wake up in a couple hours. I haven't slept the night through since ... well, you know."

"I haven't either."

She snuggled in close and laid her head in the crook of my shoulder, kissing me softly. I began lightly stroking her hair, lulling us both into sleep.

My eyes popped open, and old instincts brought me instantly alert. This time, though, I was also confused. Alert because someone had quietly called my name. Confused because I was feeling something I'd not felt in a long, long time: waking up holding someone.

At some point I must have shifted to my back because Josie was curled up into me, her head laying on my chest, one leg thrown over my legs. She was snoring, ever so quietly. I had my other arm wrapped around her, holding her close. The soft query sounded again.

"Jacob?"

I looked up to see Flora looking down at me. It was barely light enough in the house for me to—shit, we overslept. I must have gotten that panicked look in my eyes because Flora grinned and shushed her hand at me.

"It's six in the morning," she whispered, "Kaylin will be up soon.

You two are so cute all curled up together that I didn't want to wake you, but I don't want Kaylin to find you."

I pushed at Josie's shoulder a few times. "Josie, honey, wake up. Josie—"

She snorted and smacked her lips a few times before snuggling in closer. The rising sun's rays shone through a kitchen window. I could see Josie's face in the dim light, and her beauty took my breath away. On the downside, she was also drooling on me. A nice big, wet circle adorned my shirt, and I could feel it sticking to my chest.

I shifted on the couch, forcing her head to move. That did the trick. Her eyes blinked open, and she smacked her lips a few more times. She looked at me and smiled sleepily, stretching her back. The cuteness factor shot up ten-fold, and I realized that I would really like to see that sleepy smile again.

She kissed my chest, luckily not in the drool spot. "Hey, you," she said before reaching up to caress my cheek.

"Hey, yourself."

I captured her gaze, then shifted my eyes upward before looking back at her. She wasn't getting the message, so I looked up and over her shoulder again. She turned on her side enough to be able to see her mom. Flora twiddled her fingers at her, smiling. I almost lost it when she got a panicked look in her eyes.

"Oh god, we slept too long. Shit, Kaylin—" but her mom shushed her with her hand as Josie struggled to get up and out of my grasp.

Flora whispered, "Still asleep. Perhaps your boyfriend should go home before she wakes up?"

Josie untangled herself from me so that we could both stand. She took my hand and pulled me quickly to the front door. "Pick us up at five?" she asked. I nodded and kissed her again before stepping quietly out and into the cool morning air.

By the time I was finished with my coffee and reminiscing, I was hard again. I shook my head and headed to the bathroom. A shower with some personal attention was needed.

After one stress-relieving shower and a second cup of coffee, I was ready to face the day. I threw my thermos in the Gator and puttered my way up to the job site.

Today was crown molding day. I had bedrooms and bathrooms on my list, so it would be a full workday. I never really liked putting up crown molding, so of course growing up Dad made sure to give me that task on his project's checklist for every new house.

I expected to be more tired than I was, but in truth, I felt pretty good. Josie and I must have slept at least seven hours. That was more sleep than I normally got and was probably one of the best nights I'd had since Kara's death. Josie had felt good and waking up to her— nope, had to stop that line of thinking. I didn't have time for another shower.

I motored through the side yard and parked near the garage. Even though the garage was at the back end of the house, it was a good place to store my tools, set up my saws, and stack all the supplies. Much easier to haul cut pieces of wood around than lug my miter saw and other tools around the house.

Dumping my stuff on the garage floor, I stepped up through the side door into the mudroom and stopped. Every hair on my neck stood up. Something was wrong. They may not be here now, but somebody had been here recently.

I stood and listened, trying to pick out any sounds that didn't belong. Nothing stood out, so I eased from the mudroom into the kitchen. I scanned each room as I moved, looking for anything out of the usual.

Dusty footprints that didn't match mine were in several rooms. Wood that I stacked on the floors had been broken and strewn around. Great.

It got worse when I reached the first bathroom. Someone had taken a dump in the toilet without flushing. That I could have lived with. What I couldn't live with was that same someone spreading shit on the walls and the mirror. A quick check showed all the bathrooms were in the same state.

Shit. My schedule was changing for the day. Luckily, most of the pieces I needed were already in place. I would need to finish up certain things sooner than I'd expected.

It took me the rest of the day to get all the door locks installed and the rest of the security system set up. Since I'd already installed the room and window sensors, I just needed to land the wiring in the control panel, which was tedious work. I finished that up after lunch and connected the power to the panel. Now was test time and finding the things I missed or messed up. I tried each door and window individually to make sure the sensors were wired and working properly, using a small buzzer instead of the larger horn to indicate an alarm tripping.

I replaced two sensors and re-terminated three wires before the system controls announced they were happy. Grabbing my stuff from the house, I dropped what I could in the garage and the rest in the back of the Gator. A trip back into the garage and a few pokes at some buttons and the alarm panel was activated. I closed the garage doors before the alarm sounded and jumped back into the Gator. I had about an hour before I needed to pick the Callison girls up.

I was only a few minutes late when I rang the doorbell at Josie's. I chuckled as "I'LL GET IT" yelled from the inside. A few seconds later, the front door flew open, and Kaylin was looking up through the screen. She turned back, slammed the door in my face, and ran back into the house yelling "MOMMY IT'S MR. JACOBBBBB!"

I could only stand there and laugh. I could hear more muffled yelling before the door opened again and Josie ushered me in, her face a picture of exasperation.

"You want a six-year-old, low mileage, high attitude?" she asked. "I can make you a good deal."

I simply laughed and kissed her.

"Can I think about your offer? Maybe over cheap pizza and watery soda?"

"You drive a hard bargain. I accept. Give us a few minutes," she replied. I nodded as she turned back down the hallway.

'Kaylin, get your socks and shoes on so we can go."

"BUT I WANT MY RED PANDA SOCKS!" came wailing from

the back bedroom before Josie was halfway down the hall, causing her to pause for a moment before striding into what must have been her daughters' room.

"GET YOUR SOCKS ON NOW OR NO PUTT-PUTT!"

I started chuckling.

"You sure you're ready for this?" I turned at the question to see Flora standing at the dining room entrance wiping her hand on a dish towel.

I shrugged. "Hi, Flora. It's just putt-putt. I think I can handle it."

"Is that what you think this is?" she asked, smiling at me, her eyes twinkling. I was a bit confused.

"I thought that's what we were doing tonight?"

She laughed and stepped closer, putting her hand on my arm. "Promise me something?" she asked softly.

I arched a curious brow. "Sure."

"Please don't hurt her."

I understood that she wasn't talking about putt-putt. I put my hand on hers.

"I would never want to hurt either of them." She smiled and patted my arm before heading back to the kitchen just as the girls were finally coming down the hall.

"Hi, Mr. Jacob!" exclaimed Kaylin. "Look!" I laughed as she pulled up the legs of her pants to show me red socks with what appeared to be white pandas. I looked up at Josie, and she rolled her eyes.

"Slight change of plans. Bethy's now staying the night—," she said.

"Wohooo," chimed in Kaylin, interrupting Josie. "We're gonna have popcorn and watch movies and stay up all night!"

"As I was saying," Josie added, steering the bouncing Kaylin towards the door. "Pam is going to drop Bethy off with us at putt-putt, so I'll drive my car and you can follow. We'll never get the four of us in your truck. "

"Sure, works for me."

Fifteen minutes later, we pulled up to Jake's Game Shack, where we hooked up with Bethy and her mom. I stood back and marveled at the well-oiled machine of two moms transferring a kid from one sphere of control to another. I've had night maneuvers with highly trained soldiers fail to move as efficiently as these two moms. Sleeping bag, suitcase, favorite stuffed animals, car booster seat, and commands to be good, brush teeth, and a few other logistical marvels.

Josie finally caught her breath and did the introductions. "Pam, this is Jacob. Jacob, Pam, Bethy's mom," she said.

"Hello."

Pam's smile was warm and her eyes held a twinkle of amusement.

"Pleasure to finally meet you," she replied. "Her dad dropped her off the other night at Gordo's with another friend of ours. She hasn't stopped talking about the ball pit."

Both young girls broke out in "GIRLS RULE, BOYS DROOL!"

Josie blushed, and Pam laughed.

"Mr. Jacob is dating my mommy and me," piped up Kaylin. "Mommy said I don't have to kiss him. I just have to play games and skee-ball and she would do the kissing. I still don't want a baby brother. They're gross."

Josie's face turned even redder, and Pam was obviously trying her hardest not to laugh but little 'eeps' were leaking out. I decided this was a conversation that I, as a male, had no business being part of, and opted for escape.

"Come on, girls, let's go get our putters and leave your mommies to finish getting Bethy's stuff in the car." I hustled the two girls away with them chanting "girls rule" over and over.

When we got to the counter, the girls quickly educated me on the pros and cons of buying the all-access pass versus paying for a round of minigolf. The acne-plagued young man behind the counter wisely kept quiet and let the two girls do all his work.

"If we get the pass then we can play *lots* of golf and do the games inside, *and* we get free sodas!" exclaimed Kaylin, bouncing up and down with excitement.

I tapped my fingers on the counter, giving them both a wry look.

"But it's more expensive than just buying one round and paying for the games and soda."

"But we get free sodas," said both girls together.

Josie was laughing as she came up to my side.

"Give it up, Jacob. Something to quickly learn about six-year-olds: Adult logic doesn't work. Best to pick your battles," she told me with an air of wisdom.

I bowed to her superior knowledge and bought passes for everyone. The young man merely smiled and handed each of us one of those orange, self-sticking wrist bands to identify our status. He helped the girls pick out putters, which entailed a five-minute selection process on the ball color. Both girls wanted pink. Josie put a stop to it by handing them one green and one yellow ball and telling them both it was those or no putt-putt. They sulked and took the balls.

Luckily, it was a slow night. The girls wasted no time getting about a hole ahead of us. Josie seemed to be okay with it as long as she could keep an eye on them. Plus, it gave us a chance to talk.

"So, did you get in trouble with your mom this morning?"

She knocked her ball down past the clown and laughed. "My mom found it quite funny that she had to lecture me about making out with my dates on the couch. She thought she was done doing that after high school."

I glanced over at her to find she was blushing. Damn, she was even beautiful when she blushed. I looked up to see where the girls were and saw them laughing two holes in front of us.

A putter poked me in the ass, and I scowled at its wielder.

"Hey, watch where you put that thing!"

"That's *my* line," she retorted, dancing back out of range of my putter. We were two swipes into a putter duel when the speakers squealed.

"*Putters are for putting, not slaying dragons, wayward rogues, or dates who steal your fries. Please use them responsibly.*"

We both laughed, red faced, and moved onto the next hole, returning our putters to their designated use.

By the time we reached the last hole, Josie and I were tied. She berated me when she caught me missing putts on purpose so she could win, and warned me to play for real or suffer the consequences. She may have been grinning when she said it, but the glint in her eyes told me she was serious.

The girls finished their round and were now bouncing impatiently at the arcade entrance.

The last hole was your standard steep ramp up to a large putting circle, nothing fancy. It was designed to be an easy putt to collect the balls and prevent folks from playing another round for free, assuming they didn't skip the last hole and start back at the first hole.

Just as Josie was hitting her putt, I sneezed, causing her putter to jerk, smacking the carpet before it hit the ball. Her ball trickled about halfway up the ramp before rolling back down to stop at her feet.

She stared at me intently, her eyes little laser beams.

"Oh, *sniff*, I'm so sorry, Josie. Must have been a bug." I made a show of wiping at my nose as if trying to dislodge something. She glared at me, not buying my excuse. She putted again, rolling her ball up the ramp and bouncing around the back before it settled within a foot of the hole. She would have an easy three. I waited for her putter to impact my skull.

Instead, she did the scariest thing possible. She looked me right in the eye and smiled. As I stepped up to the putting line, she kissed me lightly on the cheek.

"Good luck," she told me, oozing sweetness and innocence.

As I lined up my putt, she moved behind me, snuggling up close to my right shoulder. Not close enough to mess with my swing but close enough I could feel her breath on my neck. I laughed to myself. Surely, she knew breathing on my neck, while pleasant, was something I could tune out.

I made a couple of practice swings before setting up like I was putting for real, just to see what she would do. She didn't take the bait. I lined up for my shot and let my concentration drop to my putt. Just as my putter was moving forward, she struck. A light, breathy whisper caressed my ear.

"I'm not wearing panties."

My putter slammed forward and impacted cleanly with the golf ball. The angle of the ramp provided the perfect launch platform, and we both watched as my ball cleared the back of the putting green as well as the six-foot fence on the backside of the property. The ball continued on a graceful arc into the woods. We heard several thocks as it rebounded off the tree trunks, like a pinball hitting bumpers.

As I watched, dumbfounded, Josie sashayed up the putting ramp to her ball. She calmly lined up her putt and sank it. She sashayed back to me and kissed me on the nose.

"Girl's rule," she said quietly. She strutted over to the two girls who were dancing and cheering for her. She gave them high-fives and opened up the door to the arcade. She paused and threw a glance back over her shoulder at me. She licked her lips slowly, winked, and followed the girls inside. Muttering to myself, I followed in defeat, hoping no one paid too close attention to my now-uncomfortable-fitting jeans.

A couple of hours later, we ushered the girls out of the arcade. Josie and I avoided talking about our previous night's activities and instead focused on the girls and having fun. Adult conversation in a place like that was about as productive as it had been at Gordo's.

We were about halfway to my truck when the hairs on my neck stood up and I froze. I felt someone watching me, making me a target. I let my eyes start scanning and when my gaze hit the tree line across the parking lot, every nerve in me started screaming danger.

Josie noticed and paused, calling for the girls to stop. "Jacob?"

"Take the girls to the car."

"What's wrong?" she asked, looking around.

"Please, just take the girls to the car." Something in my tone must have tipped her off because she turned and shooed the girls towards their ride. I started walking slowly towards the tree line, up on the balls of my feet and ready to bounce, mentally cursing myself for not being armed.

I was halfway to the tree line when the feeling left me. Whoever or whatever had been there had moved on. I stood for another minute, listening and waiting, but nothing else tripped my trigger. Giving the tree line one final glance, I headed back to the girls. Josie hopped out of the car to meet me.

"Okay, what's going on?" she asked, coming up close.

"Something spooked me."

"Spooked you?"

"Someone was in the trees, watching us."

"How did you know that?" Her voice hitched slightly, and she crossed her arms, glancing around. "It's barely lit up by the parking lot lights. What did you see?"

"Nothing, just a feeling." Her eyes told me she was skeptical, but she didn't press it further. Several loud 'ewwwws' came from the car when I pulled her close and kissed her goodnight. She laughed as we broke the kiss.

"You cheated tonight."

"All's fair in love, ball pits, and putt-putt," she replied, giggling and giving me an innocent look.

"Uh huh. Not buying that innocent look at all." The next kiss she gave me was far, far from innocent. I was still breathing hard when she drove off with the girls, waving out her car window at me. I hated fucking driving with a hard-on.

TWENTY-TWO

Josie

I was eating lunch Monday, but I couldn't tell you how much of it I ate, since all I could think about was the weekend. Especially Friday night. I could still feel Jacob's hands on me. I chewed absently and let my mind languish in the memories of lips and hands.

"Earth to Josie"

"Josie ..."

"JOSIE!"

I startled, blinking my eyes as I looked up to see Brianna standing at my shoulder.

"Hey, Brianna. You say something?"

She sat down at the table with me, laughing. "What's going on with you? I only called you three times. Your face looked like you were seconds away from popping an O in my chair."

I smiled, chewing some more of my sandwich. She rolled her eyes, chuckling.

"Oh, let me guess. About six foot, 210 pounds, good hands," she said.

"*Really* good hands."

Brianna's eyebrows flew up. "Oh *reeeeally*? Do tell," she teased, refilling my glass and taking a drink from it before I could grab it back. As I reached for it, she pulled the glass back out of my reach. "No more till you dish the deets."

I scoffed. "You really need to come up with a new word. You've become addicted to that one."

She took another drink from my glass and stared at me, her eyes alight with curiosity.

I cleared my throat. "Well, Jacob got back from Seattle at about ten last night and came over. I fixed him some leftover meatloaf. You know how Mom makes it. Just the right amount of ketchup."

Brianna interrupted me by smacking me with her order form.

"*Ow!* What the hell?" Brianna was glowering at me, her eyes snapping with just a hint of peeved. It was actually kind of cute.

"I'll ow you. Tell the story right," she snapped, glaring at me from behind my drink she held hostage.

"Fine." I decided to have a little fun. "Alright. He made it to the house about ten. Fed him dinner, after which we hit the couch. I was in my best flannel. He sat down, and I attacked him. Lips met and our tongues dueled fiercely. We sucked face like there was no tomorrow. Then we took the game horizontal."

I paused and pointed at my glass. She hesitated but finally gave it back to me. I took a drink, playing out some line so my fish wouldn't get too spooked.

"That's when the real game began. Batter up. His wonderful, strong hands started around first base, made multiple trips around second base —and they were really, really, good passes. Lots of squeezing, caressing, pinching, if you know what I mean."

I threw in some moans to spice up the bait. Brianna merely stared, wide-eyed.

"He was pressed into me, and I could feel him all stiff and ready. *Then* ... he went for third." I waggled my eyebrows suggestively.

Brianna took a swig of my tea and grabbed one of my fries. I was pretty sure she hadn't blinked, and her face was a bit flushed. Time to reel in the fish.

"His hand slid slowly, oh so slowly down, making little caresses at my belly button, meandered down my stomach until he slipped ever so gently into my flannel bottoms."

I threw in some small sighs before setting the hook.

"His fingers start to tickle the hair right at the very edge ... ready to make that first ... slide into home ..."

Brianna blinked and took a drink from the tea pitcher. I leaned in a bit closer, and my sucker leaned in with me. I dropped my voice to a whisper.

"I started to part my legs, and his fingers lifted a bit ..."

"And?" she asked, her voice breaking a bit as I paused.

"Kaylin got up, fixed herself a glass of water, and the game was called on account of kid." I sat back in my chair and calmly ate a few more fries.

Brianna stared at me, her mouth hanging open. I started laughing so hard I was snorting, almost peeing myself. For a second, I thought she was going to pour the tea pitcher on me. After a moment, she sniffed.

"Well, if you're not going to tell me bitch, *fine*."

I took pity on her and told her about the night, including waking up in his arms and looking up at Mom.

That got her laughing.

"Oh, it was loads of laughs. Mom had a 'talk' with me later that morning about what should and shouldn't be done in a house with Kaylin. Not to mention about not having my boyfriends sleep over. She told me it was like having the birds and bees talk again. Although she did say we looked cute. Even took a pic." I pulled out my phone and showed her the picture Mom sent me.

"Aww, you're so cute. You really were in flannel jammies. Wait, is that ... *drool* coming off your lip?" she asked, smirking.

"No," I said stiffly, "it's just the angle of the lighting."

"Uh huh." My phone ringing interrupted her. She went to check on her other customers when I answered.

"Hi, Uncle Frank."

"*Hi, Josie. Are you and your mom busy at the moment?*"

"I'm at lunch, and Mom's back at the store. What's up?"

"I need you both to come to the bank. I have some rather good news."

That had me sitting up straighter.

"You found something to help us?" I could feel my heart racing. Could we finally catch a break?

"Just bring your Mom, and we can go over everything. Say in about forty-five minutes?"

"Sure, Uncle Frank. See you then. Bye."

I stared at the phone, willing it to give me the details that Uncle Frank wouldn't share. When it didn't work, I pulled out my wallet and dropped a twenty on the table as I stood up. I waved to Brianna as I headed out the door and back to the store.

When Mom and I arrived at the bank, we were ushered into Uncle Frank's office. He got us seated across from his desk before he sat in his leather chair.

"Can I get you ladies anything? Coffee, water?" he asked. We both told him no. "Well, I'm happy you ladies could make it on such short notice. I have some exceptionally good news for you. I've found an investor who is willing to help you with your financial situation." He smiled wide.

"That's great news, Uncle Frank. What are the terms?"

"Well, that's one of the best parts of this, Josie. There are no terms. It's a grant," he explained.

"Excuse me?" Mom sputtered.

Uncle Frank nodded his head, still grinning.

"A grant. No terms. No payback," he said.

I shook my head. "Wait a minute. Some investor is going to give us free money and wants nothing in return? No stake in the store, no rebranding, nothing?"

He nodded.

"This sounds too good to be true, Frank," Mom remarked, frowning. "Even I know there is no such thing as a free lunch. There *has* to be a catch."

"No catch, Flora. I've talked with the investor and their accountant. I've also run this by our lawyer. It's all perfectly legal. You just say the word, and the money will be applied to your accounts due with the bank."

"How much are they granting?" asked Mom. "I mean, how much will it cover?"

Frank's smile got bigger. "All of it, and then some."

Mom gasped and her hand reached over to grasp mine. I stared at him, mostly in shock.

"Can ... can we talk to this investor?"

Uncle Frank's smile faltered. "No, you can't, ladies. I'm sorry, but that was the one stipulation placed on this offer. The investor wishes to remain completely anonymous. All of the financials are being handled through the investor's accountant and the bank. You can speak to the accountant if you want. I'll have all of the paperwork ready for tax time. Since you've made use of the bank for your accounting services, it will simplify things greatly."

"You said 'and then some'," Mom replied, who still had a death grip on my hand. "What does that mean?"

Uncle Frank was smiling again. "With the funds provided, I will be paying off all your current debt to the bank, as well as your suppliers and store accounts. Basically, if the store owes someone money, I will be issuing checks to pay that off."

He paused to gauge our shell-shocked expressions. When I thought he had blown my mind enough, he proved me wrong.

"Also," he added, "the investor has allotted another $50,000 to handle any unforeseen needs. The desire was for you not to incur any new debt for a short time while you digested all of this and worked out your future plans."

I thought Mom was going to faint. She paled, and her breathing was a bit shallow.

"Some water please, Uncle Frank."

He looked closer at Mom. His eyes widened in alarm, and he rushed over to his small refrigerator to get her a bottle of water. He kneeled next to her while she drank, murmuring something to her that I couldn't hear. She patted his arm, and he returned to his desk. Her color was much better. I cleared my throat.

"It just seems too good to be true. Are you sure this is legit?"

"Trust me, Josie. I wouldn't do anything that would hurt Flora or you. I checked this out completely. I verified the funding, and I spent this morning talking to our lawyer. It *is* unorthodox, but perfectly legal. So, yes, it is very true."

I didn't know what to say or feel. How do you react when all of your financial worries go away with a blink of an eye thanks to a perfect stranger? I looked at Mom, raising an eyebrow. She smiled and nodded. I turned back to Uncle Frank.

"Okay. What do we need to do?"

"Just say yes," he said, grinning.

I squeezed Mom's hand.

"Yes, Uncle Frank. We accept the offer."

He tapped several keys on his keyboard. A few seconds later, his printer kicked on. He pulled the page off the printer, glanced at it, smiled, and pushed it across the desk to me.

It was a printout of our bank financials. With zero balances due on the operational line of credit and the equity loan. Our operations account now showed a balance of $50,000.

We were debt-free. I didn't know whether to laugh or cry or scream. Maybe I needed to do all three. I think Mom was in the same boat.

I don't remember telling Uncle Frank goodbye or walking back to the store. Mom and I were now sitting in my office, staring at each other, both of us still in shock. I clutched the printout that Uncle Frank had given me.

I looked at Mom. She looked at me. Her lips twitched, then twitched again. My nose crinkled, and my lips tried to crack a smile. Finally, as if a switch had been flipped, we were up and dancing, holding each other's hands. We laughed and screamed as we jumped around.

Billy, our front counter help for the afternoon, came running back. He looked at us like we had lost our minds, which wasn't all that far from the truth.

"Um, everything okay?" he asked, staying as far away from us as he could.

I rushed over to him and grabbed him by the arm, pulling him into the celebration. His face went pale and his eyes opened wide and started darting around the room, as if looking for an escape from the crazy people.

"How many customers are in the store, Billy?" I let his hands go and started the Electric Slide, heading for the hallway. Poor Billy.

"No one," he said, trying to back up against a wall since I had the door blocked.

"Awesome! Go lock the door. Oh, and put a sign on the door that says, '*Closed until Wednesday due to Happiness!*'"

"Josie?" he asked, completely lost.

"Hop to, young Billy Boy. You have the rest of the day off with full pay! Hurry!"

Billy looked at me like he was sizing me up for a straight jacket. He glanced over at Mom. I wasn't positive, but she appeared to be doing the Lindy.

"You heard the lady. Hop to!" she shouted in glee.

I glided back into the office as Billy broke for the door and the safety of the front counter. I screamed in happiness as I ran over and wrapped Mom in a big hug.

"Can you believe it, Mom? Debt-free! No more worries about monthly payments, no more robbing Peter to pay Paul. Freeeee!"

"We need to celebrate!" she exclaimed happily. "Oh, I know, let's go out to dinner. I'm thinking steak and all the trimmings."

"Flannery's? I'll call for reservations. Can I invite Jacob?"

"Sure," she replied, laughing. "Hell, he can sleep on the couch again if you want!"

I was pretty sure the excitement covered up the blush. I danced over to my desk and grabbed my phone. With a quick call, I had a reservation for four at 6:30 p.m.

Mom was leaning against my desk, her hand on her chest, trying to catch her breath. She panted, saying, "Oh goodness, these old bones just … can't take all this excitement!"

"Oh please. You're sixty-four, not ninety-four. You're a babe!"

Mom had been ten years younger than Dad, and they'd had me when Mom was thirty-five. Mom was far from old.

"Well, this babe needs time to get all gussied up. We have three females to get ready for a big dinner and only five hours to do it. It might just be enough time."

I laughed as Mom headed home. I pulled out my phone and texted Jacob.

"Hey. What's up?"

"Are you in town?"

"Yes. Janey's updating me on some shift stuff and scheduling for when she's being lazy in a couple weeks."

"She'll be on her honeymoon, goof. She's allowed to be whatever she wants. You doing anything tonight?"

"I wasn't before, but it sounds like I might be now."

"I have some great news. Mom and I are celebrating. Reservations at Flannery's at 6:30. My treat!"

"Wow, free steak and dinner with you and Kaylin at the most high-dollar place in town? I'm in. Meet you there?"

"Yes! Great! See you there."

Several hours later, I had shaved my legs, finished my makeup, and was pondering what to wear under my dress. I hadn't dressed up much these last couple of years, but tonight's main goal was to celebrate. The second goal was to make all Jacob's blood flow to his little head. Weapon of choice tonight would be the classic LBD.

I opened my bottom dresser drawer and pulled out a small box that was tucked behind some camisoles. I laid the contents on the bed as I dropped my towel. I slipped on the silky blue thong, followed by the matching strapless push-up bra. My dress had a modest plunge to the neckline. Mom always said, *'If you got 'em, flaunt 'em.'* Tonight, I was listening to her.

I slipped my dress on and began adjusting it, making sure the girls were sitting comfortably. I was smoothing down the wrinkles when Mom appeared at the door.

"Oh dear, that poor man," she said, laughing quietly.

"Poor man?"

"He's not going to know what hit him. You're going to fry his brain cells in that outfit, sweetheart." Mom came over and finished zipping me in. I smoothed down the hips as I looked in the mirror.

The dress hugged me, but not too tight, allowing me to move comfortably. The hem hit about three inches above the knee, showing a lot of leg. The neckline was just low enough to combine with the bra to show a small amount of cleavage without being gauche.

I stepped away from the mirror and turned to face Mom. "Not too bad, huh?"

"You're beautiful. Like I said, Jacob's not going to know what hit him. Oh wait, I have just the thing for that dress." She left the room and returned with a small case. "Stand in front of the mirror," she ordered.

I moved back to the mirror, and Mom moved behind me. She reached around and brought something up to my neck. My breath caught when I saw the reflection in the mirror.

"Those are Grandma's pearls! I can't—" I began, but she shushed me. She fastened the double strand around my neck, and the necklace landed perfectly, just even with my collarbones. She put the pearl studs in my ears, completing the set.

"There, perfect. I've been meaning to give them to you. Tonight seems like the perfect time," she replied, looking at me in the mirror.

"Mom, I ... I don't know what to say. Thank you."

"Give them to Kaylin one of these days. Consider them a loan till then," she said. "Now, let's get your hair done."

Mom brushed and primped my hair until it shone. I opted to leave it down, so Mom pulled it over one shoulder.

"It's a good thing Jacob's a strong young man," she said as she gave me a final once over. "He's going to be fighting off every male in that restaurant tonight. You are just so beautiful, Josie, so beautiful." She laughed and shook her head as she went to help Kaylin put on her coat and shoes.

I added a small clutch and my three-inch, strapless black heels to the outfit and looked back at the mirror, taking in the full effect.

"No. No, he won't, Mom. He has absolutely no competition."

We arrived at the restaurant a few minutes before our reservation. By the time we wrangled Kaylin out of Mom's car, got our dresses smoothed, and made our way to the hostess, we were right on time. She greeted us cordially.

"Welcome to Flannery's, ladies. Do you have a reservation?"

"Yes, Callison."

She scanned her list.

"Party of four. One of your parties has already arrived. If you ladies will follow me?"

She picked up three menus and led us into the main dining area.

Flannery's wasn't a large place, but it still had an elegant atmosphere. A small fireplace was tucked into one corner, and a smattering of tables occupied the dining area. The place was large enough to allow for ample space between tables for the wait staff to move and to give the table's occupants a modicum of privacy. Indirect lighting allowed the candles on each table to provide a touch of warm ambiance. The owners even managed to squeeze in a small dance floor and piano in the back corner.

About half of the tables were occupied tonight. As we moved towards ours, Jacob saw us and instantly stood up, locking eyes with me. My knees weakened at the intensity of his gaze.

He looked good. Really good. He wore a grey suit, a black shirt, and a grey tie. He'd found time for a haircut because his hair looked neat and trimmed. Even from here, I could tell the shirt was fitted and fit him well.

I wanted that man. I know we had been getting closer during these few short weeks and shared some intimate moments, but that was nothing compared to what I was feeling right now. And my heart really hoped that hunger in his eyes meant he was feeling the same way.

He never broke eye contact with me as we neared. Everyone and everything in that room fell to the background. I could only see him.

The hostess guided us to our chairs and began placing menus. Jacob finally broke his gaze and rushed to pull out Kaylin's chair. She giggled as he pushed her up to the table. He picked up a small yellow rose and handed it to her.

"For a lovely princess," he said. Her face lit up as she smelled it.

"Thank you, Mr. Jacob!" she replied, beaming at him.

Jacob moved around and seated Mom. He picked up another small yellow rose and presented it with a flourish to her, eliciting a smile from her and bringing a slight blush to her cheeks.

He came around to me, again capturing my gaze with his. He took my hands and leaned in to lightly kiss my cheek before whispering in my ear, his breath sending delicious tingles everywhere.

"You're stunning. You're without a doubt the most beautiful woman in this room. Every man here wishes he were me." I felt the heat rise up inside at his words. He reached into his jacket and removed a red rose, presenting it to me.

"For a true queen," he whispered.

That did it. I had now officially fallen for this man.

He seated me and returned to his chair. The waiter had been standing by and as soon as Jacob sat, he came over and began filling water glasses.

"Good evening. My name is Oscar, and I'll be taking care of you this evening. Can I start anyone off with a cocktail, a glass of wine, and perhaps a Shirley Temple for the young lady?"

I looked at Mom and Jacob, but they said nothing, apparently deferring to me.

"Thank you, Oscar. Yes, the young lady may have a small Shirley Temple with two cherries. I think we're all going to be having steak tonight, so can you recommend a good wine?"

"Absolutely ma'am," he replied, smiling. "We have an excellent house sauvignon that would go very well with the seasonings the chef uses on our ribeye."

"Perfect."

Oscar nodded and left to attend to our drinks.

"So," said Jacob. "What are we celebrating?"

"Are we getting a dog?" asked Kaylin excitedly. "That would be a good celebration!"

Jacob and Mom laughed while I patted Kaylin's hand.

"No, sweetie, we're not getting a dog. This is a bigger celebration."

"Oh," she said, her disappointment evident but short-lived. "Big like a birthday? Is it your birthday? Grandma normally tells me when that is."

"No, pumpkin, it's not my birthday. This is more a Mommy and Grandma celebration. It's like a thousand times better than birthdays for us."

'Ohh. That's really big. What is it?" she asked excitedly.

I looked at Mom, and she nodded.

"Well, Uncle Frank worked a huge miracle, and he found an investor that can help our store. This new investor paid off all of our debt with the bank and gave us quite a bit of extra money to cover our future expenses. We're not closing."

Jacob broke out in a grin and looked from me to Mom and back to me.

"Are you serious? That's wonderful! I know you're … wait," he said, dropping the grin. "Is this just a bigger loan? Did you just shift the debt?"

"No, that's the most amazing part. It's a grant. No terms, no payback."

Before I could continue, Oscar came back to take our order. Once he had left, a young waitress brought us the bottle of wine in a wicker holder. When she offered the cork to Jacob, he held up his hand and pointed at me. The waitress nodded, moved around to my side, and offered me the cork.

"I wouldn't know what I was doing with that, to be honest." The waitress simply smiled and dropped the cork into her apron front. She poured a small amount of the wine in my glass and waited. I gave it a sniff before taking a small sip. Nodding, I placed my glass back on the table and she promptly poured for the adults, set the holder on the table near Jacob and melted into the background.

Oscar returned with Kaylin's drink. Much to her delight, it was in a wine glass, just like the adults. Once the staff left, I filled Jacob in on the full discussion we had with Uncle Frank.

He shook his head in amazement. "So, this mysterious investor basically gave you a ton of money just because?" he asked.

"That's right."

"That's unreal. You have no idea who the investor is?"

"No," Mom said with a shrug. "That was the one condition for the deal. The investor was to remain anonymous. We could not meet or converse with them. Everything was handled via their accountant in Seattle."

"Mommy, does this somehow mean I can get a dog?" asked Kaylin, slurping her drink through her straw.

"I already told you, no dog." I could tell by the set of her jaw that a rebuke was inbound. Before she could respond, Jacob rose from the table and stood next to Kaylin, bowing.

"Princess Kaylin, may I please have the honor of this dance?" She giggled, looked at me and I nodded my head. She climbed out of her chair, and Jacob took her hand, walking with her to the small dance floor. He held his hands down to her, and the two of them began to do an awkward box step. I stared at them both, my thoughts drifting to places that they really shouldn't have been going.

"You've got it bad, young lady."

Mom's words broke me from my musings, and I looked at her, a small smile on my lips.

"Does it show?"

She cocked her head at me. "No, not too much, but I'm your mother. I know you better than most, and I know that look." She sipped her wine and stared out at the two on the dance floor. "He's good with her," she said softly.

I could only nod, watching them. Jacob must have said something funny to Kaylin because I could tell she was giggling. As we watched, he pulled her up a bit so that she was now standing on his feet. She laughed as he started moving them in big steps around the floor.

Kaylin's food and our salads were just arriving when the two dancers made it back to the table. We chatted about some of Kaylin's friends' antics at daycare. As we finished the salads, Oscar and another waiter returned. Plates were whisked away, and the steaks and their sides were served.

The steaks were as good as Oscar had mentioned. 12oz, grass

feed, Angus bone-in ribeye's. All three had been cooked to perfection. I had chosen garlic butter and caramelized onions for a topping. Jacob had opted for sautéed mushrooms while mom had just gone with au jus.

Between the three of us we had chosen different sides, so that we could all sample the various dishes: cheesy scalloped potatoes, a steamed vegetable mix of cauliflower, broccoli, carrots, and a large plate of seasoned fries.

The steak virtually cut itself and that first bite melted in my mouth. Mom and Jacobs faces told me that their steaks were tasting just as good as mine. For the next few moments, we all gave the excellent food the attention it was due.

As we ate, Kaylin and Jacob kept trying to sneak food from each other's plates. Jacob had fries with his steak, and Kaylin kept doing her best to snatch one. In return, Jacob was sneaking noodles out of her mac and cheese. One pesky attempt caused a fry to fly across the table and plop right into my water glass. I started to say something to them both when Mom chimed in.

"I should tell you about the time Josie embarrassed her dad and I at a dinner party when she was about six." All eyes at the table looked at her.

"Tell us, Grandma!" squealed Kaylin, Jacob's fries now a distant memory.

"*Mommmm*," I groaned. Mom shushed me and launched into her story.

"She stood there, in just her shirt and underwear, telling her dad, me, and our other dinner guests that her pants were just too itchy to wear for dinner." Mom took another drink of wine as both Jacob and Kaylin broke out laughing. I looked at my mom sweetly.

"You know, Mom, I hear those senior retirement homes have all the best amenities for someone of your … *advanced* years." Jacob tried to stifle another laugh but was only partially successful. Mom gave him the evil eye before turning on me, smiling just as sweetly.

"Even with my *advanced* years, I've never managed to fall down a hill," she replied, smiling at me.

Jacob started to laugh, but I gave him my own evil eye. He became intensely interested in his plate. Smart man.

Kaylin's laugh turned into a slight yawn, diverting both Mom's and my attention.

"Well," Mom said, "It would seem someone might need to call it an early night."

"Awww, but I was having … fun," Kaylin tried to say, but she broke out into another yawn halfway through her complaint.

Mom suggested with a smile, "Josie, why don't I take Kaylin home and you and Jacob have some dessert?"

"But I want dessert *too*," whined the sleepy one.

"We have some ice cream at home," Mom retorted. "You can have some of that once you're ready for bed."

While I wrangled Kaylin out of her chair and cleaned up some spilled mac and cheese, Mom bid Jacob goodnight, which to my surprise included a light hug and a kiss to his cheek. As she walked out with Kaylin, Mom caught Oscar's attention. They spoke for a few moments and he nodded, directing her to the hostess.

"Would you care to dance?"

While my attention had been on Mom, Jacob had come up beside me. He was holding out his hand. I took it, and he led me to the dance floor. It felt like the most natural thing in the world for me to move in close to him. One hand held mine, and his other arm slipped around my back, light pressure keeping us together. I laid my other arm along his, my hand resting on his shoulder.

We again captured each other's gaze, moving lightly in place. I noticed the set of his jaw, the way his one eyebrow sat a bit higher than the other. Small lines in his face wrapped around his eyes.

Those eyes captivated me, held me, and caressed me all at the same time. There was so much emotion in them that it was almost overpowering. How could I be worthy of that level of feeling?

Before, his eyes always made me think of Greg. Now, staring at this man, his eyes made me think that something I'd thought I had lost was possible again.

I blinked first, smiling at him.

"You're staring."

"I can't help it," he said. "I told you earlier, you look amazing."

I shrugged, a shy grin playing on my lips. "I wore this tonight just for you."

He paused for a moment before we started moving again. He inhaled deeply before speaking to me again.

"You wore this for me? Not that I'm complaining, but why?"

I smiled up at him and moved both of my hands up and around his neck. He let his hands drop to my waist. With my heels on, I was virtually eye to eye with him. I pulled our faces closer together and let my lips brush his before whispering softly.

"Because I wanted to see if I could make it hard."

He groaned and pulled me tighter to him, kissing me.

"Damn, woman, what you do to me. I haven't felt ... damn."

I laughed softly. "Brain cells a little starved for blood?"

He groaned again before catching my meaning. He tried to back away from me, but I pulled him close and pressed into him gently. We were on a public dance floor, after all.

"I don't think so, mister. I'm perfectly happy with where your blood has been ... redirected."

Jacob inhaled a deep breath, forcing me to kiss him again.

"Josie, I think we should go sit down."

I laughed softly again.

"Having a ... *hard* time?"

He stared at me intently. "You are an evil, evil woman. Sexy as hell, but evil."

I kissed him again, adding just a light grind to the mix. I gave a slightly dramatic sigh. "I guess I'll take pity on you. Let's go sit and have dessert. Jacob?"

"Yes?"

I leaned in, placing my lips next to his ear.

"Don't watch my ass while I walk away."

I lightly licked his ear lobe and turned for the table, putting just a bit of extra sway to my step. After a few steps I looked back over my shoulder to see Jacob staring at me. I winked at him and kept walking.

The dinner dishes had been cleared away and two candles lit. The table must have had a leaf in it that allowed it to expand to seat four because it was now definitely smaller, comfortable for two. In the middle of the table was a silver coffee pot and small plate containing a chocolate-looking dessert.

When we were seated again, Oscar appeared back at our sides.

"Compliments of the madam. She said to tell you the bill has been covered and that you were to take time and enjoy a nice dessert. If you need anything else, please let us know." With that, he melted back away. It might not be a big city place, but the staff knew how to be discreet. I hoped Mom gave them a huge tip.

Jacob poured us coffee as I dug into the cake. It looked delectable. A perfectly round circle with a dimple in the top, it was a dark chocolate delight. As I sunk my fork into it, already anticipating the first bite, the molten chocolate inside, slightly darker than the cake itself, started to pour out of the hole, melting the vanilla ice cream that surrounded the edges. Chocolate and cream ran together, creating swirls as they melded. I used my fork to cut off a piece, although I was tempted to just drop the fork and dive in with my fingers.

I lifted the forkful of cake to my mouth, closing my eyes and breathing in the wonderful scent of chocolate in anticipation. As I closed my mouth over the fork, I felt the sweet deliciousness touch every taste bud on my tongue. It had just the right amount of sweet, and I detected a sharp bitter touch of dark chocolate lurking in the background. It was perfection on a plate and I couldn't help the small moan of pleasure that escaped.

I quickly opened my eyes to see Jacob watching me, a look of hunger in his eyes. My insides went weak at the intensity of his gaze.

"You really enjoy your desserts, don't you?" he asked with a devilish grin. "I wasn't too jealous of the pie, but that cake is a different story."

I finished the bite, cut another piece and offered it to him. "I'll happily share."

He shook his head. Oh, no. I would never come between a woman and her chocolate," he replied.

I finished the small piece of heaven, never taking my eyes of him. The tension between us was almost palpable. Wiping my lips, I picked up my coffee and gazed at him over the cup. I asked about something that piqued my interest early on.

"Jacob, how'd you get that scar under your eye?"

His coffee cup froze just before reaching his lips. He recovered quickly, sipped his drink, and placed it back on the table. "Oh, just a childhood accident, nothing fancy. What do you think you and your mom will do now with the store?"

Nice try, dude, but I wasn't buying that deflection again. I needed to settle this soon.

"What do you have going on tomorrow?"

He looked thoughtful for a moment. "Janey needs me to work at the hospital for the next few days while she moves some shifts around to cover her honeymoon."

"So, your next free time during the day is …?"

"Saturday," he answered. "Why?"

"What say you come pick me up Saturday around lunch time and we head over to the park next to the marina?"

"No Kaylin?"

"Nope, just you and me. I'll make some tea and we can stop and get some chicken or sandwiches. We'll have ourselves a picnic."

He grinned and cocked one eyebrow. "Are you going to wear that dress?"

I slapped his hand, and he laughed, feigning hurt. We finished our coffee, then headed for home.

After sharing another scorcher of a kiss on the porch, I was opening the door to go in when he tried one more time.

"Are you sure the dress is out for Saturday?"

I looked over my shoulder and him and smiled.

"Sorry, sweetie. But I *guess* I could wear the silky blue thong I have on now. It feels so good and covers so … little." I winked at him, closing the door and leaving him open-mouthed on the doorstep. I laughed all the way to my bedroom. He had no idea how evil I could be.

TWENTY-THREE

Jacob

Saturday was a perfect late summer day. I sat at the table under my awning, my breakfast remnants on my plate as I sipped my coffee and stared out at the trees.

I was happy that Josie and her mom had accepted the bailout, but I also felt guilty about deceiving them. I knew that if they'd realized it was coming from me, they would have turned it down.

I also didn't want them to know about my finances. Frank knowing already gave me worries. Money brings out the worst in people. I meant what I said to Marissa. Money was just a tool, and if I could bring some happiness to some who needed it, then all the more reason to do so. I'd never be able to spend all of the money I had, so why not let it do some good?

My thoughts centered on Josie. My mind didn't want to work right when I thought about her.

A month. I'd only known her for a month. We've only had a few dates and not a single one yet by ourselves. In fact, today's picnic would be our very first date with just *us*.

Even in that short of time, I was breaking the rule I set for myself after Kara's death. I swore after her death I wouldn't love again. It hurt way too much when you lost that love. My sister, my parents, Kara, my unborn daughter. Love hurt too much.

And yet here I was, breaking that rule. Hell, I was smashing it with a hammer.

I was in love with her. Not lust, although that was there as well. *Love*. How did I tell her, when should I tell her, when could I *show* her?

Her dinner invitation caught me flat-footed and, once again, sadly lacking in the wardrobe department. A mad rush out to the mall near the interstate gained me a suit, shirt, and shoes. On a whim, I hit one of those style shops and turned them loose on my hair. I wanted to impress her and show her that I was the man for her. Then I melted like ice cream when she entered the room.

Seeing her in that dress at dinner sent desire coursing through me like electricity. Holding her that close on the dance floor had been unreal. The whole thing about my blood channeling to my dick just made me want her all the more. And the panty comment at the end of the night. I have no idea why I didn't explode in my pants right then and there.

The damper to all of this was my new shadow. The house invasion was bad enough, but putt-putt the other night had been concerning. Someone had eyes on me. I'd been in that situation before, but then I'd also been in a warzone with an armed team to cover me.

Now I was in a place I called home, surrounded by folks I cared about. Why would anyone be watching me? What changed recently that would cause this now? Was I putting Josie and Kaylin in danger?

I may not know the answers, but the threat was real, and I wouldn't be caught out again. I flung my breakfast scraps out onto the ground and took my dishes back into the trailer, tossing them in the sink.

I reached under my pillow and pulled out a subcompact Smith and Wesson M$P compact .45 in an inside-the-waistband holster. It was a perfect weapon for concealed carry and I like it had the physical safety. I popped the clip out and verified the rounds were seated. I then racked the slide back, making sure no round was in the chamber. Slapping the clip back in, I set the safety and tucked the rig into my pants at the center of my back, pulling my t-shirt down and over it. Time for a picnic.

I pulled up to Josie's and parked behind their cars. I rang the doorbell and again heard the pounding of feet. The door flung open, and I found myself looking down at Kaylin. Before I could get a 'hi' out, she was already running back into the house.

"MOOOMMMM, MR. JACOB IS HERE!"

Figuring it was safe enough, I stepped into the house, closing the front door behind me. Flora poked her head out of the kitchen.

"Hey, Jacob, come on in," she greeted me, turning back into the kitchen.

I followed her as she walked back over to one of the counters and began working on something in a big plastic pitcher.

"Here," she said, nodding at a spoon that was sticking up out of the pitcher. "You stir up the tea."

I started stirring as Flora poured in a cup of sugar. The tea in the pitcher was piping hot and looked to be just the tea, no extra water. Someone had been paying attention in tea prep class.

I stirred the hot tea mix until the sugar was good and dissolved. As I tapped the spoon against the pitcher, Flora was back at my side with a big thermos full of ice.

I poured the mix into the thermos and stirred, dissolving a lot of the ice. I topped it off with cold water as Flora added a bit more ice. We now had ourselves a thermos of delicious Southern goodness.

Flora opened a cupboard next to the sink and grinned at me.

"Help a short person out?" she asked, pointing to some cups on the top shelf.

"Sure, it's what we tall people live for."

Reaching up, I grabbed the two cups she indicated and handed them to her. One of them had a small ridge on the side of it. I watched as she stacked the other cup inside that one, then slid the ridged cup into a corresponding slot on the thermos.

"What would we short people do without our tall slaves?" she asked, grinning and punching me lightly in the arm.

I glanced around but didn't see anyone. What I was about to tell her had been a slight embarrassment growing up so I didn't want anyone else to hear.

"When I started high school, I was only four foot ten. Couldn't jump up and touch a basketball net. Used to walk under the volleyball nets without touching them. Barely broke 100 pounds."

"You were such a shrimp."

I turned my head to see Josie leaning against the refrigerator.

She laughed and came over to me, leaning in for a kiss. It was a nice one, perfect for viewing by children and mothers of all ages. Her eyes sparkled as she looked up at me.

"Hey," she said, slightly breathless.

"Hey," I replied, kissing her lightly again before she stepped over to her mom.

"Tea ready?" she asked. Flora pointed at the thermos on the cabinet.

"Grab the thermos Shorty, and let's go," said Josie, heading back into the front room.

I rolled my eyes, grabbing the thermos as Flora burst out into giggles. I gave her the evil eye, and she tried to look contrite but failed miserably. It was easy to see where Josie got it from.

Flora followed us to the door. "You kids stay out of trouble," she ordered. Josie merely laughed as she hugged her, kissing her on the cheek. "Be back about three."

We stopped at Ferguson's Deli on the way out and picked up sandwiches, potato salad, and a few other odds and ends, putting them all in the blue cooler I had in the back of the truck.

Arriving at the marina, I pulled into the small gravel parking lot off to the left, where the owners had cleaned up about an acre of lakefront amongst the trees. Picnic tables dotted the area, each spaced far enough away from the others to allow some privacy.

Josie picked a table as close to the lake as she could get and still have a bit of shade. She brought out a small linen tablecloth that was decorated with delicate flowers and leaves weaving around the edge, then flipped it out over the table, using some clips to secure it in place.

I spread out the food while she poured the drinks. I smiled when she sat beside me instead of across from me.

Today. My earlier questions boiled down to right now. I was going to tell her *today*. Well, at least that was the plan. Unfortunately, I had not briefed Josie on this plan.

She took a sip of tea before twisting around so that she could straddle the bench and face me. She twirled her fingers at me. I put down the sandwich I had been about to bite into and spun on the bench so that we were now face-to-face.

Josie placed her hands on my knees, looked me right in the eye, and blasted the shit right out of me.

"You didn't answer my question the other night. So, let's try again. Jacob, how did you get that scar under your eye?"

When was I going to learn not to underestimate this woman? Before I could respond, she fired her second shot.

"You've deflected on me twice when I've asked about your past. So, let's try this. I think we both know where this thing between us seems to be going, yes?" she asked, meeting my gaze.

I nodded, not trusting myself to speak yet.

"Good. I know it's quick, fast, and hard to believe given both our histories, but I know how I feel about you, how I feel about us. However," she said, holding up her finger at me, "I'm clueless about much of your past."

She reached out and gently touched my chest with that finger, smiling.

"But I like what I *do* know about the man in front of me. The man who is fiercely protective of those he likes, who dances with a little girl and makes her feel like she is a true princess, and who rescues hiking damsels in distress. *That's* the man I know. So, if you don't want to tell me about things in your past, then don't. It doesn't change a thing. But I'm letting you know that I want to know *everything* about you."

I was clenching and unclenching my jaw, trying to get my pulse under control as she drank some of her tea. She put her glass down, and that same finger reached up to trace the scar.

"That Saturday, Ken told me some serious shit about you. He also told me I had to ask you about it if I wanted more details. Jacob, there is *nothing* you can tell me that is chasing me away," she said softly. "You and I both know how the process works, how communication is key. So, I'm asking you to trust me, and if you're good with it, tell me."

I was frozen, conflicted. What she asked required opening up a chest of very old hurts that I locked away almost fifteen years ago. I looked at her, looked into those eyes, and saw understanding, curiosity, and what I dared to hope was love.

If what I was feeling for her was true, I would have to tell her eventually. I nodded, took a deep breath, and ripped the lid open on the chest.

"I got the scar the night my sister was abducted and raped."

Her eyes widened, and she gripped my knees tightly.

"I grew up in a place called Clarksville, Tennessee. It's a medium-sized town up near the Kentucky border. Populations about 100,000. A large Army base is also there, so the count was always changing.

"My dad was a general contractor and built houses for a living. From the time I could be on a job site, he took me with him. I was helping to frame houses by the time I was fourteen, wiring electrical by fifteen. By the end of my junior year of high school, I could pretty much do anything with regards to building a house except block a foundation. I knew where my future was leading, and I was good with it.

"My sister, Joanna, was older than me by a year but was also a junior. She'd gotten really sick when she was younger. She missed so much school that they had to hold her back a year in elementary school. I loved my sister, Josie. We had our occasional spat, but overall, I loved her, and she loved me. We took care of each other, had each other's backs. I would have died for her."

I paused, taking a few more deep breaths to help the tightening in my chest. Josie gave my knees another light squeeze.

"I was working late one night. My car was in the shop, so she gave me a lift to work and was picking me up. It was a nice night, so she decided she wanted to go for a walk down by the river. We had a small park next to the water with a nice walking path, perfect for nights like that one. We had a big full moon and there wasn't anyone else around.

"As we walked into the parking area near the boat ramp, a van turned in from the street. We didn't think anything of it, as this was a popular spot. All seemed okay until the van pulled up beside us and the side door flew open. Three guys jumped out. Two of them grabbed her, and one grabbed me. She fought them as they shoved her in the van. I couldn't move; the one holding me was huge and held me like I was a baby. No matter how much I struggled and screamed, I couldn't do anything.

"Once they got her in the van, the guy holding me let go, shoving me backwards as he climbed in behind his buddies. I was jumping towards the open door when the guy backhanded me in the head. He must have been wearing a ring on that hand because something split my head open right at the eye. I slammed into the pavement, unconscious."

Josie squeezed my hands again. "Are you sure you want to continue?" she asked softly.

I nodded. "I woke up when the paramedics were working on me. Took me a few moments to figure out where I was. There was a police officer with the EMTs, and I started yelling and screaming about my sister. I managed to calm down enough to tell the officer what happened. He called in the abduction, and dispatch sent the word out to both city and county patrol units. My parents met my ambulance at the hospital. I was released around two in the morning, and we spent the rest of the night sitting in the front room staring at the phone. I wanted to go out and start looking but my mom had a death grip on my hand and wouldn't let go."

I took a moment to gaze out over the lake, memories boiling inside of me. I clenched my fists so hard that I thought my fingernails would draw blood from my hands. Josie got up to sit behind me, wrapping her arms around my torso. She hugged me, not saying anything.

"Thankfully, they found Joanna alive later that day on the other side of the river, about twelve miles from where she had been taken. The assholes dumped her on some back road. Our family was torn to shreds that day. Mom couldn't stop crying, and Joanna just stared out into nothing, not saying anything. Dad threw himself into work. I had to watch as my family slowly broke into pieces.

"Everything changed for me that night. I'd never, ever felt so helpless. I failed my sister. What happened to her was my fault because I wasn't strong enough to protect her."

Josie moved back around to sit in front of me, taking my hands as she did. Her face was wet from tears and her eyes reflected the hurt she was feeling for me. "Oh, honey, that's not true. You were what, sixteen? How were you supposed to fight off three grown men?" she asked.

"Thirty-five-year-old Jacob knows that now, but sixteen-year-old Jacob didn't. I swore an oath to myself that night. I would never, ever, be in a position that I couldn't protect my family or loved ones. I saw an Army recruiter next week. I was too young to sign up, but he told me all the things I needed to do to get ready.

"I had about a year to prepare. Weightlifting, karate, running. Anything I could do to get bigger, stronger. I quit my job and devoted myself to my goal as well as to help take care of my sister. I didn't date, didn't hang out with my friends, nothing. When school started back for our senior year, Joanna was never out of my sight for long. The counselors helped by adjusting our schedules so that she and I had every class together.

"My body finally decided it understood what I was trying to do and cooperated. I grew some in my junior year, but nothing like my senior year. By the time I graduated, I was a shade over six feet tall and weighed 220 pounds, all muscle. The army recruiter was shocked, to say the least, when I showed up the day after I graduated high school."

I paused to take a drink. My throat was dry from all the talking. But, with the tale almost finished, the telling was getting easier. Josie squeezed my hands and then reached up to caress one side of my face. She patted my cheek, then returned to holding my hands.

"I threw myself into the Army. I was the perfect soldier, focused on all aspects of the training, anything that could help me protect, to …"

"Kill," she said softly, finishing for me.

I nodded. "I would have killed all three of those men if I had been able to. I had a plan. After I was done with my training and was assigned to my first unit, I was going to go home, track them down, and kill them."

"Honey, I don't think that's what your sister or your family would have wanted you to do. That kind of revenge really fucks you up. I can only imagine what they said to you."

My jaw locked up again.

"What?" she asked.

I sighed, averting my gaze. "I never got a chance to tell them about my plan. While I was away at basic training, Joanna made all her pain go away. I wasn't there to protect her. Again."

Josie's slight gasp drew my eyes back to her. Tears were slowly falling down her cheeks. I brushed them away.

"Mom never recovered from Joanna's death. She lost her zest for life. About two years after Joanna, Mom passed in her sleep. The doctor put down natural causes, but we knew it was a broken heart."

"And your dad?"

"He sold everything and left, not saying anything to anyone. I have a post office box that I maintain in Clarksville. It's the address he had when he left. I change the forwarding directions every time I move. I usually got a postcard every year near my birthday, giving me an idea of where he was. But it's been years since I've heard from him. I can only assume he's cut all ties or has gone to meet Mom."

Josie climbed up into my lap and wrapped her arms around me, pulling my head down to her shoulder. She didn't say anything, instead simply holding me as the emotions drained away. After a few moments, she pulled back and looked at me with eyes sparkling with tears but full of caring.

"I'm sorry for making you live through that, but I'm glad you told me. It only reinforces what I said earlier."

I caressed the side of her face, and she kissed my hand.

"Josie, I want you to know something. I think I lo—" and every instinct I had from years of combat began screaming 'danger'. I pulled myself free from Josie, pushing her down onto the bench. I stood up, looking around quickly, my hand going to my waistband.

"What the *hell?*" she asked, not pleased with me dumping her to the bench.

I didn't answer because I was looking at the far tree line. A man in tactical gear stood there. He raised his hand and pointed a finger at me, like a gun. He smiled and waved at me, then beckoned to me.

I turned to Josie, drawing my weapon.

"Get in the truck and stay there. If I'm not back in twenty minutes, you get the hell out of here. Call Rick and tell him to get his Marine ass here and that I need help."

"Jacob, what the hell has got ... Is that a *gun?*" she demanded.

I jacked a round into the chamber, flipped the safety off, and looked back at her. She sat wide-eyed on the bench.

"Twenty minutes, Josie. Get to the truck. *Now!*"

I turned before she could say anything else and made my way to the tree line. Mr. Sneaky didn't wait for me, turning and melting back into the trees.

I moved low and fast, hitting the woods within seconds. I paused there and reached out with my senses. A slight sound to the left pulled my attention that way. I eased around the tree I was perched next to, weapon up and ready, eyes scanning.

I reached the area where I thought the sound came from and found nothing. No tracks, nothing out of the ordinary. Whoever this guy was, he was good. Really good.

I kept easing forward, staying on the balls of my feet, never letting my eyes linger on one spot. The undergrowth kept the sound down but it also meant there were no footprints to follow, not even a broken twig to alert me to where this asshole was hiding.

I moved forward another forty feet and paused again. Just as quickly as they had come, the danger signals died. I stayed put, listening and watching. Gradually, sounds came back to the forest. I clicked the safety on and slid my weapon back into its home at my back.

It took me a few moments to clear the tree line and make it back to the picnic table. Josie saw me coming and bailed out of the truck, making a beeline for me. She wasn't a happy camper. By the time I got to the table, she was standing there, hands on her hips and pissed.

"You want to tell me what the fuck is going on? And since when do you carry a damn *gun*?" she growled.

I held up one finger as I pulled my weapon back out. Ejecting the clip, I racked the slide back and caught the expelled round. I loaded it back into the clip, inserted the clip, made sure the safety was set, and placed the gun back into my holster. I finally looked back at her.

"What's going on is someone is stalking me. Probably the asshole I just tracked into the woods."

"Okay, why stalk you and why the damn gun?"

"Don't know why, and the gun is to protect myself and those around me."

"Just because some guy was watching us from the woods?"

"That's the third time he's ghosted me and the first time I've been able to see him. Rather, he *let* me see him."

She went pale. "When were the other two times? Wait … the other night at putt-putt. You got all weird in the parking lot. That was this guy?"

"Probably, but since I didn't see him, I can't be sure. The first time was when someone broke into my … place."

"Have you told Rick about this?"

"Talked to him after the break-in. That's when I also told him I'd be carrying."

"Were you carrying that gun at dinner the other night?" she asked, arms crossed.

"What? No. I don't usually carry. No need to."

The compressed lips and hard eyes told me she was none too pleased with me. "Well, that's good to know. I know you and Rick probably like shooting those things, but they scare me. Please, let me know if you're carrying that thing."

I simply nodded, my frustration finally boiling over.

"*Fuck!*" I turned away from her, trying to get myself under control.

"*Now* what?" she asked, glancing around.

"One date. I just wanted one damn date where I had you all to myself. I dump all that crap on you, and the asshole shows up. I swear the universe hates me."

Her arms came around me, hugging me and then gently turning me. I found myself once again gazing into her mesmerizing eyes.

"You didn't dump any shit on me; you answered my question. Later tonight, once your brain catches up, you'll realize it was a good thing. As to the date Jacob, I wanted it as much as you. We both want the same thing, but life is just getting in the way. Make no mistake, I want some alone time with you. The couch wasn't enough."

I blushed as I recalled the couch, and she chuckled.

Josie raised a brow. "Couch memories?"

I leered at her and nodded, bringing my arms around her waist.

"So, what do we do? Run off to Spokane for a weekend or worse, grab a room here in town? The gossips already have enough to talk about. Your house is out for obvious reasons, and I sleep on a bench in my trailer."

We both stood there quietly, relishing the moment before she laughed and kissed me deeply. When she broke the kiss, I pulled back a bit.

"What?"

"I just had a great idea. You are so lucky that your girlfriend is such a smart woman," she said, practically beaming.

"Girlfriend? I don't remember asking you to go steady or giving you my class ring."

She rolled her eyes. "Oh *please*. Like anyone other than my boyfriend gets to feel my boobs up."

"Then as your boyfriend I must say how wonderful they felt and how I want to feel them again."

She laughed again, although this one was throatier.

"If you liked the girls, you are gonna love my—" I stopped her talking by kissing her hard, not letting her finish that statement. I had a pretty good idea what she was about to say, and I wasn't sure I could handle that at the moment.

When we pulled apart, she laughed again.

"Chicken," she said.

"Yes, I am. Now, you were saying something about being smart?"

"Can I assume, based on our conversation and by that impressive pole poking me, that you would like to, how do they say, take our relationship to the next level? The horizontal one?"

I cracked up. "Dammit, woman. You don't beat around the bush, do you?"

She grinned at me. "I'll take that as a yes. So, we both know what's going on this Sunday, correct?"

I nodded. Ken and Janey's upcoming wedding.

"Soooo, what you don't know is that with all the planned rehearsals and bride parties, et cetera, I didn't want to have to worry about the late-night parties, getting drunk, and staggering home. Your very smart girlfriend just happens to have a hotel suite already reserved through Sunday—JACOB!"

I picked her up by the waist and swung her around several times before setting her back down to the ground. She laughed and tried to catch her breath.

"I'm guessing you're in favor of that plan—no! Leave me on the ground!" she cried out, stopping me from lifting her up again. She took a moment to catch her breath as she ran her hand idly across my chest. "Look, Mom is taking Kaylin to Seattle for a week starting Saturday. One final big trip before school starts. Do you work Saturday?"

"I do, but I should be done by four."

"Well, text me when you're done and on your way. I'll add your name to the reservation. Grab a key and come up to room 201. We have until the wedding on Sunday too, well, I'll just leave *that* to your imagination."

Her expression changed in a flash as her eyes filled with an evil glint. She reached down and grabbed me through the front of my now extremely tight and uncomfortable jeans. Slowly stroking me, her voice dropped to a throaty whisper.

"Maybe you can introduce me to this on Sunday?"

My voice rumbled low in my throat as I devoured her lips. It took all my willpower to keep from pulling her down onto the very convenient picnic table. When we parted, her expression was humorous and sexy.

"Come on, let's clean up and go take Kaylin to Gordo's," she said, her smile lighting her face.

I nodded. "Okay. I'll call Rick and update him as well."

Ten minutes later, we left to make a little girl's night and ruin a sheriff's day.

TWENTY-FOUR

Josie

"Kaylin, did you pack your toothbrush?"

My six-going-on-twenty-year-old rolled her eyes. "Yes, I did. Grandma checked my bag, and you checked my bag. I got everything. Sheesh!"

Before I could address Miss 'Tude, Mom called out from the kitchen, "Josie, can you help me for a moment?"

I glanced down at the mini-me who stood there, staring at me, daring me to ask her about anything else. I rolled my eyes all the way to the ceiling before realizing I had done it. I turned and left the battlefield to see what Mom needed.

Mom was unloading the dishwasher when I got to the kitchen. "Sweetie, can you finish this?" she asked.

"Sure." Pulling out the upper tray, I began putting the glasses away while Mom sat down at the breakfast table. I glanced at her, not paying attention to what I was supposed to be doing. I almost broke a glass against the countertop when I failed to lift it high enough to clear the counter edge.

"Josie, you need to calm down. We'll be gone in an hour, and then you can go do unspeakable things to Jacob," Mom told me, her voice carrying a hint of humor.

I whirled on her, planning to protest, but the twinkle in her eyes and the grin on her face had me quickly turning back to the dishwasher, hiding my rapidly reddening cheeks.

"How—I mean, I'm not sure what you're talking about."

I kept my tone light, neutral. She had the decency to only laugh a little bit.

"Sweetie, I haven't seen you this nervous since your junior prom when you were waiting on Randal Mattson to come pick you up."

Letting out a deep breath, I gave up on the dishes and sat across from her at the table. I toyed with the salt and pepper shakers, moving them from spot to spot. Mom grabbed them, setting them out of my reach. She fixed me with a penetrating stare, giving me the feeling that she was surveying my soul.

"What's got you so nervous? Evidence of your understanding of sex is currently sitting in the back room. I also seem to remember waking *someone* up on the couch a while ago with their clothes somewhat, shall we say, out of place."

I groaned. "Mom, that was just … I don't know, a little fun in the dark. This … this is a big step. What if he … as my voice trailed off, my heart began pounding in my chest.

"Josie, look at me."

I met her gaze and saw a look of pure love and understanding. She reached over and clasped my hand lightly, smiling softly. "Sweetheart, you're putting *way* too much pressure on yourself. Do you *honestly* think that man is going to reject you? Honestly?"

I snorted lightly at hearing Mom voice my biggest fear, feeling that emotion begin to lessen. "I guess it *does* sound kind of silly when you put it that way."

"It does. I never asked, but are you still on the pill?"

"Yeah. I needed them for a while when my periods were bad after Kaylin."

"That's one hurdle out of the way," she said. "Never really liked condoms myself. I always wanted to feel your dad when he—"

I stuck my fingers in my ears before she could embarrass me further.

"LALALALALALA. I DON'T WANT TO HEAR ABOUT MY DAD'S *ANYTHING*!"

Mom broke into laughter. "Then I guess I shouldn't tell you about the small mattress we had in the back storage room for quickies?"

I thudded my head against the table. "Great. Now I have to get some brain bleach to get rid of the imagery. Thanks, mother o' mine."

"What time are you meeting him?" she asked, interrupting my perfectly good head-clearing table bangs.

"He gets off his shift at four, and then he's coming to the hotel."

"Good. A favor, please?"

Raising my head, and trying not to wince at the pain, I glared at her. "I'm almost afraid to ask."

Mom gave me a pointed look. "If you come back here, make sure to wash the sheets and air the house out. There is to be no sex in my or your daughter's room. Oh, and if you break this table, you're buying a new one."

She gazed lovingly at the table as she softly caressed its worn surface.

"If only this table could talk," she said quietly. Her face filled with memories and longing. I then swore to myself to eat all my meals standing at the stove.

My stunned and disturbed looks only seemed to bring Mom more joy.

"What can I say sweetie? Your mom and dad had sex. A lot."

Her laughter followed me all the way to my room as I tried not to imagine this and failed miserably.

While it seemed an eternity, 3 p.m. finally arrived. Mom herded Kaylin towards the door with suitcases and stuffed animals. After many kisses, hugs, and reminders to listen to Grandma, Kaylin was buckled in and raring to go.

Mom gave me a hug as she whispered in my ear, "Tell that man if he doesn't make you scream, I'll have words with him."

My face turned beet red as she got in her car, laughing at me. I waved until they were out of sight before turning and streaking back into the house.

I packed earlier, but I was sorely lacking in the sexy clothing department. It'd been two years since I'd had sex. Single moms didn't normally spend money on teddies or corsets.

Staring at myself in the mirror, I made a wardrobe decision. Yanking my current outfit off, including my underwear, I slipped on one of the lace sets. I rifled through my closet until I found my favorite dark blue sundress. Slipping it on, I shivered at the exquisite feeling of the dress and lace caressing my skin. Finishing with the buttons, I did a small twirl, admiring myself in the mirror.

I'd shaved *everything* during my shower this morning. I hoped Jacob liked a bare woman since I hadn't had a bush since Kaylin was born. The nurses shaved me for the delivery, and Greg fell in love with the hairless me the first time he saw it. Besides, I liked the way it felt, especially wearing the current lace thong.

My toiletries and makeup were already packed in their carry case. The bag holding my dress and shoes hung on the back of the bedroom door. It took three trips to the car to get everything loaded. Sitting in the driver's seat after the last trip, I took several deep, calming breaths before pulling out of the driveway. It was a supreme effort to maintain the speed limit.

By 4 p.m., I was pacing in my hotel room, my stomach filled with overactive butterflies. Two years was a long time. I talked a big game at the park that day about being ready for the next level, but in reality, I was scared shitless.

Why was I so scared? This was Jacob. A man I was falling for with each moment together. Hell, if I was being honest with myself, I'd already fallen in love.

Could it be the thought of having sex with someone other than Greg? No, that couldn't be it. I enjoyed that time on the couch and would have kept going if not for Kaylin. But that had been in the dark.

This time, he would see me in the light. While I wasn't ashamed of my looks, let's face it, I wasn't twenty anymore, and having Kaylin had done a number on my body.

What if he didn't like the stretch marks? What about the slight droop in the girls? What if I disgusted him? Oh great, he was going to take one glance at me and run screaming.

I jumped and almost dropped my phone when it vibrated in my hand along with a chirp of an incoming text message. Tightening my grip, I pulled up the message.

"Hey, ran late. Leaving hospital now. Be there soon."

I quickly texted back one of those kissy face emojis and wondered if it was too late to call this off as I resumed my worried pacing, phone still in hand.

I was standing in the middle of the room when the lock clicked, and the door opened. Jacob took two steps in and let the door shut, his eyes focused on me. Tossing his suit bag on the bed, he walked steadily to me, his eyes locked on mine, his gaze full of promise. I never felt more desired than at that moment.

I melted into his arms. His lips met mine, our tongues wasting no time reacquainting themselves. It seemed like we kissed for hours, but I knew it had only been a few moments. He pulled back and looked at me. Damn. His eyes just pulled me in and held me.

"Hi."

"Hi."

Unbidden, I felt a tremble overtake me. My damn head was making its presence known. Jacob looked at me, confusion in his eyes.

"Josie?"

Dammit. I snuggled up to him, kissing his chin, hoping to distract him. He groaned lightly but wasn't letting it go.

"Talk to me, Josie. What's wrong?" I could hear the concern in his voice as I buried my head into his chest, muffling my own.

"Promise you won't laugh?"

"I promise. Now, what's wrong?"

"I'm nervous and a little bit scared."

"Is that all?" he said, raising a brow. "Sweetheart, I've had butter-flies doing dive bomb runs in my stomach all day."

Sweetheart? Did he just call me sweetheart?

I really liked the sound of that from him.

"Why are you scared?" I asked. "I didn't think you were scared of anything."

He softly kissed me again. Pulling back, he placed a single finger under my chin, raising my head and bringing us eye to eye.

"I'm scared because I've been given a chance to make love to the most beautiful, woman I've ever known. She is a walking ten in jeans and ponytail, hell in a ball pit, not to mention a great mother. For reasons I can't figure out, someone so far out of my league likes me enough to let me that close. That scares the shit out of me. I'm scared that I'll mess this up and disappoint her."

My mind was spinning. How could he possibly think that *I* was out of *his* league?

"Jacob, you should get your eyes checked. I'm not sure what you're seeing, but it isn't me. I'm a single mom and have the stretch marks to prove it. I don't have toned abs or a tiny waist. As to being out of your league, honey, I'm scared that you won't find me … enough. That you'll take one look at me naked and run."

He tenderly kissed me again.

"We're a pair, aren't we? This is good. We're talking and laying out our fears. If we can talk about them, we can get past them. We've both kinda got swept up fast in this thing we have going on. Maybe we're putting too much pressure on ourselves. Worrying ourselves about expectations. Maybe?"

I nodded, and he kissed me again. This man's lips could be the death of me.

"Can I ask you something?" he asked softly. I nodded, waiting expectantly.

"Have you been with anyone since Greg?" I shook my head.

He flashed a sympathetic smile. "Kara was my last. Look, we have all night and most of tomorrow to learn about each other. What say we order something light from room service and slow things down, just let things happen as they happen?"

I gave a huge mental sigh of relief. I'm sure the relief showed on my face, too, because he gave me a small smile and nodded encouragingly.

"I'd really like that."

Jacob nodded and let me go. I sat on the couch and watched as he hung his suit bag in the closet and pulled off his shoes and socks. He grabbed the room service menu and joined me. After comparing choices to tastes, we both settled on chicken Caesar salads and a nice white wine. It was light and wouldn't take long.

After placing the order, he reclined next to me on the couch. I slipped off my shoes and curled my legs underneath myself so I could lean into him. He wrapped his arm around me and took my hand in his.

Jacob's thumb lightly caressed my knuckles, sending small tingles through me. Sighing contentedly, I leaned up and kissed his jaw. He brought his hand up to cup the side of my face, pulling me into a kiss. Long, deep, slow. I'd never felt such emotion in something as simple as a kiss.

Still holding my head, he spoke softly, and I could hear the hesitancy in his voice. "I have a request."

"Yes?

"We haven't been shy about Greg and Kara and what they meant to each of us. I would very much like tonight to be just us. What we like and don't like as us, not what we liked or didn't like with them. Do you think we can do that?"

I laughed softly. "I think we can manage that."

He smiled and pulled me in for another kiss. Damn, what this man's lips did to me. My thong was proving worthless at stopping leakage. I just hoped I didn't stain the back of my dress or the couch.

Just as his hand dropped to my chest, a knock at the door announced the arrival of dinner. Jacob greeted the waiter and signed for the food. Once the door was closed, he sat the elegant silver tray on the small table near the kitchenette.

He once again held my chair out for me and seated me before he took his own place. He poured us a glass of wine and raised his for a toast.

"To us."

I smiled, clinking my glass against his. "To us."

Setting our glasses down, we turned our attention to our salads. Jacob had taken a few bites when he laid down his fork, wiping his mouth with the linen napkin.

"I guess I need to ask about protection. I brought condoms."

"We don't need them; I'm on the pill."

"Good." He nodded. "To be honest, I've never liked them."

I immediately squashed the mom flashbacks that brewed up in my head.

We ate a bit more, talking about the mundane things of our day. The salads hadn't left me feeling stuffed, and the two glasses of wine and casual conversation had gone a long way towards settling my nerves.

Jacob gathered up our dishes once we finished and sat them outside in the hallway. Sipping my wine, I watched him close the door and then begin to rearrange the furniture. Once he had a clear spot near the middle of the floor, he closed the curtains and dimmed the lights.

Satisfied with his effort, he turned on the radio and fiddled with the tuning knob until he found a station playing easy listening music. He walked back to me and held out his hand.

"Dance with me?"

I placed my hand in his and let him pull me to the middle of the room. He enveloped me in his embrace, and we began gliding softly in a small box, staying in the middle of the floor.

As we danced, I laid my head against his shoulder, deeply breathing in his scent. The feel of his chest, the press of him against me as we moved ... I'd never been more turned on, nor more scared. A sudden thought popped into my head.

"Jacob?"

"Hmm?" he said, his hand gliding up my back and sending shivers up my spine.

"What ... what is your biggest fear in a relationship?"

He stopped dancing, a curious expression on his face as he gazed at me.

"Interesting question. Why do you ask that?"

I let one finger toy with the collar of his shirt.

"Because I want this. I want it with you, and I want it to work. I don't want to fuck it up, and I'm scared I'll do just that. Does that make sense?"

He pulled me in close and started dancing again. I snuggled into his chest, placing both my hands around his waist. I felt his hands slide down my sides to rest on mine. We danced for a few more moments, no sounds other than the music and the rustle of our feet on the carpet. My mind drifted to the feel of him in my arms when his answer startled me.

"Cheating."

There was an undertone of anger and hurt in his voice. Someone had hurt him in the past, hurt him badly.

"Were you cheated on?"

He kissed me lightly on the neck, his warm lips sending chills up and down my spine. He kept up our slow, steady movements, and I felt him take in a huge breath, letting it out slowly.

"Once in high school," he answered. "But it was bad in the Army. Guys were always getting 'Dear John' letters or coming back home to find a wife or girlfriend pregnant from someone else. I watched so many marriages break and shatter."

He looked down at me, and I could see the set in his eyes.

"I never could figure out why. Why do that? If you're gonna sleep around, why get married or commit to someone?"

He stopped dancing; his eyes boring into me with his conviction. "I want to be clear, Josie. I'm a 'one and done' kinda guy. No excuses, no 'I was drunk' or 'It was just sex' or 'I was just so lonely.' That's all bullshit."

I nodded. "I agree, Jacob. High school, college, I saw it too. The drama, the hurt, the anger. If it's not working, I'll step, Jacob. I wouldn't do that to you, or to me."

"Good. Just so we're clear, are we in a relationship?"

I laughed softly. "Oh yes, Jacob Berman, we are most definitely in a relationship. One I hope to be in for a long while."

He pulled me in tighter. I looked into his eyes and felt a small shiver run down my spine at the amount of heat pouring into that gaze.

"I really like the sound of that Josie Callison," he murmured. His voice dropped in timber and set off vibrations throughout body and soul.

He kissed me again, but this time was different. Something changed after those words. This kiss held the promise of passion and soon-to-be missing underwear.

Pulling back, he kissed me lightly on the corner of my mouth before moving to my ear, sucking and nibbling the lobe. I hissed and moaned as he blew ever so gently, his hot breath caressing me.

Jacob slowly trailed small kisses along my jaw to my other ear, sometimes nipping softly as he went. My pleasure hummed in my throat, intensifying with each touch of his lips. I could feel how excited he was as I pressed into him, grinding ever so slightly, eliciting a small groan from him.

He turned me and pulled me back against him. As he drew me in tight, his length poked into my ass, and I pushed back against him. His mouth dropped to that small valley where my neck met my shoulder and began kissing my neck, teasing me with those lips.

I reached for his hands and brought them to the girls, cupping them against me. He began kneading me lightly, but I wanted more.

"Harder, baby."

He kept up the kissing and squeezed my breasts harder, pinching my nipples.

I moaned, "*Yesssss*."

Between his wondrous hands on my breasts and my bra dragging against my painfully stiff nipples, I was on fire. As he kept his hands busy, I began rubbing my ass harder against him, stroking that wonderful stiffness. I could have sworn I could feel the heat through his jeans.

I threw my hands back over my head to lay on his shoulders and neck, pushing my chest into his magical hands. I turned my head and kissed him hard, my tongue drilling into his mouth to tangle with his.

I gasped as he suddenly pulled his hands off me. Then he began working at the buttons of my dress. In seconds I felt the cool air on my skin as his hands wasted no time pushing my bra up and out of his way. He cupped me fully with both hands, pinching and pulling my nipples hard.

"Oh god, yes ... more ... more of that ..." I could only pant as he did what I asked. After Kaylin, my nipples had always been sensitive, and I could explode if they were handled right. And he was handling them oh so right.

"*Yes*, Jaco—*Oh* ..." was all I managed to say as a small but powerful orgasm rocked through me. I clamped my hands down on his, holding them tight to my breasts until I was done shuddering.

I quickly worked my dress and bra off, letting them fall to the floor as I turned inside his arms and attacked him.

I frantically tugged his shirt out of his pants, thanking his foresight in wearing a pullover. I wanted him out of these clothes, and I wanted it now.

Taking the hint, he yanked the shirt off over his head, tossing it somewhere. My now free hands tugged his belt free from his pants. My fingers fumbled with the clasp, but I finally grabbed the zipper and yanked it down.

Between me shoving and Jacob using his feet to push, his pants soon flew across the room. Our hands met at his underwear, and they speedily followed the pants.

He pulled me back to him, his mouth finding mine, our tongues renewing their frantic duel. His hands came up between us and captured my breasts, squeezing and flicking my tortured nipples.

I trailed my hand down his stomach, my fingernails grazing against his skin as I reached him and ran my hand down his full length.

Jacob shuddered and moaned into my mouth as I began to stroke him lightly. He was hot and oh so hard. Mom wouldn't have to worry about me screaming. I gripped a bit harder, and he grunted, breaking our kiss.

"That's not ... a pull toy," he growled between clenched teeth.

I stroked his warm flesh, gripping lightly.

"Oh, I don't know. I think it *could* be, don't you?"

He grunted again and stepped backwards, pulling us further into the light from the bedside lamps. For the first time, I saw him without a shirt.

I actually paused, letting go of my new toy as I focused on his scar-riddled body. It was fascinating to behold. I started tracing a small, puckered scar on the front of his left shoulder.

"Shrapnel from a roadside bomb."

"Shrapnel?"

"Fragments of metal from an explosion."

Nodding, I kissed it softly and touched the small pucker on his right shoulder.

"Bullet, through and through. Um, it hit me there, punched all the way through, and came out the back of my shoulder." His voice was growing rougher with each telling. I let my hand drift around his shoulder to confirm the larger pucker. I kissed the smaller one on the front.

I touched and kissed each and every scar as he told me what caused them, his voice growing rougher as the memories brought old pains.

Most of the scars were from shrapnel, but there was also a knife and two other bullet wounds. When I finished my tour, I gave him another deep kiss and reached down to grab him. He danced back out of reach.

"Uh-uh. My turn."

He spun us so that the dim light was more on me than him. He pushed on my shoulder, turning me around slowly and pausing when my back was facing him.

"Nice birthmark," he noted, lightly moving his fingers across the heart-shaped blemish stretching between my shoulder blades.

Jacob lightly traced his calloused fingers down my back. My skin tightened and tingled at his touch as his hands continued down until they caressed both of my cheeks. He leaned forward and whispered into my ear, causing me to moan.

"Very nice ass."

He pushed again until I was facing him. He stepped back slightly, his hands staying on my shoulders as his fingers caressed me. His eyes met mine, then traveled slowly down my body. My insecurities kicked back under his intense gaze.

"Like I said, poochy belly, slightly saggy boobs, and enough stretch marks to—" I started to say, but he held up a finger.

"Stop."

He let his gaze run over me again before he looked back into my eyes. I saw no disgust or revulsion, merely raw hunger. He wanted me as badly as I wanted him.

"You're the most beautiful woman I've ever seen."

A blush started, and my hands crossed at my belly. The heat on my face was matched only by the heat building inside me at his simple declaration. My insecurities waged with my excitement and my arms began to cover my stomach.

Jacob reached out and grabbed them, stopping me. He gently but firmly pushed my hands back down to my side. He took my face between those warm, calloused hands, sliding his thumb across my lips before he kissed them.

"I love your beautiful smile," he said. "It lights up the room when you laugh."

His hands dropped down to caress the tops of my breasts, lazily brushing his fingers down their sides as he held and lifted them. I shivered, my nipples aching for his touch. He grinned at me.

"I love the girls, very much. That miniscule sag you worry about? That's from nourishing a child who drank from them for life."

Shit, where did he come up with this stuff? No one I knew talked like this. I hungered for more.

He bent and lightly kissed and suckled each nipple, and I moaned and gasped. My legs felt weak from the intense feelings.

He dropped to his knees, his hands encircling my waist. Starting just under my breasts, he started planting small kisses. He drifted those lips to the middle of my chest before beginning a trek downward. Every kiss was like an explosion of heat on my skin.

When he got to my stomach and the stretch marks, he paused.

"See? I told you, nothing …"

I wanted to say more but my voice died away as he moved to one side of my stomach and began kissing my stretch marks. Every single one.

"Josie, the scars I have, they're from death and destruction. I got them from taking life, sometimes violently."

One finger began tracing all of my marks, causing me to groan at his teasing touch.

"These? *These* are from giving life. These are badges of the highest honor. Never, ever be ashamed of them. Especially with me."

Jacob hooked his thumbs into either side of my thong, pulling slowly downward until the soaked bit of lace lay puddled at my feet. He leaned forward until his nose almost brushed me, deeply inhaling my scent. My legs felt weak, and I grabbed his shoulders to keep myself steady.

"Intoxicating," he whispered gruffly.

Still on his knees, he turned me towards the bed. He pushed me backwards until the backs of my calves hit the mattress and I sat.

He pushed between my legs, taking a nipple into his mouth, sucking and nipping. I held him there while he switched to the other. I could feel my release building as he kept moving back and forth, keeping me in sweet agony and bringing me right to the edge.

He must have sensed something. He sucked one nipple hard and pinched and tugged the other one. I gripped his head, my fingers digging into his scalp as the muscles in my stomach tightened and rippled. My orgasm rocked through me as I tossed my head back, my eyes closed in ecstasy.

"Jaaccoobb!" was all I could scream as my pleasure rose sharply and then began to ebb. He kissed my nipples lightly, put his hands on my shoulders, and gently pushed me backwards. I took the hint and eagerly laid back. He didn't follow, staying where he was as I reclined.

He started kissing the inside of my left knee, landing two or three heated touches before working his way up my inner thigh. My breathing quickened as he got closer to my soaking lips, lips that I ached for him to kiss. Teasing me, he moved to the junction of my right thigh and started kissing down to my knee.

"You *bastard* ..."

Jacob merely laughed and began the return trip, nipping and kissing his way upwards. My heart beat faster as he again neared where I wanted him.

He gave me a light kiss and a flick of his tongue before quickly moving on his way. I was panting, my hips lifting ever so slightly towards his face.

"You ... you fucking tease."

His laugh was evil, cruel, and so damn sexy as he kept up his play, kissing my upper thigh and all the area around where I wanted his tongue. I was panting hard now.

"Jaacc ... Jacob, I swear ... oh *fuck* ... if you ... if you don't ... lick my ...YESSSSS!"

I threw my hips up as Jacob licked from the bottom of my lips all the way up, his tongue lightly tapping the nub at the top. I didn't even get to cry out again before he got serious.

His lips and tongue were in constant motion now. He sucked and licked, working me almost to the point of release before backing down. It was agony. It was the most intense pleasure I've ever felt. I was only dimly aware that he had my legs over his shoulders as he devoured me.

"Jac ... Jacob, please ... you ... *Shit* ... bastard!"

I was panting and babbling now, thrusting myself at him, willing him to finish what he kept starting.

As if reading my frustration, he sped up, his tongue tap-dancing on my clit. I could feel my release starting at my toes.

"Yes ... yes ... more ... baby ... I'm ... YESSSS!"

My orgasm crashed over me like a wave, my back arching upwards. As it rushed to its peak, he pushed one finger inside me and strummed that ridged spot. I clamped my thighs around his head, thrust hard against his mouth, and exploded.

Jacob's finger and tongue didn't stop. As his finger stroked, his lips sucked my clit in hard. A second orgasm, no less intense than the first, raced through my being. I cried out in pain. It felt so good it hurt. Jacob immediately stopped.

I dropped back against the mattress, my lungs heaving, my muscles rippling aftershocks. So good. Gods, so good.

He moved up and laid beside me, gathering me in his arms. I kissed him deeply, and our tongues dueled again. I must have gushed buckets because I could taste me all over him. I caught my breath, willing my heart rate to slow, allowing me to recover.

"Jacob ... I ... that ... *fuck* ..."

He merely chuckled, the smug bastard. Then he kissed me again. He pulled back and captured my eyes with his. Even through my orgasm induced haze, I could see a volcano of heat in that stare, that look.

"I want you."

Those three words took my heart right back to racing. I laid back, pulling at his shoulders until he moved on top of me, his hips falling naturally between my spread open legs. I grabbed that iron-hard warmth of his and placed it right at my drenched opening.

"I'm yours," I promised.

He thrust forward. As soaked as I was, he slid all the way in, burying himself completely as our hips met.

"Yess! Jacob ... *fuck* ..." I moaned, and then I stopped talking and started grunting as he started moving.

The sound of our bodies slapping together filled the room. I wrapped my legs around him, locking my ankles above his ass so I could pull him to me harder. Propping himself on his elbows to either side of me, he dropped his mouth to my chest and began ravishing my nipples.

My world centered on the point where our bodies crashed together, our passion driving us harder and faster. It didn't take long for our climax to occur.

"Now ... now, Jacob ... now, baby ... with meeeee!"

My release blasted out of and through me. I clamped down on him, squeezing him as he thrust harder into me, slamming me down against the bed and burying himself deep.

"Jooosieee," Jacob cried out as he exploded, bathing my insides with his warmth.

He collapsed, rolling us together to lay on our sides facing each other. Grabbing my ass in both his hands, he pulled me in close so that he stayed inside me. It was several moments before our breathing slowed enough to talk.

"Josie, that … I've never felt that before. You've ruined me for anyone else."

I smiled at him, bringing my hand up to caress the side of his face.

"There isn't going to be anyone else, Jacob. Like I said. You, me, relationship. And for the record, we're so going to be doing that a lot more. A hell of a lot more."

"I like the sound of that," he said with a grin. Then his eyes filled with such an intensity it made me a bit uneasy.

"Jacob?"

He captured my hand with his, bringing it between us.

"Josie, I love you."

I almost crushed his hand. My heart skipped a beat at hearing those words. I stared at him, not trusting that he actually spoke the words. His expression turned from one of love to confusion.

"Shit. I'm sorry. I shouldn't … I mean, you don't—*mmrph.*"

I crushed my mouth to his, kissing him hard. I kept kissing him until we both broke free, gasping for air. I was trying to laugh and cry at the same time. Jacob looked like he wanted to jump out of bed and run away. Laughing won out, and I kissed him again.

"Jacob, I love you too."

"You do? Really?"

I pulled him closer, letting my forehead rest gently against his. "It's scary how much I love you, Jacob, and how fast it happened. But it feels so right."

"I've argued with myself for days," he admitted. "This couldn't be, it could be. I wanted to tell you at the picnic. But tonight, with you? It was so amazing. Life's too short, and I don't want to live another moment without you."

For the next few minutes, he simply kissed me. Sometimes deep and slow, sometimes light and soft. When we finally broke apart, I felt a deep sense of unity, almost as if it were a physical connection.

His finger lightly traced my jawline, his eyes shining as he looked at me. "I love you, Josie, and I'm going to tell you that each and every day."

I grinned at him. "Say it again."

"I. Love. You," he whispered softly, kissing me between each word.

"I love you, tooorrghh." My proclamation ended in a small yawn. Some sexy wench I was.

Jacob laughed, pulling me closer.

"Maybe a short nap and then you can show me how much you love me."

He slipped out of me as he rolled onto his back. I threw my arm across his chest and curled up next to the man I loved. Sleep claimed me quickly.

A phone ringing pulled me back to consciousness. I was tucked up against warmth, my hair was everywhere, and as I shifted, a dull pain shot between my legs. Memory returned, bringing a smile to my face.

I was in a bed with Jacob, who loved me, and there had been sex. Lots and lots of sex. I dimly remembered the floor, or was it the couch? No, definitely the couch as he took me from behind. The shower was in the mix somewhere. All of that served to explain the raw feeling between my legs. I was woefully out of practice.

I poked Jacob. "If you really love me, answer that damn phone. What ungodly time is it, and who the hell is calling at this hour?"

He fumbled with the phone as I tried to keep myself plastered to him. "We need to get up. Wedding is in two and a half hours."

I grumbled as I rolled and squirmed to sit up, embarrassed to see a line of drool connecting me to him. Yep, that was sexy as all get out.

"Hello," he said.

As I watched, his sex-contented sleepy face went cold and serious in a blink of an eye. He listened for a few minutes before detangling himself from me and rolled over to sit up. "How many, Lisa?" He was sliding off the bed now, grabbing at clothes. "How long?"

He tried to hop into his underwear with one hand while the other held the phone.

"Okay, get the rooms prepped and the doctors notified. I'll be there in ten minutes." He tossed the phone down on the bed and kept dressing. "Logging accident. We've got multiple casualties coming in."

I got up, helping him gather his wayward attire. While he finished dressing, I grabbed a warm washcloth from the bathroom. I waited until his hands were free to hand it to him. One eyebrow quirked up, and I grinned.

"Wipe your face. I don't think the nurses want to smell your girlfriend."

He blushed and began washing his face. "Good thinking."

"Do you think you'll make it to the wedding?"

Jacob shrugged. "No way to tell without seeing the injuries," he said, pulling on his shoes. Dressed, he grabbed his suit bag from the closet.

I shook my head. "Leave it. Change here after you get back."

"Easier to shower and change at the hospital," he said with a smile. "Gets me back quicker to you." He grabbed me for a quick hug. My boobs pressed into his arm, and part of him woke up, tenting his pants. Grinning, I reached down, grabbing the newly awakened part of him.

"Some part of you doesn't want to go."

He groaned and pushed me away. "He doesn't get a say. I gotta go. Call you when I can. Love you."

I yanked him back to me, giving him a kiss that left him with no doubt what I was wanting. I dropped my hand down and grabbed his now full erection, squeezing and stroking it a few times before pushing him away.

"I love you too. That will have to hold you till later."

He scowled at me as he opened the door, trying to adjust himself.

"Dammit. Do you know what a pain in the ass it is to drive with a hard-on?"

I broke out laughing as the door closed. Jacob had *no* idea what evil was yet.

TWENTY-FIVE

Josie

The wedding went off without a hitch, but I honestly didn't remember one single minute of it. All I could think about was Jacob. Waking up with the man I loved, a man who loved me. Not to mention the mind-blowing sex. Walking and sitting had been a bit painful but so damn worth it.

Once the wedding party went off for pictures, the DJ set up. Music filled the hall, along with background conversations as guests began moving along the buffet line, consuming the variety of appetizers and sweets. I settled down at my table with my punch and cake. Just as I picked up my fork, I heard someone call out.

"Josie!"

I looked up to see Brianna threading her way through the tables, pausing to say hello to those she knew. When she reached mine, I stood up. She sat her plate down and gave me a hug.

"I was looking all over for you. Where have you …" Her voice trailed off. She stepped back and looked at me funny, her head cocked to one side. Then her eyebrows flew straight up.

"Oh my god, you didn't?" she squealed, squeezing both my arms.

"Didn't what?"

She answered my question by grabbing my arm at the elbow and beginning to pull me towards the back of the hall. I almost had to break out in a fast trot to keep up.

"Brianna, slow down. Brianna … this isn't a track meet!" Apparently, no one informed Brianna of the indoor speed limits at these events. She continued to drag me along until she found a door leading into a back hallway. She yanked it open and kept walking, towing me along like a pull toy.

There were several doors off the hall, and she kept trying them until one opened and she pulled me inside, closing the door behind us.

"Okay. Spill it."

I looked at her like she was crazy, and I was pretty sure she was.

"Spill what? Why the hell did you drag me here? There is a perfectly good cake back at the reception, and I was just about to try some."

Brianna rolled her eyes all the way to the ceiling and then looked at me.

"Don't make me smack you," she snapped. Then she grinned and lightly poked me in the chest. "So, did he have a big dick?"

"*Holy shit*, Bri—" was all I got out before she poked me again.

"Josie, you're lit up like a bonfire with that 'I just got the shit fucked out of me' glow. So, I repeat," she said, her voice dropping to a whisper, "does he have a big dick?"

I could feel my face heat up. Brianna cackled.

"I can't tell you that, Bri. Jacob would never forgive me." Then I held up my hands, spread apart to an approximate width to indicate the length of the object in question. Bri's eyes went big, and her mouth popped open just a bit.

"*Fuuuuck*," she said with a sigh.

"Oh, we did. A lot."

Brianna smacked me on the arm. "So, I can assume he rang your bell?"

I blushed harder as I grinned at her.

"Rang it, broke it, rebuilt it, rang it again. I'm so sore I can barely walk. Had to take a two-hour hot soak before getting dressed. Bri, where are Izzy and Riley?"

"Izzy's menfolk are all sick with some stomach thing. Seems they ate some undercooked hotdogs. Riley, her sister, and her mom took off for a weekend in Vegas. I'm just waiting for the call to wire them bail money. Why?" she asked.

"Don't tell them, okay? Especially Riley."

She grinned. "Okay, Josie. So, was it worth the wait?"

I flashed back to last night, and my thoughts solidified around one event. Jacob looked at me with such intensity right before he told me he loved me. I was lost in that moment. I relived it a thousand times in just a few seconds.

"Damnnn."

My thoughts snapped back to the present, and I saw Brianna staring at me. Her face had a look of disbelief that slowly melted into one of intense happiness. She grabbed me in a hug and squeezed hard for a second before letting me go.

"I'm so happy for you, Josie. When's the wedding?"

"It was just our first time!"

She laughed and then looked at me with an intensity I'd never seen from her. "That look in your eyes just now, when you left this world and went somewhere else. That's the look of love. That wasn't lust or like. That was pure love. Does he know?"

"He told me first. That's what I was thinking of just now. God, Bri, when he told me, I just attacked him, telling him I loved him too."

"I'm happy for you, I really am. Riley said it right. You're such a lucky bitch."

I nodded, smiling. "I know, Bri, I know." Then I yanked her into a hug of my own. She pulled back from me a step or so, smoothing her dress. She opened the door and started into the hallway, leading me back towards the main hall. Just before we entered, she turned back to me, a wicked grin on her face.

"You still owe me details, and I expect them. Soon. Told you, I'm living vicariously through you." I laughed and followed her back to our table. She picked up her cake and went back over to her hubby. I was so lucky to have her as a friend.

I was raising my fork to take a bite of cake when a muffled ringing came from my clutch. Someone really didn't want me to have cake. I put my fork down and pulled out my phone. I was surprised and delighted to see it was Gary. I eagerly clicked on the accept button.

"Hey, you!"

"Hey, yourself. What are you wasting time on?"

"I'm at a friend's wedding where I'm enjoying fine food and cake. Where are you?"

"Oh, just hanging out in your driveway, trying to figure out why you are hiding from me."

"When did you get to town, buttmunch?" An older couple at the next table looked at me, a shocked expression on their faces. I waggled my eyebrows at them and crossed my eyes. They turned away, muttering to each other.

"I finished my deal in Boston early and thought I would surprise you. Seems the surprise is on me. You're not here."

"Get yourself over here. I'm at the Azton Inn. Go back out to that service station you turned at to get to my place, hang a left, go five stop lights and turn right on Reddison. The Inn's about four blocks down; can't miss it. We're in their large event room. Oh, Gary, I have *so* much to tell you."

"Be there in a jiff."

"Bye!"

It was all I could do to not bounce in excitement. Now I could introduce Jacob to the man who was my brother in all but blood.

I kept an eye on the entrance way for Gary. He was easy to spot when he walked in. He was one of the sharpest dressers I knew. If that custom-fitted, charcoal-grey suit cost less than $5,000, I'd eat it. I stood up, waving to catch his attention. Spotting me, he grinned and headed my way.

He wrapped me up in a big hug the minute he got to me, giving me a big kiss on the lips.

I laughed and hugged him back. His holding me felt so good,

bringing back warm, happy memories. I held the hug for several seconds before pulling back to stare up at him, smiling.

"It's so good to see you, Gary!"

He held me out at arm's length, turning his head from side to side as he looked me over from head to toe.

"Girl, you look fabulous," he said. "Better than I've seen you in a long time. Something's changed from the last time I saw you. You're practically glowing! If I didn't know any better—"

I gripped his arms lightly, stopping him before he could complete that sentence. "I could never hide anything from you. Sit down; we have so much to catch up on."

He glanced around. "Wait, let me get a drink. I assume there's a bar somewhere?"

I pointed back over my shoulder. "Over on the far wall."

It only took him a few moments to reach the bar, get his drink, and make his way back to our table. He was pulling out his chair when disaster struck. Two kids ran by him being chased by a third. One of them bumped Gary's elbow.

Everything seemed to go to slow motion. Gary's arm shot forward, which was also the arm/hand combo holding the glass of red wine.

His face started to make that comical 'oh no' expression, and I could instantly see the trajectory of that explosion of red that burst out of his glass. I did attempt to do my best yoga contortion as I tried to slide away, but I wasn't fast enough.

With a nice *splash*, the wine bomb landed in my lap, drenching my nice peach-colored dress. Time sped back up.

"Oh damn, Josie, I'm so sorry. No, don't *spread* it!" Gary exclaimed, grabbing my wrist and keeping me from using my table napkin to wipe at the spill. I stood up, hoping that the wine would move downward and not soak me further.

"Great. Just great. I didn't bring another dress, and now this one is ruined."

"Bring another? Wait … do you have a room here?"

I rolled my eyes. "Yeah, for all the good it will do me."

"Come on, let's go," he said, grabbing me and pulling me towards the hallway, plowing his way through the tables and even some guests. He paused at the bar, procuring several bottles of something clear.

We took the elevators to the second floor. In the cab, I got a good glance at the bottles. Club soda. Of course.

My room was next to the elevators, so we were inside it before the car doors closed. He hauled me into the bathroom, pulling the shower curtain aside and peeking at the shower.

"Okay," he said. "Strip out of that dress and let me have it. Lose the panties and use the shower handheld to wash the wine off your legs. Snap to."

"Aye, aye, Gary, sir."

I turned and let him unzip me and stepped out of the dress. I handed it to him and got the water in the shower going.

Gary dumped the dress into the sink and began saturating it with club soda. I slipped off my panties and stepped into the shower. I talked as I washed, asking him about his husband.

"Hey, how's Jeremy?"

"He's fine," he answered, never pausing his scrubbing. "He couldn't go with me to Boston. Shuzi's puppies were due, and he didn't want to leave her. He's gonna be such an overprotective mom. It's so cute."

I rolled my eyes. "Whatever you do, *don't* mention puppies to Kaylin. She bugs me enough about dogs. If she finds out Uncle Gary and Uncle Jeremy have new puppies, I'm sunk."

He chuckled evilly. "I don't know, Josie. I think she'd be so cute with a little miniature schnauzer following her around."

I shut the water off and pulled the curtain back. I glared at Gary and shook a finger at him.

"I'm warning you, Gary. You say one word, just one, about puppies and I'll tell Jeremy *all* about that little weekend you had in Atlanta your senior year."

His head snapped up, his face in shock. "Girl, you wouldn't! You swore an oath to me."

I gave him my own evil grin. "And I'll break it. I mean it. No puppies."

He threw up his hands, flinging water everywhere. "Fine, no puppies," he retorted, returning to his work. "Damn, girl, you went nuclear in a second. Didn't even let me negotiate for my goddaughter."

"No dogs, no puppies."

"Fine." I chose to ignore the muttering he was doing under his breath.

Stepping out of the shower, I grabbed a towel to dry off. As I dried, I moved around Gary and into the bedroom. I rummaged in my bag, looking for clean underwear.

Shit, I only packed one pair of panties. The ones I had been wearing. I most definitely was not wearing the thong, given the way it smelled.

I went back to the bathroom to retrieve my panties, checking them for wine stains. Finding none, I slipped them back on and headed back to the sitting area.

Gary finished rinsing out my dress, put it on a hanger, and hung it up on the shower curtain rod. He followed me and plopped down on the end of the couch. I sat in the armchair next to it, smirking at him. This was going to be so evil of me.

"So, tell me what's happened? Something's different. What is it?" he asked, turning on the couch to face me.

"Well, sometime around four this morning, I had some really awesome sex right where you're sitting."

I burst out laughing as Gary's eyes got huge and he bounced up off the sofa. Glaring at me, he walked to the desk and grabbed the chair, wheeling it back to where I sat. He started to sit in it but paused, staring at me.

I was still laughing but shook my head. He harrumphed at me and sat down in the chair. He crossed one leg over the other and rested his hands on his knee, waiting for my juvenile laughter to come to an end.

I finally caught my breath and wiped the tears from my eyes, making sure not to streak my makeup. Feeling thirsty, I checked the bathroom to see if any club soda was left. Finding a half-empty bottle, I took a drink before setting back down.

"Feeling better?" he asked, a fake smile plastered on his face. I almost lost it again. Coughing, I took another drink and sat the bottle down on the end table.

"Yep. Feeling pretty good, actually. Sore, but good." Couch flashbacks almost had me going again.

"I'm glad. Most people would normally catch me up on their family, maybe talk about what's new with my goddaughter. But apparently some bitches like to jump right into their sex life. I'm just going to sit here and let you present your case. Not on the quality of the sex, mind you, but how you moved from not dating the last time we talked to the aforementioned act of duvet debauchery."

"Duvet debauchery?" I sputtered, lapsing back into fits of laughter. Gary sat there calmly, checking his nails and smiling slightly while he waited.

It took a few more sips of soda and some deep breaths before I was back in control. I sat up straighter and addressed Judge Gary.

"His name is Jacob Berman. I met him when I fell down a hill while on a hike and knocked myself out. I came to with him leaning over me and his hands almost on the girls. I screamed and slugged him."

He nodded. "I can so see you doing that. You never were one who liked being scared or surprised. Continue," he said, twiddling his fingers at me.

"After he checked me over, bandaged my hand, and splinted my leg, he picked me up, carrying me about a mile to his trailer. Then—"

Gary raised his hand. "Clarify. He picked you up and carried you a *mile*? Seriously?"

I nodded. "Well, to be fair, he had to take two or three breaks. But I think that was more to give my leg a rest from swinging. I believe that if he had been so inclined, he could have carried me non-stop."

Garry got a light whimsical look on his face. "You're sure he's straight?"

"Hey! You're married! But, to answer your question, oh *hell* yes. Parts of him are slightly curved but can be straight when needed, and hard!" I couldn't help it. Laughter overtook me again.

"Seriously?" he asked. "Penis jokes? Is that what we've resorted to now? I don't suppose I'm going to get any other type of answers out of your sex-addled brain, am I?"

"No, hehe, wait ... I'll be good, I promise." I don't think he believed me.

I got my juvenile antics under control and proceeded to tell him everything that happened. He stopped me again when I got to the situation with the bank.

"Wait. An investor just gave you money. No terms, no anything. Called it a grant?" he asked, his financial lawyer side perking up.

"Yep. No terms. Paid off all our bank loans as well as our vendor accounts. Even fronted us $50,000 for future operation costs."

"Josie, that's just too good to be true. I can't say that I've ever heard of anything like that. Grants, yes, but structured like that? The tax implications alone ..."

I shrugged. "Uncle Frank said the bank is handling it and that their legal department looked at it and all was okay."

"Would you mind if I took a peek as well, just for my peace of mind? The monies have been transferred, so I doubt I can cause any issues by checking."

"Sure, I can point you to Uncle Frank, and you can go from there."

"Now, please continue with the tale of this amazing Jacob," he said, wiping a dust spot off his knee.

I told him about everything that we had done during the last month, up to and including our night in the hotel, being in love, and ending with Jacob leaving for the hospital.

"So," he said, "Let me see if I have this right. You haven't dated anyone since Greg's death. You turned down multiple dates here in Azton. Then, in the span of a month, you've met someone, had a few dates, some amazing sex, and now you're both madly in love. Is that about it?"

I nodded. "Yep, that's about right."

He glanced at his watch. "It's been about an hour and a half. Think he's back yet? I really want to meet this stud of yours."

"Eek! Has it been that long? We need to get back downstairs so I can introduce you. He might be looking for me."

My dress was still slightly damp, so we used the hair dryer on it for a few minutes. I rushed around trying to get us both out of the room and downstairs. I stepped out into the hall, shoes in hand and dress still partially zipped while Gary closed the door.

The elevator dinged behind me.

"Hurry up," I said as I hugged him and gave him another quick kiss on the lips, something I always did with him from our college days. Greg thought it was cute that his gay friend was always getting lip action from his wife. We thought nothing of it. I loved Gary, as did Greg. Gary chuckled, shaking his head slightly.

"What's so funny? Here, zip me up please." I turned to him, holding my hair up out of the way as he grinned.

"Some guy stepped out of the elevator and saw us. His expression was priceless. He jumped back in the elevator before it even closed. There, all zipped."

I held on to him while I slipped my shoes on. The wine spot was hardly noticeable and barely damp. I could work with it since I'd probably be sitting down most of the time or glued to Jacob on the dance floor.

Someone had taken the elevator up to the top floor, so we had to wait for it to free up and come back down. When we finally got to the reception area, I grabbed an empty table and told Gary to hold it for us while I looked for Jacob. I didn't see him, but I did find Ken standing near the exit.

"Hey, Ken, have you seen Jacob?"

He turned to me, confused. "He just walked out. He looked really pissed. I tried to talk to him, but he wouldn't stop."

"Thanks." I rushed out the door, but the sidewalk was empty. A nearby engine rumbled to life. I ran to the side lot just in time to see Jacob's truck backing out. I started waving at him, but he never saw me as he gunned it and tore out, tires barking. Must have been another hospital emergency.

I turned to go back inside when a massive shock hit me, and everything went dark.

TWENTY-SIX

Jacob

"Later, Lisa!"

I finished scrubbing up, changed into my suit, and began making my way out for the wedding. I walked past the intake nurse on the way to the parking lot.

"Night," she said, pointing at me. "Make sure they don't eat all that cake! They're supposed to send some over for us."

"I don't know, Lisa. I *really* like cake."

She glared at me, shaking her finger. I laughed and headed out to my truck.

Tooling over to the reception, my thoughts were on Josie, the woman I loved.

I loved Josie. I was in love with Josie Callison. I was head over heels in love with someone, and it felt *great*!

I read somewhere that moms say that the love of a child makes the labor pains fade away, so having the next child is not as daunting. Maybe it worked the same with broken hearts. Maybe this feeling of love and euphoria I was feeling for Josie dulled and faded the pain from losing Kara.

Either way, I loved Josie, and she loved me. She said it and showed it. God, how she had shown it.

The sex had been out of this world. Now to figure out how to have more time alone with her. With the house basically finished except for furniture, I had someplace other than a trailer to bring Josie.

Pulling into the hotel's side parking lot, I lucked out, finding a spot near the road. After parking and sliding out of the truck, I used the side mirror to straighten my tie and run my fingers through my hair.

The reception was in full swing. Music blared from multiple speakers and lights flickered in sync with the beat. The dance floor had a smattering of couples, young and old. Walking around to the bar I ran into Ken.

"Hey man, sorry to have missed the wedding."

"Totally understand," he said, slapping me on the shoulder. "Janey and I appreciate you covering for her. If it weren't for you, she'd have missed her own wedding!" That drew a good laugh from both of us.

"So, leaving in the morning for the honeymoon?" I asked as my eyes wandered around the room looking for Josie. She was nowhere in sight.

He took a swig from his beer. "Yep, all packed and ready to go. Flight leaves Spokane at a god-awful six in the morning and by five that afternoon, we should be laying on the beach at Cancun, sipping little drinks with umbrellas in them!"

"Well, the two of you deserve it. Hey, you seen Josie anywhere?"

He glanced around the room. "Come to think of it, I haven't. Saw her at the wedding, but since we made it back to the reception from the picture taking, can't say as I've seen her."

"No worries. I'm sure she's around here somewhere, or maybe ran up to her room. I'll keep looking."

Ken started to take another sip of his drink, but Janey called out to him from the dance floor. Grinning, he sat his beer on a table and made a beeline for his new bride, leaving me forgotten in his wake.

I moved around the room, chatting with a few of the folks but not finding Josie. The only place left was her room. Maybe she was waiting there so we could have some more time together. My body responded to that thought. Damn, I was worse than a horny teenager.

The ride up in the elevator seemed to take hours, but only took seconds before there was a ding and the doors opened. I took a step towards Josie's room, stared for a second, and stepped back into the elevator before the doors even closed.

My world was shattered. My gut felt as if someone punched me in the stomach hard enough to break my spine.

Josie. *My* Josie. In another man's arms. I had only the briefest glance, but the image was burned in my brain. She was in his arms, kissing him and her dress half on. Her dress was unzipped, allowing her back to show. Which meant I could see that birthmark between her shoulder blades. She even held her shoes in one hand.

Cheating on me. Just hours after telling me she loved me, she was *cheating on me*. Guess she expected me to be gone long enough for her to fuck her other lover and be waiting for me at the reception, with me none the wiser.

I stormed out of the elevator on the first floor, heading towards the exit. I vaguely registered someone calling my name, but I didn't turn or slow down. Reaching my truck, I yanked the door open and climbed in, slamming it behind me so hard that the truck rocked. Firing the engine up with a roar, I peeled out of the parking lot, my hurt shifting to a full-blown rage.

I didn't remember driving anywhere. When I tuned back into reality, I was sitting in my truck, parked at the high school. The clock in the dash told me it had been several hours since I left the hotel. It felt like an eternity.

I stared out the window, not seeing anything, my mind numb. The only thing running through my head was a repeating question: *What had I done wrong?*

With shocking clarity, I knew *exactly* what I had done wrong. I broke my rule. I let myself feel again, to hope, to love. I swore to myself after Kara that I would never love again, never allow myself to feel that level of pain again. Within hours of telling Josie I loved her, she destroyed me, ripping my fucking heart apart and shitting on the pieces.

I screamed out my frustration, beating the dash, the steering wheel, the seats. I screamed till my throat was raw and the tears flowed freely. I thought Kara's death hurt, but this? This was a whole new level of pain. *Damn you, Josie!*

"You fucking cheater …" It came out as a croak and I repeated it over and over.

My cell phone started ringing. I ignored it. To hell with the world tonight. It rang again, and I continued ignoring it. Why couldn't people leave me the fuck alone?

The phone rang again, but it wasn't the normal ringtone. This time it was the Marine Hymn, the one I downloaded and assigned to the sheriff's personal cell. Rick didn't call me to chat or gab. If he called, it was normally an emergency. I groped my hand across the seat till I found my phone and answered.

"What?"

"I need you to come to my office," he said. That was Rick, all business.

"Ain't happening. I'm going over to Danny's to get shit faced. Hey, you should go with me. We can start a bar fight. I'll spot you two drunks."

"Jacob, cut the shit and get to my fucking office *now*! It's Josie," he snapped, his voice taking on a tone I hadn't heard out of him before.

"Fuck that bitch."

There was a drawn-out silence and for a moment I thought he'd hung up. His voice came back on the line, his tone ice cold.

"Jacob, Mad Dog's back. He has Josie and he's going to kill her. Get your fucking ass to my office now, grunt, or she's dead in twenty-four hours." The phone clicked in my ear as he hung up.

"*Fuck!*" It was the Bransons all over again. Why me? Why did it seem like I was always the one the universe dumped this shit on?

Smashing the dash one last time, I started up the truck and drove over to Rick's office. Regardless of what was going on between Josie and I, no one deserved to be in Mad Dog's hands.

Parking next to a patrol car, I slowly walked my way up the stairs and through the front doors of the station. Lacy was on duty tonight. She looked up and jerked her thumb back towards Rick's office. His door was open and when he saw me, he waved me in, gesturing for me to shut the door.

"I got a call this afternoon that Mad Dog and some of his crew managed to escape while on a hospital visit. That was eight days ago," he explained. "Some of his boys overpowered the deputies and freed them. They roughed up two nurses on their way out and had a van waiting on the street. State troopers found the van abandoned not far from the hospital. I gave the warden up at the prison a rash of shit for just now letting me know."

He took a deep, measured breath before continuing.

"Bout twenty minutes ago, a kid came in, dropped off a big mailing envelope with Lacy, and ran away before we could ask him anything. Inside the envelope was a flash drive." He motioned me around to his side of the desk so I could see his computer monitor. He started the video that was paused on the screen.

It was a cave. Weak lighting flickered from several lanterns on small boxes and camp tables spaced around the area. The camera must have had a light on it as well. Beer bottles and trash were thrown around the floor.

I took all that in, but my focus was the two figures in the middle of the screen. One was Josie, standing there in her bra and panties. She had a cut over one eye and a bruise on one cheek. Her hands appeared to be restrained behind her back, and duct tape covered her mouth. Mad Dog stood beside her with his hand clamped in her hair to hold her in place. In his other hand he held what appeared to be a large Bowie knife, and he was using it to point at the camera as he talked.

"Listen up and listen up good, Sheriff. Gonna say this once. You're gonna get five hundred grand in small bills. I don't give a shit where it comes from or what you have to do to get it, just get it. It better be loose bills, no bundles, no dye packs. Then you go find that sack of shit pussy and you tell him I got his bitch. He's gonna take that money and meet one of my boys at the marina. My boy is gonna bring him to me.

"Pussy-boy, figure by now the sheriff has got you watching this. I owe you big time, you fucker. From the day I landed in prison I spent all my time planning on fucking you up. Killing you, well, that'd be too easy, too quick. It was almost six months before I could piss without a bag and another two before I could use my arms. I'm gonna make you suffer, dickhead. But not in the way you think."

On the screen, Mad Dog brought that knife up and cut the bra off Josie. He dropped the knife in the dirt near his foot, grabbed her breasts, mauling them. She struggled to get away and he punched her in the stomach. When she doubled over, he immediately jerked her back upright. I could see the hand marks he left on her stomach. I could tell by her eyes she was pissed. Her defiance made me feel good, but I squashed that feeling before it could grow.

"Them's some nice tits. Bring me the money, pussy-boy. You're gonna watch while me and the boys show this bitch what real men are like. She'll be begging the Dog for it when we're done."

Then whoever was running the camera zoomed in on Mad Dog.

"And it better only be you pussy-boy. I got eyes on that sheriff and his crew. He so much as moves from that office or if any of his asshole deputies do anything out of the norm, I'll slice this bitch from cunt to mouth and leave her for you to find.

"If you come here without the money, I'm gonna cut your dick off and shove it down her throat. I'm gonna cuff you both to trees while you bleed out. Then I'm gonna douse her in gas, throw on a match, and burn this bitch to ash while you watch, knowing there ain't a thing you can do. You're gonna die hearing her screams.

"The money buys her life, pussy-boy. Oh, don't get me wrong. We're still gonna fuck her up, but she'll live. But you, pussy-boy, are gonna die. You got twenty-four hours. If you ain't kneeling before me in twenty-four hours, well, you know what happens. Tick tock, pussy-boy. Tick tock."

The video stopped. All that could be heard in the office was heavy breathing.

"Fuck." I wasn't sure who uttered the word, or if we both did. I started pacing.

"We have to call in the State and the Feds," Rick said. "Mine can't move."

I immediately shook my head. "You do that and she's dead. Soon as he sees the first marked or unmarked car roll in, he'll do what he said."

I continued pacing the room, thinking. I came back and leaned on Rick's desk.

"How did the ones who helped him escape know he and his boys would be at the hospital? For that matter, what idiot scheduled him and his gang to be at the same hospital at the same time."

"The warden figures it was one of the guards or nurses," he replied. "Anyone who had access to their jail system could pull up the inmates' schedules. Simple matter to text that info out. They're doing an internal investigation to find out who set it up. Their computer system should have prevented this very thing from happening. Something had to be overridden which means there will be an electronic trail."

He continued speaking as he leaned back in his chair.

"They had the setup of the hospital down, probably scouted it for days. They knew right where everyone would be and how many guards would be on duty. The van was ditched and a second vehicle ready."

I started pacing and talking. "But we know where he is, roughly, or at least where he's close to. Josie was snatched within the last few hours, so we know that wherever they're holed up is close. The only problem is that there's only 10,000 square miles of forest and hills he could be in."

He looked up at me. "How do you know ... Ah, the reception." No one ever said Rick was slow.

"They had to make the snatch, get her to a location, make that video, and get it back to us, Rick. That puts them somewhere within about sixty or seventy miles."

"I know her mom doesn't have that money, and Frank ain't gonna give that cash up unless the Feds or State get involved," Rick retorted, getting up and doing some pacing of his own.

He stopped, toe-to-toe, and looked me in the eye.

"Jacob, I don't know what happened between you and Josie, and I can't ask you to do this. But I'm gonna ask you anyway. If there is any chance of saving her, it's you."

I glared at him. "She's dead anyway. Even if he gets the money, he's gonna kill both of us."

"Son, I don't want to stare that little girl in the eye and tell her that her momma is dead. Or have to explain to Flora why that casket is closed," he said flatly.

"Dammit!" I screamed, turning away from him. Why did he have to mention Kaylin? I turned back to him, pissed. "That's a low damn blow, Marine."

He didn't even have the guts to be ashamed. "I grew up with that girl and her family. I don't know what happened between you two, but I know there is something between you, something you need. You gonna look that little girl in the eye and tell her you might have been able to save her momma but chose not to?"

Damn that Marine bastard to hell. Pulling my phone from my pocket, I flipped it open, hitting a speed dial.

"Jacob? What time ... Do you know what damn time it is?" he *growled.*

"Yes, I know what time it is. Arnie, shut up and listen because I don't have time to explain this. I'm at the sheriff's office in Azton. There's been an ... *incident* here."

"Well, an incident. Of course, that's understandable. Can you be any more flipping vague, given the hour. What the hell is going on?"

Okay, Arnie was pissed, but I didn't have time to be nice.

"Arnie, the less you know the better. Now, listen carefully. You know that funding line we set up the other day?"

"The one for your girlfriend?"

"Yes, that's the one. I need you to get to the bank first thing in the morning and get me $500,000 in unbundled bills."

"$500,000 IN UNBUNDLED BILLS? HAVE YOU LOST YOUR—"

I yanked the phone away from my ear so Arnie's roar wouldn't deafen me. Once the volume subsided, I put the phone back to my ear.

"Arnie, I don't care how many goddamn banks you have to empty or what the fuck it costs in penalties. I need that cash now. Once you have it, head out to the airport and rent a helicopter ...”

“A helicopter? Jesus Christ, Jacob. Have you got any damn idea how expensive renting a helicopter is? Have you lost your senses?” he barked.

“God damnit Arnie, I don’t care what it fucking costs. Spend every goddamn dollar I have if you have to. Charge it, pull it out your ass, I don’t fucking care. I need that money in the sheriff’s hands before noon tomorrow. I’m dead serious when I say life and death, Arnie, life and death. Get it done.”

I hung up the phone and slid it back to my pocket. Rick was staring at me, stone faced again.

“Who’s Arnie?” he asked.

“My accountant.”

He kept eyeing me. I could see those gears burning in his head. “He wouldn’t by chance be the mysterious grant source that Flora has been talking about, would he?”

I looked at him, my non-answer giving him all the answers he needed. He nodded.

“Okay, we get the money, and you meet the guy at the dock. What’s the play after that?” he asked.

The dock. Something had been nagging me about the dock ever since Mad Dog mentioned it. Why the dock? It was away from the main roads, and there was nothing around it but houses and marina slips. Maybe they had another getaway car somewhere accessible by the lake?

No, that had clearly been a cave in that video. Most of the mountain area was to the north of the lake, up near the back side of my property. The proverbial light bulb came on.

The boats on the lake late at night, all heading up to the northeast end. The rash of lakeside burglaries Rick had mentioned. My house and my ghost. It all fell together, like pieces in a jigsaw puzzle.

I looked up at Rick. He studied me and one eyebrow quirked up.

“You know where he is, don’t you?”

“A fair idea. At least, I know where to start.”

He nodded again. "What's your plan?"

"It's gonna take Arnie a while to get that money together when the banks open tomorrow. Assuming he does the job, he should have it here by noon-ish. I have that long to find her."

. "Where will you start, and what else do ya need?" he asked.

"North end of the lake. I need Lacy's civilian clothes."

I almost laughed when his eyebrows shot up.

"Josie's naked in that video."

He nodded, heading to the front desk, yelling for Lacy as he went. He was back in a few minutes.

"That's a conversation I never expected to have," he said, tossing me a gym bag. "Lacy's workout clothes. What else?"

"Think you can get out of this building without being spotted, Marine? Mad Dog said he was watching you."

"Grunt, don't tell this old dog how to hunt."

"I'll leave that to you, but if it were me, I'd get some folks on the north end of the lake and be ready for my signal.

"What do I watch for?" He asked.

"Yellow flare."

I headed for the front door before he stopped me.

"Jacob, you held back the last time. You know it, I know it. We're not doing that dance again. Weapons free, and I'll handle cleanup. Good hunting."

I nodded and headed out. He didn't need to know I already made that decision.

TWENTY-SEVEN

Jacob

I skidded to a stop at my trailer, gravel and dirt flying and pinging off the metal abode. I bailed from the truck and ran inside, tearing the door off its hinges as I went. Reaching under my bed, I pulled out a large suitcase and dropped it on top of the covers. Flicking the clasps, I opened it up and gazed at items that I never imagined wearing anymore.

My teammates and several doctors all questioned me during my career. I was one of the lucky, or unlucky, depending on your viewpoint, few that could process my actions and not be overly affected. Something inside my head switched off the emotions when it was needed. It only happened in combat, when killing had become necessary.

I had been through numerous interviews with the army's shrinks and head doctors. They thought it had to do with what happened to my sister, and I honestly couldn't disagree. I just knew that when it came time to gear up for a mission, I felt the worry and angst about the killing go away. I felt the fear and anticipation of action but not the guilt of taking life. Many thought me sociopathic. I didn't like killing; I hated it, in fact. But, just as a doctor sometimes has to take healthy flesh to ensure getting the cancer out, sometimes bad people need to die.

Either way it went, I knew for a fact that tonight, none of the assholes who had Josie would live to see the next day, and I wouldn't lose a wink of sleep over it.

I shucked out of my suit and started donning the case's contents. Jet black tactical pants. Black undershirt for sweat wicking with a black overshirt made of more tactical rip-stop. Pads for knees and elbows, balaclava. Gloves went into a side pouch.

I reached into my closet and pulled out the soft-soled black boots. Sitting on the bed, I put them on, tucking my pants legs into the boots. I tightened up the laces, then double wrapped them around the boot tops before tying them off.

Dressed, I ran back through the now dangling front door, grabbed Lacy's gym bag from my truck and jogged to my tool shed. I moved the small cement mixer and tools that stood in the back corner and yanked the heavy tarp off my gun safe.

I punched the combination into the keypad and placed my thumb on the biometric reader. Once the light turned green, I yanked open the safe door, activating the inner light.

I pulled out my equipment harness, swung it over my shoulders and let it sit on my waist, snapping the buckles. I fixed a combat holster to my belt and fastened the Velcro wrap around my right leg.

I glanced at the MP5. No. Tonight's mission was stealth. I would love to have its firepower, but it was too much for what I anticipated facing. I pulled out my custom Sig Sauer, a trusted friend that fit my hand like a glove. I'd put so many rounds through this beauty that it felt like an extension of my body.

I worked the slide several times, making sure it was smooth and clean. Pulling a clip from the ammo pouches attached to the inner safe door, I slammed a clip home, chambered a round, and engaged the safety. I attached a silencer before sliding the pistol home into the holster.

Extra clips were placed in various holders on my belt and harness.

Three different knives and a set of black cuffs all found their spots on my belt.

I looked out to the sky and observed the almost full moon with some slight clouds overhead. More than ample light for my task. I left the night vision gear where it lay.

I ticked off in my head the scenarios that might play out tonight then compared that to what was left in the safe. I picked up two small yellow signal flares and shoved them into a pants cargo pocket.

Opening Lacy's gym bag, I grabbed the clothes inside and shoved them into a backpack. I added two more flares, three additional clips, and a few little things Rick didn't need to know about. Frag grenades were not on the nice list for any civilian.

Josie would need the clothes more than I needed any other equipment. The very thought of her brought back images of her in that asshole's arms, which only fanned my anger. Closing my eyes, I took several deep breaths to center myself, then locked that anger into a small box, shoving it into the back of my mind. I needed to focus. The rest of the issues I could deal with later.

I ran to my four-wheeler and cranked it up, revving the engine and turning right towards the access road before kicking it up to full throttle. A few bumpy minutes later, I slid into the lot on the backside of the house. Killing the engine, I hopped off and walked to the clearing that overlooked the lake.

The moon's reflection on the water made for a picturesque scene while the moonlight lit up virtually the entire lake and shoreline. It was beautiful ... and it was going to make my job harder. I glanced towards the top of the lake where I spotted the boats before, about two miles away if I remembered the lake size correctly.

My best plan would be to parallel the lake as close to the shoreline as I could until I found where they were landing at, then work my way in from there.

A direct frontal approach was not the ideal way in, but doing an area search was going to take more time than I had.

'We're not doing that dance again.' It was nice of Rick to say it, but I'd known what I intended to do the minute that video stopped

playing. As I stared out over the water, I felt the emotions fade and the clarity of the task sharpen even more. Giving the lake another intense scan, I turned to the woods and went hunting.

It took about two hours of scooting and sneaking before I found their landing point. I slowed my pace in the last thirty minutes to get my breathing back under control and to make myself stealthier. I pulled the balaclava down, adjusting it so the mouth and eye holes were in the right spots. Last thing I needed was for the moonlight to wash across my face and give me away.

I fell easily into my old mode, ghosting my way through the woods, using the cover provided. My teammates always felt better when I was on point, even if I was the medic. They were the ones who nicknamed me Smoke, said I just seemed to disappear like a puff of smoke. I could think of worse names to be called.

As I got near the water again, I froze in place. Something registered on my senses. I calmly scanned the area, slowly quartering the woods, inhaling deeply as I surveyed each quarter.

I was looking slightly up the shoreline when I caught the whiff of tobacco. Someone up ahead was smoking. I focused on the area, but whoever it was knew enough to shield the burning end from sight. Adjusting my line of movement, I eased forward into the dark.

Moments later, I was close enough to see a small spit of sand, about forty yards wide. It was an open beach area that stretched up to the tree line. A path was there that led further up into the woods. A boat was pulled up onto the beach. I caught the wink of red up near the tree line. Time to introduce myself to our mystery date. Picking my path, I blended back into the trees.

Working my way up and around, I came up slightly behind the figure standing at the tree. I paused, holstered the Sig, and drew one of my knives. It was time to figure out what I was facing.

I eased up behind the small tree. Bringing the knife around quickly, I placed it against the throat of the sentry and grabbed their left arm.

"Make a noise or go for a weapon, and I'll slit your throat," I growled into his ear, keeping my voice low. I pressed the razor-sharp blade against the skin hard enough to make a small cut and emphasize the threat. The sharp smell of urine punctuated the air. It would seem I had my target's attention.

"Put your hands back and around the tree, slowly."

Mr. Urine complied. I let go of his arm and pulled the cuffs out from my back holder. Two clicks later, I had him cuffed to the tree. Keeping the knife at his throat I slid around to face him, pulling a red penlight from my harness with my other hand. Even in the moonlight, I could see the small rivulet of blood trickling down his neck from the shallow cut.

"You make a sound other than answering my questions, and I'll bleed you like a pig. Nod if you understand." He nodded multiple times. I sheathed the knife, pulled up my balaclava and clicked on the red light.

His eyes locked with mine as I studied his face. Even in the red light, I recognized this one, the scar on his jawline was hard to forget. He was one of the original assholes that assaulted the Branson sisters.

"How many of you are there?"

"I can't tell you shit, man. He'll kill me if I do."

I smashed my hand against his mouth, drew my Sig and shot him through the right foot. He screamed as his eyes bugged out and sweat popped out on his forehead. I leaned in close and brought the silencer up to press into his wet crotch.

All of the blood drained from his face as I whispered to him quietly, "You have more personal worries right now. I'm going to remove my hand and ask you again. Fail to answer, and, well, do I really need to say it?"

He shook his head quickly. I removed my hand but left the silencer in place, pushing gently.

"How many?"

"Ten counting me," he said, the words rushing out.

"How far is the cave?"

"About a thousand yards or so up that trail."

"Any type of a guard?"

"Couple outside the cave, one or two inside it. The rest are spread around the woods between here and the cave. Mad Dog makes them stay out there watching for you."

"Anyone due to relieve you?"

"Murph should be down in a bit."

As if the gods were listening, someone was coming down the trail, making no effort to keep himself quiet. I could only assume it was Murph, the relief. I looked back at my captive.

"Don't call out, don't make a sound." I pressed the silencer into his balls, and he nodded rapidly in agreement. I clicked off the red light, pulled myself to the side and slid the balaclava back down over my face.

Moments later, another figure stumbled out of the trees, cursing a root that apparently tripped him. He was calling out for his pal.

"Jer, where are you? Come on, asshole. I ain't got no fucking time for this hide and seek bullshit, motherfucker."

I watched as he continued down towards where Jer was cuffed to the tree.

"Hey, dickhead, I see you by that tree. You fucking better not be asleep. I warned you—"

He never finished his warning as the Sig fired twice, the silencer reducing the sound of each shot to a small cough. Both rounds took Murph in the head, a classic double-tap. One round to kill, second round to make sure the first round did its job. I heard puking followed by Jer whimpering. I stood back up and stared at him again.

"What weapons do they have?"

"Shit, man … you killed him. You blew his fucking brains out. Don't kill me, man, *please*. I told ya what you wanted. Please, don't kill me. Let me go and you'll never see me. *shitohshitohshit*." Jer was babbling and crying now.

I smacked the silencer against his crotch again, shutting up his whining.

"What weapons?"

"Uh … pistols, knives. One of the guys has an Uzi or some kind of machine gun pistol thing. See, I'm telling you everything. Don't kill me man …"

"You know, Jer, I wonder how much Jenny begged you to let her go as you raped her?" His eyes grew wide, and his mouth started to open, but I wasn't in the mood to listen anymore.

The double-tap stood him up against the tree and smashed his head backwards. His bowels gave way as he slid down the trunk, the cuffs keeping him from pitching over. I moved behind the tree and uncuffed him, letting his body fall to the side. Ejecting the clip from my Sig, I fed in a new one, jacked a round in, and slipped it back into my holster. I slid the partial clip into the holder that the full clip had been in. I gave Jer's corpse one final glance.

"That's for Jenny," I said softly.

With the moon straight overhead, I eased up the trail that Murph had come down. If I believed Jer, there were seven more guards to get through before I could get to Mad Dog. I was betting that he would have one or two in the cave with him. That still left plenty to find and eliminate.

What was really worrying me was the guy from the picnic. He was good. If he was part of this bunch, and I assumed he was, he would be a big problem.

I'd traveled about seventy-five yards when the path began to rise and the moonlight was not as bright. I crested near two large cedars, one to either side of the trail. I was almost even with them when my leg froze on its own in mid-step.

One of the skills that I picked up during my time in conflict was the ability for my body to work on its own. When I stalked, my senses tended to take control sometimes. This skill saved me and others countless times.

I let my leg drift slowly backwards to the spot it had been. I scanned the area closely, working slowly from left to right, inhaling softly and deeply as I did.

No new smells tickled my nose and at first pass, I didn't see anything out of the ordinary.

I started forward and again stopped. I may not have been able to recognize the threat, but my body knew something bad was ahead of me. As I started looking again, the trees rustled slightly in the wind, letting the moonlight hit the path in front of me. As it did, I caught a glint of reflection.

Dropping to my knees, I stretched out my hand, my fingers pointed down. Within a few inches I touched a wire. I moved forward on my knees, making sure to keep my hand away from what I assumed was a tripwire.

Glancing to my left, I could now see the wire anchored to that tree in some kind of enclosed pulley. I moved my head to the right, following the wire to a small pulley and then up to some brush hanging around waist high on the tree.

Scooting back on my knees, I stood and slowly crept to the cedar on the right. I carefully moved the brush aside and followed the wire up and around the trunk. There on the back side of the trunk was the booby trap. I pulled out my small penlight again, shielding it with my body so no one up the path could see it.

It seemed that this guy with Mad Dog had some smarts. The trap was a sophisticated blow gun.

A small metal cylinder was strapped to the tree. My guess was that it was full of compressed air since there appeared to be a release mechanism attached to the end of the tank. An air hose led from the mechanism into the back of a capped-off PVC pipe, about an inch in diameter.

Without looking inside that pipe, I would bet there was a rigid foam rubber plug on the other side of that cap that would act as a pusher when the compressed air hit it. The ammo would be some form of bolt, either a crossbow bolt or possibly a large sharpened dowl that was smaller than the tube. Either one would be very light and very deadly.

Trip the wire, release the air in the tank, and viola, a big dart gun. I had to give its creator credit; it was a pretty smart trap.

Reaching with my pliers, I was ready to cut the trigger wire when I saw the other wire. Pulling back the small tool, 1 visually traced this new wrinkle around to the other side of the air tank and froze.

A black box, barely visible in my red light, was affixed to the tree.

The new wire disappeared inside the box. This was a wrinkle I didn't need.

I sat back for a second, studying the new-found problem. Whoever created this, and I'd bet money on my ghost, knew who I was, and probably had an inkling about my past. If I were building this, I'd make sure no one would mess with my trap. Like say, cutting the trigger wire.

I studied the wiring setup for a minute or so before I figured out what he had done. I'd bet money the pulley on the other tree was spring-loaded. Cut the tripwire and it gets reeled back to the other pulley. That action would then yank the second wire from the little box, which I was pretty sure would set off an electric detonator and a clump of plastic explosive. Just enough to ruin the day of anyone staring at the trap.

I'd disarm this, but I wasn't entirely sure I found all of Mr. Sneaky's little toys. I didn't have time. I hated leaving a trap behind me, but now that I knew it was there, I could come back later and take care of it.

As if to emphasize my timeline, another voice came drifting down the trail, calling for Murph. I stowed my pliers and drew my Sig. Time to find out who the new mystery guest was.

It seemed like hours, but was probably only forty minutes before I reached where Jer said the cave was located. I could start to see dim lights through the trees. Along with the one who disturbed me at the trap, I found two other gang members along the way, all three now bodies laying out near the trail. It hadn't been difficult to find them. Mystery Guest walked right up to me, and the other two had been standing right beside big trees. Both had been focused on the trail, talking and drinking, making no effort to be quiet or hide. Stupid on their part, fatally stupid.

Five down, five to go.

Moving out to the left of the trail, I eased into a small clearing, looking for an obstructed path to the cave. The hairs on my neck shot out. A rustle of fabric was my only other warning. I threw myself to the side as a sharp burning pain sliced down the side of my head, and I felt a heavy thud on the ground. Rolling quickly, I came up with my Sig extended only to find myself staring down the barrel of another silencer.

The man behind the silencer was about my height, but at a glance, had me by about forty pounds. He was also dressed in what appeared to be black tactical gear.

"Holster it and drop the backpack," he ordered, waving his pistol at me. I calculated how fast it would take me to dive to the side if I decided to shoot. "I know what you're thinking, fuckwad. You'll never make the roll."

I slowly slipped the Sig into the holster, my hand staying near it. I shrugged off the backpack and let it hit the ground.

He slowly circled around me, and I turned to meet him, always maintaining eye contact. I could feel the wetness on the side of my head trickling down into the collar of my shirt. I hated head cuts. So damn bloody.

The trees were rustling softly as we stared at each other. Put us in western gear and dusty street and we could have been having a showdown.

"You're the one who's been watching me. The guy from the park that day. And the putt-putt place before that."

"Yep, and you're good, I'll give ya that. You knew I was there at that golf place," he said. "You've spent some time in the mix. Ranger?"

"No. SF."

"Fucking green beenies. I ate your kind for lunch," he said with a sneer. Given his overall appearance, I was betting he didn't miss many lunches.

"Why are you working with this trash?"

"Money, plain and simple," he said. "The asshole in charge told me what happened last time. He figured he needed some insurance. That's me."

"Cheap skills at a cheap price is what I'm thinking." That scored a hit as I watched his jaw tighten. Maybe I could goad him a bit more, get him off his game.

"Pick a knife," he said, and with a twist in my gut, I knew where this was heading.

Standing up straighter, I pulled the knife from the sheath at my hip. I reversed the blade, setting the spine along my forearm, the edge facing outward like a fin. I let my hands drop loosely by my side and eased up on the ball of my feet. My ghost holstered his weapon. I saw the knife already in his other hand, blade resting up against his forearm.

We began circling. He started the dance with a series of lunges and feints, testing for a weakness or slow response. His first real strike was lightning fast, going for my face. I turned away and lashed out with my own blade, aiming for his head even as I was blocking his kick.

He backed off, still circling. "Not bad. Almost a shame to kill you. Almost."

I could hear a small wheeze to his voice. Someone hadn't been keeping up with their cardio. I needed to keep him moving and wait for him to get sloppy.

Time and time again he came at me, pushing and moving us around the small clearing, the only sound the shuffle of our feet and the metallic clicks as our blades met.

Then he got lucky. I misread his strike and his blade came straight at my face. I barely got my head turned before the blade sliced just above my eye. It wasn't a deep cut, but it stung like fire. As I stumbled back, blocking another kick, I missed the strike to my right arm.

"Gonna slice … you … into … pieces," he panted. Even from the blood trickling into my left eye, I could see the sweat on his face. I needed to end this. While we had small cuts and bruises, neither of us had landed a crippling cut or hit.

I launched multiple attacks at him. He grunted as he blocked, stumbling around the clearing. I kept pressing, nicking his jaw, slicing his wrist, and catching him with a side kick to his thigh.

He stumbled backwards, and I struck out with my left leg, aiming for his stomach. Too late; I realized it was a feint. Before I could pull the kick back, his blade flew down, catching my left thigh. I grunted as his edge opened up my pants and flesh.

He didn't bother to gloat or mouth off with any more threats. The way he was huffing, he needed all his air just to stay upright. Time to end this and find Josie.

I took a deep breath to center myself and began mentally blocking the pain. Once I was more focused, I began stalking towards him.

I don't know what tell of his I picked up on, but I was moving before I registered that I had tossed the knife at him and was pulling my Sig from its holster. Throwing myself to the left, the cough of his shot barely beat mine. I rolled quickly as I hit the ground, firing three more times in his general area. A burning along my right leg as I rolled again told me one of his shots landed. Finishing the roll, I came into a kneeling stance, pistol extended.

He was staggering back against a tree, gun hanging to his side. Keeping my sights on him, I stood up, wincing at the pain in my leg. Easing over to him, never letting my gun waver from his head, I watched as he slowly slid down the tree to collapse on the ground, the pistol falling from his hands. I kept moving.

His hand was pressed to his gut, but then it slid away, flopping to the ground, lifeless. Ready for any sudden move, I knelt on the sodden ground next to him. His head had fallen to the side, and I could see where one of my shots apparently sliced through his neck, cutting the carotid artery. The two in his stomach had been the icing on the cake.

I staggered over to where I dropped my backpack, using the trunk of the tree for support as I slid down to the ground, exhausted and battered. Digging through my pack, I pulled out some clean rags, a bottle of water, some cloth strips, and a tube of surgical glue.

I worked my way around the cuts, rinsing them with the water and cleaning them with a rag. I filled each cut with the glue and then squeezed the skin edges together, gritting my teeth at the pain. Once I was sure it was sealed, I wrapped a cloth strip around it to apply pressure to the cut. The cuts on my head were going to have to live with only being glued.

Stowing my supplies, I pulled out a small, single-shot energy drink from my pack and downed its contents in one slug. I gave myself about ten minutes for the caffeine and B12 to hit my system.

I stood up, again using the tree to steady myself as I clung to it for support. I worked each limb, making sure the glue would hold. I picked up my pack, grabbed the new corpse's collar, and started dragging it to the trail.

Taking a moment behind a tree, I popped the clip in my Sig out. Reaching to my waist, I grabbed the clip from earlier. Working quickly, I consolidated rounds until one clip was full and the other almost empty.

I put the full clip back into my weapon and put the other one back into my belt.

Six down, four to go.

Nearing the cave, there was a disturbance of some kind, and a female voice cried out. *Josie*. I crept up as quickly as I could, getting in view just in time to see her get yanked back into the cave by one ugly piece of shit who I recognized immediately as Mad Dog.

I waited for the guards to settle back into place and the laughter and yelling to die down. Determining it was as calm as it would get, I moved up to the cave entrance from the left side until I had both guards in line with each other.

I must have made a noise or stepped wrong because the guard closest to me began turning his head in my direction. The two shots took him in the temple and, as he collapsed, he cleared my sight line to his buddy, who stood there with his mouth hanging open, unbelieving. He died that way. All that was left now were those in the cave. Taking a deep breath, I slipped into the entrance.

TWENTY-EIGHT

Josie

Awareness slowly came back with a pounding in my head and my body feeling like I stuck my finger in a light socket. I knew my eyes were open, but everything was pitch black. It came rushing back to me. Running out to find Jacob and a shocking feeling, followed by darkness. I groaned as I tried to sit up, but something shoved me back down.

"Keep your ass still, bitch," growled a nearby male voice, deep and rough.

I could make out the growl of an engine and a rushing sound, almost like water. Was I in a boat? That might explain the rocking feeling and the queasiness in my stomach.

I took several deep, calming breaths. As I did, the pounding in my head began to lessen, and the all-over body tingle began to fade. I debated trying to sit up again when the engine's high, whining pitch started to wind down. Someone grabbed me, pulling me to my knees. Something, some type of hood, was yanked from my head. I darted my eyes everywhere, not moving my head.

Moonlight streamed down on the water, confirming that I was on the lake and in some kind of boat. I'd never seen this type before. It appeared to be made up of two large tubes of hard rubber with a floor between them. One person appeared to be in the front of the boat, and I guessed someone must have been behind me, driving the boat.

I could see what looked like a stretch of bank in front of us, and a faint shape was moving back and forth. Whoever was running the boat drove us up onto the bank, causing me to fall forward, but hands kept me from hitting the floor again. The engine sound died abruptly.

"Let's go, bitch. You try anything and I'll put a bullet in your fucking head," said my handler.

Someone yanked and pulled me around until I was out of the boat. I stumbled when my feet hit the ground, my legs not wanting to work. Hands jerked me back upright, and I found myself looking at a sneering, ugly face. They were also in serious need of a breath mint. Possibly ten.

"Walk on your own or else I'll drag your fucking ass," said the asshole. I almost fainted from the rolling stench that washed over me.

I didn't know who this guy was, but I had a serious desire to cave his face in. With his attitude and stench, I decided to call him Assface. Unfortunately, my hands were tied, and somewhere in the process, I lost my shoes. Doing anything would have to wait.

I could barely see the ground but that didn't seem to matter to the dickheads pushing me along. They were wearing some kind of lights on their head that were shining red, allowing them to apparently see where they were going. I tripped and stumbled uphill, following some path that wound up through the woods.

"Who the hell are you people?" I asked. Someone grabbed me and spun me around. I couldn't see his face, but the same overall smell of booze and filth from his mouth was almost staggering. I almost threw up right on him.

"Not your fucking concern, bitch. Keep your fucking mouth shut and get the fuck to walking. The Dog is waiting," he growled, shoving me back up the path when he was finished. I tagged *this* guy as Shitface.

Who the hell was Dog? Something was tickling my back brain about that name.

I don't know how long it was before we came upon what appeared to be a cave, two men standing on either side of its entrance. The only light for the area came from the opening. One of the figures moved forward to meet us. The left side of his face was scarred up and he wore and eyepatch on his left eye."

"This her? Any problems?" Eyepatch asked.

One of my captors hocked up a wad of gunk and spat to the side.

"Nah, bitch ran right into our arms," said Assface. "Dropped like a rock when we tased her ass."

That explained the light socket feeling.

"Dog's inside. Been waiting." said Eyepatch as he leered at me. "Hope he lets us fuck her later. Ain't had no pussy in weeks."

Assface laughed as he shoved me forward.

I felt my blood turn cold in my veins, bile rushing up my throat as fear rose in me. What the hell was going on?

I hadn't taken more than a dozen steps before we came into the cave proper, stopping near the middle of the area.

The place was littered with trash, sleeping bags, and other junk. Lanterns were hanging around the wall, others sitting on crates. I took in my surroundings, but what I mainly saw was some large ugly man sitting in a chair, beer bottle in his hand.

This man was seriously ugly. We're talking 'tie a pork chop around your neck to get the dogs to play with you' ugly. Someone had busted his face up good in the past. His nose was crooked and covered in scars, as was the skin around his eyes. I guessed he was also missing several front teeth. He wore some kind of leather vest, leaving his arms bare. They were covered in tattoos, mostly skulls, flames, and knives.

He watched us for a few moments before he stood up, drained his beer, and tossed the bottle behind him. Taking his time, he walked over to stand within a couple feet of me, his gaze making my skin crawl.

I barely saw his shoulder flinch before my jaw exploded in pain as his hand struck me, sending me to the ground. Someone yanked me back up to my feet. Ugly man got up close, his hot breath causing the bile to threaten to rise again.

"So, you're pussy-boy's piece of ass. Well, yar mine now. What's your name, bitch?"

My face was in agony and the world was spinning around me like a top. I wanted to collapse to the ground and curl into a ball, but something or someone was keeping me up. I tried to speak, but couldn't get the words out past the pain.

The punch to my gut lifted me off my feet and dropped me to the ground again. I started retching, trying to catch my breath. Then I began sobbing, the pain in my gut and the fear giving way to tears. I was hauled back to my feet, sagging against the arms holding me. Ugly man was back in my face.

"I can beat you all day, cunt, and never get tired. Now, one more fucking time. What's your name?"

"Jo … Josie."

He smiled, and my blood chilled. It was like having the devil smile at you.

"Now, was that so hard, bitch? I guess you're wondering what's going on, hmm?" He looked at me expectantly, but I didn't rise to his bait. After a moment, he nodded. "Well, because I'm feeling so *gracious*, I'll clue you in. You've got yourself a new dick. Goes by the name of Jacob, yes?"

Jacob? How did they know about Jacob? My silence just made the guy angrier. He reached out and grabbed my jaw, hard, twisting the skin.

"Yes?" he asked again, his eyes hard as stone. I could only nod. He wrenched his hand off my face. It felt like he ripped my jaw off. The tears began falling faster as I quietly sobbed.

"Good. Well, me and Jacob, we have some unfinished business. 'Cuz of him sticking his fucking nose in where it didn't belong, me and a few of my boy's here spent some time in the pen."

He rubbed his very crooked nose. "He busted me and the boys up good. I owe him for that, and then some."

The connections finally clicked in my memory. "You're Mad Dog," I managed to say through the sobs.

The slap rocked me, but the arms holding me kept me from hitting the ground again. I tasted blood as I was jerked back upright, and Mad Dog was nose-to-nose with me. A very large, shiny knife, at least a foot long, was held up between us, its point laying on my cheek.

"Bitch, don't you *ever* fucking call me that again or I'll carve your god damn tits off," he said, his voice quivering with barely restrained rage.

I looked into those eyes, and I knew he meant every word he said because all I could see in those black, blood-shot orbs was insanity and my death.

He turned to where another man stood. "Jer, get the camera setup!" he shouted as he pulled me back to his chair. He pointed at me as he addressed the others.

"Strip that dress off her."

I tried struggling as they pawed at me, groping me everywhere as they ripped and pulled at my dress. I screamed and scratched at them to no avail. I was soon standing in only my underwear and feeling like I needed ten showers to get clean again. I managed to stop crying, even though my whole body hurt.

Mad Dog stood in front of me again, his eyes traveling over me. Make that twelve showers.

"You're not bad looking for an older bitch. Me and the boys? We're gonna love playing with you. The last girl I fucked in this town was a young piece of ass but you? You got some meat to you. I'm gonna feast on them tits … oh, I most certainly am, right before I fuck your brains out."

I cringed as he groped my breasts through my bra, mashing them hard. Maybe I could get the fire department to use a hose on me to strip away the top few layers of my skin along with this unclean feeling.

"Camera's ready, Dog," said the one called Jer.

"Gag her."

The other guy slapped a piece of duct tape on my mouth. Once finished, he grabbed one of my boobs, twisting as he laughed and walked away from me.

Mad Dog pulled me over in front of a camera that was setup on a tripod. It had a light that was shining on us. I listened as he made his demands to Jacob. I couldn't do anything when he cut my bra off and hit me again. I was hurting so much already, that I barely felt the new hit.

Once the light cut off, Mad Dog kept his grip on me as he spoke to his crew.

"Jer, get that video to that rat-fuck sheriff and let the boys know to get ready. You stay down at the boat and wait for Frank. Murphy will be along in a bit to relieve you."

Jer nodded and left. Mad Dog pulled me across the cave to a rusty bed frame in the corner with a mattress that looked to be a home to rats. Fear gripped me as I thought this would be the start. He ripped the tape off my mouth and tossed me down on the mattress. I squirmed as far away from him as I could, putting my back against the rock wall.

"Like your bed? Well, get comfy cuz in a few hours, the boys and I are going to put it to good use." He pulled that big knife back out and told me to turn around. I hesitated, eyes on the knife. "Bitch," was all he said as he twisted that knife a bit, letting it catch the light, causing it to reflect on me. Swallowing hard, I turned around.

He grabbed my hands, I felt a quick tug, and my wrists were suddenly free. He shoved me forward on the mattress. I quickly turned, rubbing my wrists as I put my back against the wall, pulling my knees up, and wrapping my arms around them.

Mad Dog stared at me for a moment before grunting and walking back to his chair. He opened a cooler and rummaged around in it. Lifting out a clear plastic bottle, he threw it at me. I caught it before it could hit me in the face. A bottle of water. I opened it and drank half before putting the lid back on.

I watched him as he sat and popped open another beer. There were two other men on the other side of the cave. They were sitting at an old table, playing some card game while they swilled beer. It must have been an hour or more since the guy left with the video. I moved forward to sit on the edge of the bed.

All I could think about was my mom and Kaylin. What would they do without me? How would my daughter grow up without me? I didn't want to die and leave Kaylin alone. No child that young should have to lose both parents. My fear gave me a bit of strength.

"I hope Jacob comes and kills you all."

The two guys at the table grunted out harsh laughs, and Mad Dog turned his gaze on me.

"That so, bitch?" he asked, smirking.

"He was in the Army. He knows how to kill, and he's going to fuck you all up while I laugh. If I were you, I'd leave now while I still had the chance."

Mad Dog turned to the other two.

"You scared, boys?" he asked. The two at the table started laughing and telling Mad Dog what they were going to do to Jacob if he showed up. He turned back to me, looking anything but amused. "I'll give pussy-boy some credit. He fucked us up good the last time. But we were drunk," he said, followed by a belch. "I got armed men out there waiting for him. I hired me an Army man of my own. He's itching to get a crack at your boy."

"I'm going to enjoy watching him kill you."

He laughed and started drinking his beer. A few minutes later, he turned to the card players.

"Murphy! Go relieve Jer."

One of the guys got up and rambled towards the cave mouth. The other guy reached into a stack of stuff and pulled out a small handheld device. I soon heard the opening music of a video game startup. Gamer joined the list of named assholes.

For the next hour or so, I watched as Mad Dog sat and drank beers almost non-stop. He mostly stared at the floor, but every so often he would glare or sometimes leer at me. I glanced at the cave opening, but making a break meant running right by him.

After what must have been his sixth or seventh beer, he got up, belching as he stood. He tossed his empty beer bottle towards the pile of others, causing several to shatter. He glared at me again. After a few seconds he turned and shuffled towards the back of the cave, working at the zipper of his pants. Apparently, it was time to get rid of the beer.

Soon as his piss hit the cave wall, I exploded off the bed, heading for the cave entrance. Gamer and Mad Dog both yelled, but I was already in the tunnel. the opening just steps away.

As I took my first step out of the cave, I collided with someone, falling to the ground with them. I struggled, rolling and kicking, trying to break free. A hand snagged into my hair and yanked my head back, and something metal laid against my throat.

"Stop, bitch, or I'll cut your fucking throat right now."

Mad Dog yanked me to my feet and dragged me back into the cave, pulling me by my hair. When we got back to where his chair was, he lifted me fully up on my toes by my hair. His face was beet red.

"You try that fucking shit again, and I'll cut your feet right off," he growled, beer breath blasting me in the face.

Gamer started laughing as he walked back towards his chair. I could see the cave entrance and almost cried out when a figure appeared. A mask may have covered the face, but those eyes locked with mine, and I instantly knew them. *Jacob was here.*

Gamer must have sensed something too, because he yelled and reached for the gun at his waist.

Mad Dog spun me around just as Jacob's gun made two funny noises. Gamer's head snapped backwards, spraying blood on the wall and floor. Jacob swung his gun straight at us. Mad Dog gripped my hair and held me right in front of him tight, the knife still at my throat. All I wanted to do was puke from watching a man's head explode.

"Well, well, look who's here. Where's my money, pussy-boy?"

I could see Jacob was bleeding from several spots, including a nasty dried patch on his mask. I struggled, but Mad Dog held me tight. Jacob pulled his mask up and off his head, dropping it to the ground.

"In the bank where it's staying." Jacob's voice was hard and flat.

Mad Dog moved his knife to my chest. It wouldn't take much for him to drive the blade up into my throat.

"I told you what I'd do to your bitch here if you didn't bring it. Drop that gun, pussy-boy," he ordered.

"Not happening."

"I'll slit her throat clean open."

"First drop of blood I see, and your brains are on the floor behind you. One more time, Let. Her. Go." I shivered at the timbre of Jacob's voice. I'd never heard that before, and something deep in me said I never wanted to again.

"Oh, and I suppose I just get to walk out of here, pretty as you please?"

Jacob's stare was cold and calculating. "No, you don't."

Mad Dog grunted out a laugh. "Ain't seeing much of a reason to let the bitch go then. Any of my boys alive?"

"Not a one."

"Guess I'm just gonna have to cut this bitch to pieces right in front of you."

Before Mad Dog could act, Jacob's gun made that huffing noise again. Mad Dog screamed and the knife fell out of his hand.

"DROP, JOSIE!"

I pulled my knees up and let my weight drop straight down. Breaking out of Mad Dog's grip, I rolled several times as soon as I hit the dirt. Jacob's gun sounded again, and Mad Dog screams became shrill, high-pitched screeches.

Getting back to my feet, I started towards Jacob, but he threw his hand up at me, stopping me in place. Mad Dog was on his knees screaming, his knife arm hanging and flapping by the elbow. His other hand held his crotch, blood flowing through his fingers.

"YOU FUCKING ASSHOLE! I'm gonna rip your head off. I'm gonna fuck your bitch till she begs for my dick. I'm gonna—" Jacob's gun made two more funny sounds. Mad Dog's head snapped back as blood and other stuff I didn't want to think about sprayed the dirt behind him before he collapsed to the ground. Unrestrained, I turned my head and vomited up my guts.

Jacob checked on the other body, nudging it with his foot before slipping his gun into a pouch on the side of his leg. He opened the cooler and grabbed a bottle of water. Opening it, he bent and handed it to me. I did my best to rinse out the bile and taste from my mouth.

He gave me a second, then helped me to my feet. I threw myself on him and hugged him hard as the tears started to fall. I sobbed quietly for a moment, letting the terror that had built up inside me flow away. I let him go and started to kiss him when he pushed me back. I must not have gotten the vomit smell totally washed out.

"You hurt, cut, bleeding?" he asked. His voice was flat, emotionless.

"No, nothing bad. They didn't really do anything to me, just hit me a few times. You're the one hurt, you're bleeding. Let me—" I began, but he cut me off.

"Can you walk?" he asked, ignoring me as he shrugged off his backpack. Dropping to one knee, he began rooting through it.

"I think so. I mean, I don't have any clothes. Jacob, what's wrong?"

"Here."

He thrust a bundle of clothing in my hands. There was a shirt, some shorts, and a pair of sneakers. I dressed as quickly as I could. The clothes mostly fit, but the shoes were about a half size too big. I laced them as tight as I could.

While I was dressing, I watched Jacob do something to his gun that caused another metal piece to fall out. Oh, a clip. I'd seen them on TV shows. They held the bullets. He reached to his waist and pulled another clip out which he then slid into his gun. He pulled back on the top, then released it, and it clacked back into position. He dropped the other clip into his backpack and stood up, swinging it onto his back and clicking the buckles.

"Let's get out of here. I should have gotten them all, but the guy might have been lying about how many are here," he said, turning towards the cave.

I followed as he stepped out of the cave and paused, looking around. He had his gun still out, but he kept it pointed at the ground.

"He said he hired someone like you."

"Yeah, I found his merc. He wasn't as good as he thought. Good, but not good enough," he said quietly, still looking around.

I could see blood on his face, and a bandage around his leg. I reached up to his hair, trying to move it aside.

"You're hurt. Let me clean—" I tried to say, but he moved his head away from my hand and stepped to the side.

"No time for that. I need to get you out of here. Come on."

Ignoring the two bodies by the opening, I followed Jacob, trying to make out anything that was in my path. The moonlight gave me some view of the trail, but stones and branches still blended into things that I tripped on occasionally.

As we moved down the trail, we came across more bodies.

"Jesus, Jacob, did you kill all of these men?"

He kept moving forward, not looking at me.

"Yes, I did. Now be quiet," he whispered. "Sound carries in these woods, and if there are any others, they'll home right in on us."

"Sorry, I didn't—" but I clamped my mouth shut as he turned and glared at me, his face looking distorted and evil in the moonlight. What the hell was going on with him? Was this the side of him that Mom was so worried about.

We continued moving down the trail. We finally reached the point where the path started to go downhill. If I remembered right, the lake was not too far from here. Good. I wanted out of these woods and away from all of this crap.

"We're almost back to the water. I remember this part—" was all I got out before he whirled on me, moving until our faces were almost touching.

"Will you please shut your fucking mouth," he snapped, whispering harshly.

I stepped back, stunned at the venom in his tone.

"Look, I don't know what your problem is here, but you don't have to bite my head off. I'm sorry, I didn't mean to be loud."

"Josie, for the love of god shut your damn mouth," he growled.

That was it. First it was being kidnapped, then bound, stripped, beaten, and fondled by that diseased scumbag and his fellow bastards.

Now the love of my life was growling and snapping at me like I was a piece of shit on the bottom of his shoe.

"Fuck you, asshole." I slammed into him, shoving him out of my way, and started trotting down the trail. Once I got to water, I could try to follow the shoreline back to the marina. Shit, I'd walk all the way back to town if I had to.

"Josie, stop. Wait—" I barely heard his muffled cries from behind me. I flipped him the bird and jogged faster. I was almost to a couple of big trees when the sounds of his feet slapping the ground were close behind me.

"JOSIE STOP!"

Fuck that. I wasn't stopping for him or anyone else. Just as I snagged something with my foot, Jacob slammed into my back, shoving me forward and knocking me to my knees. A big whoosh and a thud filled the air, followed by Jacob crying out.

I skidded down the trail a few feet, tearing up my knees and hands. It took me a moment to catch my breath, but I hopped up, pissed. I stomped back up the trail towards Jacob, not caring who heard me.

"I don't know what crawled up your fucking ass, but shoving me is —oh ... shit, shit, shit." I didn't have to look at my face to know the blood had drained out of it.

The moonlight was bright as day in that section of the path, shining down on the tree where Jacob stood, not moving. I could see a large spike or something like it sticking into his left side.

"Oh god. No, no ... shit. What ..." I was babbling, my anger now long forgotten. Blood was soaking his side and working down his pants leg. I started to grab the thing to yank it out.

"Don't, Josie, don't ... touch it. Fuck me," Jacob gasped out, panting like he had run a long race.

I yanked my hand back but my eyes were drawn to the blood. God it was so much blood.

"Oh my god, Jacob. What should I do? Shit the blood ..." I babbled. I tried to catch my breath, but the sight of all the blood and that huge thing sticking out of his side were freaking me out. I was starting to feel lightheaded. I reached up to hold his face but he cried out again.

"Shit, I'm sorry. I'm sorry, Jacob. I don't know ... what can I do?"

"Josie ... I ... shit," he gasped. My hands flew to his face, trying to pull his head up so he could see me. I could feel my vision starting to grey. A corner of my mind was yelling at me not to pass out.

I groaned and sank to my knees, trying to breathe deep. The greyness around my vision slowly went away and my head began to clear.

"Jo ... Josie ..."

I lurched back to my feet, my hands going to his chest. "Here, I'm here, Jacob. Hold on. I ... I can go get help. Don't die on me. Please, don't die." I pleaded, my grip on sanity slipping. Jacob was dying and I was helpless.

"Josie, focus. I ... my backpack ... need it off." He was trying to undo the belly snap, but his hands kept slipping.

"Yes ... yes. I can do that."

I tried not to jostle him as I got the backpack undone and pulled down off his back. Unfortunately, I bumped the thing sticking out his side, causing him to groan in pain.

"Sorry, sorry. What now?"

He was panting as he talked, the words coming in spurts.

"Inside ... t-shirt ..."

I opened the pack and rummaged around till I found the shirt. I pulled it out and showed him.

"Good ... come ... wrap it around ... shaft ... push it against skin."

I did what he wanted, but when I pushed it up against his skin, he cried out.

"Oh god, Jacob. I'm sorry, I—"

His lips quivered with pain. "S'okay ... knew it would hurt. Need ... pressure."

I could see him taking some deep breaths before he brought his left hand up and pressed it against the shirt. He cried out again.

"Josie ... on the ground ... gun ... don't grab by trigger."

I looked around and spotted the pistol on the ground under his right hand. I picked it up by the grip, using two fingers. He reached out his shaking hand, and I handed it to him. He let go of the t-shirt and brought his left hand around. He did something with his right hand, and I heard a light click. He dropped the gun down and put it into that pouch on his right leg. Oh, it was a holster of some kind.

He collapsed back against the tree, panting. His left hand went back against the t-shirt, and I could see he was pressing it again.

"Front … front pants pocket … at knee. There's a tube in there. Get it."

It took me a moment to undo the buttons, but I got the pocket open and pulled out a small tube with a pull loop of some kind at the bottom.

"Go down the trail to the water. Nothing … there's nothing in your way. Two … bodies." He paused and took some breaths. "Point end of … the tube straight out over … lake. Hold tube tight … pull the loop. It … it will pop and a … yellow ball of light will … shoot out. Help … help should come."

I hesitated, not wanting to leave him.

"Go … go Josie. *Hurry.*" His head slumped to his chest as he said those words. I turned and ran down the trail, trying not to stumble. The boat came into view as I neared the water. Two bodies were on the ground near a tree. Ignoring them, I pointed the tube up towards the sky over the lake and pulled the loop.

As Jacob warned me, there was a loud pop and a showering hiss as something like a roman candle shot up in a yellow trail. A boat motor roared to life and two lights popped on out on the lake.

The lights played over me, blinding me, forcing me back up into the trees as I shielded my eyes. Within seconds, the engine cut out, and the boat slid hard up into the bank. Several shapes jumped out, and something large was thrown down on the shore near the other boat.

"Jacob, where are you?" A flashlight popped on, aiming at the beach and the bodies.

I knew that voice! I rushed towards it.

"Rick! Rick! I'm over here."

I collided with a dark shape, and he grunted, wrapping me up in his arms.

"God, girl, are you okay? Where's Jacob? Shit, you've got blood all over you."

"Oh, Rick. Hurry. It's Jacob. He's hurt bad. He's bleeding all over the place."

"Ken, Perry, stay here. Show me, Josie," he ordered, his hand pushing me back the way I came.

I took off back up the trail with Rick close behind, shining a big light out in front of us. We were back to Jacob in seconds.

Rick dropped the big flashlight and did something to his head. A smaller light popped on and he played it over Jacob and the tree.

"Shit, grunt, you're stuck like a pig." Rick moved up closer to Jacob, shining the light behind him. "Well, pig fuck. Broadhead welded to the bolt, and it's buried in the tree trunk. I'll tear him open if I try to pull that back through him. You with me Jacob? Jacob?"

Rick lightly slapped Jacob's face and his eyes blinked open.

"You with me, grunt?" Rick asked. Even in the moonlight I could make out the worry in his eyes but the complete lack of any other expression. It was as if the rest of his face was carved in stone.

"Not ... doing good. Lot of blood," was all Jacob could get out before he slumped again.

"Oh, please tell me he's not ..." I couldn't get the words out as something cold gripped my chest. Not again. Please God, not again.

"Nope, but we've got to get him out of here or else he'll bleed out. Okay Josie, this is going to get messy," Rick said, shrugging off his backpack and pulling a knife from something on his belt. "Josie, in my pack near the bottom are some tampons and a couple of maxi pads. Get them," he said as he aimed his headlamp at the front part of the bolt.

"You carry tampons—" I started, but he cut me off.

"Dammit. Focus, Josie. I'm going to have to pull him off this thing, and he's gonna bleed like crazy. We have to stop it, or he dies."

Nodding, I dug through his pack and pulled out what he was asking for. Why he had them was a story for another time.

I watched as he used his knife to cut what looked to be plastic fins off the end of the bolt. He also cut away Jacob's shirt, working his way around the bloody t-shirt until Jacob's side and back were bare. He shoved his knife back in its place on his belt.

"Josie, open those tampons. I'm going to pull him off this bolt and hold him up. You're gonna shove one of those tampons in that hole in his back and slap on a pad. I'll spin him around and we repeat. Understand? It's gonna be bloody but think of it as a really messy period. Okay?"

"Okay, su—sure."

"He needs you, Josie. You can do this. All right, here we go," he said.

Rick got as close as he could to Jacob and put his arms around him, just under Jacob's arms. He did a couple of deep breaths and suddenly stepped straight back.

Jacob cried out in pain as slid off the bolt, and Rick turned him towards me.

"Hurry, Josie," he grunted.

Rick was leaning his head over Jacob's shoulder so that his light shot downwards. Taking a deep breath, I held the skin near the bloody hole and pushed the tampon in like I had been doing to myself for all these years. Jacob didn't make a sound this time.

"Now the pad, right on it. Sticky side on the skin."

I opened a pad and slapped it over the tampon. Rick maneuvered Jacob around to bring his front out to me.

"Same thing." Rick grunted. I repeated the process.

"Okay, pick up the backpacks and let's go."

"But what about …" I stopped because Rick maneuvered Jacob around, bent, hoisted him up and over his shoulder, and took off down the trail towards the water. I grabbed both backpacks and the flashlight and followed.

We got to the boat and with the others' help got Jacob in and settled before we loaded up ourselves.

"Josie, my car is at the dock. We'll get him to the hospital quickly." Rick said, shining his light up and down me.

"He saved me again, Rick. He killed Mad Dog and all those men,

then he shoved me aside on the trail and got shot with that thing. I ...
I'm not ..."

Rick put a blanket around me. "Easy, girl, easy. It's okay. We've
got him. We've got you, and you're safe. Are you hurt? Cut, bleeding?" I shook my head no.

Ken piped up next. He had his own light shining down on Jacob.
"Is that a maxi pad?"

"Yep," Rick replied. "Trick I learned from a SEAL buddy. Field
expedited way of patching bullet holes till you can get to a medic.
Works for women, works for bullet holes. Get us out of here."

"Learn something new every day," Ken muttered, turning his light
back to the front and getting us moving. I was numb; the only thing I
felt was Jacob's hand in mine.

When we got to the hospital, I tried to go back with him, but they
stopped me at the door and took me to my own exam room. Other than
some scrapes and bruises, and the small cut above my eye, I was fine,
and they made me go back out to the waiting room.

I guess someone at the hospital called her because Janey showed up
within minutes of me sitting back down. When I complained about her
honeymoon, she shut me right up.

She dragged me back to the nurses' locker room. Grabbing a pair of
scrubs, she dug through her locker and handed me soap and shampoo.
She waited while I showered and dressed, then took me back to the
waiting room, plopping down next to me.

When the doctor came out to let us know the surgery was over and
Jacob was in recovery, Janey found out what room they were going to
move him to. I was waiting in his room when they wheeled him in. My
heart stopped when I saw all the bandages, tubes, and wires adorning
him.

I sat there every day, holding his hand and talking to him. The
nursing staff brought me food and drinks, but I didn't remember eating
or drinking. I held on to the sound of that stupid beep because it told
me his heart still beat and that he was still here with me.

TWENTY-NINE

Jacob

My head hurt. That was the first thing I realized as I swam up out of the darkness. It felt like someone had a small mallet and was attempting to smash their way out of my head.

Pain. Pain was good. Pain meant I was alive.

I could also hear a soft, rhythmic beeping. As I tried to convince the remodeler in my head to stop, the beeping became a bit more insistent. I prayed the mallet holder would go and smash whatever was causing the beeping.

The overzealous mallet wielder finally managed to break through a wall, and the memories came rushing back. The cave, the standoff, Josie. Along with those memories came a crushing wave of pain. The pain in my heart radiated out through my pores and through my soul. The beeping became faster and more insistent.

My nose twitched as smells assaulted it. Hospital. I was in a hospital. They all had that same sterile, antiseptic smell. The beeping must be from a vitals monitor connected to the sticky pads and leads I could now feel on my chest.

I tried to move my hands, but the left one wouldn't budge. It took everything I had to get the right to raise a small bit before it flopped back down to the bed. I could wiggle my toes and, even if I couldn't move my left hand, I could move my fingers a bit and could feel the IV lines sticking in me. That damn beeping was really getting annoying.

I forced my eyes open. Blinding white light speared my brain, and my eyes instantly slammed shut. After a few hundred blinks and tears sliding down my cheeks, I managed to get them to stay open.

Without moving my head, I could take in most of the room. Same cookie-cutter room that you would find in any hospital. I saw an IV tree on my left, with bags hanging from its hooks. I followed the lines from the bags to the back of my left hand, which rested on an immobilization board. I must have been moving enough while unconscious that the staff had been afraid I would pull out the lines.

The door opened, and Janey bustled into the room. Janey. Wedding. Honeymoon. Shit, how long had I been here?

"Well, lazy bones, it's about time you woke up!" She smiled, coming around to the side of my bed to check my IV bags while recording information on her chart.

"How ..." was all I managed to get out. My mouth and throat felt like someone had dumped a sandbox in it. Janey picked up a cup off the side table and brought a straw to my lips. I sipped and cold wetness slid down my throat. I'd never tasted anything sweeter.

"Ho ... how long?" I croaked.

"Three days," she answered.

"You ... should be on your honeymoon."

She simply smirked at me. "Person covering for me got a boo-boo, so I had to postpone. Let me get the doctor." Patting me on the arm, she bustled out of the room and returned in a few minutes with Dr. Murray. He glanced at me as he took the chart from Janey and perused the latest entries.

"How's the pain?" he asked, flipping through the pages on the clipboard.

"Okay. Not really feeling anything at the moment. Feel a little disconnected. What's the damage?"

"Five stitches on the outside thigh of your left leg, nasty crease on the right leg that needed eight stitches, five stitches on your upper right arm, six more on the left side of your head, a couple at your front hairline," he recited. "The real damage was that nasty puncture wound. Not sure who did it, but someone slapped two tampons in you and covered them with maxi pads. Kept you from bleeding out. Heard about that trick, but I'd never seen it before now."

He consulted the clipboard again before continuing.

"Even still," he went on, "you'd lost quite a bit of blood by the time we got you in here and on a table. We were in surgery for about four hours getting that hole in your side taken care of. Luckily whatever it was missed your vital organs, but it nicked your intestine. Fairly easy fix. As if you weren't giving us enough of a challenge, you developed a small infection. Probably from dirt and crap on whatever put that hole in you. We've kept you under while we worked on cleaning that up, not to mention to keep you from ripping out all that work I did."

"How much longer am I gonna be here?" I asked.

He studied the clipboard a bit more, took out a pen, and made some notations, then he signed off on the chart and handed it back to Janey as she stepped back into the room. He stuck his hands in the pockets of his white lab coat and gave me that generic stare doctors adopt when delivering news to their patients.

"Your infection is still hanging around, and your temp is up a bit," he explained. "I've ordered up more bloodwork and another round of antibiotics. You know the drill as well as any of us, Jacob. I'd like to keep you a few more days to get that infection under control and your temp down. Overall, you're in surprisingly good shape, so other than being sore, I think you're going to be just fine. I'll drop by again tomorrow during rounds and see how things are going. If you have any questions, let the nurses know and they'll track me down."

He nodded at me, talked quietly with Janey, and left the room. She came and checked the drips again.

"You're fussing, Mom." I smiled up at her. "I'm sorry about the honeymoon. I'll make it up to you both."

"You scared the shit out of us," she said, her voice choking up.

"Sorry." A one-word answer was about all that I could manage now that I was more alert, my head clearer, and my heart feeling like someone sucker punched it. Well, in reality, that was pretty close. I was surprised that the monitor was not beeping more than it was.

There was a knock at the door as it opened, and Rick stepped in. Janey smiled as she greeted him.

"Hi, Janey, how's he doing?" he asked pleasantly, smiling as he removed his hat.

"He's fine," she said brightly.

He glanced over at me. "Is he going to be here much longer?"

"I'm right here, you know." I could do grumpy with the best of them.

"Hush you," she chided, squeezing my shoulder. "Be a good patient and lie there while the adults talk." She gave Rick a generic rundown and told him I'd be there for a few more days. He nodded as she wrapped up her recap.

"Janey, wonder if you could give us a moment. And make sure no one disturbs us, please?" he asked. She nodded, gently squeezed my shoulder again, and left the room.

Rick studied me for a second, his gaze just as penetrating as the first time I met him. Like he was looking right through me. I took the offensive.

"Tampons?"

"Sorry. I only had the slims," he replied. "Didn't know what size you Army pussies normally used."

"Asshole." I started to laugh, but the pain brought that to a quick halt.

Rick smiled for a second before his gaze turned serious.

"Me and a few buddies of mine took a little stroll up that path to the cave, which is indeed on the backside of your property. Found the first two bodies right at the shoreline."

"You here to arrest me today?"

He continued as if I hadn't spoken, "Followed the trail up and into the cave. I counted ten. That about right?" he asked.

"Yeah. Two at the beach, other three at various points along the path, the one about a hundred yards out from the cave, two outside the cave entrance, and one inside with Mad Dog. The one near the cave, he was the one that had been stalking me. He'd had some special forces training, I'm just not sure which one. The air cannon was his trap. What about the guy at the marina?"

"He came along in the boat with us. He's with the rest of his buddies. You ever explored that cave?" he asked.

"No. Didn't even know it was up there."

"Inside, about 120 feet back, there are a couple of side passages. One of them ends at an old shaft. May have been natural, not sure. Never heard of any mining work in that area. Estimated that shaft to be about 200' deep. We gathered all of the stuff in that cave and dumped all of it down that shaft."

"What about the bodies?" I knew ways to hide a body, but not ten and not once they had been found.

"Dumped in the shaft. Figured it was as good a grave as any. One of the boys with me is a pyro nut. Seems he has quite the stockpile of things that no law-abiding citizen should have. When I contacted him for help, he packed up some special supplies, just in case. We dropped a few pounds of thermite powder down on top of everything, then lobbed in a couple of thermite grenades. When the fire burned itself out, we repeated the process just to be safe. Once the fireworks were done and the area cooled enough so we could get back near it, we dumped a ton of dirt down the hole. Figured it was enough to keep the trash covered."

"Rick," I started, but he waved his hand at me before giving me that direct stare again.

"Told you I would handle cleanup," he said. "We watch out for our own up here, Jacob. You've put it out there a time or two, helped the town out, helped the people. You helped those girls when those bastards were here before. You saved Josie. *Twice*. You've damn near died for her and this town."

He paused and watched me for a moment, jaw muscle working, before continuing.

"Me and you are the only ones who saw that video, and I've already deleted it and destroyed the thumb drive. Ken and Perry were in the boat with me. Both of them remember those shitholes from before and those sisters. We had us a little talk, and there will be no worries there.

"I had a talk with Josie while you were taking your nap. She's good, and you know the hospital staff would die before saying anything. Then again, all they know is you came in needing stitches and some body work. Some kind of accident you had while working up in the woods. You really need to be more careful with your power tools," he said.

Rick sighed, running a hand down his face.

"The friends that helped me have chewed enough dirt in shitholes around the world that they have no problem dealing with the cleanup and keeping quiet about it. Come by the office when you get a chance and pick up your stuff. I took your gear off you before we got you to the hospital. And just so you know, your grenades ended up in the pit. Didn't think you'd be needing those anymore."

"What about Arnie and the money?" That got a grin out of him.

"That was one pissed off fellow. I talked to him when he finally got here with the money. He and Frank worked something out, and he took off back to Seattle. Said to tell you his wife would be having some words for you the next time you saw her. Guess he missed some big charity thing."

He picked up his hat and walked to the door. He glanced back at me, nodded, and left the room. I stared at the closing door, my mind lost in the magnitude of what he told me, what he and others did for me. Then the door opened, Josie walked in, and acid boiled up in my stomach.

She rushed to the bed, throwing herself on me. I could feel her quietly sobbing. I should have felt warmed by her emotion and outpouring, but all I felt was hurt and anger.

She kissed me, but I didn't respond. She pulled back, puzzled.

"Jacob? Love? What's wrong? Did I hurt you?" She stared at me, worried.

"Why are you here?"

"What?" She laughed. "What do you mean 'why am I here?'"

"It's a simple question. Why are you here?"

Her head cocked to the side as if trying to determine if I was serious. "Why *shouldn't* I be here? I've been here every day and night, right here next to this bed, waiting for you to wake up. I'd only gone home to shower and change. When Janey called, I rushed right back."

"Still doesn't answer my question. Why are you here? Shouldn't you be somewhere else?"

She stared at me, studying me. The beeping of the monitor filled the silence.

"I don't understand. Where else would I be?" she finally asked, confused.

"Oh, I don't know. How about with your other lover?"

She stepped back as if she had been slapped. I watched as her expression changed quickly from love to anger.

"What do you mean 'my other lover'?"

"You seemed to have a problem with simple questions today. I'll speak slower. Your. Other. Lover. Man other than me that you are fucking."

Her cheeks became flushed, and her eyes became daggers. Damn, she was beautiful when she was angry. I crushed that thought before it could go any further.

"Who's been telling you this shit? Has Riley been talking to you? Because that's what it is. Bullshit. I only have one lover, and that's you."

"Liar. Were you lying when you told me you loved me? I'll give you this much, you had me fooled." That damn beeping was speeding up again as my heart raced and my head pounded.

"Are you drugged? Is that what's going on? Jacob, I've never lied to you, and there is no one else. I told you I loved you, only you. I'm going to kick someone's fucking ass for feeding you these lies," she snarled.

"Then you better get busy kicking your own ass. I saw you in his arms. I guess I really blame myself more than you. You never said we were exclusive, I just assumed we were." I could feel the first tear running down my cheek. Damn her to hell.

"Jacob, there has been no one—" she started, but I cut her off.

"DON'T FUCKING LIE TO ME!"

She backed up several steps, and I tried to sit up but almost passed out. I fell back against the covers. The monitor was sounding like an engine. Janey came rushing into the room.

"What in the hell is going on here?" she asked, hurrying over to my monitor and checking. "Jacob, if you don't calm down, you're gonna stroke out."

"Then tell the cheater to get out of my room."

Both women just stared at me, both looking like I was a raving idiot.

"Jacob … I … who …"

"I. Saw. You. Right down to that damn birthmark between your shoulder blades. A birthmark I could see because your dress was hanging open as you were in his arms and *kissing him*!"

Josie stood there, stunned. Her mouth opened a few times, like a fish gasping for air. All of the anger and hurt just spewed out of me. I was just sorry that Janey was there to see it.

"Guess the two of you had a good time talking about how you fooled me. Good old, stupid Jacob. I swore to myself after Kara that there would be no one else, that I could never go through that pain again. Then you came along, and I fucking let my guard down, let myself love someone again.

"God *damn*. I'm so stupid. But I promise you, this dumb boy has learned his lesson. Leave. Now!"

The monitor shifted into overdrive. She was crying, still struggling to speak.

"But … but you came—"

I cut her off again, "I did that for Kaylin. No child should lose both parents. I may hate you, but that little girl didn't need to lose her other parent."

"Hate?" she whispered, choking on the word.

"Jacob! What the hell are you talking about?" asked Janey, looking between both of us. I ignored her.

"It sure as shit isn't love. I guess in a way I should thank you. You showed me I should have trusted my instincts. Be a cold day in hell before I ever love again. Now get out of here. I'm sure he and his dick are waiting for you."

She stood there, tears flowing like rivers down her cheeks. Zombie-like, she turned and left the room. Before the door clicked closed, Janey turned on me and she was *pissed.*

"You want to tell me why the hell you just did that to her?"

I gave her the condensed version. Her face turned pale, and she let her hand flutter to her mouth before dropping it to my arm.

"No, Jacob. No. I refuse to believe it. I can't believe it. You saw wrong or something. Are you sure about what you saw?" she asked.

"Absolutely positive. Now, if you will excuse me, I'm tired and I need to rest."

Janey looked at me like she wanted to say something else, then headed to the door. I called out to her before she could open it.

"Janey? She's not to be allowed in here, nor is Flora."

"You're serious, aren't you?" she asked. "Jacob, she's been here virtually all day, every day since you were brought in. She's sat there in that chair next to your bed, holding your hand. Hell, it was all we could do to keep her from crawling up in the bed with you. Why the hell am I keeping her out?"

"Because I'm telling you. No protected information goes out to her, and she and her family are not allowed in this room. I mean it, Janey. If she opens that door, I'm done here. I'll never step foot back in this hospital."

Janey's mouth thinned, and her jaw clenched. I knew she was pissed, and I really couldn't blame her, but I could deal with a pissed-off Janey later. She kept staring for a few more seconds and then nodded her head.

"Fine. If that's the way you want it, I'll pass the word. Will that be all, Mr. Berman?"

I guess I deserved that. I nodded, watching as she glared at me for a few more seconds before leaving the room, her posture stiff and unyielding. I gave her another few moments before I turned to stare at the closet door, letting the tears slowly fall.

THIRTY

Josie

I ran from the hospital, crying. I could hear Janey calling to me, but I didn't stop. Once in my car, I lost it. I wrapped my arms around my chest and held myself as deep, racking sobs consumed me.

Figures he would wake up while I was at home cleaning up. When I got back to the hospital, Janey told me he would be there for a few more days but all was good.

Only when he woke up did things go horribly off-course.

How could I have read someone so wrong? That first kiss, when he held my head and looked me in the eye, I felt it in my *soul*. I loved Greg deeply, but that first kiss from Jacob caused something to break open inside of me. I never felt so complete in my life as I had at that moment. Making love to him, hearing him return my love, I finally felt whole again.

Now I didn't know what to think. What had he seen? I hadn't been with any man other than him. I knew it for a fact, but he was adamant and seething with anger. It radiated from him like heat from the sun.

I don't remember starting my car or driving home. Mom and Kaylin wouldn't be back for a few days. Someone had called Mom to tell her what happened, and she called me while I was in the waiting room. I was able to convince her to finish her trip, that I was fine, and that her coming home wouldn't change anything. She reluctantly agreed.

I didn't leave the house. Hours, days, I had no idea how long I grieved. I only remembered walking into my bedroom and falling onto my bed, curling up into a fetal ball. Crying, lots and lots of crying. It hurt. Oh god, it hurt. A part of me died, and I didn't know why, which only made the pain worse.

It was the ringing of the damn doorbell that pulled me up out of my stupor. I ignored it. It finally stopped, and I was sighing with relief before the pounding started. No matter how much I ignored it, it wouldn't go away. God, I fucking hate people.

I finally gave up and staggered to the front door, opening it. I threw up my hands to block out the bright sunlight blinding me, trying to see who it was through the halo of light and tears.

"Girl, you look like warmed-over shit," said the voice at the door as hands started pushing me back. I didn't offer Gary any resistance as he closed the door and began dragging me through the house.

I followed like a zombie as he pulled me along, opening and checking doors until he found my room. He pushed me into my bathroom and let go of me. I sank to the floor.

He opened the shower door and started the water. It didn't take long for steam to start wafting up towards the ceiling. Satisfied, he came back and pulled me up off the floor.

"I want you to strip, get in that shower, wash everything twice, including your hair, and stand there until the water goes cold. Get out, dry off, put on that nice pink robe I see on the back of the door, and meet me in the kitchen," he said, rattling off orders like a drill sergeant addressing new recruits.

"Don't wanna," I muttered. I had wanted it to sound forceful and defiant, but I failed miserably, which was par for the way my life was going. Pity party, table for one.

He reached out and took my chin in one hand, pulling it up and forcing me to look him in the eye.

"Do you want me to strip you and shove you in there?" he asked, his eyes taking on an evil glint.

"You would, wouldn't you?"

He nodded. Bastard.

"Fine." I didn't have the energy to argue with him. He kissed me on the forehead and left the room.

I wandered into the kitchen thirty minutes later wrapped in the requested robe. He was leaning against the sink but pointed at the table where a steaming bowl of tomato soup, two grilled cheese sandwiches, and a glass of iced tea waited. All of my comfort foods. Okay, maybe he wasn't such a bastard. Maybe.

"Eat," he snapped, giving me a glare that said, *'Don't even try to argue with me.'*

I had no appetite, but I knew he would hold me down and force-feed me the soup if I didn't eat it on my own. I flopped down at the table and reluctantly slurped down the first spoonful.

I must have zoned out and my stomach took over. When I zoned back in, the bowl and glass were empty, and the sandwiches were gone. I actually felt better, both from the shower and the food. Bastard.

Gary grabbed the dishes and dropped them into the sink. He must have made coffee because he poured two cups, set one in front of me, and sat down opposite me at the table. He took a sip before setting it back down in front of him. He reached into his pocket and handed me a handkerchief.

"Talk," he said softly as I took the small, folded piece of pristine white cloth from him. "I want to know everything from the time you ran out that hotel front door three days ago until now."

I talked. I told him everything. He didn't interrupt, didn't ask questions, just sat there listening, like he always had done when I had a problem.

His only reaction was a widening of his eyes and a heavy intake of breath when I described Jacob blowing Mad Dog's brains out, followed by the trap that he saved me from on the walk back to the water. I didn't start crying until I talked about the hospital and him telling me to leave, that I lied to him and cheated on him. That he hated me.

"Why would he say that?" he asked. He took a sip of his coffee, grimaced, and pushed it aside. It was probably cold by now.

My voice cracked. "I don't know why. There's only been him, Gary."

He sat there for a moment, stroking his goatee. He had a habit of doing that when he was thinking deeply. It was one of the things that made him the best at what he did. His mind was like a Ferrari when it came to processing data; seeing pathways, variables, and pairings faster than any other person I knew.

He stared at me again, squinting slightly, his fingers tapping on the tabletop.

"We're missing something," he said. "Something big."

"Shit, Gary, don't you think I know that? I've gone over everything for the last week and I don't have a clue as to what's going on." I sat there and let the tears fall. *Damn you, Jacob.*

He got up and paced the kitchen, muttering to himself. He stopped after a few minutes and looked at me in a funny manner.

"You know," he began, "We talked in the hotel about what happened with him up to the wedding. Is there anything else I should know?"

"No. How could I have misread him so badly? How could I have fallen in love with him so fast if he was this bad."

"Josie, dear, love knows no timeline. I know you. I was there when you met Greg. I watched you two live and love until life took us on different paths. But this thing with Jacob is nothing like that. When we were talking at the hotel, your face lit up. You were damn near *glowing*. I just assumed it was the 'I've just been fucked' look but now I think it was more you being totally and completely in love with that man.

"Everyone knew you loved Greg. But baby girl, I've only seen that glow one other time on you, and it was the first time you introduced me to Kaylin. She was a piece of you that you didn't know was missing until she came along. I suspect Jacob is another piece. And a love like that? There's no way to kill it. Oh, you may damage it, smash it around with anger, but you don't kill it. We *are* going to figure this out," he said, sitting down and putting his hand on top of mine.

He frowned, deep in thought.

"But we're missing something. Something happened from the time he left you until you got nabbed. Something that tore him up. Where could he have seen you?"

I flopped back into my chair, waving my hand around the kitchen.

"That's just it. He left that morning and I never saw him again until the cave. I have no idea what or who he saw but it couldn't be me."

"But he said he saw the birthmark. That's pretty specific."

I started to cry yet again. Gary reached over and patted my hands, rubbing them.

"Well then, Josie, I guess we're just going to have to go ask him. Go get dressed, and we'll go to the hospital together."

I nodded and went back to my bedroom. Gary always knew how to help, and I could only hope that he could get the answers I desperately needed.

THIRTY-ONE

Jacob

Getting up and out of the patrol cruiser hurt more than I thought it would. I had taken half of one of the pain pills Janey gave me. The pills made me feel like my head was stuffed with cotton. I'd rather deal with the pain than deal with that. Rick got out the driver's side and looked at me over the dusty top of the car.

"You're sure I can't help you with anything?" he asked, concerned.

"Nope, the ride home was all I needed. I'm just gonna take it easy for a few days. Thanks, though."

Rick walked around the cruiser to stand in front of me. Pushing his hat back on his head, he glanced at the trailer and sheds before looking me in the eye.

"Look," he said quietly. "I don't know what happened between you and Josie. Janey wouldn't tell me the details, just that the two of you had a blowout after I left. She said Josie ran from the hospital crying and you looked like someone shot your dog. Jacob, for your own good, you need to fix this."

I tensed up, and he saw it. He held up his hands, palms out.

"I don't know what happened after the wedding, but Ken said he could damn near see the pain and anger rolling off you when you left that reception. Then when you found out she was in trouble, you whistled up half a million dollars and didn't blink an eye. You told that Arnie fellow to spend every penny you had if it took it. You saved her ass from that piece of shit and almost bled out taking that hit for her. Are you really going to stand there and tell me that you don't love her?" he demanded.

I looked at the ground because I couldn't handle looking him in the eye. I couldn't say a word because if I did, I would have lost it right there. I heard his question, but I didn't know the answer.

But that was a lie. I knew the answer. I was too much of a coward and had too much pride to admit it.

His hand came up and gripped my shoulder, giving it a good squeeze to acknowledge the agony he could see washing over me.

"Son, you and I have had the fortune of loving good women, good women that we lost. You've found another good woman. Talk to her, Jacob. Fix it, for both of you." He squeezed my shoulder again and headed back around to the driver's side of the car, sliding back into his seat. He fired up the big cruiser, rolling down the passenger window. "You need something, you get word to me, hear?" he said.

I nodded, still unable to trust my voice. He put the cruiser in gear and headed back down the road to town, leaving a dust cloud in his wake.

He wasn't wrong. I did love her. That first kiss filled holes in me that I didn't know existed. When we made love, it felt like a banked fire exploding into raw flames. It felt right, so good, even more right than Kara. But watching her in that other man's arms and thinking about what she had done with him in that hotel room just destroyed me.

I stepped under the awning of my trailer, fishing out my keys and swearing as they slipped to the ground. I bent over without thinking, grunting as my side ached and reminded me why I shouldn't be bending at this time. Squatting, I picked up my keys and stood back up. Better.

Without thinking, I reached out with the key and then noticed the door, remembering what I had done to it a few short nights ago. Sighing, I pushed the broken door aside, mentally adding it to my to-do list to fix, and stepped up into my small abode. It wasn't much, but then again, it was only temporary. The house was finished except for the furniture. Tonight. I'd move up there tonight. I had a sleeping bag and had slept on harder surfaces than a wood floor.

I tossed my keys on the counter and reached into my little fridge. Pulling out a bottle of apple juice, I knocked back a few swallows before replacing it in the fridge.

With dying of thirst stalled, a nap was in order. While my bed was softer, the bench was closer, and I eased myself down on its worn, cracked surface.

I was pretty sure I only blinked when my driveway beeper went off. One of the first things I did after setting up the trailer was to string wire about two hundred feet down the driveway and rigged up some hidden infrared eyebeams. Anyone coming up the drive would trigger a beeper in the trailer.

I groaned as I forced myself back to my feet and over to my door. I stepped out under the awning and watched a late model BMW pull up and stop a few feet from the end of the trailer. I glanced to the driver's side, but the tinting of the front window and the angle of the sun hitting it kept the occupants hidden.

The passenger door flew open, and Josie stepped out. Shit. Not her, not now. Why did the universe fucking hate me?

Slamming the car door shut, she marched right up to me, her eyes alight with anger, her hair flowing behind her. She was what Valkyries aspire to be. God help me but I both wanted her and hated her right at that moment.

"Have you lost your mind?" she growled.

"Not sure what you're talking about." My voice stayed steady, thankfully. My gaze flicked to the car and back to her. I turned myself just enough to keep her and the driver door in view.

"You're supposed to be in the *hospital*. You were pinned to a tree and damn near bled to death!"

"As you can see, I'm just fine. No need for you to be concerned." I knew it sounded cold and petty, but I wasn't in the mood to be chummy and chatty. Then it dawned on me finally that she knew I had left the hospital and followed me here.

"Wait. How did you … Damn it. Janey. I told her not to tell you. God dammit." I wiped my hand down my face, wondering who was going to be the next person to betray me.

"Janey didn't break your stupid rule," she said, glaring at me. "She didn't call me until *after* you left. You owe her an apology, by the way, for putting her in that situation."

"Why are you here? Shouldn't you be somewhere else, or rather, with someone else?"

"And *that* is what we're going to talk about. I want to know why you think I cheated on you. Let me say it yet again, *I did not cheat on you.*"

I took a step closer to her. She must have read how angry I was because her face paled slightly, and she took a step back.

"I saw you. I saw you with him, in his arms, half dressed. It was pretty clear what had been going on."

"I swear there has been—" she started to say, but I cut her off.

"Don't lie to me. I told you about cheating, but you just didn't listen. I sure hope he was worth it because we're through." I took another step forward, and she stepped back.

Tears started falling down her cheeks. "Jacob, I swear, no one—"

I cut her off again, "I. Saw. You. In his arms, half dressed, shoes in hand. That birthmark on your back was clear as day."

I took another step forward, and she fell back again. We were almost up to the front of the car.

"Just get the hell out of here and leave me the fuck alone."

At this point, she was sobbing. I pointed to the car. As I did, the driver's door opened, and her lover boy stepped out.

I couldn't believe her nerve. She had her new lover drive her up here. Now I was really pissed. Before I could even speak, he beat me to the punch.

"Josie, it's him."

Josie turned to the asshole. "What?" she asked with a sob.

The guy pointed his finger at me. "Him. Remember the guy I told you about from the elevator? That's him."

I watched Josie's head move back to me, glance back at the guy, then back to me. She cocked her head at me, and I exploded on her.

"It's bad enough you fucked him, but did you have to bring him up here to rub it in. Tearing my heart out wasn't enough?"

Josie bowed her head, and I could see her shoulders shaking as she sobbed. It tore at me to see her suffer, but she had brought this on herself.

"Just get back in lover boy's car and go. Don't come back here again. Just leave me the fuck alone." I turned to go back to my trailer, not wanting her to see how the whole situation was killing me. I stopped when I heard her start to laugh.

I couldn't believe it. Laughter. She thought this was funny. I turned back on her. She was just looking at me, smiling and laughing.

"You think this is funny?"

She nodded, still laughing as she clutched her stomach.

"You think cheating on me and ripping my heart out is funny?" It was all I could do to not begin screaming at her.

"No, Jacob, that's not funny. Not at all," she said, her laughter abating, but her smile still stretched across her face. She looked back over at the driver, who merely rolled his eyes. "Jacob, help me understand. Where did you see what you think you saw?" she asked, waving her hand over towards the driver.

"Outside your hotel room, right after the wedding. Don't try to deny it."

She just laughed again but cut it short when I glared at her.

"No, I can't deny what you saw. I can only tell you that what you saw isn't what you think. It's the fact that you think it about him and me is what's funny."

Before I could respond, she took two steps forward and put her hand on my chest.

"Don't touch me."

"Jacob, love, I need you to listen," she said softly, staring up at me with those eyes, the same way she had looked when she told me she loved me. My heart shredded all over again.

"Don't call me that."

"It's what you are. My love. And if you give me a few seconds, I'll explain how what you saw was right, and very wrong, at the same time," she replied, looking at me expectantly. I stared at her, willing my face to remain still and stoic. She took my silence as permission. "Yes, you did see me just like you said. But what you saw was me thanking Gary."

I heard her, but it didn't make sense. She had talked about Gary, but as a family friend, not a former lover.

"But … your room … and you were undressed …" I couldn't force the facts to line up. Things weren't making sense. The pain meds must have still been screwing with me.

"Yes, I was, kind of," she said. "Gary showed up and spilled his wine on my dress. We came up to the room and he helped me get it clean. We also talked about you and how important you were to me and how we were doing. We talked so long, and I let the time slip away, so we were rushing to get back downstairs to be there if you got back."

"But … kissed … you were in your room with another man, undressed …"

My mind wasn't firing clearly. Something wasn't right.

Josie got a questioning look on her face as if trying to recall something before looking at me with a perplexed expression on her face.

"I guess in all my talks about Gary, I never told you he was gay, did I?" she asked.

I drew in a pained breath, my eyes searching hers. Was this the truth? Had I been a colossal idiot? "No. I think you left that little important fact out."

I looked up at the driver again and back to Josie, who moved closer and let her arms slide around my waist. God, she felt good. I looked down at her and felt the anger flow away, only to be filled with intense shame.

"Josie, I'm so …" I began, but she stopped me with a finger to my lips.

A single tear rolled down her cheek, and I reached up, gently wiping it away. She clasped my hand and pressed her face into my palm, her eyes closing and a slight smile on her lips. She took a deep breath and looked back at me.

"I've been through *hell* these last few days," she whispered. "It hurt so bad, much worse than when Greg died. You threw me out of the hospital with those vile words and accusations and I just died. You were so angry at me, and I couldn't figure out why. I can see exactly why you thought what you did after seeing us in that hallway."

She took a deep, shuddering breath before continuing.

"But even as angry as you were, you came for me. You saved me. I will spend the rest of my life proving to you that I am worthy of that love and that you hopefully will feel it for me again."

Josie took another breath, her hand squeezing my cheek again.

"Jacob, we have to promise each other. From this point forward, no more assumptions. We have to talk to each other when something seems off. I'll start that right now," she said. "I've always kissed Gary like you saw. Just a peck on the lips. It's like kissing any other guy on the cheek. Greg and I used to joke about his gay friend getting lip action from his wife. But if it makes you uncomfortable, then I'll never do it again."

I shook my head, not trusting myself to really speak. My mind was still trying to wrap my hands around the whole twisted situation and how badly I fucked up. How close I came to losing her.

She caressed the side of my face, letting her fingers linger along my cheek as she did. I couldn't help but shiver. Her touch was like a drug, and I wanted more. She brought both hands to my cheeks and pulled me forward so that she could kiss me, and when her lips touched mine, I was lost all over again.

It wasn't a passionate, lustful kiss. It was just her lips on mine, a reconnection of two halves, making us whole again. My universe recentered, and she pulled back far enough to capture my eyes.

"I told you in bed, and I told you before you left that morning. I even told you constantly at the hospital, but you couldn't hear me. I'm going to tell you every day from now on. I love you, Jacob. *Only* you.

There is no one else, and there will never be anyone else. Can we please, I don't know, reset back to waking up in each other's arms a few days ago? Can we both forget all of the rest of the shit after that and just go from there? Please?" she asked quietly, her eyes begging along with her words.

"Josie, I'm so sorry—" I tried to say, but she kissed me again, and this time her tongue lightly brushed my lips until I parted them and let her in. The other kiss may have reconnected our souls, but this kiss welded them back together with its heat. When we broke apart, we were both out of breath.

"No. No apologies. Reset, love. Reset," she said firmly.

I inhaled deeply and slowly brought my own arms around her, leaning forward to let my forehead touch hers. No words, nothing else, just us. I'm not sure how long we were like that before a throat clearing brought us back.

She kissed me lightly again and stepped to my side, keeping one hand wrapped around my waist but being careful of my wound. She glanced towards Gary and looked back up at me, smiling now.

"Come on, let me introduce you."

THIRTY-TWO

Josie

"Jacob, this is Gary, the brother I never had. Gary, this is Jacob, the father of my future children." I laughed as Jacob's hand jerked on my hip and he gave me a rather startled look. I patted his arm. "We'll talk later."

"Glad to finally meet you, Jacob. Josie's told me *all* about you," Gary said. I could tell by the slight uptick of his smile and the slight squint of his eyes that the *'all'* Gary was thinking about would make Jacob blush or possibly punch Gary.

"You, too. Sorry about—OW!" Jacob exclaimed, holding his side where I pinched him.

"Reset means reset," I said, preparing to pinch him again. He nodded, and I could feel his shoulders as they relaxed. He was trying hard, so I reached up and kissed his ear, nibbling the lobe slightly. I chuckled when he groaned.

"Glad to finally meet you, Gary. Josie told me about you as well, except for one *small* detail," said Jacob, smirking as he glanced at me.

Gary looked at me and glared. "Did it ever occur to you to tell him I was gay the first time you mentioned me?" he asked.

I shrugged my shoulders. "Nope, never even crossed my mind. I didn't think it was any big deal."

Gary threw up his arms. I simply shrugged again, grinning at him. Rolling his eyes, he nodded as if he expected no less from me and let his gaze wander around the lot. "You building something somewhere?" he asked, waving his hand around at the supplies stacked in the area.

I did my own look around. The last time I had been up here was when Jacob brought me here that Saturday when I took my tumble. At the time, I really hadn't noticed what was around me. But now I could see what Gary was referring to. There were piles of supplies around the area and inside several sheds.

"A house, back up in the woods," Jacob explained, pointing back towards a small dirt road leading off into the forest.

I poked him on the arm. "Why didn't you tell me? Everyone builds houses." I tried to glower at him, but my heart wasn't in it.

"It was a promise I made to myself, and I didn't want anyone to offer help. I needed to build it on my own. It was kinda like my therapy," he offered quietly.

"A promise for Kara?"

Jacob looked at me and nodded.

"Ah," Gary said. He and I talked about Kara, so he understood. "How much more do you have left to do?"

"Some trim work, couple of small things with the flooring, then a final cleanup. Finish the road leading to it, and buy furniture," Jacob said.

I pulled Jacob's hand so that he turned towards me. "Can I see?"

I could tell he was hesitant. This was something very important to him. His jaw clenched, and I knew he battled some inner demon. I placed my hand on his arm and smiled.

"Please?"

Taking a deep breath, he nodded. "Okay. I'd planned to show it to you at some point, and I guess today is as good a day as any."

Taking my hand and catching Gary's eye, he indicated with his head that Gary should follow before leading us to a large Gator. It had two bench seats and a cargo box with some building materials and tools in it. Once we were seated, Jacob and I in the front and Gary behind us, Jacob cranked it up and headed up the small road at the back of the clearing.

The road was bumpy, so Jacob was taking it slow. I could see him wince when some of the deeper ruts caused us to bounce and his stomach muscles to clinch.

About five minutes later, we came out into a large clearing, and I saw the house for the first time. It was a good size, maybe 3000-4000 square feet if I had to guess. I could see a pool and pool house behind it. I kept looking at its lines, something about them tugging at the back of my brain.

Jacob drove us through a large side yard and up to the house. Easing out with a slight grunt, he reached back for my hand. By the time I was out, Gary jumped out the back and was standing with us.

Jacob then led us up onto a large deck. Overall, it was probably sixty feet long, about fourteen feet deep, and looked to be made up of rough-hewn cedar. The house side facing the deck was made up of large, single-pane windows, eight to ten feet high, and they covered pretty much the entire side of the house. My subconscious was screaming at me, but I couldn't hear it. He took us to the railing, and I gasped, my hand coming to my mouth.

The view took in a huge expanse of the lake, clear blue water stretching out as far as the eye could see. Not to mention the forest and hills rising above the other side of the lake.

As I looked to either side, I could tell that the trees had been cleared in an angle away from the house to enhance the view. That alone must have taken months. It was breathtaking. I could imagine standing on this deck on a cool spring morning, coffee in hand, breathing in the crisp, clean air. Heaven. I could hear Gary telling Jacob what a beautiful, peaceful sight it was.

"Let me show you inside," Jacob said, turning us back to the house. As he did, sunlight broke through the partially clouded sky and hit the glass house front. My mouth dropped open as that nagging in my head broke through and exploded my brain. I stepped back, stumbled, and fell flat on my ass. Jacob and Gary were both there in a flash, pulling me back up.

"Walk much?" Gary quipped. I didn't say anything, still staring at the house. Jacob squeezed my hand, bringing my attention back to him.

"Josie? What's wrong?" he asked, his eyes full of concern.

I looked at the house for a few more minutes before turning my attention to him.

"Where did ... where did you get the plans?"

He shrugged. "Kara and I talked about what we wanted, but we never really did anything about it. I hired an architect and described what we talked about. Took about five months, but when they showed me the finished plans, I knew it was right. Why?"

I shook my head, looking back at the large glass front, the roof line. I walked to each side of the deck, taking in the angles and views of the house, the placement of windows for the rooms. I walked back to the guys, both of them staring at me like I had lost my mind. Funny thing was, I thought maybe I had.

"Gary, can you do me a huge favor?"

He nodded and I handed him my keys.

"Take the Gator back to your car and run back to town and the store. Tell the clerk I sent you and that you're getting something for me. In my office, you will find a montage mounted on the wall over my desk and a yellow binder sitting under it. Bring them both, please."

"Josie?" he questioned, taking the keys.

"Please hurry, Gary. If Ken or the sheriff pulls you over, tell them I sent you and I'll cover any tickets."

I'd give Gary one thing. He didn't ask a lot of useless questions. He simply nodded and took off. I turned and walked back to the deck railing, feeling Jacob follow.

At the railing, I stared out at the lake. Jacob came up beside me, pulling me into his arms and turning me to face him. I could see the worry in his eyes. I wrapped my arms around his waist, smiling at him.

"Tell me about you and Kara talking about the house. What you liked, what she liked. Tell me as much as you can remember."

He gave me a quizzical little look but then nodded and began talking. I soaked up those words, hearing the love they shared in those discussions. It didn't take long to determine he had been the driving force in how the house looked. She had given her inputs but seemed to have deferred to him on many occasions.

He was still talking an hour later when we heard the Gator coming back. Gary walked up on the deck towards us, binder in one hand and my board in his other. He handed me the board and gave me a strange look. He started to say something, but I shook my head. I thanked him and stepped back slightly from Jacob, the board between us so he couldn't see the front.

"Jacob, have you ever heard of a vision board?"

He shook his head. "Nope."

I gave him a brief vision board lesson. He listened, nodding occasionally.

"Then I'm guessing that's your vision board?" he asked, pointing to the board between us.

I nodded. "Greg and I always dreamed of coming back to Azton to make our home. My parents were going to help us get a piece of land so we could build our house and raise our family. Honestly, I think it was more my dream than Greg's, but he said he would follow me wherever I wanted to go. He would have been happy to have lived in a square box in a quiet suburb as long as he was with me and Kaylin and could work in the forest.

"I started the vision board the year we got married. It's gone through some revisions over time. When I got back to Azton, I began tweaking it. I'd wake up some morning and have an urge to make an adjustment."

He rubbed his chin and cocked his head at me. "Okay, since I've built my house, you want me to help you build yours?" he asked. Off to the side, Gary started to laugh and coughed to cover it when I gave him an evil stare. He made a zipping motion across his mouth but kept a know-it-all grin on his face.

"No, you don't need to do that. You've *already* built it."

He looked confused, glanced at the house and back at me.

"Already built? What are you ..." he started to ask, but his voice trailed off into silence as I turned the vision board around. He stared at it for several moments, then looked back at the house and back to the board again. Finally, he looked back at me. "Did you come up here and take pictures?" he asked, his voice taking a very ominous undertone.

I shook my head several times. "No, sweetheart, not at all. These are photos and sketches I made or clipped out of magazines. Some are years old."

"Impossible," he breathed.

I knew it was possible. Because the house of my vision board stood before us. The deck I sketched we now stood on. The deck to roof glass windows from my board stretched before us.

I laughed and sat the board down against the deck rail.

"What say we see just how freaky and weird this can really get?"

I walked over to Gary and took the yellow binder from him. "You're a scary woman," he said, grinning at me.

"You have *no* idea."

I walked up to the large French doors leading into the house and paused to glance back at Jacob, grinning.

"Come on. Let me show you my house."

"But ... this is my ... and how ..." Jacob sputtered as he followed. With the way I was whipping his brain around today, I wasn't surprised by his inability to form coherent sentences. I would make it up to him later when speaking was optional.

Opening the binder, I took out a sheet protector that had a sketch, color palette, and layout of a front room. I handed it to him as he followed me into the house. He stopped dead in his tracks, looking first at the sheet, then at the room.

"*Fuck*," he whispered quietly, unable to believe that he held in his hand a virtual match to the room he now stood in.

I just laughed and headed to the first doorway off to the left.

"That's the ..."

"Kitchen, yes, I know. Here's the layout." I handed him another page. "Let's see if you got the tile and backsplash right, love." I marched into the kitchen, looking around. All as it should be except for the floor tile. "Hey, where's the white checkered slate? This diamond pattern is okay, but it's not the right one for this layout and color palette."

I didn't think his face could get any paler.

"Um ... they were out of it and I didn't want to wait for a back order," he said meekly.

"No worries; we can fix it later. Chop chop, let's go." I took off for the laundry room, which I knew was through the next door.

It took us about forty minutes to get through the house. I kept handing Jacob sheets as I walked from room to room. With very few exceptions, my sheets matched his layout. The only major difference had been when he combined two smaller bedrooms with a Jack and Jill bath into a large guest suite. I could live with that.

After the third room, he started muttering under his breath. I chose not to hear his mumblings about 'demon woman' and 'devil' as he was following. After all, I was getting my house. I figured me and the universe were coming square.

We ended up back on the deck, Jacob holding a bunch of page protectors and looking shell-shocked. Gary still had that smug look on his face.

"Well," Gary said, rubbing his hands together. "Let's talk about the wedding. I'm thinking that clearing here beside the house will work just fine for the seating. We can set up a nice flower arch here on the deck with the lake in the background ..."

EPILOGUE

Josie

(Two years later, late spring)

I sipped my decaf coffee as I stood at the deck railing looking out at the side yard. I reached down and rubbed Dora's head, scratching between her ears as she sat beside me, rubbing her head against my leg. We obtained the German Shepherd puppy a few months after moving in, and she and Kaylin were inseparable.

The fresh morning air was clean smelling and the temperature a pleasant seventy-two degrees. I could smell the new forest growth and feel a slight breeze across my face. I was in heaven.

Jacob was working through his katas, wearing only sweatpants and light sneakers. I watched the play of muscles as he moved effortlessly through his routine. My already screwy hormones shifted into high gear as I watched my soulmate work, knowing that all of that fineness on display was mine. The scars made him all the hotter to me, especially the large one on his left side. An eternal reminder of his love and protection for me.

We had gotten married, just not as quickly as Gary wanted. We waited another eight months. We used that time to get past the trauma of the events surrounding Ken and Janey's wedding. We both had issues with trust and communication that we had to address. Those few days following the hospital had been emotionally draining for all of us. We took the time to make sure that we were okay both individually and as a couple.

When we brought Kaylin up here to see the house, she was hooked the minute she saw the pool. Her only question had been if she could have a dog now. I gave in. All my previous arguments against one just didn't seem important anymore.

One night while at Mom's for dinner, Jacob officially asked me to marry him. He had already talked with Kaylin to make sure she was on board with it. Mom cried when he eased to one knee and proposed. Kaylin squealed and danced around when I told him yes. Like I was going to say anything else.

Jacob and I grew closer. Our days and nights were devoted to each other and Kaylin. We talked about our pasts and he answered every question I had regarding his time in the Army and with Kara. We promised ourselves that there would be no more secrets.

With the house finished and us engaged, I began floating ideas about furnishing it. I'd said something about using some of our current furniture to fill in while we saved up to get what we wanted. Jacob simply started laughing and told me to hold that thought while he pulled out his cell phone and made a call.

The next morning, Jacob had taken me to Seattle to meet Arnie and Peggy. I'd sat there in Arnie's office and just stared at him, refusing to believe the words coming out of his mouth. *Millions*. Jacob was worth *millions*. After signing my name on a mountain of paperwork, *I* was worth millions too. And after all of that, Arnie gave me a stack of papers that were copies of the same ones I'd just signed. It seemed that I had to do them again if I changed my name after the wedding.

I wasn't happy when they told me Jacob had been the source of our life-saving grant. In fact, I had been *pissed* and made sure Jacob knew it.

But, after talking more with Jacob and Arnie, and Arnie showing me how Jacob helped others, I realized that it was just his way. He truly wanted to help Mom and me, and the money really didn't mean anything to him. His desire to not have others know about his money made sense. I got over myself quickly.

When he told me about the Bransons, I fell even more in love with him, if that was at all possible.

Eight months after his cash infusion, Mom and I finally acknowledged what the numbers were still telling us. Much to the dismay of the town, Markinson's Emporium started a going-out-of-business sale. We managed to clear most of the inventory in about three months. What was left was sold off in bulk to other area distributors and businesses. We gave the employees a six-month severance package to tide them over until they found new work.

When the dust settled, Mom still owned the building. She decided to rent it out and put the money, above what was needed to maintain it, into a trust fund for Kaylin, not knowing that Kaylin was set for life. We let her feel good about it because it was a good thing to do for her granddaughter.

Mom declined our offer for her to move in with us, saying that her life and friends were in town and she was content. I secretly thought it had more to do with a certain post office manager who had recently been spotted around town with her. My sources indicated that these visits sometimes included breakfast at Mom's place. Go Mom. Maybe the table was finally getting a workout.

Jacob occasionally took solo trips out to the woods. I never asked where or why, knowing that it was something he needed and that he would tell me when the time was right.

Jacob's laughter drew my attention back to the side yard. Kaylin tripped trying to follow one of his movements. He stood her back up and had her repeat it, showing her how to do it correctly.

The first morning she had seen what he was doing, she'd immediately begged him to teach her. He gave in without a fight, knowing full well he could never deny her anything.

The two were thick as thieves. I might have been jealous if I didn't love them both to pieces. God help any boy who ever hurt that girl. When she got done with him, Jacob would bury the remains, and no one would be the wiser. For her sake, I hope it didn't scare the boys off.

I watched her repeat the movement several times, her face lighting up when she finally got it right and he gave her a high five.

"Breakfast, you two! And make sure you shower before you track your sweaty carcasses into my clean kitchen or else no pancakes for either of you!"

They both just laughed, knowing it was an empty threat. Jacob grabbed Kaylin, throwing her over his shoulder, her shrieking laughter music to my ears as she yelled at him to put her down. Dora barked and jumped up at them as they followed me into the house.

Twenty minutes later, two freshly showered hooligans descended upon the kitchen table. Breakfast was consumed in its normal, noisy fashion. The hooligans talked about what they planned for the day, and I reminded them about the chores that needed doing before they took off rampaging through the woods. Given that Jacob had just finished building his gun range last week, my suspicion was that shooting would be involved.

I'm sure there would be some parents that would freak out about an eight-year-old girl learning to shoot pistols and other firearms. If I were being honest, I would have been one of them. Life has a way of altering your thinking, though, and I was more than happy for her to learn as many ways to protect herself as she could. My daughter would *never* be a victim. Jacob and Rick would see to that.

As we were clearing the table, Jacob stopped us both.

"Once we get the dishes done, I'd like you both to get dressed. I need to take you on a short hike," he stated, glancing back and forth between us. I knew my husband, and I could tell he was nervous.

"Honey, I'm not sure I'm in the best shape for a hike."

He simply smiled. "Short, easy hike. I promise. We will be in the Gator most of the way. It'll do you good to get out and get some fresh air and exercise," he said.

I gave him the evil eye. "Did you just call me fat and lazy?"

Kaylin broke out laughing. "Ohhhh, you stepped in it now, Pops."

He shook his finger at me. "Don't put words in my mouth," he chided. "You've been working too hard, and it's a beautiful spring day. Even goddesses such as yourself deserve a break."

"I don't know. I'm pretty sure you just called me fat."

He slowly moved in my direction. His eyes locked with mine and never wavered, like a cat stalking his prey. A very hungry, lustful cat. I backed up slowly.

"Jacob ..."

Kaylin giggled at the table. She was no help, the little traitor. My husband cornered me near the stove, pressing himself up against me. He put an arm around me and pulled me in tight. One of us whimpered. I'm pretty sure it was me.

He brought the back of his hand up to my temple and slowly ran a finger around my ear, meandering down my jawline. I moaned as his caress caused a molten fire to ignite in my panties. The bastard knew what caressing my face did in normal times. In my current state, it was like tossing gas on a fire. Everything inside me heated up.

"Please," he whispered, lightly kissing me. His tongue teased my lips, pulling back before I could capture it. I moaned and sagged against him.

"Hey! There are young kids present!" came wafting over from the peanut gallery.

I sighed. "Fine. I'll go. But when we get back, you're finishing what you started."

He grinned, gave me a quick kiss, and turned back to Kaylin, scolding her for feeding Dora bacon and wrangling her to help with the dishes. I waddled to the bedroom to change clothes, including panties, fanning myself and plotting my husband's death by sex.

Twenty minutes later, we were in the Gator and heading into the woods. Dora was in the cargo box, barking at all the animals she saw invading her kingdom. We motored along several trails before hanging a left onto one I didn't recognize, finally reaching a point where the Gator couldn't go any further. We got out, and Jacob snagged his backpack out of the back, slinging it up on his shoulders and snapping the straps.

Taking my hand, he led me on a smaller trail. A few minutes of easy walking brought us to a glade I had never been to before. Kaylin and Dora ran off ahead of us, and I could hear her yelling at Dora to "leave that bunny alone" as we made our way deeper into the clearing, heading towards what appeared to be a large tree of a type I didn't recognize. It stood alone in the center of the glade.

Jacob led me to the mystery tree, whose branches spread out to shade a large portion of the ground around it. As we got closer, I could see some kind of metal near the trunk.

"Give me a moment?" he asked. I nodded and he moved closer, where he began picking up and cleaning around the tree. This early in spring, there weren't a lot of leaves or sticks. Satisfied, he pulled out a blanket from his backpack, folded it into a nice pad, and placed it on the ground near him. He motioned me forward and helped me kneel down and get myself comfortable. I groaned a bit as I settled into a good position, letting my swollen belly nestle down on my thighs. I couldn't wait for this kid to be born. Between driving my hormones amok and turning my bladder into its personal squeeze toy, this kid was killing me.

As I looked down, I noticed two small metal markers and an area of ground that had a cloth over it. My breath caught in my throat at the simple wording on them.

Kara Berman
  Loving Wife

Karen Berman
  Beloved Daughter

.   .   .

I reached out to clasp Jacob's hand as he knelt beside me. He started to speak in a quiet, reflective tone.

"She and I found this glade the first time we visited this land after she inherited it. We sat here under this tree and talked about our future. We could see our kids running around this glade. She thought it was the most peaceful place she had ever been. She told me she could lay here forever with me and be content. We made love here."

Jacob paused to run a finger across Kara's marker.

"When I finally made it home and they were already buried, I was lost and hurt. I never told you before about the shitstorm that occurred with her parents and the land. I was almost ready to give them the land back, even had a pen in hand to sign the quitclaim when I got the strongest urge to not do it. I've learned to trust my gut, and my gut was telling me loud and clear that giving them the land was wrong.

"I walked out of the lawyer's office and never looked back. I drove here, got a room, and came up here to this glade. When I sat down and leaned back against this tree, I felt the first real peace since that terrible call telling me they were gone. Since I knew I would never go back to where they were buried, I made them a new resting place here with me. I buried a picture of her and I, and one of her pregnant, along with some of our letters and emails here under the markers. I come here every few weeks to clean the area. I woke up this morning, and my gut was telling me it was time to bring you and Kaylin here, along with another."

"Another?"

He nodded. "About two months ago, I had a dream about this glade but there was something different, something new."

I watched as he pulled the cloth away, revealing another marker. I felt the tears on my cheek before I realized I was crying. I blinked to clear my vision and read the simple, powerful words.

Kara Berman
 Loving Wife

. . .

Karen Berman
  Beloved Daughter

Greg Callison
  Loving Husband and Father

I put my arms around him and held him as the tears flowed freely for both of us. Kaylin and Dora came flying up to where we knelt. As if by some basic instinct, they knew that something was going on, something that was affecting me deeply.

They sat down next to us quietly. Jacob pulled Kaylin into the hug, and we took a moment to share our love.

After a few moments, Kaylin reached her limit of inactivity and wiggled out of our embrace, asking about the markers. Giving me a final squeeze, Jacob pulled some cleaner and rags out of his pack and began scrubbing Kara's marker. As he did, he explained their meaning and who they represented. She listened for a moment then took some rags and cleaner and began wiping Greg's marker.

When Jacob finished Kara's marker and started to clean Karen's, Kaylin stopped him, letting him know that she would do this from now on "cuz sisters were supposed to watch out after each other." Jacob stopped his cleaning and his hand trembled for a moment, the only outward sign of the emotional effect that simple statement had on him.

He put his rags down and started to tell Karen about the things that he and Kaylin had done over the last few weeks. Soon, it turned into a back and forth as Kaylin corrected him, telling Karen that he always got things wrong.

As I listened to the banter between my daughter and husband, I rested my hand on our unborn son. I thought back to that day that Jacob and I first met and all of the events leading up to this day, this moment.

Folks talk about the universe and life and how all manner of unusual things occur in the name of Fate. Missed airline flights, a flat tire on the road, change in a work schedule. All shining examples of where Fate lent a hand to make one's life better or save oneself from a calamity.

I smiled to myself because in our case, the only thing needed to create our future was for Fate to take a hike. Oh, and a bunny. Can't forget him.

ACKNOWLEDGMENTS

No book is truly a solo effort, and this, my first book, is a shining example of that process.

I'd like to thank my wife, Pam, for her support and understanding when I would confine myself to my office for hours at a time. For being my social media manager, setting up my website and media pages. But most of all, for agreeing from the start NOT to talk about, edit, offer suggestions, or in any way influence the story coming out of my brain for the sake of our marriage. She knew we would argue and fuss if I included her early. She was right. Once finished, she beat on it, did editing, and made me rethink several of my scenes. Thanks sweetheart. Love ya.

I'd also like to give a special thanks to my very first alpha readers, Caitie Seagroves and Katy Kendricks (The Cats). They didn't know me from Adam but when I contacted them about taking a first read of my book, they were thrilled to read a new writer. They flipped out over my first chapters, screaming at me to publish. They also tried to teach me to speak "30" at the same time helping me to 'Un-Dad' and take the "old" out of my story. Where I failed is on me. I tried ladies.

To Amy Ryding, who gave me an unbiased and detailed review of my plot and story. A writer herself, she forced me to look at my words in a different way. She provided me an unvarnished truth, which was GREATLY appreciated, along with encouragement to finish my project.

To Tori Linville Hopper, a young lady I had the pleasure of watching grow up. Thanks for showing me the '4th Wall' as well as the places in the story that broke it. Her insights into phrasing and voice usage, along with her feedback made this a much better story.

Also, a special thanks for two of my author friends from the Nashville Authors Indie group, Shannon Brown and Kelly Utt-Grub, for their priceless help in guiding me through the process of developing a new cover and title for this book

This amazing cover was developed by Elizabeth Mackey. You can see more of her work at https://www.elizabethmackeygraphics.com/

Someone had to take a fine tooth comb through my ramblings and ensure they were in good grammatical order. The dubious task fell up on my editor, Ashley Oliver. Sorry for all the work Ashley. You definitely earned your money with me. Oh, and if you're looking for an editor, I highly recommend her. You can find her at:

https://www.Facebook.com/AshleyOlivierAuthor
https://www.Instagram.com/AshleyOlivierAuthor
https://www.Instagram.com/_AshleyOlivierEdits
ashleyolivierauthor@gmail.com

ABOUT THE AUTHOR

When he's not writing, or working his day job, Bob spends his time helping his wife take care of their three horses, four cats and the multitude of chores one finds around the farm. When there is free time left, he enjoys playing golf, video games, and DnD with his friends on the west coast, and watching their three kids grow up and explore life.

ALSO BY B.D. STOREY

Read on for a small excerpt of the exciting new second chance, small town romance *When Love Comes Knocking*.

****

PROLOGUE

The old wooden porch swing creaked comfortably as I slowly rocked, staring at the papers in my hand. I tried to come up with some feeling with regard to the small stack of documents that I held, but nothing came. It was as if I was numb. I let my hand drop back to my lap, the bundle of papers slipping from my fingers and fluttering down to the dirty porch.

I let my gaze travel out across the yard and trees, and then up into the clear evening sky. The stars were so bright they almost overshadowed the moon. I felt like I could reach up and pluck them right out of the sky.

I could hear soft nickers from the barn and side pastures out behind the house. Like most animals at this late hour, or early, depending on your viewpoint, sleep was for some, but there were always one or two horses awake, herd instincts ensuring that someone was always awake and protecting the others.

A shadow flicked across my vision. I turned my eyes just enough to catch a large winged presence gliding through the still night. Must be Owen. It was a silly name for a barn owl, but he and I had an easy truce now. I stayed away from his corner of the barn loft, and in return, he kept the barn area reasonably free from field mice and didn't rip my face off.

I glanced down at the papers scattered on the porch. *Dissolution of Marriage.* Seemed like such a cold and legal statement, but I guess that's what it needed to be when those words signaled the death of a marriage and the love it contained.

Normally, when something dies, there's a reason or cause. Trauma, illness, some tragic reason. In this case, nothing. When I got back from Ft. Collins five months ago, my wife of almost two years, Julia, was gone. No note, no message. Nothing. Her closet and drawers were empty. Anything that was hers was gone. Mom had been away visiting her sister and my barn manager, John, was out checking the back pastures and never saw her leave.

I tried multiple times a day for a month to get in touch with her. I needed to find out what was going on. Her cell was disconnected and her family shut me out. I'd driven to her parent's place in Denver but couldn't get past the security at the entrance to their gated community. When I told the rent-a-cop at the gate I wasn't leaving until I spoke to Julia, the real cops were called. That resulted in a restraining order preventing me from being anywhere within 500 feet of Julia, her parents, their home, or their place of business.

The divorce papers showed up the day after I was served the restraining order; a one-two punch. Her parents were well off and they'd apparently bought some fast talent. Their lawyer drove his black Mercedes to the farm and politely told me that all future contact would be through him.

I never saw Julia again.

After examining the papers, my lawyer advised me to just sign. Colorado was a no-fault state. Julia didn't ask for anything. She just wanted out of the marriage. Finally, after yet another meeting with her lawyer, where he again denied my request for a meeting with her, he informed me that if I did not sign the papers, Julia would re-file paperwork and go after everything, including 50% of anything associated with my family's business. This would be in addition to alimony. I was shocked. The Julia I knew would have never been that cold-hearted.

So I signed. And today, months later, my copy of the final paperwork arrived in the mail.

I slowly rocked and gazed out at the night sky. I didn't stop the tears as they fell. Until this moment, I'd held out a sliver of hope that some miracle would happen and that Julia would change her mind. She would come back and we would have hours of makeup sex, laugh, and move on with our life together.

Owen hooted off in the distance as a Julia-sized hole in my heart, held together with hope, ripped open.

Made in the USA
Columbia, SC
28 April 2023

15614123R00189